RAVES FOR **Cops and Robbers** and Donald E. Westlake

"The rougher the going gets, the more intrigued you'll become. Westlake's uniformed duo is definitely cops with cachet."

—***Saturday Review***

"Excitement and super-entertainment."

—***Publishers Weekly***

"Everything about *Cops and Robbers* is first-rate—the plotting is ingenious, the suspense is intense and sustained, the point of view is manipulated expertly, and the ending is surprisingly gratifying. . . . Westlake successfully breaks the mold, retaining enough humor to satisfy his longtime fans but adding sufficient depth for those of us who want a bit more."

—**John R. Coyne, Jr., *National Review***

"Nerve-end entertainment!"

—***Kirkus Reviews***

"Westlake's strongest qualities remain his wild but seamless plotting and his tape-recorder ears, but this time his characterizations are more dimensional and compassionate . . . and the exciting ending is a jewel of complexity."

—*Library Journal*

"Through sheer craftsmanship, Westlake makes us say 'of course' to the most preposterous of happenstances . . . a writer of uncommon talent, imagination, flair and unpredictability."

—*Los Angeles Times*

"Westlake writes in an idiom of controlled comic hysteria . . . he has a wonderful feeling for the absurd, revels in farce and slapstick, and piles complication upon complication."

—*New York Times Book Review*

"Westlake doesn't miss a comic beat or a funny line."

—*Playboy*

"Westlake is always original."

—**Elmore Leonard**

"If there is any funnier mystery novelist around, I can't imagine who it might be."

—*USA Today*

"Westlake can wring humor out of a situation until an appreciative chortle becomes a hopeless snort of oxygen deprivation."
—*Newsday*

"The master of the rolling scam."
—**James Grady**

"Donald Westlake keeps showing me people I'd like to meet."
—**Rex Stout**

"Westlake is among the smoothest, most engaging writers on the planet."
—*San Diego Tribune*

"Donald E. Westlake [is] the Noel Coward of crime. . . . He displays an excellent ear for bitter-salty urban humor, composed of equal parts of raunch and cynicism."
—*Chicago Sun-Times*

"Westlake probably is the best practitioner we have of the craft of writing about subjects that should be grim and tense but turn out only to be ridiculous."
—*Kansas City Star*

By Donald E. Westlake

NOVELS

Humans • Sacred Monster • A Likely Story
Kahawa • Brothers Keepers • I Gave at the Office
Adios, Scheherazade • Up Your Banners

COMIC CRIME NOVELS

Trust Me on This • High Adventure
Castle in the Air • Enough • Dancing Aztecs
Two Much • *Help* I Am Being Held Prisoner
Cops and Robbers • Somebody Owes Me Money
Who Stole Sassi Manoon? • God Save the Mark
The Spy in the Ointment • The Busy Body
The Fugitive Pigeon

THE DORTMUNDER SERIES

Don't Ask • Drowned Hopes • Good Behavior
Why Me • Nobody's Perfect
Jimmy the Kid • Bank Shot • The Hot Rock

CRIME NOVELS

Pity Him Afterwards • Killy • 361
Killing Time • The Mercenaries

JUVENILE

Philip

WESTERN

Gangway (with Brian Garfield)

REPORTAGE

Under an English Heaven

SHORT STORIES

Tomorrow's Crimes • Levine
The Curious Facts Preceeding My Execution and Other Fictions

ANTHOLOGY

Once Against the Law (edited by William Tenn)

DONALD E. WESTLAKE

COPS AND ROBBERS

THE MYSTERIOUS PRESS
New York • Tokyo • Sweden
Published by Warner Books
A Time Warner Company

MYSTERIOUS PRESS EDITION

Cover design by Jackie Merri Meyer
Cover illustration by Wilson McLean

The Mysterious Press name and logo are trademarks of Warner Books, Inc.

This Warner Books Edition is published by arrangement with the author.

Mysterious Press Books are published by
Warner Books, Inc.
1271 Avenue of the Americas
New York, NY 10020

A Time Warner Company

Printed in the United States of America

First Warner Books Printing: April, 1993
10 9 8 7 6 5 4 3 2 1

For Sandy

Prologue

I left the car on Amsterdam Avenue and walked around the corner onto West 72nd Street. With the heat the way it was, I was glad the Police Department let its people wear a short-sleeved shirt in the summer, open at the neck, but I could have done without all that weight around my middle. Pistol, holster, gunbelt, flashlight, one thing after another, all dragging down on my pants and giving me an uncomfortable bunched-up feeling around the waist. What I would have liked most of all right then would have been to take all my clothes off and just stand there in the street and scratch. But in a way that would have been more against the rules than what I had in mind.

At the corner of Amsterdam and 72nd is the Lucerne Hotel, one of the spots where the bar-flies live who hang out along Broadway. Broadway between 72nd and 79th streets is lined with those narrow little bars, and every one of them is the same; the same loud jukebox, the same formica-and-plastic fixtures, the same fake Spanish decorations, the same big-breasted Puerto Rican girl behind the bar. All the losers from the single-occupancy hotels in the neighborhood spend their nights with their elbows on those bars, mooning at the barmaids, and then at closing time going back alone to their rooms to dream great seduction scenes before going to sleep. Or, if they have the money, which they usually don't, they take home with them one of the fourth-rate hookers who walk up and down Broadway waiting to substitute for the barmaids, who have lives of their own.

Along the block from the Lucerne to Broadway are a bunch of old buildings with small business on the ground floor and old-line tenants in the apartments upstairs; school-teachers' widows, retired grocers, aging garment workers. The small businesses include a couple of bars, a delicatessen, a dry cleaner, a liquor store; the usual collection, each with its piece of red neon in the window. *Schlitz. Hebrew National. Shirts Cleaned.* It was ten-thirty at night, so most of them were closed now with just the neon and their night lights glowing. Except the bars and the liquor store, of course, and they weren't very lively either, not on a hot midweek night in June.

Very few people were out tonight. A few kids ran around on the sidewalks, and cruising cabs ricocheted by at forty miles an hour, the drivers cooling their left elbows; everybody else was at home, in front of a fan.

The liquor store was midway to Broadway. When I reached it, one look through the window past the animated snowman display told me there were no customers in there; just the Puerto Rican clerk, reading one of those illustrated paperbacks in Spanish, and a pair of winos stocking shelves in the back. I unsnapped my holster flap and went in.

All three of them glanced at me when I pushed open the door. The winos went right back to work, but the clerk kept watching me, his face empty, like everybody when they look at a cop.

The place was air-conditioned. Sweat cooled on my back, where I'd been sitting in the car. I walked over to the counter.

The PR was as neutral as gray paint. "Yes, officer?"

I took out the pistol and pointed it generally at his stomach. I said, "Give me all you got in the drawer."

I watched his face. For the first second or two, it was just shock, pure and simple. Then he made the switch of identities in his head—I was not a cop, I was a robber—and he clicked over to the new right response. "Yes, sir," he said, very fast, and turned toward the cash register. He just worked here, it wasn't his money.

In the back, the winos had stopped. They were standing there like a couple of part-melted wax statues, each of them holding two bottles of sweet vermouth. They were facing mostly toward each other, giving me their profiles, but they weren't looking at anything in particular. They definitely weren't looking toward me.

The PR was pulling stacks of bills out of the cash register and putting them on the counter; ones, then fives, then tens, then twenties. I grabbed the first stack left-handed and shoved it into my pants pocket, then switched the pistol to my left hand and did the rest with my right. Fives in my other pants pocket, tens and twenties inside my shirt.

The PR left the cash register open, and stood there with his hands at his sides, showing me he didn't have any immediate plans. I switched the pistol back to my right hand and put it away, but left the flap open. Then I turned around and walked to the door.

I could see them reflected in the windows in front of me. The PR didn't move a muscle. The winos were staring at me now. One of them made some sort of unfocused arm movement, gesturing with the vermouth bottle. The other one shook his head and the bottles in both his hands, and the movement died.

I left the store, and turned back toward Amsterdam. On the way, I closed the holster flap. Around the corner, I got back into the car and drove away.

1

They were on day shift then, which meant they had to face all that morning traffic on the Long Island Expressway. That was the only bad thing about living out on the Island, bucking that rush-hour traffic whenever they had day shift.

One of them was Joe Loomis; thirty-two years of age, he was a uniformed patrolman assigned to a squad-car beat with a partner named Paul Goldberg. The other was Tom Garrity; thirty-four years old, he was a detective third-grade usually partnered with a guy named Ed Dantino. They were both stationed at the 15th Precinct on the West Side of Manhattan, and lived next door to one another on Mary Ellen Drive in Monequois, Long Island, twenty-seven miles from the Midtown Tunnel.

They drove into town together like this whenever their schedules worked that way, taking turns at whose car they'd use. This morning they were in Joe's Plymouth, with Joe at the wheel, dressed in uniform. Except for the hat, which he'd tossed on the back seat. Tom was in the passenger seat in his usual work clothes; a brown suit, white shirt, thin yellow tie.

Physically, they were more or less the same type, though there wouldn't be any trouble telling them apart. They were both just about six feet tall, and both a little overweight; Tom maybe twenty pounds, Joe maybe fifteen. In Tom, the weight concentrated mostly in his stomach and behind, while in Joe it spread out all over him, like baby fat. Neither of them liked to admit to themselves that they'd gained weight. Without saying anything to anybody, both of them had tried to go on diets a couple of times, but the diets never seemed to work.

Joe's hair was black, and very thick, and worn a little longer than it used to be; not so much because he wanted to be stylish with the new trends, as because it was always a boring pain in the ass to get a haircut, and these days it was possible to get pretty shaggy before anybody noticed or commented. So Joe ran longer between haircuts than he used to.

Tom's hair was brown, and thinning badly. He'd read a few years ago that taking a lot of showers sometimes caused baldness, so he'd been secretly using his wife's shower cap ever since, but the hair was still coming out. The top of his head was very thin now, with long roads of scalp showing where there used to be only a forest of hair.

Joe had the quicker personality of the two, rough and pragmatic, while Tom was more thoughtful and more imaginative. Joe was the one likely to get into brawls, and Tom was the one likely to calm everybody down again. And while Tom could sit almost anywhere and keep company with his thoughts, Joe needed action and movement or he'd get bored, he'd start to fidget.

As he was fidgeting now. They'd been sitting in this one spot in stalled traffic for almost five minutes, and now Joe was craning his head this way and that, trying to stare past the cars in front of him to see what was causing the tie-up. But there wasn't anything special to see; just three lanes of nobody moving. Finally, out of anger and frustration, he leaned on the horn.

The sound went through Tom's head like a blunt nail.

"Don't," he said, waving one hand. "Forget it, Joe." He was too weary to be bugged by stalled traffic.

"Bastards," Joe said, and looked to his right. Over there, past Tom, he saw the car in the next lane; a pale blue brand new Cadillac Eldorado. The windows were all rolled up, and the driver was sitting in there in his air-conditioned comfort as neat and unruffled as a banker turning down a second mortgage. "Look at that son of a bitch," Joe said, and pointed with his jaw at the Caddy and the man in it.

Tom glanced over. "Yeah, I know," he said.

They both looked at him for a few seconds, envying him. He looked to be in his forties, very neatly dressed, and he faced front looking calm and untroubled; he didn't care if there was a traffic jam or not. And the way his one finger was tapping lightly on the steering wheel, he had a radio in there that worked. Probably even his dashboard clock worked.

Joe rested his left forearm on the steering wheel and glared at his watch. He said, "If we stay here without moving another sixty seconds by my watch, I'm going over there and study that Caddy and find a violation and give that son of a bitch a ticket."

Tom grinned. "Sure, sure," he said.

Joe kept frowning at his watch, but gradually his expression changed and he started to grin instead, remembering something he still couldn't get over. Still looking at the watch, but not really counting anymore, he said, "Tom?"

"Yeah?"

"You remember that liquor store a couple of weeks ago, the guy that held it up disguised as a cop?"

"Sure."

Joe turned his head and looked at Tom. He was grinning very broadly now. "That was me," he said.

Tom laughed. "Sure it was," he said.

Joe moved his arm down from the steering wheel. He'd forgotten all about his watch. "No, I mean it," he said. "I had to tell somebody, you know? And who else but you?"

Tom didn't know whether he was supposed to believe it or

not. Squinting at Joe as though that would help him see better, he said, "You putting me on?"

"I swear to God." Joe shrugged. "You know Grace lost her job."

"Sure."

"And Jackie's supposed to have swimming lessons this summer. Dinero, you know?" He rubbed his thumb and finger together, in the gesture that means money.

Tom was beginning to think it might be the truth. "Yeah?" he said. "So?"

"So I was thinking about it. The whole thing, the payments and the problems and the whole mess, and I just walked in and did it."

Meaning it as a question, but phrasing it like a statement, Tom said, "On the level."

"On a stack of Bibles. I got two hundred thirty-three bucks."

Tom started to grin. "You really did it," he said.

"Damn right."

A horn honked behind them. Joe looked front, and the traffic had moved maybe three car lengths. He shifted into drive, caught up, and shifted back into park.

Tom said, in a bemused kind of way, "Two hundred thirty-three dollars."

"That's right." Joe was feeling great, having the chance to talk about it. He said, "And you know what really amazed me?"

"No."

"Well, two things. That I'd even do it at all. The whole time, I couldn't believe it. I'm pointing a gun at this guy, I just can't believe it."

Tom nodded, encouraging him. "Yeah, yeah . . ."

"But the thing that really got me is how easy it was. You know? No resistance, no trouble, no sweat. Walk in, take it, walk out."

Tom said, "What about the guy in the store?"

Joe shrugged. "He works there. I'm pointing a gun at him. He's gonna get a medal saving the boss's dough?"

Tom shook his head. He was grinning from ear to ear, as though he'd just been told his daughter was head of her class. "I can't get over it," he said. "You really did it, you just walked in and did it."

"It was so *easy*," Joe said. "You know? To this day I can't believe how easy it was."

The traffic moved a little again. They were both quiet for a minute, but they were still both thinking about Joe's robbery. Finally Tom looked over at him, his expression serious, and said, "Joe? What do you do now?"

Joe frowned at him, not understanding the question. "What?"

Tom shrugged, not knowing any other way to say it. "What do you *do?* I mean, is that it?"

Joe made a barking kind of laugh. "I'm not giving it back, if that's what you mean. I spent it."

"No, I don't mean . . ." Tom shook his head, trying to find what he meant. Then he said, "Will you do it again?"

Joe started to shake his head, but then stopped and frowned, thinking it over. "Christ alone knows," he said.

Tom

My first squeal of the day was a robbery with assault, in an apartment over on Central Park West. Actually it was my partner, Ed Dantino, that took the call. Ed is a couple inches shorter than me and maybe ten pounds heavier, but he still has all his hair. Maybe he started using his wife's shower cap earlier than I did.

Finishing the call, Ed hung up the phone and said, "Okay, Tom. We're going for a ride."

"In this heat?" I was feeling a little queasy today, from the beer last night. Usually a feeling like that goes away toward midmorning, but the heat and the humidity were keeping me from shaking it today. I'd been looking forward to a couple hours of relaxation in the squadroom until I felt better.

The squadroom isn't all that great. It's a big square room with plaster walls painted a really sickening green, and big globe lights hanging down from the ceiling. The room is full of desks, all of them old, no two of them alike, and a general smell of old cigars and used socks. But it's up on the second floor of the precinct house, and there's a big fan in the corner near the windows, and on hot humid days there's a little breath of air that passes through from time to time, giving a promise that life may be possible after all, if we just hang in there.

But Ed said, "It's on Central Park West, Tom."

"Oh," I said. With rich people, we make house calls. So I got to my feet and followed Ed downstairs. When we got to our car, an unmarked green Ford, he volunteered to drive and I didn't argue with him.

Going across town, I started thinking again about what Joe had told me this morning in the car. I still thought sometimes he was pulling my leg, but then I'd remember the way he'd talked about it, and I'd know for sure he'd been telling the truth.

What a crazy thing to do! Thinking of it was the only thing to make me forget my stomach. I'd be sitting there, trying to burp and not being able to, and the first thing you know I'd be grinning instead, thinking about Joe and the liquor store.

I almost told Ed, in the car, while we drove over, but finally decided not to. Actually it hadn't been very smart of Joe even to tell *me*, and God knows I wasn't going to turn him in. But the more people that know a thing, the more chance that the wrong people can find it out. Like, if I told Ed, I could be sure he wouldn't report it, but he just might tell somebody else. Who would tell somebody else, who would tell somebody else, and who knew where it would end?

But I could understand why Joe hadn't been able to stop himself from telling at least one other person about it, and I was kind of flattered I'd been the one he'd picked. I mean, we'd been friends for years, we lived next door to each other, we worked out of the same precinct, but when a guy trusts you with a secret that could put him away for maybe twenty years you *know* you've got a friend.

And a pretty wild-ass friend at that. Imagine going into a liquor store, *in uniform*, and pulling out a gun and just taking everything in the cash register! And he had to get away with it because who would believe a robber in a policeman's uniform was really a policeman?

While I meditated about Joe's Great Liquor Store Robbery, Ed drove directly over to Central Park West and turned south toward the address we wanted. He didn't have the siren on; where we were going, the crime had already been committed and the criminals had already gotten away, so there wasn't any sense of urgency. They were reporting the robbery because their insurance required it, and we were making a house call because they were rich.

I love Central Park West. On the one side there's the park, green and rolling, and on the other side the apartment buildings full of rich people, rolling in green. The East Side has become more fashionable in the last few years, as the slums of Harlem have crowded down from the north and the Puerto Rican slum of Amsterdam and Columbus Avenues has crowded over from the west, but there's still plenty of wealth to be found on Central Park West, particularly toward the southern end.

We parked in front of the address. It had a canopy and a doorman, both of which I liked. We went inside, and going up in the elevator I said, "You do the talking, okay?"

I'd already told Ed I was under the weather, so he just said, "Sure."

It was a very expensive apartment we were headed for, on a high floor. The woman herself let us in, opening the door as though she weren't used to that kind of manual labor. She was about forty-five, and holding time away with every pill and diet and exercise she could find. She looked expensive but old, like her apartment.

She took us into the living room, but didn't suggest we sit down. It was a beautiful room, all golden and brown, with high windows overlooking the park. An air-conditioner hummed, and the sun shone through the windows, and you could almost hear the buzz of lazy insects. You get the idea; everything sun-dappled and rich and comfortable and beautiful and easy. It was just a great room to be in.

Ed did the talking for both of us, while I wandered around the room, digging how good it felt to be there. She had knickknacks and whatnots all over the place, in marble and onyx and different kinds of wood, and some in chrome or glass or green stone, and every one of them was just a pleasure to be with.

Over by the window, Ed and the woman were talking, their voices seeming to be muffled by the sunlight, muted and indistinct, like voices in another room when you're sick in bed in the daytime. From time to time I'd tune in on what they were saying, but I just couldn't build up any interest. It was the room I cared about, I didn't give a shit about the two spades that had busted in here.

At one point, I heard Ed say, "And they came in through the service entrance?"

"Yes," she said. She had a voice like a prune, very offensive. "They struck my maid," she said. "They cut the inside of her mouth, I sent her downstairs to my doctor. I could have her sent back up if you need a statement."

"Maybe later," Ed said.

"I can't think why they struck her," she said. "She is black, after all."

Ed said, "Then they came in here, is that it?"

"No," she said, "they never came in here at all, thank goodness. I have some rather valuable things in here. They went from the kitchen into the bedroom."

"Where were you?"

On a glass coffee table was an ornate lacquered Oriental wooden box. I picked it up and opened it, and it had half a dozen cigarettes inside. Virginia Slims. The wood inside the box was a warm golden color, like imported beer.

The woman was saying, "I was in my office. It connects with the bedroom. I heard them rummaging around, and went to the door. As soon as I saw them, of course, I realized what they were doing."

"Can you give me a description?"

"I honestly didn't—"

I said, "How much would a thing like this cost?"

The woman looked at me, baffled. "I beg your pardon?"

I showed her the Oriental box. "This thing," I said. "How much would it go for?"

She talked down her nose at me. "I believe that was thirty-seven hundred dollars. Under four thousand."

What a great thing! Four thousand dollars for this little box. "To hold cigarettes in," I said, mainly to myself, and turned away again to put it back on the coffee table.

Behind me, the woman was being a little miffed, saying to Ed, "Where were we?"

I looked at the things on the coffee table. It made me happy to be with them. I couldn't help smiling.

Joe

I don't know why, for some reason I'd been pissed off all day. It had started right from the time I got out of bed this morning. If Grace hadn't avoided me, we would have had us a good old-fashioned fight, because I was really in the mood for it.

Then the car, and the traffic, none of that helped. And the heat. It felt good telling Tom about the liquor store, a thing I'd been bottling up inside me for a couple weeks, but a little while after I told him and we'd stopped talking about it I was in a rotten mood again. Only now I had something to hook onto, because I just kept thinking about that comfortable bastard in his air-conditioned Cadillac out there on the Long Island Expressway this morning. I was sorry I hadn't ticketed him for something; anything. I hated the idea that somebody was better off than me.

For me, the best way to work off a mad is to drive. Not in that stop-and-go traffic like on the Expressway this morning; that just makes things worse. But in ordinary traffic, where I can move, use my skills. I get behind the wheel, I push it a little hard, win some contests, and pretty soon I feel better. So I volunteered to drive today, and my partner, Paul Goldberg, just shrugged and said it was fine with him. Which I knew he would; he has no feeling for cars, Paul. He'd rather I drove all the time, so he could sit beside me and chew gum. I never saw anybody in my life who could chew so much gum. He went through Chiclets like kids through Kleenex.

He's a couple years younger than me, Paul is, and slender and wiry, with more strength than he looks. His name is Goldberg, but he looks Italian. He has that curly kind of black hair, and an olive complexion, and those big brown doe eyes the chicks love so much. He's a bachelor, and I guess he makes out pretty good with the women. He ought to, given his looks and potential. I don't know for sure; I hinted around a couple of times, but he never talked about his personal life while we were on patrol together. Which was only fair, since I never talked about mine either.

On the other hand, what kind of personal life does a married man with kids have to talk about?

We did a little driving around the neighborhoods to begin with today, but it wasn't the kind of movement I needed to unload the irritable feeling in my chest. It was also too hot for mooching along down side streets; what we needed was to be where we could move fast enough to create a breeze for ourselves, keep ourselves a little cooled off. Me, especially, keep me cooled off.

So I headed us west over 79th Street and got on the Henry Hudson Parkway northbound. Way up ahead you could see the George Washington Bridge. On our left was the Hudson River, looking better than it really is, and across on the other side New Jersey. There were little puffs of white cloud in the blue sky, boats of different sizes were on the river, and even the city, off to our right, looked clean in the sunlight. For looking at, it was a really nice day. Of course, you can't see humidity, or a temperature in the high eighties.

I got off the Parkway at 96th Street and hit the neighborhoods again for a while. Now I was having second thoughts about telling Tom about the liquor store. Could I really trust him? What if he told somebody else, what if the word got around? Sooner or later it would reach the Captain, once it got started, and if that ever happened I was finished. The 15th Precinct had a couple of very hairy Captains for a while, guys who were in on the take, guys you could have bought off on a baby rape with a bottle of Scotch, but the boom got lowered all of a sudden, on the Captain we had at the time and also the one who'd been there before him and was assigned some place else and about to retire, and they both got their heads handed to them. Now we had a Captain who was out to make King of the Angels; spit on the sidewalk off duty and he'd write you up. Think what he'd do to a patrolman who held up a liquor store while driving his beat.

But Tom wouldn't say anything, he'd have more sense than that. I could trust him; that's why I'd told him. And face it, I'd had to tell somebody, I couldn't keep it tied up inside me much longer. Sooner or later I'd have told somebody like Grace, for God's sake, and Grace would never in a million *years* understand. With Tom, no matter what else he might think, I knew he'd understand.

And keep his mouth shut. Right?

Christ, I hoped so.

I was really feeling bugged. Frustrated and irritable and about ready to punch somebody in the mouth. I'd been having days like this every once in a while for the last few months, and I didn't know what to do about them, how to deal with them. Except wait them out, wait for it all to go away, which sooner or later it always did.

Down on 72nd Street, I went over to the Parkway again. Paul had tried starting a couple of conversations, but I didn't feel like talking. I'd come close, a few times in the last week, to telling Paul about the liquor store, but I didn't really know Paul as well as I knew Tom, I didn't have that same sense of closeness with him. And now that I'd told Tom, I didn't want to tell anyone else at all. Or talk to anyone else at all. In fact, part of me was sorry I'd talked to Tom.

We got back up on the Parkway, and rolled along. The air was a little better over the river, and the motion of the car made a breeze that at least blew the stink off. My mood was picking up.

Then I spotted the white Cadillac Eldorado up ahead, moving right along. It was the same model as the one this morning, but a different color. I saw him up there, looking so cute and arrogant and rich, and all the bile came right back into me again, stronger than ever.

I eased up on him and saw he had New York plates. Good. If I gave him a ticket he couldn't be a scofflaw, fade away into some other state and thumb his nose at me. He'd have to pay up or have a mess on his hands when it came time to renew his license.

I clocked him a mile, and he was doing fifty-four. Good enough.

"I'm taking the Caddy," I said.

I guess Paul had been half-asleep, sitting there in the silence next to me. He sat up straighter and looked ahead and said, "The what?"

"That white Caddy."

Paul studied the Cad, and raised his eyebrows at me. "How come?"

"I feel like it. He's doing fifty-four."

I hit the dome light, but not the siren. He could see me, he wouldn't need a lot of noise. He slowed right away, and I crowded him off onto the shoulder.

Paul said, "You cut him a little close there."

"He should of braked harder." I looked at Paul, waiting for him to say something else, but all he did was shrug, as though to say he didn't care, it wasn't his business—which it wasn't—so I got out of the car and went back to talk to the driver of the Cad.

He was about forty, with those pop-eyes called thyroid. He was wearing a suit and a tie, and when I went back to talk to him he opened his window by pushing a button. I asked to see his license and registration, and stood there a long time reading them, waiting for him to start a conversation. His name was Daniel Mossman, and he leased the Cad from a company in Tarrytown. And he didn't have anything to say for himself at all. I said, "You know the speed limit along this stretch, Dan?"

"Fifty," he said.

"You know what speed I clocked you at, Dan?"

"I believe I was doing about fifty-five." There was no expression in his voice, nothing in his face, and those pop-eyes just looked at me like a fish.

I said, "What do you do for a living, Dan?"

"I'm an attorney," he said.

An attorney. He couldn't even say lawyer. I was twice as irritable as before. I went back to the patrol car and got behind the wheel, holding Mossman's license and registration.

Paul looked over at me, and rubbed his thumb and finger together. "Anything?"

I shook my head. "No," I said. "I'm giving the bastard a ticket."

2

They co-hosted a barbecue for some friends in the neighborhood. The grill was in Tom's backyard, so that's where the party was, but they both pitched in for the food and drink, and both wives worked on the salads and the desserts and in setting things up. The first humid hot spell of the summer had broken the day before with one of those real drenching summer downpours, but by the morning of the barbecue the yard was almost completely dry. Also, the humidity was way down, and the temperature had dropped into the high seventies. Perfect weather for a party in the backyard.

There were four other couples invited, all from the same block, plus their kids. None of them were on the force, and in fact only one of them even worked in the city; Tom and Joe liked them all mostly because they could forget their own jobs while with them.

Before the party, they'd brought all the kitchen chairs and folding chairs out of both houses and scattered them around Tom's yard, and set up a bar on a card table back by the grill. They had gin and vodka and scotch, plus soft drinks for the kids. Mary had put a sheet over the card table instead of a tablecloth, one of those printed sheets with a flower design all over it, and it really looked nice there.

Before dinner, Tom and Joe took turns being bartender, one serving the drinks while the other wandered around the yard playing host. But Tom was the official chef, like it said on his apron, so while he was doing the chicken quarters and the hamburgers on the outdoor grill Joe became the bartender full time. Then, after everybody had eaten, Tom became bartender again and Joe just stood around or occasionally went to one kitchen or the other for more ice. They both had ice-makers in their refrigerators, but with fifteen or twenty people all drinking iced drinks at once—and the kids mostly spilling theirs out on the grass—you can use ice faster than any refrigerator on earth can make it. It was a good thing to have two.

It was a good party, as that kind of party goes. That is, there weren't any long uncomfortable silences, and there weren't any fist-fights. In fact, nobody got falling down drunk, which was kind of unusual. The people on the block, mostly the men, tended to be pretty two-fisted drinkers, and the way the summertime parties usually went, the survivors carried the others home. Maybe it was because it was so early in the season, and the group wasn't into the swing of things yet. Or maybe it was simply the nice weather after the long stretch of humidity; everybody was feeling so pleasant and comfortable that nobody wanted to spoil it with a hangover.

It was getting toward evening when Joe wandered over to the bar again and said, "How's the ice holding out?"

"We need some."

"No sooner said," Joe told him, and went over to his own kitchen, and brought back a glass pitcher full of the little half-moon cubes. He worked his way through the guests to the card table, where Tom was standing with his chef's apron still on. He didn't have any customers right at that moment. Joe put the pitcher down and said, "There you go."

Tom began to switch the ice cubes to his Colonial ice-bucket. Joe rooted around among all the dirty glasses on the card table, and finally said, "What did I do with my drink?"

"I'll make you another."

"Thanks."

Joe was drinking scotch and soda. Tom knew that wasn't considered a summertime drink, but he'd never said anything; it was what Joe liked all year 'round, so why pester him?

Tom started making the drink, and Joe turned to look at the freeloaders all over the lawn in the gloom of twilight. The men were talking with men, the women were talking with women, the kids were running around the adults like motorcycles around traffic stanchions. It occurred to Joe that of all the women currently in the backyard the only one he really wanted to ball was Mary, who was Tom's wife. Then she turned, and he realized in the half-light he'd made a mistake and it was Grace he'd been staring at, his own wife. He grinned and shook his head, and almost turned to tell Tom what he'd just done when he realized that wouldn't be a good idea.

He looked around some more, and at last saw Mary way over by the house. Both women were wearing slacks with stripes, and fuzzy sweaters; Mary's pink, Grace's white. Because of the party they'd both gone off to the beauty parlor this morning and had come back with hairdos that sat up on top of their heads like Venusian helmets, hair styles that had absolutely nothing to do with who they really were. But that was women for you, they did that sort of thing.

Tom said, "Joe?"

Joe turned. "Yeah?"

"You remember that— Here." Tom handed over the fresh drink.

"Thanks."

"You remember," Tom said, "that thing you told me the other day about the liquor store?"

Joe pulled at his drink, and grinned. "Sure."

Tom hesitated, biting his lower lip, looking worriedly at

the people at the other end of the yard. Finally, all in a rush, he said, "Have you done it again?"

Joe frowned, not sure what he was getting at. "No. Why?"

"You thought about it?"

With a little shrug, Joe looked away. "A couple times, I guess. I didn't want to push my luck."

Tom nodded. "Yeah, I guess so."

One of the guests came up then, stopping the conversation for a while. He was named George Hendricks, and he ran a supermarket over in the five towns. He was a little drunk now, not terrible, and he came up with a loose grin on his face and said, "Time for a refill."

"You're a screwdriver," Tom said, and took his glass.

"You're goddam right I am," George said. He was about thirty pounds overweight, and always hinting about what a sex maniac he was. Now he said, mostly to Joe, since Tom was busy making his drink, "You two both still work in the city, huh?"

Joe nodded. "Yeah, we do."

"Not me," George said. "I'm out of that rat-race for good." Up till a few years ago, he'd managed a Finast in Queens.

Drunks always irritated Joe, even when he was off duty. Skeptical, a little bored, he said to George, "It's that different out here?"

"Hell, yes. You know that yourself, you moved out here."

"Grace and the kids are out here," Joe said. "I'm still in the city."

Tom held George's fresh drink out to him: "Here."

"Thanks." George took the glass, but didn't drink yet. He was still involved in his conversation with Joe. He said, "I don't see how you guys stand it. The city is nothing but wall-to-wall crooks. Everybody out to chisel a dollar."

Joe merely shrugged, but Tom said, "It's the way of the world, George."

"Not out here," George said. He made it one of those definite, don't-argue-with-me statements.

"Out here," Tom said, "just like any place else. It's all the same."

"You guys," George said, and shook his head. "You think everybody's crooked in the whole world. It's being in the city gives you that idea." He gave a knowing grin, and rubbed his thumb and finger together. "Being in on it a little."

Joe, who'd been looking at the women again, trying without success to develop an interest in George's wife, turned his head and gave George a flat stare. "Is that right?"

"One hundred per cent," George said. "I know about New York City cops."

"That's the same everywhere, too," Tom said. He wasn't offended; he'd given up being sore about slurs like that years ago. He said, "You think the guys in the precinct out here could make it on their salaries?"

George laughed and pointed his drink at Tom. "See what I mean? The city corrupts your mind, you think everybody in the world is a crook."

Suddenly irritated, Joe said, "George, you come home every night with a sack of groceries. You don't do that on any employee discount, you just pack up those groceries and walk out of the store."

George was outraged. He stood up straighter, and got drunker. "I work for them!" he said, his voice loud enough to carry to the far end of the yard. "If the chain paid a man a decent salary—"

"You'd do the same thing," Joe said.

Smoothly, Tom said, "Not necessarily, Joe." He was a natural host, he eased groups through the rough spots. He said to Joe, but for George's benefit, "Everybody hustles, but nobody wants to. I don't want Mary to work, you don't want Grace to work, George doesn't want Phyllis to work, but what are you gonna do?"

George probably embarrassed at having gotten mad, made a heavy attempt at humor. "Lose the house to the bank," he said.

Tom said, "The way I see it, the problem is really very

simple. There's so and so much money, and there's so and so many people. And there isn't quite enough money to go around. So you do the only thing that's left; you steal to make up the difference."

Joe gave Tom a warning look, but Tom hadn't been thinking about the liquor store just then, and in any case didn't notice him.

George, still trying to make up for his bad temper, said, "Okay. I can go along with that. You got to make up the difference, and you do a little of this and that. Like me with the groceries." Then, with a smirk, and another heavy attempt at humor, he added, "And you guys with whatever you can get."

"Don't kid yourself," Joe said. He was still serious. He said, "In our position, we could get whatever we wanted. We restrain ourselves, that's all."

George laughed, and Tom gave Joe a thoughtful look. But Joe was moodily glaring at George; he was thinking he'd like to give him a ticket.

Tom

The way to take somebody out of a place full of his friends is to do it fast. This was a coffee shop on Macdougal Street in Greenwich Village, a hangout of several different kinds of freaks, and at one o'clock on a Saturday night it was full; college students, tourists, local citizens, hippies passing through town, a general cross-section of people who don't like cops.

Ed waited outside on the sidewalk. If worse came to worse, I'd push Lambeth into running and he'd run straight into Ed's arms.

He was at a table midway along on the right, just as the finger had said. He was with four other people, two male and two female, and he had a bunched-up handkerchief in his left hand and kept patting his nose with it. Either he had a cold or he was on something; most of them sooner or later try a free sample of what they sell.

I stopped behind his chair, and leaned over him slightly. "Lambeth?"

When he looked up over his shoulder, I saw that his eyes

were watery and red-lined. It was still maybe a cold, but it was still more likely heroin. He said, "Yeah?"

Despite what they say in the movies, a plainclothes detective is not instantly recognizable as a cop. "Police," I said, low enough so he'd be the only one to hear the word clearly. "Come on along with me."

He had a loose kind of grin. "I don't think so, man," he said, and faced around to his friends again.

He was wearing a fringed deerskin vest. I reached over his shoulders and yanked the vest back around his arms, pinning him like a straitjacket. At the same time, I lifted him and kicked the chair out from under him.

Nobody thinks faster than his body. If he'd just let himself drop to the floor then, he would have gotten away from me. Maybe long enough for his friends and some busybody bystanders to louse me up. But his body reacted automatically, getting his feet under him, helping him to stand, and the instant he had his balance I turned him toward the front and ran him full speed at the door.

He yelled, and tried to squirm to the side, but I had him pinned and moving. The door was closed, but would open with a push; I pushed it with his head. We'd gone through so fast there hadn't been time for anybody to react along the way.

Lambeth was still struggling when we hit the street. Ed was standing there, and our Ford was parked right in front. I didn't slow down, but kept running across the sidewalk and slammed Lambeth into the side of the car. I wanted the wind and the fight out of him. I pulled him back a foot or two, and bounced him off the car again, and this time he sagged and quit fighting.

Ed was beside me with the cuffs. I let go of the vest, slid my hands down Lambeth's arms, and lifted his arms up behind him like pump handles, bending him over the trunk of the car. Ed clicked the cuffs on, and opened the Ford's rear door.

I was shifting Lambeth over into position to shove him into

the car when somebody tapped me on the upper arm, and a female voice said, "Officer?"

I looked around at a middle-aged tourist woman in a red-and-white flowered dress and a straw purse. She looked angry, but as though she was making a great effort to be reasonable. She said, "Are you absolutely sure that much violence was necessary?"

Lambeth's friends would be coming out any second. "I don't know, lady," I said. "It's how much I used." Then I turned away from her again and kicked Lambeth into the car and followed him in. Ed shut the door behind me, got behind the wheel, and we pulled away from there as the coffee-shop door opened and people began to pile out into the street.

Lambeth was crumpled up on the right side of the rear seat like a dead dog. I adjusted him around into a sitting position. He looked dazed, and he mumbled something, but I couldn't tell what.

Up front, Ed said, "Tom?"

"Yeah?"

"Looks like you're gonna get another letter in your file."

I looked at him, and he was checking the rear-view mirror, looking at the situation behind us. "Is that right," I said.

"She's taking down the license number," he said.

"I'll blame you," I said.

Ed chuckled, and we turned a corner, and headed uptown.

After a couple of blocks, Lambeth suddenly said, "My arms hurt, man."

I looked at him. He was wide awake, and apparently rational. You don't switch off a cold that easily. I said, "Don't stick needles in them."

"With these cuffs on, man," he said. "I'm all twisted around."

"Sorry," I said.

"Will you take them off?"

"At the station."

"If I give you my word of honor, I won't try—"

I laughed at him. "Forget it," I said.

He gave me a level look, and then a sad kind of smile. "That's right," he said. "Nobody's got any honor around here, do they?"

"Not the last time I looked."

He wriggled around for thirty seconds or so, and apparently finally got himself into a more comfortable position, because he stopped moving, and sighed, and settled down to watch the city go by.

I settled down, too, but not that much. We were traveling without siren or flashing light, in an unmarked green car, which meant we were going with the general flow of the traffic. Unless there's a specific reason to make a fuss, it's better not to. But the result was, we were from time to time being stopped by red lights, and from time to time crawling along in very slow traffic, and I didn't want Lambeth to suddenly decide to jump out of the car and make a run for it with Ed's cuffs. The door was locked, and he seemed quiet, but I nevertheless kept my eye on him.

After three or four minutes of watching the world outside the window, Lambeth sighed and looked at me, and said, "I'm ready to get out of this city, man."

I had to laugh again. "You'll get your wish," I told him. "It'll probably be ten years before you see New York again."

He nodded, grinning at himself. He seemed less freaky, more human, than he'd been back in the coffee shop. "I dig," he said. Then he gave me a serious look, and said, "Tell me something, man. Give me your opinion on a question I have in my mind."

"If I can."

"What do you say; is it the bigger punishment to get sent out of this city, or to stay here?"

"You tell me," I said. "Why'd you stay here long enough to get yourself into a bind like this?"

He shrugged. "Why do you stay, man?"

"I'm not dealing," I said.

"Sure you are," he said. "You're dealing in machismo, man, just like I'm dealing in scat."

Ever since drugs got tied in with the cultural revolution, the junkies have had a richer line of horseshit. "Anything you say," I said, and turned away to look out my own window.

"None of us started out this way, man," he said. "We all started out as babies, innocent and pure."

I looked at him again. "One time," I said, "a guy a lot like you, full of talk, he showed me a picture of his mother. And while I was looking at it he made a grab at my hip for my gun."

He gave a big broad grin; he was delighted. "You stay in this town, man," he said. "You're gonna like what it does to you."

Joe

The woman was all right coming down the stairs. She was bleeding from a long cut on her right arm, and she had blood all over her face and hands and clothes, some of it her own and some of it her husband's and I guess she was still dazed by it all. But when we went out the front door and she looked down the tenement steps and saw the crowd of people standing around gaping at her, she flipped her lid. She started screaming and struggling and carrying on, and it was hell to get her down the steps to the sidewalk, particularly because all the blood made her slippery and tough to hold onto.

I didn't like that situation at all. Two uniformed white cops dragging a bloody black woman down the steps into a crowd in Harlem. I didn't like any part of it, and from the expression on Paul's face he didn't like it either.

The woman was yelling, "Let me go! Let me go! He cut me first, let me go! I got a right, I got a right, let me go!" And finally, as we neared the bottom of the stoop, I could hear over her yelling the sound of a siren coming. It was an ambulance, and I was glad to see it.

We got to the sidewalk just as the ambulance came to a stop at the curb. The crowd was keeping out of it so far, giving us a big open space on the sidewalk, moving out of the way of the ambulance. All I wanted was to get this over with and go away somewhere for a while. The woman was wriggling and squirming like an eel, a long black eel covered with blood and screaming with a voice like a fingernail on a blackboard.

It was one of those high-sided ambulances, a boxy van, and it carried four attendants, two in front and two in the back, all dressed in white. But not for long. The four of them climbed out and came running over to us and got hold of the woman. One of them said, "All right, we've got her."

"About time you got here," I said. I knew they'd been as fast as could be expected, but the situation had me scared, and when I'm scared I get mad, and when I'm mad I sound off.

They didn't pay any attention to me, which was the right thing to do. One of them said to the woman, "Come on, honey, let's fix the old arm."

Their being dressed in white had made a connection with the woman, because now she started to yell, "I want my own doctor. You take me to my own doctor!"

The four attendants hustled the woman to the ambulance, having as much trouble with her as we'd had, and a second ambulance arrived, pulling in behind the first. Two guys came out of this one, both also dressed in white, and came over to us. One of them said, "Where's the stiff?"

I couldn't say anything; I was having trouble breathing. I just pointed at the building, and Paul said, "Third floor rear. In the kitchen. She really cut him to pieces."

Two more had come out of the back of the second ambulance, carrying a rolled-up stretcher. The four of them went up the stoop and into the building. At the same time, the first four were getting the woman into the first ambulance, with some trouble. So much movement, so many flashing red lights, kept the crowd from deciding to join in; they'd just be spectators this time.

Paul and I were finished with this one, for right now. We still had to call in, and later on there'd be forms to do at the station, but for the next couple minutes the action had moved away from us. And it hadn't happened any too soon.

Excitement carries you through the tense parts. It had been that way from the beginning, from the first time I was around at a violent situation, which was a ten-year-old kid hit by a cab on Central Park West. He was still alive, the kid, and when you looked at him you wished he wasn't. But the excitement and noise and movement had carried me through the whole scene, and it wasn't until we were driving away from it that I had Jerry, an older cop who was my first partner, pull the car over to the curb and stop so I could get out and up-chuck.

That's never changed, from that day to this. I don't up-chuck anymore, but the run of emotions is still the same; the excitement carries me through the tense part or the ugly part or the violent part, and then there's a sick queasy letdown that comes after it.

The patrol car was across the street where we'd left it, with its engine off and its flasher on. The two of us went over there, pushing our way through the crowd, ignoring the questions they were asking us and ignoring what was going on behind us. When we got to the car, we stood beside it a minute, not talking or moving or doing anything. I don't know what Paul was looking at; I was looking at the car roof.

A siren started again. I looked around, and the first ambulance was leaving, taking the woman to Bellevue. I turned to look at Paul, and he had blood smeared all over his shirt-front, and dotted on his face and arms like measles. "You got blood on you," I said.

"You, too," he said.

I looked down at myself. When we'd come down from the third floor, I'd been on the side of the woman where her cut arm was, and I had even more blood on me than Paul did. My bare arms, from elbow to wrist, were soaked in blood, the hair all matted, like a cat that's been run over. Now that

I was looking at myself, with the sun beating down on me, I could feel the blood drying against my skin, shrinking up into a thin wrinkled layer of scab.

"Christ," I said. I turned away from Paul and leaned my left side against the car and stretched my left arm away from me across the white car roof, where the flashing light kept changing the color of it. I couldn't think about getting clean, I couldn't think about what I was supposed to do next, all I could think was, *I've got to get out of this. I've got to get out of this.*

3

They were both on the four-to-midnight shift that time, so they got to drive home pretty late at night, after most of the traffic had thinned out. That was the advantage of the four-to-twelve; they got to drive into town in the middle of the afternoon, before the rush hour, and in any case in the opposite direction from most of the traffic, and then at the other end of the shift they could drive home along practically empty roads.

The disadvantage of the four-to-midnight was that it was the busiest shift of all. They weren't driving during the rush hour, but they were *working* during it, and then on into the evening, the high-crime period of the day. Muggings hit their peak between six and eight, when people are coming home from work. Around the same time, the husbands and wives start fighting with each other, and a little later the drunks join in. And store robberies—like the one Joe had pulled—occur most frequently in that period between sundown and ten o'clock, when most of the stores finally close. So when they were on the four-to-midnight shift they tended to spend most of their time working, and very little of it sitting down.

But then midnight would come around at last, and this shift too would come to an end, and they would get to sail home along practically deserted highways once they'd left Manhattan, all by themselves, thinking their thoughts. Which is what they were doing now.

Tom was driving his Chevrolet tonight; six years old, bought used, a gas burner and an oil eater, with bad springs and a loose clutch. He kept talking about trading it in on something a little newer, but he couldn't bring himself to take it to a used-car dealer and try to get a price on it. He knew too well what this car was worth.

They were riding along without any conversation between them, both tired from the long day, both remembering things that had happened earlier in the week. Tom was going over in his head the conversation with the hippie junk dealer, trying to find better answers to the things the guy had said, and also trying to figure out why he couldn't seem to get that conversation out of his mind. And Joe was remembering the blood drying on his arm in the sun, stretched out across the roof of the patrol car, looking like something from a monster movie and not anything that could ever have been a part of himself at all. He didn't particularly want to remember that scene, but it just seemed to stay in his head, no matter what.

Gradually, as they left the city behind them, Tom's thoughts shifted away from the hippie, roamed around, touched on this and that, and settled on a new subject. It wasn't exactly Joe's liquor store, though the liquor store was behind what he was thinking about now. All at once he broke the silence, saying, "Joe?"

Joe blinked. It was like coming out of sleep, or a dentist's anesthetic. He looked at Tom's profile and said, "Yeah?"

"Let me ask you a question."

"Sure."

Tom kept looking straight ahead through the windshield. "What would you do," he said, "if you had a million dollars?"

Joe's answer was immediate, as if he'd been ready for this question all of his life. "Go to Montana with Chet Huntley," he said.

Tom frowned slightly and shook his head. "No," he said. "I mean really."

"So do I."

Tom turned his head and studied Joe's face—they both had very serious expressions—and then he looked out the windshield again and said, "Not me. I'd go to the Caribbean."

Joe watched him. "You would, huh?"

"That's right." Tom grinned a little, thinking about it. "One of those islands down there. Trinidad." He stretched the word out, pronouncing it as though saying it was tasting something sweet.

Joe nodded, and looked around at the glove compartment. "But here we are instead," he said.

Tom glanced at him again, then faced front. He felt very cautious now, like a man with a bag of groceries walking on ice. He said, "Remember what you told George last week?"

"Big mouth? No, what did I tell him?"

"That we could get anything we want," Tom said, "only we restrain ourselves."

Joe grinned. "I remember. I thought you were gonna tell him about my liquor store."

Tom wasn't going to get distracted by side issues now; he'd started moving, and he was going to keep moving. Ignoring the liquor-store remark, he said, "Well, what the hell, why don't we?"

Joe didn't get it. "Why don't we what?"

"*Do* it!" Tom said. He'd been bottling this up for days, his voice was vibrating with it. "Get everything we want," he said, "just like you said."

Skeptical, Joe said, "Like how? Liquor stores?"

Tom took one hand off the wheel to wave that away, impatient with it. "That's nothing, Joe," he said, "that's crap! That stinking city back there is full of money, and in our position by God we really *can* get anything we want. A million dollars apiece, in one job.''

Joe didn't believe it yet, but he was interested. ''What job?''

Tom shrugged. ''We've got our choice. Anything we want to work out. Some big jewelry company. A bank. Whatever we want.''

Suddenly Joe saw it, and he started to laugh. ''Disguised as cops!''

''That's right!'' Tom said. He was laughing, too. ''Disguised as cops!''

The two of them sat in the car and just laughed.

Joe

The subway had fucked up again. Paul and I were positioned at a manhole on Broadway, where the people were coming up. They'd been down there for over an hour, and there'd been some smoke, and now they'd had to walk single file in the tunnel for a ways, and come up a metal ladder, and at last out onto the street. It was nine-thirty at night, traffic was being detoured around us, and we had our patrol car between the manhole and the street, flasher going.

Most of the people coming up were just stunned, all they wanted was to get the hell away from there. A few were grateful and said thank you to Paul or me for helping them up the last few steps. And a few were pissed off and wanted to take it out on a representative of the municipal government, which at the moment was Paul and me. These last few we ignored; they'd make an angry remark or two, and then they'd stomp off, and that would be the end of it.

Except this one guy. He stood around on the other side of us, away from the manhole, and yammered at us. He was about fifty, dressed in a suit, carrying an attaché case. He was like a manager or supervisor type, and all he wanted to do was stand there and yell, while Paul and I helped the rest of the people up out of the manhole.

He went on like this: "This city is a disgrace! It's a disgrace! You aren't safe here! And who cares? Does anybody care? Everything breaks down, and nobody gives a God damn! Everybody's in the *union*! Teachers on strike, subways on strike, cops on strike, sanitation on strike. Money money money, and when they work do they *do* anything? Do they teach? Don't make me laugh! The subways are a menace, they're a menace! Sanitation? Look at the streets! Big raises, big pay, and look at the streets! And you *cops*! Gimmie gimme gimme, and where are you? Your apartment gets robbed, and where *are* you? Some dope addict attacks your wife in the street, and where's the *cops*?"

Up till then we ignored him, the both of us; like he was a regular part of the city noise. Which in a way he was. But then he made a mistake, he overstepped himself. He reached out and tugged at my elbow, and he yelled, "Are you listening to me?"

They're not going to start grabbing me. I turned around and looked at him, and he was so amazed he went back a step. The city had finally noticed him. I said to him, "I'm coming to the conclusion you fell coming up those stairs and broke your nose."

It took him a second to work it out, and then he backpedaled some more, and yelled, "You mustn't care much about keeping that badge of yours."

I was about to tell him what he could do with the badge, pin first, but he was still backing away, and the hell with him. I turned back and helped Paul with a fat old lady who was having trouble climbing because of bad ankles. But I kept thinking about what the guy had said.

4

It was a hot sunny day, and they were both in Joe's backyard. Where the barbecue was in Tom's backyard, Joe had put in a pool; one of those above-the-ground pools, four foot high and ten foot across. They were both drinking beer, Joe was in a bathing suit and Tom was in slacks and shirt, and Joe was trying to fix the pool filter. The damn thing was always getting screwed up one way or another, it was about the most delicate machine ever made. It sometimes seemed as though Joe spent his entire summers fixing the pool filter.

They'd lived next door to one another for nine years now. Tom had bought his house first, eleven years ago, and when Joe wanted to move out of the city after Jackie was born it happened the house next door to Tom was just going on the market. Back then, they'd both been in uniform, and sometimes even partnered. They'd known each other for years, liked one another, it seemed they ought to make good neighbors. And they did.

The houses weren't the greatest in the world, but they were livable. They were in a development put up right after the war, back when the notion of curving streets was still new. They had three bedrooms, all on one floor, and a smallish attic that a lot of the guys in the neighborhood had converted to a fourth bedroom. Fortunately, neither Tom nor Joe had families big enough to need that, and neither intended to have families any bigger than they already had, so they could keep their attics as attics, and fill them with all that junk everybody gradually collects through life, that nobody has any use for anymore, but that nobody wants to throw away.

The houses weren't bad. They were old enough to have been built before plastics were really big, which meant they were constructed fairly well, mostly of wood. They had clapboard siding that had to be painted every few years, they had half-basements for the utilities, the backyards were a pretty good size, and there was a detached one-car garage at the rear of each and every property. Gravel driveways separated the houses and defined the property lines, and every house in three or four blocks in all directions looked exactly the same, except for color of paint job or any special additions or changes that anybody might have made. Neither Tom nor Joe had made any special changes, so they both had the original basic house, just the way it had come from the architect's drawing board; only a little older.

Most people put up fences along the sides of their backyards, mostly to keep little kids inside, but Tom and Joe hadn't done that. Between Tom and his neighbor on the right there was a basket-weave wooden fence put up by the neighbor, and between Joe and his neighbor on the left there was a chain-link fence covered with vines put up by that neighbor, but between their own two yards there was nothing but the remains of a hedge planted by some previous owner of one of their houses. The hedge had big gaps in it where they walked back and forth all the time, and they could never agree who was supposed to keep it trimmed, so nobody did, and it was gradually dying. And taking years to do it.

In every single house in the development that either of them had ever heard of, the kitchen linoleum was all cracked and buckled. In a lot of houses, including both of theirs, the basement leaked.

They hadn't done any more talking about the robbery idea since that one time in the car, but they'd both been thinking about it. Not that it was real, not that they thought they would actually commit a major robbery somewhere, but just that it was nice to daydream about a possible way of getting themselves out of this grind.

Joe wasn't thinking about the robbery idea at the moment, mostly because his mind was taken up with the problem of the pool filter, but Tom's mind was ticking along on the subject, and all at once he said, "Hey."

Joe was sitting cross-legged on the ground, surrounded by hoses and washers and nuts. He put a double handful of parts down, wiped his face with his hand, drank beer, looked over at Tom, and said, "What?"

"What do you think the Russians would pay for him," Tom said, "if we kidnapped their ambassador?"

Joe squinted at him in the sunlight. "You serious?"

"Why not? Profitable and patriotic both."

Joe thought about it for a couple of seconds, and then he looked all around the backyard and said, "Where the hell are we going to keep the Russian ambassador?"

Tom looked off toward his own yard next door. "Yeah," he said. "That's a problem."

Joe shook his head and went back to the pool filter. Tom drank some more beer. They both thought their thoughts.

Tom

The squeal was at a junior high school; they'd found a missing teacher, dead.

It was about eleven in the morning, a cloudy day that promised rain for later on. Ed and I drove over in the Ford and parked in the school zone out front. It was one of the old gray stone school buildings, three stories high, looking more like a fortress than a place for kids. A concrete-covered play yard was on the right, surrounded by eight-foot-high chain link fence. Nobody was in it.

A recent fad among the kids has been to write nicknames on walls and subways and all over the damn place in either spray paint or felt-tip pen, both of which are very tough to get rid of, particularly from a porous surface like stone. The fad is for a kid to write his name or his nickname or some magic name he's worked out for himself, and then under it write the number of the street he lives on. "JUAN 135," for instance, or "BOSS ZOOM 92," that kind of thing.

The fad had hit the school building. As high as a child's

arm could reach, the names and numbers were scrawled everywhere on the walls, in black and red and blue and green and yellow. Some of the signatures were like little paintings, carefully and lovingly done, and some of them were just splashed and scrawled on, with runlets of paint dripping down from the bottoms of the letters, but most of them were simply reports of name and number, without flair or imagination: "Andy 87," "Beth 81," "Moro 103."

At first, all of that paintwork looked like vandalism and nothing more. But as I got used to it, to seeing it around, I realized it gave a brightly colored hem to the gray stone skirt of a building like this, that it had a very sunny Latin American flavor to it, and that once you got past the prejudice against marking up public property it wasn't that bad at all. Of course, I never said this to anybody.

Inside, we went to the principal's office, and he said he'd show us where the body was. Walking down the corridor with us, he said, "The room *was* a girl's lavatory, but all of the plumbing is out of it now. That's as far as they got with the modernizing plan." He was balding, about forty, with a moustache and horn-rim glasses and a slightly prissy manner, as though he were more sinned against than sinning.

We got curious stares from the teen-agers we passed, so apparently the news wasn't general yet about the discovery of the teacher's body.

Ed said, "Why didn't you report her missing?"

"So many of these younger teachers," the principal said, "they're apt to take two or three days off without warning, we didn't think a thing of it. Another teacher noticed the smell this morning, that's why she happened to look."

I said, "We'll want to talk to her. The other teacher."

"Of course," he said. "She's in the building at the moment. With Miss Evans, what we think happened, a group of them must have decided to rape her, and took her in there. At some point she must have fought back. I don't think they brought her in there with the intention of killing her."

Intentions didn't matter, if she was dead. None of us said

any more, until the principal stopped and pointed at a door and said, "She's in there."

I went to the door as Ed said to the principal, "What about her family? You try calling her at home?"

I opened the door and took a step in, and the smell hit me in the face. Then, in the dim light through the dirty translucent windows, I saw her lying on the floor over against the green wall. Plaster showed white where they'd pulled the sinks out. She'd been there for a week, and there were rats in the building. "God," I said, and backed out, and slammed the door.

The principal was answering Ed's question, saying, "She lived alone in—" Then he noticed, and said, "Oh, I'm terribly sorry! I should have warned you, I suppose."

Ed took a step toward me, looking worried. "You okay, Tom?"

I waved my hand at him, to keep back away from the room. "Leave it for the ambulance." I could feel the blood draining out of my head, a sensation of coldness in my arms and feet.

The principal, still prissy but bewildered, said, "I'm really very sorry. I took it for granted you were hardened to that sort of thing."

I pushed past the two of them, needing to get outdoors. Hardened to that sort of thing. Jesus H. Christ!

5

They had the midnight-to-eight shift that week. It's the quietest of the three shifts, but at eight o'clock in the morning, driving home eastward into the rising sun, a man's eyes feel covered with sand and he thinks his stomach will never be comfortable again.

Joe left the station first and got the Plymouth out of the lot and drove down the block to double-park across the street from the precinct house. He had to wait ten minutes before Tom came out, looking disgusted, and slid into the passenger seat.

Joe said, "What's the problem?"

"Little talk from the Lieutenant," Tom said. "Some damn thing about narcotics."

"What about it?"

Tom yawned, fighting it, and gave an angry shrug. "Anything you pick up, be sure you turn it in. The usual noise."

Joe put the Plymouth in gear and started through the maze crosstown and downtown to the Midtown Tunnel. "I wonder who they caught," he said.

"Nobody from this house," Tom said. He yawned again, giving in to it this time, and rubbed his face with both hands. "Boy, am I ready for sleep."

"I got me an idea," Joe said.

Tom knew at once what he meant. Looking at him, interested, he said, "You do? What?"

"Paintings from a museum."

Tom frowned. "I don't follow."

"Listen," Joe said. "They got paintings in those museums, they're worth a million dollars each. We take ten, we sell them back for four million. That's two million for each of us."

Tom's frown deepened. He scratched the side of his jaw, making a sound like sandpaper. "I don't know," he said. "Ten paintings. They'd be as tough to hide as my Russian ambassador."

"I could put them in my garage," Joe said. "Who's gonna look in a garage?"

"Your kids would wreck them in a day."

Joe didn't want to give this up; it was the only idea he'd managed to come up with. "Five paintings," he said. "One million apiece."

Tom didn't answer right away. He chewed the inside of his cheek and brooded out at the traffic and tried to figure out not only what was specifically wrong with the paintings idea, but also a general rule to live by, to guide his thinking on the subject of the robbery. It was a way of taking it seriously and yet not taking it seriously at the same time. Finally he said, "We don't want something we have to give back. Nothing we have to keep around us or hide for a while. We want something with fast turnover."

Reluctantly, Joe nodded. "Yeah, I guess you're right," he said, admitting it. "We're not in a position for that kind of thing."

"That's right."

"But we don't want cash. We talked about that."

Tom nodded. "I know. Everybody keeps serial numbers."

Joe said, "So it isn't that easy."

"I never said it was."

They were both quiet for a while, thinking it over. They were practically to the tunnel when Tom spoke up again, restating the rule he'd worked out earlier; narrowing the range of it, refining it. Gazing out the windshield, he said, "What we want is something we can unload fast, for big money."

"Right," Joe said. "*And* a buyer. Some rich person with a lot of cash."

They were about to enter the tunnel. "Rich people," Tom said. He was thinking very hard. They both were.

Joe

There were camera crews from two of the television news programs that showed up to cover it. The way we handled that, Paul and I were the first car that reached the scene after the call came in, so Paul got interviewed by the one crew and I got interviewed by the other.

I wasn't nervous at all. I'd never been interviewed personally on television before, but of course I'd watched the news sometimes when other guys did it, at the scene of an explosion or a big water-main break or something like that. Three times I'd seen guys I actually knew in real life being interviewed. Also, sometimes while taking a shower I'd run a fantasy kind of interview in my head, the questions and the answers and all, and how I'd hold my face. So you might say I was pretty well rehearsed.

The way they set things up for the interview, they put the camera so it was facing the building, so the building would show behind me and the interviewer while we were doing our thing. It was one of those huge office buildings being constructed there, and the hardhats kept steady working away at it all through the interview. One of their number had got himself killed, but that had only held their interest for maybe five minutes. Where money is concerned, you keep your mind on the job, you get it done.

These buildings are going up all over town, big glass and stone boxes full of office space. Practically none of them have apartments in them, because who wants to live in Manhattan? Manhattan is a place you work in, that's all.

The buildings have been going up ever since the end of the Second World War. Good times, bad times, boom, recession, it doesn't matter, they just keep going up. For the last ten years or so, most of them have been on the east side of midtown, Third Avenue and Lexington Avenue, around there. The first thing you know, they'll give Third Avenue a classier name, the way they did with Fourth Avenue when the big office buildings went up on it and it was turned into Park Avenue South.

Anyway, that's the section where most of the new buildings are concentrated, but there's others going up all over the place. The World Trade Center way downtown. Sixth Avenue across from Rockefeller Center. And a couple up in my precinct, including this one where they'd just had the death and where I was going to get myself interviewed.

A guy I was talking to in a bar a couple years ago said it was his opinion that the main characteristic of New York is that it's going through all the phases of the phoenix at once. You remember reading about the phoenix in high school? That's what he said New York was; but all at once. New York is living, and it's on fire, and it's dying, and it's ashes, and it's being reborn, all at the same time and all the time. And boy, those buildings look it, coming up out of brick rubble where yesterday's buildings were knocked down, coming up new and clean and pretty, and every once in a while killing somebody along the way.

The interviewer was a light-colored spade, with a moustache. You could see he thought he was the hottest thing in Bigtown. He and the director and the sound man and a couple other people fussed around a while, getting everything set, and then they started the interview. Somebody had written a little lead-in paragraph for the interviewer to say, and he had it on a clipboard he held in his other hand. The hand without the microphone, I mean. He had it on the clipboard, but he'd memorized it, because once he started talking he never looked at the clipboard at all.

Here's how it went: "Tragedy struck today at the site of the new Transcontinental Airlines Building on Columbus Avenue when a worker fell thirty-seven stories within the uncompleted building to his death. Patrolman Joseph Loomis was among the first at the scene." Then he turned to me and said, "Officer Loomis, could you describe what happened?"

I said, "The decedent was a full-blooded Mohawk Indian employed in putting the steel framework of the building up. What they call working the high iron. His name was George Brook. He was forty-three years of age."

The interviewer had been looking me straight in the eye the whole time I talked, as though I was hypnotizing him. As soon as I stopped, he whipped the microphone from my mouth back to his and said, "What apparently went wrong, Officer Loomis?"

I said, "Apparently his foot slipped. He was on the fifty-second story, which is as high as they have so far reached, and he fell thirty-seven stories and landed on the concrete floor at the fifteenth. He fell through the interior of the building, and the fifteenth is the highest story that they have a floor finished and put down."

Zip, the microphone went back over to him, and he said, "He found death thirty-seven stories down." *Zip*, the microphone came back to me.

I said, "No, he was probably dead from about the fortieth story on down. He kept hitting different metal beams on the way. They knocked some parts off him."

A spade can't turn white, but he tried. His eyes looked panicky, and very fast he said, "There are many full-blooded

Mohawk Indians working the high iron, aren't there, Officer Loomis?"

He wanted to change the subject? I didn't give a damn. I said, "That's right. There's a couple tribes of them live over in Brooklyn, they're all steelworkers."

Zip. "That's because they have a special affinity for heights, isn't it?" *Zip*.

I said, "I don't think so. They come down pretty often. About as often as anybody else."

You could see I'd suddenly caught his attention. He was interested in spite of himself. He said, "Then why do they do it?"

I shrugged. I said, "I suppose they have to make a living."

Not on television. His eyes filmed over, and in the furriest of brush-off voices he said, "Thank you very much, Officer Loomis," and turned away from me, ready to go into a close-out spiel.

Screw him. Just to louse up his timing, I said, "My pleasure," as he was opening his mouth again. Then I turned around and walked off.

I watched it that night, and all they used was the very first part of what I'd said. The rest was something the interviewer did on his own after I'd left; he stood in the same spot, with the construction going on behind him, and told you what happened. He said, among other things, "He found death thirty-seven stories down." So much for accuracy, the bastards.

I don't know what Paul said, but he didn't get on the tube at all. He claimed afterwards it was anti-Semitism.

Tom

Two big Mafia men had got picked up in our area the night before, and Ed and I were among the six plainclothesmen assigned to take them downtown this morning. These were really very big important Mafia people from New Jersey, and it was rare to find them actually in the city like this, where we could get hold of them. One of them was named Anthony Vigano and the other was named Louis Sambella.

Nobody knew if there was going to be any trouble or not. It wasn't too likely anybody would try to break them loose from us, but it was just possible some enemies of theirs might take a shot at them while they weren't surrounded by their bodyguards. So a lot of precautions were taken, including transporting them in two different unmarked cars, with three officers in each car.

I was driving one of the cars. I was alone in the front seat, and Vigano was squeezed in the back seat with Ed on his left and a detective named Charles Reddy on his right. We drove downtown without any incident, and then we had to take them up to a hearing room on the fourth floor. Arrangement had been made ahead of time, so we were met by a couple of uniformed cops at the side entrance and taken to an elevator already waiting for us.

Vigano and Sambella were very similar types; heavy-set, florid, their faces fixed in that expression of contempt that people get when they've been bossing other people around for a long time. They were expensively dressed, but maybe overdressed, the stripes a little too dominant on their suits, the cufflinks a little too big and shiny. And too many rings on their fingers. They smelled of after-shave and cologne and deodorant and haircream, and they weren't fazed a bit.

Nobody had said a word all the way down in the car, but now, once we were in the elevator and headed up for the fourth floor, Charles Reddy suddenly said, "You don't seem worried, Tony."

Vigano gave him a casual glance. If it bugged him to be called by his first name he didn't show it. He said, "Worried? I could buy you and sell you, what's to worry? I'll be home with my family tonight, and four years from now when the case is over in the courts I won't lose."

Nobody said anything back. What was there to say? "I could buy you and sell you." All I could do was stand there and look at him.

6

They both had the day off, and were at home. There was a birthday party going on in the kitchen of Joe's house. It was his daughter Jackie's ninth birthday, and the kitchen was crammed with kids and mothers, a lot more of them than the room could really hold. But nobody seemed to mind. The kids seemed to enjoy being squeezed in together like that, and the mothers were having a good time pretending to be working too hard.

Joe stood in the kitchen doorway, watching with a little grin on his face. He got a kick out of the racket and the mess the kids were making, and he also liked looking at the mothers' bodies as they moved around trying to keep things organized. It was a hot day anyway, and the kitchen was small, and everybody was sweating, and nobody was wearing a lot of extra clothing in the heat. The women were very sexy moving around, with their hair plastered to their foreheads and their faces shiny and their dresses wet in the small of the back and their legs making brushing sounds against each other as they walked.

Joe had a little fantasy going in the back of his head, in which he would catch the eye of one of the mothers and give her a little come-here kind of head gesture, and she'd come over and say, "What is it?"

"Telephone," he'd say.

"For me?" she'd say.

"Come take it in the bedroom," he'd say. (He grinned to himself at that sentence, he really liked it.)

So they'd go into the bedroom and she'd pick up the phone and turn to him a little confused and say, "There isn't anybody here."

And he'd grin at her, and maybe wink, and say, "I know. What do you say we rest a minute?"

And she'd grin back, and give him a look, and say, "What do you have in mind, Joe?"

And he'd say, "You know what I have in mind," and he'd put her down on the bed and fuck her into the basement.

All of which was going on in the back of his mind, while mainly he was just standing there, leaning against the doorjamb, getting a kick out of watching all the kids at their birthday party.

Tom came into the house, coming in the front way for once, because he knew the birthday party was going on in the kitchen and he'd figured Joe would be staying far away from it. He searched the house, and was surprised at last to find Joe practically inside the kitchen, standing there in the doorway and letting the waves of heat and noise roll over him.

Tom tugged at his elbow. Joe, enjoying the party and his fantasy, gave him an irritable look and didn't move, but Tom made a head gesture meaning come-with-me-I-want-to-talk. Joe nodded at the kitchen, meaning he wanted to stay and watch the party, but Tom jabbed his thumb urgently toward the living room and finally Joe gave up and went with him.

The two of them walked into the living room, where it was a lot quieter, and where Joe said, "Okay, what is it?"

Excited, talking in a half-whisper, Tom said, "I've got it!"

Joe was feeling very irritable. "You got what?"

Tom held up one finger and grinned. "Half," he said. "I've got our problem half-solved."

Joe displayed his irritation by humoring Tom in a heavy-handed way. "Which problem was that, Tom?" he said.

"The heist."

Suddenly Joe was frightened of being overheard. "For Christ's sake!" he said, and looked over his shoulder toward the kitchen.

"It's okay, they can't hear us with that racket."

Joe hadn't been thinking about the robbery idea, and he didn't want to think about it. To get it over with, he moved in closer to Tom and said in a low voice, "All right, what is it?"

This time, Tom held up two fingers. He said, "You remember, we decided we needed two things. Something we could turn over right away for a lot of money, and somebody with a lot of money to do the buying."

Joe nodded, listening but not really involved. His attention was still back with the party and his fantasy. Up till now, they'd both enjoyed talking about the robbery at dull times when there was nothing else to do, like while driving in to the city to go to work, but it was only a theoretical kind of thing that they said they were going to do but that neither one of them really intended to pull off. Now there'd been a change, and the robbery had grown more real to Tom. That hadn't happened yet with Joe, so he just nodded, listening with half of his attention, and said, "Yeah, I remember."

"I've got the buyer," Tom said.

Joe frowned at him, and didn't bother to hide his skepticism. "Who?"

"The Mafia."

"What?" Joe stared at him. "Are you crazy?"

"Who else has two million dollars cash? Who else buys hot goods at that volume?"

Joe looked away, gazing across the living room, starting to think about it. "Christ, Tom," he said, "they do, don't they?"

Tom said, "I told you about those cargo heists on the piers that I worked on that time. It all went straight to the Mafia. Four million a year, they figured that was worth."

Joe thought about it, looking for flaws. "But that wasn't one robbery," he said. "That's over a whole year."

"They're in the business." Tom said. "That's the point."

"All right," Joe said. "So what do we sell them?"

"Whatever they want to buy," Tom said.

Tom

Joe and I had talked it over and decided together how best to approach the Mafia. We decided we didn't want to go through channels, starting with some rank and file punk on the streets. That way, either we wouldn't get to the top at all, or the word would filter out through some informer somewhere along the line, and we'd be in trouble before we even did anything. Besides, the Mafia is always talked about as though it's a business, and in any business, if you've got a problem or a proposition, you should go to the top and leave the clerks strictly alone.

So we decided the thing to do was make our pitch directly to Anthony Vigano. He was, as he'd said he would be, out on bail, so it should be possible to get to see him. We decided it would be better if just one of us approached him, and since it had been my idea in the first place I was the one who would go. Also, Joe didn't feel very much like doing it. It wasn't his kind of thing.

There were files on Vigano downtown, and because of my identification I had simple and easy access to the files. They included Vigano's address, over in Red Bank, New Jersey, plus a lot of other information about the things he'd been involved with over the years. He'd spent eight months in jail when he was twenty-two years old, for assault with a dangerous weapon. Other than that, he had more arrests than I had hairs on my head, but no convictions. He'd been a union officer a few times in his life, and he had an import-export business for a while, and he was a major stockholder in a New Jersey brewery, and he was a part-owner of a trucking company down in Trenton. The arrests had involved drugs and extortion and receiving stolen goods and bribery and just about every crime on the books except playing hookey. There had even been two attempts to get him on income-tax charges, but he'd wriggled out of both of them, too.

There had been three attempts on his life over the years, the last one nine years before, in Brooklyn. He traveled with bodyguards, one of which had been killed that time in Brooklyn, and so far he didn't have a scratch on him. And apparently there hadn't been any more internal disputes since the Brooklyn incident.

His place in Red Bank was an estate near the shore there, a full square block surrounded by a high iron fence and eight-foot-tall hedges. I got the Chevvy and drove over to New Jersey and took a spin around the place once, by day, just checking it out, and through the closed iron gates you could see the black-top road curving in through crew-cut lawn with big oak trees on it, and leading over to a three-story-high brick mansion with white trim and four white pillars on the front. There were two or three expensive-looking cars parked in front of the house, and a casual-looking guy dressed like a gardener was hanging around just inside the iron gates. Gardener, hell.

A part of our thinking in this situation all along had been that in our position we could get supplies for the robbery right from the force itself, from the Police Department, and now for the first time we put that idea into effect. There's a room upstairs at the precinct full of disguises, including dresses and false stomachs and all kinds of things; I went up and checked out a moustache and a wig and a set of horn-rim glasses with clear lenses. Then I turned over all my identification to Joe, and took the train down to Red Bank. The idea was, I wanted to visit Vigano without him being able to return the favor.

I took a cab from the station to Vigano's place. If the driver knew anything about the address, he gave no sign of it. I paid him, got out of the car, waited for him to drive away, and then walked over to the gate.

Somebody inside the gate suddenly flashed a light in my eyes. I put my forearm up to block it, and said, "Hey! You don't have to blind me."

A voice said, "Whadya want?" It was a gravel voice, the kind you make with pizza and cigars.

I kept my forearm up. I didn't want all that light on my face out here. I said, "Get that God damn light out of my eyes."

It took him a couple seconds longer; then he lowered the flashlight beam till it was aimed at about my belt-buckle. I still couldn't see anything past it, but at least it wasn't blinding me. And it wasn't showing my features big and clear to anybody observing.

He said, "I still want to know what you want."

I lowered my forearm. "I want to see Mister Vigano," I said. I was suddenly feeling very nervous. I was here without any of the protection I usually carry. Not so much the gun, as the status of being a police officer.

He said, "I don't recognize you."

I said, "I'm a New York City cop, with a proposition."

He said, "We don't take defectors."

"A proposition, that's all," I said. "I'm willing to go see somebody else."

Nothing happened for maybe ten seconds, and then all of a sudden the light went out. Now I couldn't see anything at all. "Wait there," the voice said, and footsteps went away.

After a minute or so my eyes adjusted to the dark again,

and I could make out lights in the house inside there. I didn't know if there was anybody standing inside the gate or not.

I waited nearly five minutes. That gave me plenty of time to come to the conclusion that I was an idiot. What the hell was I doing here in the first place? This whole robbery thing was just something Joe and I talked about in the car, going into the city and going home. Sometimes we talked and thought as though we were serious about it, but were we? Was I really going to steal something and collect a million dollars and go live in Trinidad? That's just daydreams.

The reason I became a policeman is because I wanted a civil-service job. I took a couple of the state civil-service exams, and I became a clerk in an Unemployment Insurance office in Queens, and one day when I had nothing to do I read a police-recruiting poster on the billboard in the office. The idea I got from the poster was that being a policeman combined civil service with a little bit of glamour or excitement. The clerk job was too boring to put up with anymore, so I switched over. And the poster didn't lie. Being a policeman is exactly that; civil service plus excitement.

But I don't know, the last few years everything seems to be going to hell. Sometimes I think it's just me getting older, but other times I look around and I notice everybody else has the same attitude. Like New York is getting crappier by the second, and money is getting tighter, and everything is just more tense and troubled and futile than it used to be.

It's been coming this way for a long time, I don't mean this is any sudden change. I mean, the reason I moved my family out to Long Island eleven years ago was because already by then New York was a place where you didn't want to bring up your children. Everybody else moved out then too. We all knew the city was getting impossible, and we all freely admitted to one another that we were moving out because of the kids.

Well, now the city *is* impossible. It isn't even a place for adults any more. I hate driving in there every workday, I don't even like to look in that direction. But what am I going to do? You get married, you have kids, you commit yourself to a mortgage on a house, payments on the car and the furniture; all of a sudden there aren't any more decisions you can make. I couldn't decide tomorrow morning to stop being a New York City cop. Give up my seniority, my civil-service status? Give up my years toward the pension? And where would I find another job at the same pay? And would it be any better?

You go along and go along, and it seems as though you're running your own life, and it never occurs to you that your life has gradually closed around you like a Venus flytrap and *it's* running you.

During this whole period of time, while the idea of the robbery was still theoretical, I found myself remembering over and over what that hippie pusher had said, about all of us having started out different from this. It's true. I'd find myself sometimes doing things, or saying things, or just thinking things, and I'd suddenly look around at myself and not believe it was me. If I could have looked ahead when I was ten years old to the man I was going to turn out to be, would I have been pleased?

And I just have this vague feeling that it isn't necessary, that this isn't who I have to be. Joe and me both, my partner Ed, all of us, we've narrowed ourselves down, we've made ourselves blunt and tough because that's the only way to survive. But what if we were in a different kind of setting? Even that hippie was a ten-year-old kid once. But we all of us get together in that city like hungry animals jammed in together in a pit, and we beat on each other because that's all we know how to do, and after a while all of us have turned ourselves into people you don't want to bring your kids up among.

So you sit in the car on the way to work, and you fantasize a million-dollar robbery, life in a Caribbean island, out and away from all this lousy stuff. They make movies about robberies, and people go to them and love them. Or watch them when they show up on television. And every once in a while somebody tries it in real life.

A flashlight was coming down the drive from the house. I tensed up, seeing it come. I could still turn around and walk away from this, let it stay in the land of fantasy. I think it was only the idea of facing Joe that kept me from doing it.

There were several people behind the flashlight, I couldn't be sure how many. The flashlight didn't point at me at all now; first it pointed at the ground, and then it pointed at the gate as it was being unlocked. A voice said, "Come in." It wasn't the gravel voice from before, but a different one, smoother, oilier.

I stepped in, and they shut the gate behind me. I was frisked, fast and expert, and then hands held my arms just above the elbows and I was walked up to the house.

I didn't get to use the front entrance. They took me around the side and into an entrance with snow shovels and overcoats and overshoes in the small room inside. We went through that into an empty kitchen, and they frisked me again, more thoroughly, going through all my pockets. There were three of them, and two searched me while the other stood off a ways behind me. They were dressed in suits and ties, but they were unmistakably hoods.

When they finished with the second search, one of the friskers went out of the room. The other two and I waited. I looked around the kitchen, which was like the kind you see in a fairly small restaurant. Big chopping-block table in the middle, with copper pans hanging from racks over it. Stainless-steel ovens and grill and sinks. Apparently Mr. Vigano did a lot of entertaining.

It had occurred to me there was a possibility Mr. Vigano might decide to kill me. I couldn't think of any reason for him to do it, but I couldn't discount the possibility. I admired the kitchen rather than think about that.

The frisker came back and said to the other two, "We take him to Mr. Vigano."

"Fine," I said. I said it partly because I wanted to be sure my voice was still working.

The frisker led the way. The other two took my arms again, and we left the kitchen in a group.

It was a weird sort of stop-and-go method we had, the four of us, traveling through the house. First the frisker would go on ahead through a doorway or around a corner, and then he'd come back and nod to us, and the rest of us would move forward and catch up with him. At which point we'd stop again, and he'd go on to the next phase of the trip. It was like being a piece on a board game, something like Monopoly or Sorry, moving one square at a time. I don't know if the idea was that they didn't want me to be seen by members of Vigano's family who weren't a part of the mob operation, or if he had Mafia people staying with him that I wasn't supposed to see and maybe identify. But whatever their intention the result was that I got a slow-paced guided tour of the first floor of Vigano's house.

It was a strange house. Either Vigano had bought it furnished from the previous owner, who had been somebody with a lot of good taste, or he'd had the thing done for him by an expensive decorator. We went through rooms filled with obviously valuable antiques, graceful furniture, flocked wallpaper, crystal chandeliers, heavy draperies, all sorts of tasteful and quietly expensive things; just the kind of surroundings I'm happiest among. But then on the wall there'd be hanging some lousy painting of a crying clown, with real rhinestones sprinkled on his hat. Or a lovely marble-topped table would have one of those ashtrays on it made of a flattened gin bottle. Or a modern black parson's table would have a lamp on it composed of a fake brass statue of two lions trying to climb up the trunk of a tree and the shade would be cream-colored with purple fringe. Or a room with a beautiful wallpaper would have one of those porcelain light-switch plates in a free-form star shape. Absolutely the most amateurishly done bust of President Kennedy I've ever seen was sitting on a huge gleaming grand piano, next to a green glass vase with pussy willows in it.

And finally, at the end of the guided tour, they took me through another door and down a flight of stairs and into a bowling alley.

It was amazing. A one-lane bowling alley in the basement, a long narrow brightly lighted room like a pistol-practice range. There was the normal kind of curved leatherette settee behind the lane, and Vigano himself was sitting there alone. He was wearing a gray sweatsuit and black sneakers and a white towel around his neck, and he was drinking beer from a Pilsner glass. A bottle of Michelob was on the score table.

Down at the far end of the lane, a heavy thirtyish guy in a black suit was setting up the pins. He was another hood, like the two who'd brought me in and who now stood back by the door, waiting to be called on.

I moved forward to the settee. Vigano turned his head around and gave me a heavy smile. He had heavy-lidded eyes; it was as though he only allowed the dead part of his eyes to show, the living parts were hidden away behind the lids. He looked at me for a few seconds, and then put the smile away and nodded at the settee. "Sit down," he said. It was a command, not hospitality.

I stepped through the central opening in the settee and sat on the side opposite Vigano. Down at the other end of the lane, the hood in the black suit finished setting up the pins and hoisted himself up onto a seat hidden away out of sight. Only his highly polished shoes showed, hanging down over the black valley where the ball would stop.

Vigano was studying me. "You're wearing a wig," he said.

I said, "The story is, the FBI takes movies of your visitors. I don't want to be identified."

He nodded. "The moustache phony too?"

"Sure."

"It looks better than the wig." He drank some beer. "You're a cop, huh?"

"Detective Third Grade," I said. "Assigned in Manhattan."

He emptied the rest of the beer from the bottle into the glass. Not looking directly at me, he said, "I'm told you don't have any papers on you. Wallet, driver's license, nothing like that."

I said, "I don't want you to know who I am."

He nodded again. Now he did look at me. He said, "But you want to do something for me."

"I want to sell something to you."

He squinted slightly. "Sell?"

I said, "I want to sell you something for two million dollars cash."

He didn't know whether he was supposed to laugh or take me seriously. He said, "Sell me what?"

"Whatever you want to buy," I told him.

I could see him deciding to get annoyed. "What bullshit is this?"

I talked as fast as I knew how. "You buy things," I said. "I've got a friend, he's also a cop. In our position, with what we know about how things work, we can go anywhere in New York you want and get you anything you want. You just tell us what it is you'll pay two million dollars for, and we'll go get it."

Shaking his head, seeming to be talking more to himself than to me, Vigano said, "I can't believe any DA in the world would be this dumb. This is a stunt you worked out for yourself."

"Sure it is," I said. "And how can it hurt you? Your boys frisked me on the way in, I don't have a recorder on me, and if I did it's entrapment. I'm not crazy enough to just hand stuff over to you and expect two million dollars in cash right back, so we'll have to work out intermediaries, safe methods, and that means you can't possibly get picked up for fencing stolen goods."

He was studying me hard now, trying to work me out.

He said, "You mean you're actually offering to go steal something, anything I want."

"That you'll pay two million for," I said. "And that we can handle; I'm not going to get you an airplane."

"I've got an airplane," he said, and turned away from me to look toward the pins set up at the far end of the lane.

I could see him thinking it over. I felt I hadn't said enough, hadn't explained it right, but at the same time I knew the best thing to do right now was keep my mouth shut and let him work it out for himself.

The fact was, he had nothing to lose, and he should be smart enough to see it. If I was crazy or stupid or just a horse's ass kidding around, it still wouldn't cost Vigano anything to tell me what he'd be willing to buy from me. So long as I didn't ask for an advance payment, it was strictly to Vigano's advantage to play along with me.

I saw that understanding come into his face before he said anything. I watched him work it out, slowly and cautiously, looking for traps and mines the way somebody in his position would have to do, and I saw him come around finally to the understanding that there was nothing hidden underneath at all. I had come here asking a question, which it wouldn't hurt him to answer. And if I was telling him a straight story, it might eventually profit him to answer. So why not?

He gave a sudden decisive nod, and looked at me with his heavy-lidded eyes, and said, "Securities."

The word didn't immediately make sense to me. All I could think of was security guards in stores and banks. I said, "Securities?"

"Treasury bonds," he said. "Bearer bonds. No common stocks. Can you do it with an inside man?"

I said, "You mean Wall Street?"

"Sure Wall Street. You know anybody in a brokerage?"

I had been thinking all along it would be something in our own precinct, where we knew the territory. "No, I don't," I said. "Do I have to?"

Vigano shrugged and waved it away. His hands were surprisingly big and flat. "We'll change the numbers," he said. "Just make sure you don't get me anything with a name on it."

I said, "I don't follow you."

He breathed heavily, to show me how patient he was being. "If a certificate has the owner's name on it," he said, "I don't want it. Only papers that say, 'Pay to the bearer.' "

"Did you say Treasury bonds?"

"Right," he said. "Them, or any other kind of bearer bond."

I found myself interested in this in a separate way from the question of stealing things. I'd never heard of bearer bonds. I said, "You mean they're like a different kind of money."

Vigano grunted, with a little smile. "They *are* money," he said.

I felt happy at the thought, the way I'd been happy in that rich woman's apartment on Central Park West. "Rich people's money," I said.

Vigano grinned at me. I think we were both surprised at how well we were getting along with one another. "That's right," he said. "Rich people's money."

I said, "And you'll buy them from us."

"Twenty cents on the dollar," he said.

That startled me. "A fifth?"

He shrugged. "I'm giving you a good price because you're gonna deal in volume. Usually it's ten cents on the dollar."

I'd meant the percentage was low, not high. I said, "If it's pay to bearer, why don't I sell it myself?"

"You don't know how to change the numbers," he said. "And you don't have the contacts to get the paper back into legitimate trade."

He was right, on both counts. "All right," I said. "So we'll have to take ten-million-dollars' worth to get two million from you."

"Nothing too big," he said. "No certificate over a hundred thousand."

"How big do they get?" I asked him. This whole thing was heady stuff.

"U.S. Treasury bonds go up to a million," he said. "But they're impossible to peddle."

I couldn't help it; I was awed and I had to show it. "A million dollars," I said.

"Stick to the small stuff," Vigano told me. "Hundred grand and down."

A hundred thousand dollars was small stuff. I felt my mind shifting around to that point of view, and doing it with the greatest pleasure. Years ago there was a show on Broadway called *Beyond the Fringe* and they did a bit from it on television one time that I saw. (I've never seen a Broadway show.) The bit was a monologue by an English miner, and at one point he said something like, "In my childhood I wasn't surrounded by the trappings of luxury, I was surrounded by the trappings of poverty. My problem is I had the wrong trappings." That line stayed with me over the years because it was exactly the way I felt; I was surrounded by the wrong trappings. And any time I found myself in the midst of the right trappings, it made me very happy.

Vigano was watching me. "You got the idea now?" he said.

Business; back to business. "Yes," I said. "Bearer bonds, no larger than a hundred thousand dollars."

"Right."

"Now," I said, "about payment."

"Get the stuff first," he said.

"Give me a number to call. One that isn't tapped."

Vigano said, "Give me your number."

"Not a chance," I said. "I already said I don't want you to know who I am. Besides, my wife isn't in on it."

He looked at me with a surprised grin. "Your wife isn't in on it," he said. The grin got wider, and then he laughed out loud, and then he said, "Your wife isn't in on it. All of a sudden, I believe you're on the level."

Everything had shifted. He'd made me feel like a fool, and

I wasn't even sure why. Angry, but trying not to show it, I said, "I am on the level."

His grin faded away and he got serious again. Reaching over to the score table, he picked up a ballpoint pen and a small blank memo pad. He extended them to me, saying, "Here. I'll give you a number to write down."

He wouldn't put his own handwriting on even a telephone number. I took the pad and pen and waited.

He said, "It's in Manhattan. Six nine one, nine nine seven oh."

I wrote it down.

He said, "You call that number from inside Manhattan; no interborough, no long distance. You ask is Arthur there, they'll say no. You call from a phone booth, or some phone you're sure of. You leave your number, Arthur should call you back. You'll hear from me within fifteen minutes. If you don't, I'm not around, try again later."

I nodded. "All right."

"When you call," he said, "you say your name is Mister Kopp. K-O-P-P."

I grinned a little. "That's easy to remember."

"But don't call me with questions," he said. "You do it or you don't. If you take ten million in securities from Wall Street, I'll read about it in the paper. Otherwise, if I get a message from you I don't answer."

"Sure," I said. "That's okay."

"Nice talking to you," he said, and picked up his beer glass again. He hadn't offered me one.

He wanted the conversation to be finished, so I got to my feet. "You'll be hearing from me," I said. I knew it was bravado to say it, and that it didn't make me look any better, but I went ahead and said it anyway.

He shrugged. He wasn't interested in me anymore. "That's fine," he said.

Vigano

Vigano watched the visitor leave with his escorts. He waited thirty seconds, brooding, sipping at his Michelob, and then pressed the intercom button on the scoreboard.

Waiting for Marty to come in, he thought back over the conversation. Could the guy have been on the level? It was hard to believe, and yet anything else was even harder to believe. What other reason could he have for pulling a stunt like this, coming here cold with such an off-the-wall idea? There was no profit for any law-enforcement agency in it, and nothing to be gained by any potential competitor.

After all, he wouldn't ever have anything else to do with the guy unless there really was a multi-million-dollar bond theft on Wall Street. Which would get into the papers and onto the television news, no doubt about it. Anybody calling up and claiming to be Mr. Kopp and claiming to have stolen bonds would be given the brush-off right away unless there had been a robbery to match, one that Vigano knew about from his own sources.

So assume the guy was on the level. What was the likelihood he'd actually go through with a robbery and get away with it? Very very thin. And if he didn't do it, Vigano wouldn't have lost anything.

But if he did really pull it off, Vigano would stand to gain a hell of a lot.

It was a nice position to be in. Vigano toasted himself with Michelob, and Marty came in, saying, "Yes, sir, Mr. Vigano?"

Vigano turned to him. "The guy that's going out now," he said. "I want his name and address and what he does for a living."

"Yes, sir," Marty said, and left again.

It would probably come to nothing. But just in case something good did come out of it, Vigano wanted to have his homework done. It's the details, he thought, that make the difference between a winner and a punk.

He got to his feet, selected a ball, and bowled a strike.

Joe

When Tom and I talked over the Mafia idea, one thing we agreed on right away was that if the mob found out who we were, there was no way we could go through with it. Neither of us wanted mobsters around with that kind of hold over us. Either we could contact Vigano and stay anonymous, or we'd have to give up that idea and try to think of something else.

We took it for granted, the two of us, that Vigano would have Tom followed after their conversation; if he talked to Tom at all. So the first most necessary thing was to break Tom loose from the people tailing him.

The last train to Penn Station from Red Bank pulls in to New York at twelve-forty. There aren't many people on that train, particularly on a week night, which was part of the reason we'd picked it. Also, where it came in at Penn Station there was only one staircase up to the terminal.

I was in uniform, and I got to the station fifteen minutes ahead of time. We'd rehearsed this three times, and the train had never been anywhere near this early, but we wanted to be absolutely sure. I went to the head of the stairs leading up from that platform, and stood there, waiting.

Standing there, it occurred to me this was the first time in my life I'd worn the uniform when I wasn't on duty. I've never been exactly gung ho for the force. The only reason I was in that uniform at all was because the Army didn't need any tank drivers the day in basic training when I got classified. The choices open to me were cook or military policeman or something else, I forget what. Something crappy. They were also picking orderly-room clerks and finance clerks that day, but my test profile wasn't too good in the right areas for those jobs. What I really wanted was to drive a tank, but I wound up an MP.

I was an MP for a year and a half, eleven months of it assigned to the Vogelweh dependent housing area outside Kaiserlautern, Germany. I dug it. I got a kick out of carrying a .45 around on my hip, and doing the target shooting, and driving around town in a jeep at night to keep the white troops and the black troops from beating each other's head in. I hadn't had any job at all before I was drafted, I mean nothing that I wanted to get back to, and I never had any interest in college, so when I got out of the Army the question was what would I do for a living, and the answer was plain and simple. Go on the same as before. The uniform changed from brown to blue, the sidearm changed from a .45 automatic to a .38 revolver, and you had to be a little more careful how you dealt with people, but otherwise it was pretty much the same job.

Which was nice at first, it made for a nice transition from soldier to civilian. But after a while the same job gets to be a drag and a bore and a pain in the ass, no matter what it is. Whether you're carrying a gun or not, driving around the city or not, it doesn't matter; it gets boring.

For a long time, it seemed as though there was always something else to take up the slack, keep me interested in life even when the job was dull. Getting married, for instance. Having kids. Moving out of the apartment out to Long Island.

Those are like the mountains, and the valley is your dull everyday life.

It had been a long time between mountains.

For the last couple years, I'd been thinking about women, about maybe shacking up with somebody somewhere. Get me a girl in town, somewhere in my precinct. I was pretty sure a girl on the side would drain off all this stored-up boredom again, at least for a while, but somehow I never seemed to get started at it. My heart wasn't in it. I knew it was possible, I personally knew four guys in the precinct who had exactly that kind of arrangement, but it was like I didn't have the energy to make the first moves, to look around in any way more than just eyeing my friends' wives and wondering how they'd be in the sack. Maybe I was trying to keep myself from disappointment, maybe down in the bottom of my brain I had the idea a girl on the side would finally be the biggest letdown of all. With no place left to go from there.

I heard the train come in, down below; the way the brakes squealed, they could probably hear it up on 42nd Street. I stood at the head of the stairs, just to one side, looking down. The stairs were concrete, and wide enough for three people abreast, and they were flanked on both sides by amber tile walls.

Tom got to the stairs first, the way he was supposed to. If I hadn't already seen him in the disguise I wouldn't have recognized him. The wig was a different hair color, and longer than his usual hair, and it seemed to change the whole shape of his head. Then he had a David Niven kind of moustache, which made his face look younger for some reason. And the horn-rim glasses changed his eyes entirely, so he looked like an accountant somewhere.

As for me, the uniform was my main disguise. People rarely look past the uniform to see the individual man. The only extra disguise I wore was a droopy moustache, like a western sheriff's, and I'd put that on more for the hell of it than because I thought I really needed it. There wouldn't be any reason for anybody to tie me up with Tom.

About a dozen other passengers came along behind Tom, the usual number for this train, and it wasn't hard at all to pick out Vigano's men from among them. Three of them, all dressed differently but all unmistakably hoods, with hard faces and hunched shoulders.

I was surprised at how hard it hit me, when I saw those three guys among the bunch of people coming up the stairs behind Tom. Up till that second, I guess I really hadn't believed it; that Tom would go through with it, or that he'd get in to see Vigano, or that Vigano would wind up listening to him and believing him. But it must have happened, or those three guys wouldn't have taken the train.

Tom was moving fast, coming up the stairs two and three at a time. The three shadows were mixed in with the pack, all of it moving more slowly; when Tom reached the head of the stairs, the nearest other passenger was still eight steps down.

Tom went by me without a look, the way he was supposed to. He went past, and I immediately stepped forward to block the staircase. I held my arms out and said, "Hold up a minute. Hold it, there."

Momentum kept them coming up a few more steps, but then they stopped and all looked up at me. People obey the uniform. I saw two of Vigano's men pushing their way up past the other passengers toward me, and the third one going back down the stairs; probably to look for another way up. But there wasn't any, not from that platform. By the time he found another exit it would be too late, and he'd come up in the wrong place anyway.

They were all milling around on the stairs, a dozen of them packed in tight together. New Yorkers expect that kind of thing, so there wasn't any major complaint. One of Vigano's men, having shoved himself up to the front of the pack, where his head was at the level of my elbow, looked past me down the corridor, watching Tom hustle away. He made an irritated face, but tried to keep his voice neutral when he said to me, "What's the problem, officer?"

"Only be a minute," I told him.

His eyes kept flicking back and forth between the corridor and me, and I could tell by his expression when Tom turned the corner down there. But still I held them all, while I counted to thirty slowly. The third hood reappeared at the foot of the stairs and trotted up them, looking disgusted.

I stepped to the side, slow and casual. "Okay," I said. "Go ahead."

They streamed past me, Vigano's men moving at a dead run. I watched them go, and I knew they were wasting their time. We'd practiced this enough, Tom and I, so that we knew how long it would take him to get to the nearest exit and out to where his car was parked, with the special police permit showing on the sun visor. By now, he was probably already making the turn onto Ninth Avenue.

I strolled the other way.

7

There was a certain amount of leeway in setting up the work schedules at the precinct, so Tom and Joe could usually adjust things around to be on duty at the same hours. They got cooperation from the precinct because it was understood they had a car pool together. If they'd both been patrolmen, or both on the detective squad, they could probably have worked it out one hundred per cent of the time, but operating out of two different offices the way they did there were bound to be times when the work schedules were in conflict, with nothing to be done about it.

Because of one of those conflicts, it was three days before they got to talk about Tom's meeting with Vigano, and when at last they did get together Joe was too worn out to pay much attention. He'd been on a double shift, sixteen hours straight, caused by some special activity over at the United Nations. In fact, it was the stuff at the United Nations, involving a couple of African countries and the Jewish Defense League and some anti-Communist Polish group and who knows what all, that had created the conflict in the work schedule in the first place.

It wasn't that Joe himself had had to go over to the UN, but a lot of uniformed men from the precinct had been sent down there for the duration of the special circumstances, and that meant the guys who were left had to double up to cover the territory.

That was one of the big differences between the patrolmen and the detective squad. The detectives were chronically short-handed, and used to it, but there was never any time when orders would come down that would strip out half the men from the squad and leave the rest to take up the slack. The patrolmen though, were under normal circumstances up pretty close to full strength, until every once in a while the phone would ring in the Lieutenant's office, a couple of buses would pull up out front to take the boys away, and the ones left would have to start scrambling. Like today.

Today, the result was that they rode back together in Tom's car that afternoon with Tom excited and ready to talk, and Joe just sitting there as though he'd been hit by a fire hydrant. In fact, having come to work eight hours before Tom, he had his own car in the city, the Plymouth, and was just leaving it there, because he didn't think he had the stamina to drive it all the way home. He'd come back in with Tom tomorrow, and drive the Plymouth home tomorrow night, if all went well.

At first, Tom didn't realize just how far out of it Joe was. They got into the car together and Tom headed for the tunnel, and as they drove he gave a quick rundown on what Vigano had said. Joe didn't make any response, mostly because he was barely listening. Tom tried to capture his attention by talking louder and faster, trying to push some of his own enthusiasm into Joe's ear. "It's simple," he said. "What are bonds? They're just pieces of paper." He glanced over at Joe. "Joe?"

Joe nodded. "Pieces of paper," he said.

"And the great thing is," Tom said, "we can actually do it." He gave Joe another look, with some annoyance in it. "Joe, you with me?"

Joe shifted around in his seat, moving his body like a sleeper who doesn't want to wake up. "For Christ's sake, Tom," he said, "I'm dead on my feet."

"You aren't on your feet."

Joe was too tired for humor; it just made him grouchy. "I *been* on my feet," he said. "Double shift."

"If you pay attention to me," Tom said, "you can say good-bye to all that."

They were just entering the Midtown Tunnel. Joe said, "You really believe in this?"

"Naturally."

Joe didn't make any answer, and Tom didn't say anything else while they were in the tunnel. Coming out the other side, Tom said, "You got change?"

Joe roused himself and patted his pockets, while Tom slowed for the toll booths. Joe didn't have any change, so he got out his wallet. "Here's a dollar," he said.

"Thanks." Tom took the dollar, gave it to the attendant, got the change back, and passed it to Joe, who sat there looking at the coins in his palm as though he didn't know what he was supposed to do with them.

Driving away from the booth, Tom said, "How'd you like a job like that?"

"I don't want any job at all," Joe said. He dropped the coins in his shirt pocket and rubbed his face with his palm.

"Just standing there all day," Tom said, "taking money in."

"They all rake off a little," Joe said.

"Yeah, and they get caught."

Joe squinted at him. "We won't?"

"No, we won't," Tom said.

Joe shrugged, and looked out the side window at the black buildings and brick smokestacks of Long Island City.

Tom said, "The big difference is, we won't do it over and over. One big job, and quit. I go to Trinidad, you go to Montana."

Joe turned his head to Tom again. "Saskatchewan," he said.

Tom, thrown off the track, frowned at the trucks he was driving among, and said, "What?"

"I thought it over," Joe told him. He was beginning to wake up despite himself, though he was still in a bad mood. He said, "What I'd really like to do is get Grace and the kids out of this country entirely. But completely out, before it goes to hell altogether."

"Where's this you want to go?"

"Saskatchewan." Joe made a vague gesture, as though pointing northward. "It's in Canada," he said. "They give you land if you want to be a farmer."

Tom gave him a grin of surprise and disbelief. "What do you know about farming?"

"A hell of a lot less than I'll know next year." They were now on that part of the Expressway lined on both sides with cemeteries, and Joe brooded out at it all. It's like somebody's idea of a sick joke, all those tombstones stretching away on both sides of the Expressway just a couple miles from Manhattan; like a parody of a city, in bad taste. Neither of them had ever mentioned it to the other, but those damn cemeteries had bugged them both from time to time, over the years of driving back and forth. And the funny thing was, they bothered the both of them more in the daytime than at night. And more on sunny days than rainy days. And more in the summer than in the winter.

This was a sunny day in July.

Neither of them said any more until they were past the cemeteries. Then Joe said, "I'm really thinking about that, you know. Just pack everybody in the car and take off for Canada. Except with my luck, it'd break down before we got to the border."

"Not if you had a million dollars," Tom said.

Joe shook his head. "There are times," he said, "I almost believe we're gonna do it."

Tom frowned at him. "What's the matter with you? You're the one that's *done* it already."

"You mean the liquor store?"

"What else?"

"That was a different thing," Joe said. "That was—" He moved his hands, trying to think of the word.

"Small-time," Tom said. "I'm telling you to think big-time. You know what Vigano had?"

Small-time wasn't the word Joe had been looking for. Irritated, he said, "What did he have?"

"His own bowling alley. Right in the house."

Joe just stared. "A bowling alley?"

"Regulation bowling alley. One lane. Right in the house."

Joe grinned. That was the kind of high life he could understand. "Son of a bitch," he said.

"Go tell *him* crime doesn't pay," Tom said.

Joe nodded, thinking it over. He said, "And he told you securities, huh?"

"Bearer bonds," Tom said. "Just pieces of paper. Not heavy, no trouble, we turn them right over."

Joe was wide awake now, interested, his irritation forgotten. "Tell me the whole thing," he said. "What he said, what you said. What's his house look like?"

Joe

To me, Broadway in the Seventies and Eighties is the only part of Manhattan that's worth anything at all. Paul and I cover that area in the squad car a lot, and I kind of like it. The people are maybe a little uglier-looking than the average, but at least they're human; not like the freaks in the Village or the Lower East Side. Midtown has all the pretty people, all those marching men in their suits and good-looking girl secretaries out wandering around during lunch, but that isn't where they *live*. There isn't anything human or livable in that area at all; it's just stone and glass boxes that the white-collar people work in all day. On their own time, they go somewhere else.

Anyway, we're supposed to cover the cross-streets and West End Avenue and Columbus and Amsterdam and Central Park West, but whenever I'm at the wheel I tend to be on Broadway. Unless I feel like doing some fun driving or giving out some tickets, in which case I go over to Henry Hudson Parkway.

Two days after Tom and I had our talk in his car about

Vigano, Paul and I were heading south on Broadway, me driving, when all of a sudden, half a block ahead of us, two people came struggling out of a hardware store onto the sidewalk. They were both male, both Caucasian. One was short, heavy-set, fiftyish, wearing gray workpants and a white shirt with the sleeves rolled up above his elbows. The other was tall, lanky, twentyish, wearing army boots and khaki pants and a green polo shirt. At first, all I could see was that they were struggling with one another, going around in a circle as though they were dancing.

Paul saw it too. "There!" he said pointing.

I accelerated, then hit the brakes as we got closer. I could see now that the tall young one had a small zippered bag in one hand and a small pistol in the other. The short guy was clinging to the tall guy's waist, holding on for dear life, and the tall guy was trying to club him with the pistol. There were a lot of pedestrians on the sidewalk, as usual, but they were falling back, giving the two men plenty of room.

Paul and I both jumped out of the car at the same time. He was closer to the curb, while I had to run around the front of the car. At the same time, the tall guy finally managed to break loose from the short one. He gave him a shove backwards, and the short guy staggered a couple of steps and then sat down hard. The tall guy had seen us coming, and he waved the pistol at us.

I yelled, "Drop it! Drop it!"

All of a sudden the son of a bitch fired two shots. Out of the corner of my eye I saw Paul go down, but I had to keep my mind on the guy with the gun. He'd turned and started to run southward along the sidewalk.

I reached the sidewalk, went down on my left knee, propped my forearm on my raised right knee; all those years of practice paid off after all. I was sighted on his back, with the green polo shirt, and then on his legs. But the sidewalks were full, there were too many faces and bodies past him, right in the line of fire. And he was smart enough not to run in a straight line but to shift back and forth as he went.

I kept the pistol aimed, in case I could get a clear shot with nobody beyond him, but it didn't happen. "Damn it." I whispered. "Damn it." And he disappeared around the corner.

I got back to my feet. Over by the storefront, the older man was also getting up. Paul was on his back on the sidewalk, but struggling to sit up, moving like a turtle on its back. I moved to him, holstering the pistol, and crouched beside him as he finished sitting up. He looked stunned, as though he didn't know where he was. I said, "Paul?"

"Jesus," he said. His voice was slurred. "Jesus."

His left trouser leg was wet, stained dark, sodden with blood, midway between the knee and the crotch. "Lie down," I said, and poked at his near shoulder. But he wasn't really conscious at all; he didn't hear me, or didn't understand me. He just went on sitting there, his mouth hanging open, his eyes blinking very slowly.

I got up again, turning toward the squad car, and the old man clutched at my arm. When I looked at him, pulling my arm away, he shouted, "The money! The money!"

I could have killed him. "Shut up about money!" I yelled, and ran to the car to call in.

8

They both had that afternoon off. Tom was mowing his front lawn, wearing just a bathing suit in the sunshine, when Joe came around from between the houses and said, "Hey, Tom." He too was dressed in a bathing suit, and he was carrying two open cans of Budweiser beer.

Tom stopped. He was panting and sweating. "What?"

"Come take a break."

Tom pointed at the beer. "Is that for me?"

"I even opened it for you," Joe said, and handed him one of the beers. "Come on, the kids are out of the pool for once."

Tom took a swig of beer, and they walked down the driveway between the houses and over into Joe's backyard. It was a really hot sunny day in July, and the pool looked great to the both of them. Cool water in a container of light blue, nothing looks better than that on a hot day. Except a beer.

Tom said, "The filter's working?"

Joe put his finger to his lips. "Easy, it'll hear you. Come on, cool off."

Joe had a short sturdy wooden ladder in an A shape over the side of the pool; you went up three steps on one side of the A, and down three steps into the water on the other side. They both climbed up and over, Joe first, and while Joe waded around the four-foot-deep water throwing out leaves and sticks and pieces of paper and dead bugs, Tom sat back on one of the steps of the ladder, so he was in water up to his neck. With his right hand he held the beer can up out of the water.

Joe looked over at him and laughed. "You look like the Statue of Liberty."

Tom grinned, saluted with the beer, and took a swig. It was tough to drink in that position, but Joe was watching, so Tom did it for the effect. Then he said, "You know what I was thinking before? When I was over there with the lawn-mower?"

"What?"

"Remember I told you I used to go to City College nights?"

Joe waded over to lean against the side of the pool to Tom's left. "So?"

Tom moved up a step, so the water was only chest-high and it was easier to drink. "What I was thinking," he said, "if I'd kept at it, you know where I'd be today?"

"Where?"

"Right here. I *still* wouldn't be a lawyer, not for two more years."

"Sure," Joe said. He nodded. "You put a penny away every day, at the end of the year you're still poor. It's the same principle."

Tom stared at him. "It is?"

They looked at one another, both bewildered, until Tom lost interest in the subject and changed it, saying, "Listen, what about the wives?"

Joe switched his bewilderment to the new topic. "What?"

"What do we tell the wives?"

"Oh," Joe said. "About the robbery, you mean."

"Naturally."

Joe didn't see any problem. He shrugged and said, "Nothing."

"Nothing? I don't know about you and Grace," Tom said, "but if I put Mary in Trinidad, she's going to know she's in Trinidad."

"Sure," Joe said. "Then. When we're ready to move, that's when we tell them. After it's all over."

Tom hadn't made up his own mind about that yet. There were times, particularly at night, when he very strongly wanted to tell Mary about it, talk it over with her, see what she had to say. Frowning, he said, "Not now at all?"

"In the first place," Joe said, "they'd worry. In the second place, they'd be against it, you know they would."

Tom nodded; that was what had kept him quiet up till now. "I know," he said. "Mary wouldn't approve, not ahead of time."

"They'd throw cold water on the whole idea," Joe said. "If we tell the wives, we'll *never* do it."

"You're right," Tom said. He was disappointed, but he was also relieved that the question was resolved. "Not till it's all over," he said. "Then we tell them."

"When we're ready to take off out of here," Joe said.

"Right," Tom said. Then he said. "The thing is, you know we can't leave the country right away."

"Oh, sure," Joe said. "I know that. They'd be on our asses in five minutes."

"What we've got to agree right now," Tom said, "is that we bury the money and neither one of us goes near it until we're ready to leave."

"That's fine with me."

"The big advantage we've got," Tom said, "is that we've seen every mistake there is."

"That's right. And we know how not to make them."

Tom took a deep breath. "Two years," he said.

Joe winced. "Two years?"

"We've got to play it cool," Tom said.

Joe looked pained, as though he had an ankle cramp down underwater. He wanted to argue against it, but on the other hand he had to agree with the theory of it; so he was stuck. Reluctantly, but giving in, he said, "Yeah, I suppose. Okay, two years it is."

Tom

In the weeks after my visit with Vigano, I got to learn an awful lot about stocks and bonds, and about brokerages, and about Wall Street. I had to, if we were going to take ten million dollars away from there.

Wall Street itself is only about five blocks long, but the brokerages are scattered all around that whole area down there below City Hall; on Pine Street and Exchange Place, on William Street and Nassau Street and Maiden Lane.

I've heard the Wall Street district described as the only part of New York that looks like London. I can't say about that, since I've never been to London, but I do know it has the narrowest and crookedest streets of any part of the city, with narrow sidewalks, and the big bank buildings crowding as close to the curb and each other as they can get. Writers all the time talk about that section in terms of "canyons," and I can see why. With the streets so narrow and the stone buildings so tall and close together, the only time the sun shines on Wall Street is high noon.

For the first time in my life I was beginning to see that

breaking the law could be just as complicated as upholding it. I'd always thought of the police side of things as being tougher than the crook side, but maybe I'd been wrong; there's nothing like standing in the other guy's shoes to make you sympathize with him.

There were so many *details* to figure out. How to do the robbery, for instance; whether it should be day or night, whether we should try for a diversion, just exactly how we were going to work it. And how to be sure we were taking the right bonds; before this, neither one of us had known zip about stocks and bonds. And how to make a getaway after the robbery in those narrow crowded streets. And how to hide the loot afterward until we sold it to Vigano; which was ironic, since all along we'd been telling each other we had to steal something that didn't need to be held onto or stowed out of sight.

But there it was. And the brokerages didn't make it any easier. They were guarded like banks; no, they were tougher than banks.

Let me tell you just how tough they were. First of all, there's a special section of the Police Department with headquarters down in the Wall Street area that deals with nothing at all except stock market crime. There are cops in that section that know more about the financial world than the editor of the *Wall Street Journal*, and those cops keep tabs on the brokerages all the time, talking to the personnel directors, talking to the security directors, checking up on their ways of handling things and protecting themselves, and always no more than one phone call away in case there's any kind of trouble.

And then there's the internal security departments. All the big brokerages have them; private uniformed guards, security files, closed-circuit TV, and all of it run usually by an ex-cop or an ex-FBI man. Guys that treat a stock brokerage as though it were a top-secret atomic-testing laboratory, and whose entire job is to see to it that none of the millions of pieces of paper that flow through Wall Street every day ever gets stolen.

Of course, some do. But most stock market robberies are inside jobs, and there's a good reason for it. Stocks and bonds, like dollar bills, carry serial numbers. Usually, the only way to steal securities and get something for your pains is to be an employee of a stock brokerage and alter the records so the brokerage isn't aware that anything has been stolen. With bearer bonds, it's possible for somebody like Anthony Vigano, with his expertise and his contacts, to alter the numbers and peddle the bonds back into legitimate channels, but other than that an inside job is the only kind of job possible on Wall Street.

But even if it weren't, even if there were any point in breaking into a stock brokerage and stripping the vault, they've gone out of their way to make things tough. For instance, a couple of years ago a bank down in that area closed down, and a restaurant was going to move into the space they left vacant. Before they could, though, they had to pull the vault out, and they had one hell of a time doing it. Not only was it wired with all kinds of alarms, not only did it have sixteen-inch-thick concrete walls reinforced with steel rods, but it actually had two separate walls all the way around the vault, and the area between the two walls was filled with poison gas. The workmen taking the vault walls down had to wear gas masks.

That isn't merely being tough; it's being insane.

Still, Joe and I had an edge over the normal safecracker or the normal dishonest employee. We had the facilities of the Police Department to help us, to provide us with material for the robbery and specific information—such as blueprints of alarm systems and other security measures—on whichever brokerage we finally decided to concentrate on.

There was one that looked promising, called Parker, Tobin, Eastpoole & Co. They were in a building near the corner of John and Pearl streets, and I went down there one day to check them out. The building had the typical small lobby of that area—they really don't like to waste space, those financial people—and three elevators. Parker, Tobin, Eastpoole

& Co. was on the sixth and seventh and eighth floors, but I already knew it was the seventh floor I wanted, since I'd checked out the alarm-system on file at Police Headquarters downtown.

The elevator was pretty full, and three of us got off together at the seventh floor. Which was good; it gave me a chance to hang back and look at things while the other two went forward to the counter.

The elevator had opened onto a fairly large room, much wider than deep, divided the long way by a chest-high counter. The security arrangements seemed to be typical for a large brokerage. Two armed and uniformed private guards were on duty behind the counter. On the wall in back of them was a large pegboard with maybe twenty plastic ID tags hanging from it, plus room for about a hundred more. Each tag had a color photograph on it of the person it belonged to, plus a signature written underneath. Mounted on the short wall down to the right were six closed-circuit television sets, each showing a different area of the brokerage, including one showing this reception area I was standing in. Above the sets was the TV camera, turning slowly back and forth like a fan. On the other short wall, the one down to my left, was a second pegboard, smaller than the first, holding about twenty-five ID tags marked in big letters: VISITOR. Doorways at both ends of the room led into the work areas.

There was a steady stream of activity around the counter. Arriving employees were picking up their ID tags, departing employees were turning them in, messengers were delivering manila envelopes. I got to stand there for maybe a full two minutes, checking things out.

The first thing I noticed was that only one of the guards dealt with the people who came to the counter. The other one stood back by the rear wall, keeping an eye on things; watching the people, looking over at the television sets, staying alert while his partner did the detail work.

Then there were the television sets. They were in black-and-white, but the pictures were crisp and clear. You could see the people moving around in different rooms, and you could make out their faces with no trouble at all. And I knew this bank of six sets would be repeated probably three or four other places on this floor; in the boss's office, in the security chief's office, in the vault anteroom, maybe one or two other places.

It was also more than likely to be going on video tape. They have video tape now that can be erased and recorded on again, the same as regular sound tape, and that's what they'd have. They might keep the tape for a week or a month or maybe even longer, so that if it turned out later that somebody had pulled a fast one, they could run the tapes through again and see who was where at what time.

"Can I help you?"

It was the guard, the one who dealt with people, looking across the counter at me. He was brusque and impatient, because of the amount of work he had to do, but he wasn't suspicious. I stepped forward to the counter, trying for the world's most innocent and stupid smile. Pointing at the television sets, I said, "Is that me?"

He gave a brief bored look at the screens. "That's you," he said. "What can I do for you?"

"I've never been on television before," I said. I looked at the screen as though I was fascinated; and to tell the truth, I was. I'd worn the moustache again, and I was amazed at what I looked like with a moustache. Totally different. I wouldn't have recognized me if I met me walking down the street.

The guard was getting impatient. He looked me over for manila envelopes and said, "You a messenger?"

I didn't want to hang around and pester him for so long that I became memorable. Besides, I'd seen all I was going to see out here, and there was no way I was going to get inside. Not today. I said, "No, I'm looking for the personnel office. I'm supposed to come to work here."

"That's on the eighth floor," the guard said, and jabbed a thumb toward the ceiling.

"Oh," I said. "Then I'm in the wrong place."

"That's right," he said.

"Thanks," I said, and went back over to the elevators and pushed the button. While waiting, I looked around some more. You sure had to admire their security. And yet, this was the likeliest prospect.

Joe

I didn't much like visiting Paul in the hospital. I don't like hospitals anyway, but I particularly don't like them when there's a brother officer in there. I don't like that reminder.

Did you ever watch pro football on television, and notice what happens when one of the players gets hurt? He's laying there on the ground, moving his knees a little, and maybe one or two other players go over to see what the story is, but all the rest kind of walk off by themselves and pretend they have a problem with their shoes. I know exactly how they feel, I do. It isn't they're heartless or anything, it's just they don't like to be reminded how easy it could turn out to be one of them.

Same with me. I had plenty of chances to visit Paul, but until I was feeling really good and guilty I wouldn't go at all. Then I'd finally go and there'd be nothing to say, and we'd sit around and watch soap operas together for half an hour. It's a funny thing, we always had plenty to talk about in the car, but not in the hospital. The hospital is death on conversation.

So I was there again, going back and forth at the foot of the bed. Paul was in a semiprivate room, but the other bed was empty right now. His windows gave a good clear view of a brick wall. If you stood right next to the window and looked down you could see green grass, but if Paul could have stood next to the window he wouldn't have to be in the hospital, and from the bed what you saw was brick wall.

The television set mounted on the wall was turned on, but the sound was off. Paul was sitting up in bed, newspapers and magazines all around him, and he kept sneaking glances at the TV.

I was trying to think of something to say. I hate long uncomfortable silences.

Paul said, "Listen, Joe, if you want to get back out there, it's okay."

I stopped walking, and tried to look interested. "No, no, this is fine. What the hell, let Lou drive around a while." Lou was Paul's replacement in the car, a rookie.

Paul said, "How's he doing?"

"He's okay," I said. I shrugged, not much caring. Then I tried to keep the conversation alive, saying, "He's too gung ho, that's all. I'll be glad to get you back."

"Me too." He grinned and said, "Can you believe it? I *want* to go to work."

"A couple of times," I told him, "I would have traded places with you."

All of a sudden he started scratching his leg through the covers. "They keep telling me it won't itch anymore," he said.

"I haven't seen the doctor yet," I said, "that knew his ass from his elbow." I nodded at the other bed. "At least you don't have the old geek around anymore. They send him home?"

"Naw," Paul said. "He died." He was still scratching through the covers.

"That must have been fun."

"Middle of the night." He stopped scratching, and

yawned. "He fell right out of bed," he said. "Woke me up. Scared the crap out of me."

"Nice little vacation for you," I said. And I thought, *Nice little conversation we're having.*

"Oh, it's great," he said.

I didn't have anything else I wanted to say about an old man falling out of bed and dropping dead, so the silence came back again for a while. I looked up at the television set, and it showed a guy in a rowboat floating around in a toilet tank. Television is fucking incredible sometimes.

Paul shifted around in the bed, kicking his legs out this way and that, and a couple of his magazines slid off onto the floor. *Like the old man,* I thought. "Boy, my ass gets to hurting," he said. He couldn't seem to decide what position he wanted to be in. "Pins and needles, you know?"

"I know," I said. I picked the magazines up and tossed them on the bed again. "You ought to roll over on your other side," I told him. "Lie on a nurse, that'll help."

"Have you seen the beasts around here?"

"I've seen them."

And so much for that conversation. I looked at the television set again, and the commercial was over—I *hope* that was a commercial—and what was up there on the screen? A hospital room, one guy in the bed and one guy walking around the room, talking to him. "We're on television," I said.

Paul said, "The guy in the bed has amnesia."

I looked at him. "Where'd you get it?"

He grinned at me. "I forgot."

No place to go from there either. Christ, conversation is impossible in the hospital, it really is.

Paul glanced over at the empty bed. He had a thoughtful look on his face, and he said, "You know what used to get me about him?"

"What, the old guy?"

"He was always saying he hadn't done anything yet." Paul gave me a look, with this strange-looking kind of crooked smile on his face. He said, "He'd wasted his life, that's what he thought, he hadn't done anything with himself. He was older'n hell, but all he wanted was to get healthy and get out of here, so he could start doing something."

"Like what?"

"*He* didn't know, the poor old fart." Paul shrugged. "Just something different, I guess."

I looked at the other bed. I could almost see the old man falling out of it onto the floor. I wondered what he'd done for a living.

9

They both had that Saturday off, so they took the families to Jones Beach, using both cars. The beach was hot and crowded, the way it always is, but the kids liked the chance to run around in the sand sometimes instead of just jumping in and out of the pool in the backyard, and the wives liked any excuse at all that would get them out of the house. And Tom and Joe liked to look at women in bathing suits.

After a while, the two men were the only ones left on the blankets, spread out well back from the ocean. Mary and Grace were both down by the water's edge with the smallest kids, and the other kids were all off running around somewhere, pestering people. Tom was sprawled on his stomach on the blanket with his chin propped on his forearms so he could look at the girls in bikinis, and Joe was sitting cross-legged on the next blanket over, reading the *News*.

The planning of the robbery had settled into a sort of hobby they had, like two guys who operate a model railroad set together. Tom had been casing the brokerages and the general Wall Street area, checking out possible getaway routes, collecting maps of the financial district and writing out long descriptions of the security arrangements at various brokerages. Joe had been raiding the Police Department files downtown for information on burglar alarms and any special police surveillance arrangements there might be in that area. The two of them had maps and charts and memos and lists enough to choke a whale, a huge growing pile of paperwork they kept locked away in the liquor closet in the game room in Tom's basement. They'd thought it over and decided that was the best place to keep it all because nobody ever went down into the game room, and Tom was the only one with a key to that closet. Mary had had a key at one time, but she'd lost it a couple of years ago and hadn't ever replaced it because she didn't have any need for it.

In a way, the planning of the robbery had by now become an end in itself. When they'd first started talking about it there hadn't been any reality in the plans at all, it had just been a funny and interesting thing to talk about on the way to work. But gradually it had become more real to both of them, and the way it had become real was that now they were really doing the preliminaries. They would go out and talk to the Mafia, they would study different brokerages, they would make lists and keep records, they would talk over various plans for the robbery; they would do everything except the robbery itself. Although they never acknowledged that to themselves, not consciously.

The thought of the robbery was never very far from either of their minds these days; it gave them an interest in life. Including while they were at the beach.

"Well, here's one thing," Joe said, tapping the newspaper. "We don't do it the seventeenth."

Idle, unalert, still looking at girls in bikinis but automatically knowing what Joe was talking about, Tom said, "How come?"

"Parade for the astronauts."

A vision came into Tom's head; narrow streets, filled with crowds and bands. "Oh, yeah," he said.

Joe folded the paper and put it down. He was feeling vaguely irritable, as though some of the sand here had gotten into his brain. He said, "When the hell *are* we gonna do it?"

Tom shrugged one shoulder, and kept on watching the bodies all around him. "When we figure out how," he said. "Look at that one with the volley ball."

"Fuck the one with the volley ball," Joe said. He didn't feel like listening to a lot of horseshit.

"Gladly," Tom said.

Joe said, "Listen, I'm serious." He said it low-voiced and tense, and held his newspaper tight in his right fist.

Tom rolled over onto his side and gave Joe a look. He was vaguely surprised, and still feeling lazy and at peace with the world. He said, "What happened to you all of a sudden?"

What had happened to Joe, he hadn't been able to get out of his mind the vision of the old man in the hospital, dying and falling out of bed. It seemed to him when he thought about it that the old man had been making one last desperate leap toward life, and had fallen, and it had been all over for him; too late. Usually, Joe was more interested even than Tom in looking at girls in bikinis, but for the last few days it seemed that all he could think about was time going by.

But he couldn't very well talk about all of that, Tom would think he was crazy. Or turning into a weak sister. He shrugged, irritable and angry and frustrated, and said, "Nothing happened to me. We just keep fucking around on the fringes, that's all."

Tom frowned. Joe was talking very tough and mean, and Tom wasn't sure yet whether he wanted to take offense or not. Holding that issue in abeyance for a second, he said, "So what do you want to do?"

"The robbery," Joe said. "Or at least get moving on it." He slapped the newspaper down onto the blanket with a disgusted gesture.

"Fine," Tom said. He was beginning to get a little irritated himself. "Like how?" he said.

"You've been checking out the brokerages. What's the story?"

Tom sat up, grudgingly giving up his leisure. "The story," he said, "is that they're very tough."

"Tell me." Joe wanted action, he wanted movement, he wanted the sense that something was happening *now*.

"Well," Tom said, "half of them are no good to begin with."

"Why not?"

"In a brokerage," Tom told him, "there's two places where they have guards. I mean, in addition to the main entrance. And the two places are the cage and the vault."

"The cage?"

"That's what they call the place where they do the paperwork, where they move the stocks and bonds in and out of the company. And the vault is where they store them."

"So we want the vault," Joe said. Simplicity, that was what he wanted, simple questions and simple answers.

"That's right," Tom said. "We want the vault. But with half of them, the vault is down in the basement and the cage is up on some other floor, and they've got closed-circuit TV between them."

Joe made a face. "Ow," he said.

"You see the problem," Tom said. "While we're taking care of the guards down in the basement, there's some clown up on the seventh floor watching us do it. And taking pictures of it."

"Taking pictures?"

"They put it all on video tape." Tom made a sour smile, and said, "Which they can run for the jury at our trial."

"Okay," Joe said. "So the ones with the cage and the vault on different floors, they're out."

"With the rest of them," Tom said, "where the cage and the vault are both on the same floor, you've still got guards in both places, plus guards at the entrance, and you've still got closed-circuit TV."

Joe frowned. None of this was making him feel any better. He had, "They've *all* got that?"

Tom nodded. "Any outfit big enough to have what we want," he said, "has TV. The little companies don't, but we're not going to find ten million dollars in bearer bonds lying around at one of the little companies."

"Then we can't do it at all," Joe said. "It just can't be done." There was an angry sense of relief in that, in giving it up for good and for all, and knowing there wasn't any hope.

A voice behind them suddenly said, "Are you robbers?"

They both turned around, and there was a little kid standing there behind them, a little boy of maybe five or six. He had a shovel in his hand, and he was covered with sand, and he was looking at them with bright curious eyes like a parrot. Tom just sat there staring at him, but Joe quickly said, "No, we're the cops. *You're* the robber."

"Okay," the kid said. He was agreeable.

"You better take off now," Joe said, "before you get arrested."

"Okay," the kid said again, and turned around, and toddled off through the sand.

They both looked after him. Their hearts were pounding like sixty, it was amazing. "Christ," Joe said.

Tom said, "We better do our talking in the car from now on."

"What talking?" Joe was bitter, and he let it show. "You already described the situation, and it can't be done."

"Maybe it can," Tom said. "As long as the cage and the vault are both on the same floor, there's a chance we can pull it off."

Joe studied his face. "You think so?"

"People commit robberies all the time. *We* should be able to."

"Maybe," Joe said.

"What bothers me most," Tom said, "is how we're going to stash the bonds after we get them. Remember, we kept saying we didn't want anything we were going to have to hold onto."

Joe shrugged. "We can only sell Vigano what he wants to buy," he said. "Besides, we can call him right away afterward, we won't have to keep the bonds very long at all."

"I suppose so."

"The time that bothers me," Joe said, looking away toward the water, "is the two years."

Tom gave him a warning look. "We agreed, Joe."

"Yeah, I know we did. But look what happened to Paul. Shot in the leg. Another eight inches, he'd be shot in the balls. A little higher, he's shot in the heart, he's dead."

Tom shrugged that off, saying, "Paul's going to be okay, you said so yourself."

"That isn't the question," Joe said. "I don't want a million dollars buried in the ground, with me buried right next to it."

"We can't do it and run, we talked that over—"

Joe interrupted, saying, "Yeah yeah yeah, I know we did. I still think that's a good idea. But not for two years, that's too long."

Tom said, "What, then?"

"One year."

"What, cut it in half?"

"A year is a long time, Tom," Joe said. "You want to live like this any longer than you absolutely have to?"

Tom frowned, looking away. He was staring at a girl in a bikini, without seeing her.

"The idea is to get out of this," Joe said. "Remember?"

Tempted against all his resolves, Tom shook his head and said, "Ahhh, Christ."

"One year," Joe said.

Tom held out a few seconds longer, but finally he shrugged and said, "All right. One year."

"Good," Joe said. He grinned, a lot happier than before, and grudgingly Tom grinned back.

Tom

That was one of the days when our schedules didn't match. Joe was in the city working, and I had the day off. Naturally it was raining, so I moped around the house and read a paperback and watched some of the game shows on television. Mary took off in the car for the Grand Union in the middle of the day, so when the show I was watching came to an end I wandered back into the bedroom to take a look at my old uniform. If we ever really did do this robbery, that's what I'd be wearing for my disguise.

I hadn't worn the uniform in three or four years, but it was still there, hanging in the bedroom closet, pushed way down to one end, behind the raincoat liner for the raincoat I left in a restaurant two years ago. I laid it out on the bed and looked it over for a minute; no holes, no buttons missing, everything fine. I changed into it, and studied myself in the mirror on the back of the closet door.

Yeah, that was me, I remembered that guy. The years I'd worn this blue suit, hot weather and cold, rain and sun. For some damn reason I suddenly found myself feeling gloomy, really sad about something. As though I'd lost something somewhere along the line, and even though I didn't know what it was I felt its absence. I don't know how to explain it any better than that; it was a sense of loss I felt.

Well, crap, I didn't come in here to get the rainy-day blues. I came in here to check out my disguise for the big robbery. And it looked fine, it was in perfect shape, no problem.

I was still standing there, trying to forget that I was feeling sad about something I couldn't remember, when all of a sudden Mary came walking in, and looked at me with her mouth hanging open.

I'd thought she'd be at the store at least another hour. I turned and gave her a sheepish grin, and tried to figure out what the hell I was going to say to her. But I couldn't think of a thing, not a single word came into my mind to explain what I was doing here in the bedroom in my old uniform.

After her first surprise, she helped me out of my paralysis by making a joke out of it, coming farther into the bedroom and saying, "What's this? You've been demoted?"

"Uh," I said, and then finally my brain and my tongue started working again. "I just wanted to see how I looked in it," I said, and turned to study myself in the mirror again. "See if it still fit."

"It doesn't," she said.

"Sure it does." I turned sideways and gave myself a good view of my profile. "Well, it's maybe a little tight," I admitted. "Not much."

Past me in the mirror I could see her smiling at me and shaking her head. She'd kept her own figure almost exactly the same, in spite of having kids and being a housewife for years, so she was in a good position to be thinner-than-thou if she wanted. And even though it was ridiculous, I felt defensive on the subject. I turned and said, "Listen, I could still wear it. If I had to, I could. It wouldn't look that bad."

"No, you're right," she said. "It isn't terrible." I couldn't tell if she meant it or if she was humoring me.

Being agreed with was just as bad as having an argument.

I patted my stomach, looking at it in the mirror, and said, "I've been drinking too much beer, that's the trouble."

She made an I-wouldn't-argue-with-you face, and walked over to the dresser. I watched her in the mirror. She picked up her watch from the dresser top and headed for the door, winding it. In the doorway, she looked back at me and said, "Lunch in fifteen minutes."

I said, "I'll have iced tea today."

She laughed. "All right," she said.

After she went out, I gave myself another critical look. It wasn't that bad. A little tight, that's all. Not bad.

10

There's a strange sense of dislocation in leaving one's family at ten or eleven o'clock at night and going off to work. There's more of a feeling of *leaving* them, of a deep break between family life and job life. Neither Tom nor Joe had ever gotten over that atmosphere of loss, but it was another of the things they'd never discussed together.

Maybe if they'd worked the midnight-to-eight shift all the time they would have gotten used to it, and not felt any stranger about it than a guy who leaves for work at eight in the morning. But constantly switching around from shift to shift the way they did, they never really got a chance to become used to the idiosyncracies of any one schedule.

Since the incident with the little kid out at Jones Beach, they'd done most of their talking about the robbery in the car on the way to or from work, and they both seemed to prefer for that the drive at eleven o'clock at night, heading in toward the city. The sense of dislocation from home and family probably helped, and so did the darkness, the interior of the car lit by nothing but the dashboard and oncoming headlights.

It was as though they were isolated then, separate from everything, capable of concentrating their minds on the question of committing the robbery.

This night, they were both quiet for the first ten or fifteen minutes in the car, westbound on the Long Island Expressway. Traffic was moderate coming out of the city, but light in the direction they were going. There was plenty of leisure to think.

Joe was driving his Plymouth, his mind only very slightly on the road and the car, but mostly away, on Wall Street, in brokerage offices. Suddenly he said, "I go back to the bomb scare."

Tom's mind had been full of his own thoughts, involving burying the bonds and calling Vigano and figuring out the safest way to make the switch for the two million dollars. He blinked over toward Joe's profile in the darkness and said, "What?"

"We ought to be able to do that," Joe said. "Phone in, tell them there's a bomb in the vault, then answer the squeal ourselves."

Tom shook his head. "Won't work."

"But it gets us in, that's the beauty."

"Sure," Tom said. "And then a couple other guys come to answer the squeal before we get out again."

"There ought to be a way around that," Joe said.

"There isn't."

"Bribe a dispatcher to give the squeal to us instead of one of their own cars."

"Which dispatcher? And how much do you bribe him? We get a million and he gets a hundred? He'd turn us in within a week. Or blackmail us."

"There's got to be a way," Joe said. The bomb-scare idea appealed to him on general dramatic grounds.

"The problem isn't to get in," Tom said. "The problem is to get away afterwards with the bonds, and where we stash them, and how we make the switch with Vigano."

But Joe didn't want to listen to any of that. He insisted on the primacy of his own area of research. "We've still got to get in," he said.

"We'll get in," Tom said, and all of a sudden the idea hit him. He sat up straighter in the car, and stared straight ahead out the windshield. "Son of a bitch," he said.

Joe glanced at him. "Now what?"

"When's that parade? Remember, there was a thing in the paper about a parade for some astronauts."

Joe frowned, trying to remember. "Next week sometime." It had been on Wednesday, he remembered that. "Uhhh, the seventeenth. Why?"

"That's when we do it," Tom said. He was grinning from ear to ear.

"During the parade?"

Tom was so excited he couldn't sit still. "Joe," he said, "I am a goddam mastermind!"

Skeptical, Joe said, "You are, huh?"

"Listen to me," Tom said. "What are we going to steal?"

Joe gave him a disgusted look. "What?"

"Give me a break," Tom said. "Just tell me, what are we going to steal?"

Shrugging, Joe said, "Bearer bonds, like the man said."

"Money," Tom said.

Joe nodded, being weary and long-suffering. "Okay, okay, money."

"Only *not* money," Tom said. He kept grinning, as though his cheeks would stretch permanently out of shape. "You see? We still got to turn it over before it's money."

"In a minute," Joe told him, "I'm going to stop this car and punch your head."

"Listen to me, Joe. The idea is, money isn't just dollar bills. It's all kinds of things. Checking accounts. Credit cards. Stock certificates."

"Will you for Christ's sake get to the point?"

"Here's the point," Tom said. "Anything is money, if you *think* it's money. Like Vigano thinks those bearer bonds are money."

"He's right," Joe said.

"Sure, he's right. And that's what solves all our problems."

"It does?"

"Absolutely," Tom said. "It gets us in, gets us out, solves the problem of hiding the loot, solves *everything*."

"That's fucking wonderful," Joe said.

"You're damn right it is." Tom played a paradiddle on on the dashboard with his fingertips. "And that," he said, "is why we're going to pull off that robbery during the parade."

Joe

I drove the squad car down Columbus Avenue to a Puerto Rican grocery near 86th Street. I pulled in to the curb there and said to Lou, "Why don't you get us a coke?"

"Good idea," he said. He was a young guy, twenty-four years of age, his second year on the force. He wore his hair a little too long, to my way of thinking, and I almost never saw him without razor cuts all over his chin. But he was all right; he was quiet, he minded his own business, and he had no bad habits in the car. At one time or another I've had them all, the farters and the nose-pickers and the ear-benders and everything else. Lou wasn't the good friend that Paul was, but I have done a lot worse.

I'd picked a Puerto Rican store because it would take him longer in there to buy two cokes than in a regular store. The little Puerto Rican groceries all over town are filled with men and women, all of them four feet tall, most of them sitting on the freezer case, all of them yammering away at top speed in that language they claim is Spanish. Before anybody can hit a cash-register key and take your dollar and give you your change, he has to yell louder than everybody else for a minute or two, to make sure he's got his point across. Then, with your change in his hand, he thinks of the clincher argument and starts to yell again. So I was going to have all the time I needed.

I'd switched off the engine before Lou got out of the car. I watched him crossing the sidewalk in the sunlight, hitching his gunbelt, and once he was inside the store I opened my door, stepped out, went around to the front of the car, lifted the hood, and removed the distributor cap. Then I shut the hood again, and got back behind the wheel.

We had a heat wave starting. It wasn't eleven in the morning yet, and already the temperature was almost ninety. From the feeling of my shirt-collar on the back of my neck, the humidity was up over the top of the scale. A hell of a day to be at work.

Hell of a day for a parade, too. They wouldn't call it off, would they?

No. The Wall Street ticker-tape parade is a tradition, and traditions don't care about the weather. They'd have their parade.

And Tom and me, we'd get our two million.

Lou came out with the two cans of soda. He got into the car, handing me mine, and said, "They sure do like to talk."

"They got more energy than I do," I said. "In this heat."

We popped the tops, and the both of us drank. I was in no hurry for the next step. I scrunched down in the seat a little, putting my face over by the open window, looking for a breeze. There wasn't any.

"It's too hot for crime," Lou said. "A nice lazy day."

"It's never too hot for crime," I asked.

"I'll bet you," he said. "I'll bet you there isn't one major crime in this city today. Not before, say, four o'clock this afternoon."

Talk about a sure thing. I almost took him up on it, except I didn't want him remembering the conversation afterward and starting to wonder why I'd been so eager to take his money. But talk about a lock!

What I did, I said, "What about crimes of passion? A husband and wife get mad at each other, they're irritated anyway because of the heat, and *pop*, one of them goes for the butcher knife."

"All right," he said, conceding the point. "Except for that kind of thing."

"Oh," I said, "now you're making exceptions. No major crime, except this kind and that kind and the other kind." I grinned at him, to show him I was kidding and that he shouldn't get sore.

He grinned back and said, "I notice you don't want to take the bet."

"Gambling's illegal," I told him. "Except OTB." I straightened up and took another swig of soda and said, "Time to move on. We got an hour before we're off duty."

"At least when we're moving there's a breeze," he said.

"Check."

I hit the ignition key, and of course nothing happened. "Now what?" I said.

Lou gave the key a disgusted look. "Again?" he said. Because this would be the third time in a month we'd had a car break down on us; which was what had given me the idea.

I fiddled with the key. Nothing. "I told them they didn't fix it," I said.

"Well, shit," Lou said.

"Call in," I told him. "I've had it."

While he called in to the precinct, I sat there on my side of the car looking long-suffering and drinking my coke. He finished and said, "They'll send a tow truck."

"We ought to *drive* a tow truck," I said.

He looked at his watch. "You know how long they'll take to get here."

"Listen," I said. "We don't both have to hang around. Why don't you shlep on back to the station and sign us both out?"

"What, and leave you here?"

"It doesn't matter to me," I said. "No crap. There's no need us both being stuck here."

He wanted to take me up on it, but he didn't want to look too eager about it, so I had to persuade him a little more. Finally he said, "You really don't mind?"

"I got no place to go anyway."

"Well . . . Okay."

"Fine," I said. And, as he was getting out of the car, I said, "Be sure to sign me out. I won't go straight back."

"Will do," he said. He climbed out to the sidewalk, bent to look in the car at me, and said, "Thanks, Joe."

"You'll do the same for me next time."

"Yeah, and there will be a next time, won't there?"

"Count on it," I said.

He laughed, and shook his head, and shut the car door. I watched him in the rear-view mirror as he walked away; around the corner and out of sight.

I sat there almost half an hour before the tow truck showed up. They use them all the time in midtown these days, towing the tourists' cars away. But this one finally got there, and the two guys got out of it, and one of them said to me, "What's the problem?"

"It won't start, that's all."

He gave the car a squint, like he was a doctor and this was the patient. "I wonder why."

That's all I needed, an amateur mechanic. All the towman is supposed to do is tow the car off to where it can be fixed. I said, "Who knows? The heat maybe. Let's take the thing in and get it over with."

"Keep your shirt on," he said.

"I don't want to," I said. I looked at my watch. "I'm off-duty in fifteen minutes."

So they put the hook on the front, and I sat behind the wheel of the squad car, and they towed me over to the police garage on the West Side, over near the docks. That block is practically nothing but Police Department, with police warehouses on the north side and the garage in the middle of the block on the south side. The garage is a sprawling red-brick building, three stories high, with ramps inside so you can drive all the way up to the roof. It's an old building, with black metal window frames, and I've heard it was once used to stable police horses. I don't know if that's true or not, I was just told it one time.

Extending westward from the garage to the far corner is a fenced-in area full of patrol cars and emergency vehicles and paddywagons and even a bomb-squad truck, looking like a big red wicker basket. Most of those vehicles are junk, and are kept around simply so that the mechanics can cannibalize parts off them to keep clunkers like the car I was sitting in more or less in running order.

Extending eastward from the garage to the corner are three or four more warehouse buildings, partly owned or leased by the Department, and partly civilian. About five or six years ago somebody found a load of slot machines in one of those buildings, down in the basement. Nobody *ever* figured that one out.

The block is one-way, and runs west to east, and both curbs were lined with police vehicles, most of them not working right now. The entrance to the garage was also clogged with vehicles, and more of them were parked on the sidewalk between the front of the garage and the cars parked at the curb. This is a block that cabdrivers avoid like the Black Death, because you can get stuck in a traffic jam here forever, and which civilian driver is going to honk at a traffic jam caused by the Police Department?

Like the jam we caused right now. The tow truck came down the one open lane in the middle of the street, and stopped in front of the garage. I looked in the rear-view mirror to see if we were blocking anybody behind us, but with the front end of the car up in the air all I could see was a rectangle of blacktop directly behind me. I didn't much care anyway, one way or the other. If somebody was behind us, tough.

A mechanic came wandering out of the garage with a

clipboard in his hand. He was a colored guy, short and heavy-set, wearing police trousers and a sleeveless undershirt. It was a filthy undershirt. He walked around the tow truck and came ambling down to the squad car, and said to me, "Problems, Mac?"

"Won't start," I said. "Dropped dead on me."

"Give it a try," he said.

Now, that was stupid. Did he think we would have gone through all of this, dragging this car downtown on a hot day like this, without first having given it a try. But that was what they always said, every time, and there was no point arguing with them. I gave it a try, and all it did was click. I spread my hands and said, "See?"

"Can't do anything with it today," he said.

"I don't care," I said. "I'm off-duty two minutes ago. My partner went on in already."

He sighed, and got his clipboard and a pencil ready. "Name?"

"Patrolman Joseph Loomis, Fifteenth Precinct."

He wrote that down, then went around to the back of the car to copy down all the appropriate numbers. I waited, knowing the routine because I'd been through it too many times already, and when he came back I already had my hands ready to take the clipboard before he started extending it to me. "John Hancock," he said, and I nodded and took the clipboard and signed my name in the line where it said *Signature*.

I handed him the clipboard back, and he turned and waved it at the driver of the tow truck. "Put it down there somewhere," he said, and waved toward the far end of the block.

The truck started forward with a jerk, and a second later so did the squad car. It snapped my head back, but not very much. I held onto the steering wheel for balance, and out of habit, and we rolled on down the block. The mechanic stood where he was until we went by, and the look he gave the car was weary and irritated.

The nose of the squad car bobbed a little as we moved, as

though I was in a speedboat. The front being angled up so high gave the same idea, and all of a sudden I remembered a summer vacation when I was a kid, maybe ten or eleven, and the whole family went up in the Adirondacks somewhere for a week. We rented a cabin on a lake. I mean, near the lake; you had to walk down this dirt path between two other cabins to get to the water, and I can still remember the way those stones felt under my bare feet. And there was a rich man there that owned a house at the other end of the lake, a white house bigger than the house I lived in back home in Brooklyn, and he had a speedboat. Red and white. He gave me a ride once, two other kids and me. We put on these orange life vests and sat in the back seat, and when the boat started up I was scared out of my mind. We went like a bat out of hell, and the front was up so high I couldn't see where we were going. But at the same time, it was really great; the wind and the noise and the spray, and the shore being so far away. Afterwards, remembering it while safe on dry land, it was even greater, and I spent the rest of that week wondering why we weren't rich, too. Rich was obviously a better thing to be, so why weren't we? That's the way kids think.

I hadn't remembered that for maybe twenty years.

There was a free space against the curb down near the corner. They stopped the truck and I got out of the car to watch them jockey it into place. I looked at my watch when they were finishing up, and it was ten after twelve. Plenty of time.

The driver of the tow truck said, "You want a lift back to the station?"

I almost said yes, I almost forgot the situation that much. But I caught myself in time and said, "No, I'll walk."

"Up to you."

I gave them a wave and they drove off, and I watched them go. Sometimes I amaze myself. Could it be this whole business still wasn't real to me, that I could forget it that easy? I'd damn near gotten into that truck to ride back to the station with them, just as though this was any other day and

I didn't have anything else on my mind at all. Amazing. Shaking my head, I turned and walked over to Eleventh Avenue and headed south.

My role now was just to walk around for about ten minutes. One of the secondary advantages of pulling this caper in uniform is the fact that a cop is the only guy on earth who can stand around a street corner loitering and not attract any attention. It's his *job* to loiter. Anybody else, somebody's likely to say, "Who's the guy on the corner? What's he up to?" But not a cop.

I'm surprised criminals don't pull *all* their jobs wearing the blue.

After ten minutes, I headed back around to where I'd left the car. Now, who's going to look twice at a cop doing something to a patrol car? I opened the hood, put the distributor cap back on, got behind the wheel, started the car, and headed down to where I was supposed to meet Tom.

Tom

The difference between committing a crime and planning a crime is the difference between being in a snowstorm and looking at a picture of the blizzard of 'eighty-eight. Joe and I had spent a long time planning this robbery, organizing things, working out the details, and none of it had ever bothered me; but all of a sudden we were in the storm, and no fooling.

I slept lousy the night before. I kept waking up and being afraid there was somebody in the house. I never felt so defenseless in my life, lying there in the darkness, listening, trying to hear whoever it was that was in the next room. Then I'd drift off again and have bad dreams, and wake up once more.

I only remember one of the dreams. Or just one part. I was very small, and I was in a very big empty dark room, and the walls were falling outward. Slowly. Just falling out and back. Terrifying.

We'd picked a day that I had off and Joe was working, so I spent the morning hanging around on my own, trying not to show Mary how tense and irritable I was. Joe had already told Grace he'd be on double shift today, and Mary thought I was supposed to be working this afternoon, so we were both covered for the time of the robbery.

But how the early part of the day dragged on! Half a dozen times, I was on the verge of getting into the car and driving on into the city just to be doing something, even though it would be hours before I was supposed to meet Joe, and I'd have a tougher job killing time in New York than at home. But it was just impossible to sit still, I had to be up and around and moving. I took the Chevvy down to the local car wash and then drove around for half an hour, I spent some time cleaning out the garage, I even took a walk around the neighborhood, something I've never done in my life before. And it was weird how close to the house I became a stranger, walking past houses that looked like mine but that didn't have any more to do with my life than some shepherd's hut in Outer Mongolia. That walk did more harm than good, and I was glad when I got back to my own block, to houses I knew, and the sense of safety that comes from being where you belong.

Then, when it was finally time to go, I got very jittery and nervous, and couldn't seem to get myself organized to leave the house. I kept forgetting things and having to come back. Including the uniform. I had it packed in a little canvas bag, and I damn near left without it. That would have been bright.

Did you ever have a tense situation sometime in your life, and you turn on the radio, and all the song lyrics seem to refer directly to the problem you're going through? That's what happened on the drive into the city. Every song that came on was either about somebody making a mistake that loused up his whole life, or somebody who has to give up his home and go wandering around the world, or somebody putting himself in danger even though this girl that loves him doesn't want him to do it.

I was almost sorry we hadn't told Mary and Grace what we were doing, because they really *would* have talked us out of it. That way, neither one of us would have backed down, but I still wouldn't be driving west on the Long Island Expressway this morning, with my old patrolman's uniform in a canvas bag beside me on the seat.

Don't get me wrong. I don't mean I wanted to give it up. I still wanted to do it, the reasons for doing it were still just as valid as they'd ever been, and my plans for afterward still excited me as much as when I'd first worked them out. But if the situation had been taken out of my hands one way or another, and I'd been *forced* to turn back, I admit I wouldn't have put up too much of a fight.

Well. I got to Manhattan with time to spare, drove over to the West Side, and parked in the low Forties, near Tenth Avenue. Then I walked down to the Port Authority terminal, carrying the bag with the uniform in it, and changed clothes in a pay stall in the men's room there.

Leaving, heading across the main terminal floor for the Ninth Avenue exit, I was stopped by a short old woman wearing a black coat—in weather like this—who wanted to know where to buy tickets for a Public Service bus. She irritated me at first, distracting me when I was so tense anyway, and I couldn't figure out why she was bothering me with questions like that when just ahead of us there was a huge sign reading: INFORMATION; but then I remembered I was in uniform. I shifted gears, became a cop, and gave her courteous directions over to the ticket windows along the side wall. She thanked me and scurried away, pulling the coat tight around her as though she were in a high wind that nobody else could feel. Then I walked on, left the building without being asked any more questions, and headed back for the car.

Walking along, I got this sudden vision in my head of the same thing happening again, only in a more serious way than with the old woman. I could see Joe and me on our way to commit a felony and being stopped by somebody who'd just been mugged, or getting mixed up with a lost child, or being the first cops on the scene at a serious automobile accident.

And what could we do if something like that happened? We'd have to stay, we'd have to play out the policeman's role. There just wouldn't be any choice, it would be far too suspicious for us to refuse to have anything to do with whatever it might be. The next cops to come along would surely be told about it, and we didn't want the idea getting around ahead of time that there were a couple of fake cops up to something in the city.

That would be damn ironic; kept from committing a robbery by the call of duty. I grinned as I walked along, thinking I would tell Joe about it when I saw him. I could just see his face.

At the Chevvy, I opened the trunk and put the canvas bag in it, with my other clothes. The license plates and numbers were in there, in a shopping bag; they'd been there for a week, ever since we'd picked them up.

I shut the trunk, got behind the wheel, and drove over by the piers. The New York City piers have gone to hell in the last ten years or so, with most of the harbor business now being done over in Jersey, so there's plenty of places in through there, particularly under the West Side Highway, where you can have all the privacy you want. Some of the trucking companies store empty trailers there, which form walls to shield you from the sight of the occasional car or truck heading down Twelfth Avenue.

I tucked the Chevvy in by a highway stanchion, next to a parked trailer, and looked at my watch. I was still running ahead of schedule, but that was all right. And now that I was really committed to it, and I'd made the first couple of moves in the planned operation, I was actually calming down, getting less and less nervous. The buildup had made me tense, but now the tension was draining away and I felt as easy in my mind as if I was just waiting here for Ed Dantino to show up so we could go on duty. Very strange.

It was a hot day, too hot to sit in the car. I got out of it, locked it, and leaned against the fender to wait for Joe.

11

They could hear the parade before they saw it; crowd noises, march music, and drums. Mostly the drums, you could hear them from blocks and blocks away.

There's a feeling about the sound of a parade that something is about to happen, something fast and dramatic and maybe hard to deal with. It's the drums that do it, hundreds and hundreds of drums stretched away for blocks, all thumping out the same steady beat. It's a little faster than a normal heartbeat, so if you're not marching along with it you can find it making you a little tense or excited.

Of course, if you're tense or excited to begin with, because you're about to commit your first grand larceny, drums like that can just about give you a coronary.

Both of them felt that, but neither said anything about it. They were pretending with one another that they were calm and businesslike, which was probably a good way to behave, since keeping up the facade seemed to help them deal with their nervousness and not get immobilized by it.

Back when they'd met over by the piers, the fact was they

really had both been calm. Each of them had successfully done the first simple step of the plan—Joe in getting the squad car, Tom in switching into uniform and finding the place to stash the Chevvy—and there was a sense they shared of having accomplished something and of being in control of the situation. Then, when they'd first met, they'd busily switched the license plates on the squad car and put the new peel-off numbers on its sides, and they'd still had that same feeling of being smart and organized and well-prepared and in control.

But as they drove downtown, and particularly when they got down into the narrow streets of the financial section, they both got to thinking about accidents and unforeseen circumstances and all the things that can go wrong with the best plan in the world. The tension started in them again, and the pounding of the drums didn't help.

Parker, Tobin, Eastpoole & Company was in a corner building, with the front facing onto the street where the parade was going by. Down the block, another building had an arcade that ran through to the next street over. It was that street they were heading for, a block away from the crowds and jam-up of the parade, but close enough so they could hear it loud and clear.

There was a fire hydrant near the arcade entrance. Joe parked the car there, and they got out and walked through the arcade, both automatically pacing themselves to the sound of the drums. Ahead of them, the arched opening of the arcade framed a black mass of people facing the other way; past them and over their heads, they could see flags being carried by.

As they walked along, Joe suddenly burped. It was incredibly loud, it seemed to bounce off the windows of the shops along both sides of the arcade, it echoed like a cathedral bell. Tom gave him a look of astonishment, and Joe rubbed his front and said, "I've got a very nervous stomach."

"Don't think about it," Tom said. He meant he didn't want to think about his own nervousness.

Joe gave him a one-sided grin and said, "You give great advice."

They came to the end of the arcade and stepped out onto the sidewalk, and the parade noise was suddenly much louder, as though a radio had been turned up. A band was going by, in red and white uniforms; they could catch glimpses of it through spaces between the people on the sidewalk. Another band had just passed by and was half a block away to the left, playing a different marching song but with the beat of the drums at the same time. A third band was down to the right, coming this way, its sounds buried within those made by the first two, plus the talking and yelling and laughing of the onlookers. Police officers in uniform were placed here and there, but they were concentrating on crowd control and paid no attention to Tom and Joe; in any case, what were they but just two more cops assigned to the parade?

There was a narrow cleared strip of sidewalk along between the building fronts and the massed people watching the parade. They turned left and walked in single file along that strip, moving now in the same direction as the band on the other side of the people, but because they were striding out they were moving just a little faster. Joe went first, marching steadily along in time to the music and the drums, and watching everything at eye level; the people, the cops, the building entrances. Tom followed moving in a more easy-going way, looking up at the people gawking out of all the windows above street level; practically every window in every building had at least one person standing in it or leaning out of it.

No one paid any attention to them. They went into the corner building and took the self-service elevator. They were alone in it, and on the way up they put on the moustaches and plain-lensed horn-rim glasses they'd been carrying in their pockets. Those were the minor parts of their disguises, the uniforms being the main part; nobody looks past a uniform. The people outside looking at the parade were watching uniforms go by, not faces, and wouldn't be able later on to identify one single musician who'd walked past.

With his glasses and moustache on, Tom said, "You do the talking when we get up there, okay?"

Joe gave him a grin. "Why? You got stage-fright?"

Tom didn't let himself be aggravated. "No," he said. "I'm just out of practice, is all."

Joe shrugged. "Sure," he said. "No problem."

At that point, the elevator stopped, the door opened, and they both stepped out. Tom had been here before, of course, and had described it all to Joe and drawn him rough sketches of what the guarded reception area looked like, but this was Joe's first actual sight of the place, and he gave it a fast once-over, orienting the reality to his previous mental picture.

There was none of the activity around the counter now that there'd been when Tom had come here the last time; that would be because everybody was watching the parade. And now there was only one guard on duty. He was leaning on the counter, looking over toward the six television screens that showed the different parts of the brokerage. On three or four of the screens windows showed, and people could be seen looking out at the parade. From the expression on the guard's face, he was wishing he could be at a window, too.

That was one of the extra advantages of pulling this job during the parade; the route to the money would be much less populated than usual. It wasn't the main reason for doing it now, but it was an extra little bonus, and they were glad to have it.

The guard looked over when they came out of the elevator, and they could see his face relax when he saw the uniforms. He'd been resting his elbows on the counter, but now he straightened up and said, "Yes, officers?"

Walking forward to the counter, Joe said, "We had a complaint about items ejected from the windows."

The guard blinked, not understanding. "You what?"

"Objectionable articles," Joe said. "Ejected from windows near the northeast corner of the building."

Tom had to admire the toneless neutrality of Joe's voice,

he sounded just like a patrolman on the beat. That only came with practice, as Tom had said in the elevator.

The guard had finally figured out what Joe was talking about, but he still couldn't believe it. He said, "From *this* floor?"

"We got to check it out," Joe said.

The guard glanced at the television screens, but of course none of them showed anybody throwing objectionable articles out the windows. A little later they'd be throwing paper, confetti, ticker tape, but those aren't objectionable articles, except to the Sanitation Department. That's the trademark of a parade in the Wall Street area; a snowstorm of paper when the hero goes by that the parade is in honor of. Or this time, the heroes, in the plural; a group of astronauts who'd been on the moon.

The guard said, "I'll call Mr. Eastpoole."

"Go ahead," Joe said.

The phone was on a table by the rear wall, near the pegboard with the ID tags on it. The guard made his phone call with his back turned, and Tom and Joe took the opportunity to relieve the tension a little; yawning, moving their shoulders around, shifting their feet, hitching their gunbelts, scratching their necks.

He talked low-voiced, the guard did, but they could hear what he was saying. First he had to explain things to a secretary, and then he had to explain things all over again to somebody named Eastpoole. That was the third name in the company's brand-name, so Eastpoole had to be one of the major bosses, and you could tell it by how respectful and soft-pedaled the guard's voice became as he described the problem.

Finally, he hung up the phone and turned back, saying, "He'll be right out."

"We'll go in to meet him," Joe said.

The guard shook his head. He was apologetic, but firm. "I'm sorry," he said, "I can't let you in without an escort."

They'd already suspected that, but Tom made his voice sound incredulous when he broke in, saying, "You can't let *us* in?"

The guard looked more apologetic than ever, but still just as firm. "I'm sorry, officer," he said, "but that's my instructions."

Movement on one of the TV screens down at the end of the counter attracted everybody's attention then, and they all turned their heads and watched a man crossing a room from left to right. He looked to be in his middle fifties, slightly heavy-set, thick gray hair, jowly face, very expensive well-tailored suit, narrow dark tie, white shirt. He had a long stride, moving as though he was a man who got annoyed easily and was used to getting his own way. He'd get waiters fired in restaurants.

"He's coming now," the guard said. You could see he didn't like the position he was in; cops in front of him, and a tough boss behind him. He said, "Mr. Eastpoole's one of the partners here. He'll take care of you."

Tom always had a habit of empathizing with the working stiff. Now, trying to make conversation and put the guard at his ease a little, he said, "Not much doing around here today."

"Not with the parade," the guard said. He grinned and shrugged, saying, "They might as well close up, days like this."

Joe was suddenly feeling cute. "Good time for a robbery," he said.

Tom gave him a fast angry look, but the thing had already been said. The guard didn't see the look, and apparently Joe didn't either.

The guard was shaking his head. "They'd never get away," he said, "not with that crowd out there."

Joe nodded, as though he was thinking it over. "That's right, too," he said.

The guard glanced at the TV screens, and Eastpoole was

just crossing another of them. Apparently feeling he had the time to relax, the guard leaned on his elbows on the counter again and said, "Biggest robbery they ever had in the world was right down here in the financial section."

Tom, really interested, said, "Is that right?"

The guard nodded, for emphasis, and said, "That's right. It was in the World Series. Remember the year the Mets won the pennant?"

Joe laughed and said, "Who'll ever forget?"

"That's right," the guard said. "It was in the last game, the ninth inning, everybody in New York City was at their radio. Somebody walked into a vault at one of the firms on the Street, and walked out with thirteen million dollars in bearer bonds."

They looked at one another. Joe turned back to the guard and said, "They ever get him?"

"Nope," said the guard.

At that point, Eastpoole came in from the door on the right. He was being brisk, impatient, slightly hostile. He probably didn't like his employees gawking out of windows instead of getting their work done, and he surely didn't like a couple of cops coming around and telling him there's something wrong going on in his shop. He strode over, efficient, in a hurry to give them the brush-off, and said, "Yes, officer?"

Joe had a natural talent for people like this. He just slowed himself down and became very official and very dense; it drove the hurry-up types right up the wall. Joe gave this one a suspicious look and said, "You Eastpoole?"

Eastpoole made an impatient little hand gesture, brushing a minor annoyance away. "Yes," he said, "I'm Raymond Eastpoole. What can I do for you?"

"We got a complaint," Joe said, taking his time about it. "Items ejected from the windows."

Eastpoole didn't believe it, and made no attempt to hide the fact. Frowning, he said, "From these offices?"

Joe nodded. "That's the report we got," he said. He was

showing that nothing would either ruffle him or hurry him up. He said, "We want to check out the northeast corner of the building, all the windows over on that side."

Eastpoole would rather have had nothing to do with them or their complaint or anything else concerned with today. He glanced over at the guard behind the counter, but there was obviously no help there, so finally he gave an angry shrug and said, "Very well. I'll accompany you myself. Come along."

Joe nodded, still taking his time. "Thank you," he said, but not as though anybody had done anybody any favors. His style was that they were all equals in this room. It was a style guaranteed to rub somebody like Raymond Eastpoole the wrong way.

Which it did. Eastpoole turned away, to lead them on their tour of the northeast corner of the building, and then turned back to frown at the guard again and say, "Where's your partner?"

The guard hesitated, showing his embarrassment. And when he lied, he did a lousy job of it, saying, "Uh, he's, uh, he's to the men's room."

Eastpoole couldn't show his anger in the cops' direction, but he could aim it at the guard. His voice taut with fury, he said, "You mean he's leaning out a window somewhere, watching the parade."

The guard was blinking, scared of this bastard. "He'll be right back, Mr. Eastpoole," he said.

Eastpoole thumped a fist onto the counter. "We pay," he said, "for two men at this counter, twenty-four hours a day."

"He just went off a minute ago," the guard said. He was really sweating.

Partly to get the guard off the hook, and partly because they had their own schedule to think about, Joe broke in at that point, saying, "We'd like to check things out, Mr. Eastpoole, before anything else gets dropped."

Eastpoole would clearly have preferred to keep nagging at the guard. He glowered at Joe, glowered at the guard, and then mulishly gave in, turned on his heel and led the way from the room. They followed him, Joe going first and then Tom coming along behind. Passing through the doorway, Tom glanced back and saw the guard hurriedly reaching for the phone; to call his partner to haul ass away from the window, no doubt.

They walked down a fairly long corridor, and then through several large offices, each of them full of desks and filing cabinets, and all of them lined with windows along one wall. The desks were all unoccupied, and people were standing looking out of all the windows.

They hadn't heard the drums or the music from the time they'd gotten into the elevator to come up here, but now the sound was with them again, and they walked automatically to the rhythm of the drums. Tension seemed to shimmer upward from the street outside those windows like heat waves off asphalt paving in the summertime. Both of them were tense again, walking along in Eastpoole's wake, the drums echoing in their bloodstreams.

And yet, they still hadn't reached the point of no return. They could still even at this late date change their minds and not go through with it. They could do an inspection tour of the windows with Eastpoole, find nothing, give him a lecture, and walk out. Return the squad car, drive home, forget the whole thing; it was still possible. But any second now, it would stop being possible for good and all.

Twice, as they walked along, they saw TV cameras mounted high on the wall in the corner of a room. The camera would turn slowly back and forth, like a fan, angled shallowly downward so as to get a good view of the entire room. These two were among the six that showed up on the screens out by the reception area. And on other sets of screens on this floor, as well. One of the big advantages of this brokerage for Tom and Joe was that their check into the security systems showed there wasn't any closed-circuit TV communication to any other floor; it was all confined to this one level.

From the office with the second camera in it, they passed

on to a short empty corridor. They entered it, and Joe made the decision that moved them finally over the line, making them criminals in fact as well as in theory. And he did it with two words: "Hold it," he said, and reached out to take Eastpoole by the elbow and stop him from walking on.

Eastpoole stopped, and you could see he was offended at being touched. When he turned around to find out what the problem was, he jerked his elbow free again. "What is it?" he said. He sounded very petulant for a grown man.

Joe looked around the corridor and said, "Is there a camera in here? Can that guard check this area?"

"No," Eastpoole said. "There's no need for it. And there are no windows here, if you'll notice." He half-turned away again, gesturing at the far end of the corridor. "What you want is—"

Joe put an edge in his voice, saying, "We know what we want. Let's go to your office."

"My office?" Eastpoole didn't have the first idea what was going on. Staring at them both, he said, "What for?"

Tom said, "We don't have to show you guns, do we?" He spoke calmly, not wanting Eastpoole to be so upset he'd lose control.

Eastpoole kept staring. He said, "What is this?"

"It's a robbery," Tom said. "What do you think it is?"

"But—" Eastpoole gestured at them, at their uniforms. "You two—"

"You can't tell a book by its cover," Tom said.

Joe poked Eastpoole's arm, prodding him a little. "Come on," he said, "let's move. To your office."

Eastpoole, starting to get over his shock, said, "You can't believe you can get away with—"

Joe gave him a shove that pushed him into the corridor wall. "Stop wasting our time," he said. "I'm feeling very tense right now, and when I'm tense sometimes I hit people."

Eastpoole's skin was turning pale under the eyes and around the mouth. He almost looked as though he might faint, and yet there was still arrogance in him, he might still be stupid enough to talk back. Tom, moving forward between Joe and Eastpoole, being the calm and reasonable one, said, "Come on, Mr. Eastpoole, take it easy. You're insured, and it isn't your job to deal with people like us. Be sensible. Do what we want, and let it go."

Eastpoole was nodding before Tom had finished talking. "That's just what I'll do," he said. "And later, I'll see to it you get the maximum penalty of the law."

"You do that," Joe said.

Tom, turning to Joe, said, "It's all right, now. Mr. Eastpoole's going to be sensible." He looked back. "Aren't you, Mr. Eastpoole?"

Eastpoole was looking sullen, but subdued. Half-gritting his teeth, he looked at Tom and said, "What do you want?"

"To go to your office. You lead the way."

Joe said, "And don't be cute."

"He won't be cute," Tom said. "Go ahead, Mr. Eastpoole."

Eastpoole turned and started walking again, and they both followed him. It's such an old tried-and-true technique, one partner hard and one partner soft, that it's become a cliché in the television police shows. But the fact is, it works. You give a guy one person to be friends with and one person to be scared of, and between the two you'll most of the time get whatever you want.

This time, what they wanted was Eastpoole's office, and that's what they got. They walked there, and the outer office was empty, and they went directly on through. Eastpoole's secretary, who should have been at the desk in the outer office, was in here, looking out a window at the parade. Her own room didn't have any windows in it.

Eastpoole's office looked like half of a living room and half of a rich man's den. It was a corner office, with windows in two walls, and near the juncture of those two walls was the desk, a big free-form mahogany thing with an onyx desk set and two telephones—one white, one red—and only a few neatly stacked pieces of paper. A couple of chairs with upholstered seats and backs in a blue-and-white vertical-stripe cloth were near the desk, and a large antique refectory table was over against the inner wall.

Down at the end of the room opposite the desk there was a white latticework divider that separated off about a third of the floor space. Behind it was a glass and chrome dining-room table, several chrome chairs with white vinyl seats, and a bar with fluorescent lights on each shelf. Some kind of real ivy growing out of pots on the floor had been trained to grow up the latticework, giving the glass-and-chrome section behind it the look of a special private nook, the kind of secret place that shows up in children's stories.

In front of the latticework on this side was a long blue sofa, with an octagonal wooden coffee table in front of it, and a pair of armchairs nearby. There were lamps and end tables and heavy ashtrays. Spotted on the walls around the room were half a dozen paintings, probably original, probably valuable. And amid them, positioned for easy viewing from the desk, was the double rank of six television screens. Tom and Joe looked at those screens the instant they walked into the room, and there was no unusual activity showing on any of them. So far, so good.

They both noticed that there were now two guards showing on the screen for the reception area.

Eastpoole's secretary belonged in this setting. She was a tall, cool, beautiful girl in a beige knit dress. She turned away from the window now and came walking over, saying to her boss, "Mr. Eas—"

Eastpoole, angry, not wanting to hear whatever normal business the secretary had been about to discuss with him, interrupted her, gesturing over his shoulder at the two cops and saying, "These people are—"

Not that way. Tom overrode him, pushing forward and saying, "It's okay, Miss. Nothing to worry about."

The secretary, looking from face to face, was beginning to get alarmed, but not yet really frightened. Addressing the question to all of them equally, she said, "What's the matter?"

Bitterly, Eastpoole said, "They aren't really police."

Tom made a kind of joke of it, to keep the girl from going into panic. "We're desperate criminals, mam," he said. "We're engaged in a major robbery."

Whenever Joe was confronted by a woman he wanted to get into bed with and knew it wasn't possible to he got hostile, and showed it in a kind of angry smiling manner. As he did now, coming forward and saying, "They'll ask you questions on TV, just like a stewardess."

With an unconscious automatic gesture, she reached up and patted her hair. At the same time, her eyes were getting more frightened, and there was a tremor in her voice when she said, "Mr. Eastpoole, is this really—"

"Yes, it's really," Tom said. "But you yourself are in absolutely no danger. Mr. Eastpoole, you sit down at your desk."

The secretary stared at everybody. "But—" she said, and then ran down, unable to formulate the question. She moved her hands vaguely, and stared, and looked frightened.

Eastpoole did what he was told. Sitting down behind the desk, he said, "There's no way you can get away with this, you know. You're just endangering people's lives."

"Oh, my God," the secretary said. Her right hand fluttered upward to her throat.

Joe pointed at the guards on the TV screens, and said to Eastpoole, "Any of them gets excited while we're here, you're all through."

Eastpoole tried to give him a scornful stare, but he was blinking too much. "You don't have to threaten me," he said. "I'll let the authorities pick you up later."

Nodding, Tom said, "That's the way to think, all right."

Joe pulled one of the blue-and-white striped chairs around behind Eastpoole's desk, so he could sit beside him. But he didn't sit yet; instead, he stood next to the chair and said to

Eastpoole, "You and me are going to wait here. My partner and your lady friend are going to the vault."

The secretary's head jerked back and forth. "I—I can't," she said, in a thin voice. "I'll faint."

Reassuring her, Tom said gently, "No, you won't. You'll do just fine, don't worry about a thing."

Joe told her, "You just do what your boss tells you to do." Then he gave Eastpoole a hard meaningful look.

Eastpoole's response was surly, but defeated. Gazing down at his neat desktop, he said, "We'll do what they want, Miss Emerson. Let the police handle it later."

"Right," Joe said.

Tom, looking at the secretary, gestured toward the door. "Let's go, Miss," he said.

She gave one last appealing look in Eastpoole's direction, but Eastpoole was still brooding at his desktop. Her hands fluttered again, as though in accompaniment to the statement she hadn't quite found the words for; but then she turned and walked obediently to the door, and she and Tom went out together.

Tom

Until the second Joe reached out and grabbed Eastpoole's elbow and said, "Hold it," I still hadn't been one hundred per cent sure we were actually going to go through with this. Maybe it had been necessary that I keep some doubt in my mind, maybe that was what had made it possible for me to go on moving along through all the preparations and then get out of bed today and come to New York and in real life start step by step to do the things we'd decided on. That small uncertainty had been a kind of escape hatch for me, I suppose, to keep me from getting too nervous and frightened of what we had in mind.

Well, now the escape hatch was gone. We were in it now, we'd started. If there was anything we hadn't thought of, it was too late to think of it. If there was any fact that we should know that we hadn't picked up in our studies, it was too late to find it out. If there was any flaw in our plan, anything at all, it was too late now to fix it. It would fix us instead.

The first part, escorting Eastpoole to his office and keeping him calm and tractable, hadn't been too bad. It wasn't that different, really, from dealing with a suspect about whose guilt you weren't really sure, but who could possibly make things very tough if he weren't handled just right. It was like a variation on a part of my job I already knew about, so I could almost let automatic responses do it for me.

Besides, Joe and I had been working together at that point. I don't know if my presence made things easier for him, but his presence definitely made things easier for me. Seeing him in the same position I was in, knowing we were locked into this together, had made it easier to keep moving.

But now I was on my own. Eastpoole's secretary, that he'd called Miss Emerson, was walking with me through offices filled with people. What if she suddenly panicked, started to scream? What if her fright was only an act, and she was just waiting her chance to pull a fast one? What if a thousand different things happened that weren't supposed to happen? I hadn't the first idea how I'd handle it if she didn't obey orders, and I wasn't sure anymore what was the best way to treat her to make sure she would obey. Her physical being, walking beside me, terrified me, and all I knew for sure was that I couldn't let her know how nervous I was. It would either throw her into a complete panic or make her start thinking she could outsmart me, and I didn't want either of those things to happen.

There was a sexual element, too, which surprised me; I hadn't expected anything like that. I don't mean my sexual instincts are dead, or that my awareness is limited to Mary. I covet other women as much as any man, and in fact several years ago I had an affair with a woman in the neighborhood. She lived down the block from us, her husband worked for Grumman Aircraft. They're gone now, they left a few years ago and moved out to California. It happened in the fall, early in October, and it was possible because of the funny shifts I work that have me around the house a lot in the daytime. This woman—Nancy, her name was—came around one day setting up a car pool for something with the kids. Mary wasn't home but I was, and Nancy had just the night before had a big fight with her husband, and all of a sudden there we were screwing on the living-room floor. It was amazing.

It was also the only time we made it in my house. From then on, if I was home in the daytime and felt like it, I'd drift on down to her place and we'd have sex in her bedroom, on the bed. She had slightly different preferences and manners from Mary, and newness makes things exciting, and for a while I was really pleased with myself, having two women on the same block. Then the holidays came along, and there was a whole different mental attitude developed in both our minds, where we both grew much more interested in our own families again, and it all sort of faded away. We never had a fight or anything, we never officially broke it off, but by the middle of December I wasn't making any more visits and she wasn't calling up—as she'd done a couple times in October and November—to suggest it was a nice day for a bounce on the bed.

Nevertheless, good-looking women definitely still turn me on, and I can get a real letch for something tall and slender with a good figure and a good walk, all of which is a pretty good summation of Miss Emerson. I'd noticed her in the usual sexual way when I'd first walked into Eastpoole's office, but then my mind had been distracted by the problems of dealing with Eastpoole, and in the normal course of events that would have been the end of it.

Which was why I was so surprised and troubled at the sexual aura that hung between us now. It was a different sort of thing from my usual awareness, it was both stronger and unhealthier, and the most embarrassing thing about it was that I knew what was doing it. She was my prisoner. "Ah, me proud beauty, you are in my power!" It was that number. It wasn't really true that she was my prisoner in the sense that I could do anything I wanted with her, but there was a feeling of that between us, of her actually being in my power and of me being in the role of the villain.

And of course, I *was* in the role of villain, wasn't I? I was there to commit, as I'd told her, a major robbery. Which helped to make the situation different from those rare times when I actually have had good-looking female prisoners in my control, in the course of my working life. In those instances I haven't been the villain, I've been on the good guy's side. Also, I've been limited by the rules of my profession and the laws of the land. None of which applied this time.

Well, I wasn't going to rape her, though God knows she had a body I would have liked to touch. But it was much more important to keep her calm than to satisfy irrelevant bodily urges of my own that I didn't really want to have in the first place. So I wanted to talk to her, to ease her tension a little, but I wasn't sure what to say that wouldn't just increase the sexual discomfort hanging around us, so for too long a time I walked beside her in silence; which couldn't have been very reassuring.

Finally I decided the best thing to do was to be brisk and businesslike, so I said, "I'm going to tell you exactly what we want. You'll have to go into the vault alone, so I'll tell you what to get from it."

She didn't look at me. Facing front as she walked along next to me, she nodded and said, "Yes." Her face showed strain, the skin stretched tight over her cheekbones, her eyes open a little too wide.

I said, "We want bearer bonds. You know what I mean?"

"Yes," she said.

Of course she knew what I meant, she worked here. "Right," I said. "Now, we don't want any of them with a face value over a hundred thousand dollars, and nothing under twenty thousand, and we want them all together to add up to ten million."

She gave me a surprised look then, but immediately faced front again and nodded and said, "All right."

I said, "Now, I know you're going to be smart and do things right, but I just want to remind you. My partner's in your boss's office, and he can see the vault on one of the TV screens there, and the vault anteroom with the guard. If you try talking to the guard, or doing anything you shouldn't in the vault, he'll be able to see you."

"I won't do anything," she said. She sounded terrified again, and on the verge of tears.

"I know you won't," I said. "I just thought I should remind you, that's all, but I know you won't do anything."

We'd been passing through one of the big offices with all the empty desks and crowded windows. Thirty or forty people in the room, all with their backs to us, looking out the windows at the parade going by. I was still marching along in time to the drums, whether I liked it or not, but Miss Emerson was walking in an erratic sort of way, quick steps and then an occasional slow step, no consistent rhythm at all. I supposed it was part of her nervousness that made her walk like that, and I did my best to adjust my speed to hers, though I still paced myself to the sound of the parade.

In the doorway, leaving that office and entering a corridor that led away to the right, she suddenly stumbled. I automatically reached out to grab her arm and help her keep her feet, and she pulled away from me, terrified, wide-eyed. Keeping her balance by fear alone, she staggered backwards across the corridor and brought up against the wall on the other side.

I followed her into the corridor, looked down to the right, and saw we were alone. "Take it easy," I said, fast and low. I was afraid there was a scream in her throat just dying to come out. "Take it easy, nobody's going to hurt you."

Her right hand went up to her throat again, as it had in the office. I could see her forcing herself to take long deep breaths, to get control. She was really very good, she got hold of the reins herself and pulled the whole thing back together. I stood there, waiting it out, and finally she said, in a low voice, "I'm all right now."

"Of course you are," I said. "You're doing fine. There's nothing to worry about, I promise you. All we want is money, and none of it is yours, so what's there to be afraid of?" I grinned at her, spreading my hands.

She nodded, and came away from the wall at last, but she wouldn't respond to my grin, and as much as possible she avoided meeting my eye. How much of that was simple fear and how much the sexual overlay I don't know, but there was no point trying to calm her entirely. It wouldn't have been possible anyway, and all I really needed was her functional and rational.

Which she was, again. We walked down the corridor together, and then she gestured at a closed door ahead of us and said, "That's the anteroom."

Where the vault guard would be stationed. The vault itself would be just beyond. "I'll wait out here," I said. "Now, you know what I want."

Not looking at me, she nodded her head, a sudden jerky movement.

I said, "Tell me. Take it easy, don't get upset, just tell me what I said."

She had to clear her throat before she could talk. Then she said, "You want bearer bonds. Nothing over a hundred thousand dollars, nothing less than twenty thousand."

"Adding up to?"

"Ten million dollars," she said.

I nodded. "That's right," I said. "And remember, my partner can watch you."

"I won't do anything," she said. She still didn't look at me. "Should I go in now?"

"Sure."

She opened the door and went inside, and I leaned against the wall to wait; either for ten million dollars or the roof to fall in.

Joe

When I pulled the chair over behind Eastpoole's desk, it was strictly bravado. I didn't plan on using it; the truth is, I was too tense to sit. If I couldn't be up and moving around, I'd bust every blood vessel I had.

Still, the best place to keep an eye both on Eastpoole and the television screens was from back around behind his desk. So I let him go on sitting there, and I stood behind him, leaning my back against the corner of the wall, between windows facing out in two directions, where I could watch what was happening both inside the room and out on the street.

The arrangement of the TV sets was the same as the six out in the reception area. The one on the top right showed the reception area itself, with the two guards behind the counter there. The top middle, top left, and bottom right showed three different offices, two of which we'd gone through when we'd come in here. The bottom middle screen showed the vault, and the bottom left showed the anteroom that led to the vault.

The vault was empty of people, and looked like a deep walk-in closet. You couldn't see a door in any part that showed on the screen, so the door was probably directly under the camera. The three walls visible to the camera were all lined from floor to ceiling with letter-size file drawers. The open space in the middle of the room was only about six feet square, and there wasn't any furniture in there at all.

The anteroom wasn't very big either. Where the camera was positioned, you could see the heavy vault door standing open in the far wall. A desk was to the left where the only guard was sitting, facing toward the camera. He had an ordinary wooden chair, without arms, and he was sitting there reading the *Daily News*. There was nothing on his desk but a telephone and a sign-in sheet with a ballpoint pen. A second wooden chair stood beside the desk, and that was it for the furniture. The same as with the vault, the entrance must have been under the camera.

After Tom and the secretary left, I took up my position behind Eastpoole, checked out the TV screens, and then took a quick gander out the window on my left, the one facing the street with the parade. The bands were still going by, thumping away, like the world's longest half-time show. Way down to the right, blocks away, it looked like it was snowing; in July. That was the ticker tape and paper coming down, marking where the astronauts were. You couldn't see them yet, they were still too far away.

I checked out Eastpoole, then. He was sitting there with his head a little forward and down. His palms were flat on the desk in front of him, and I guess he was studying his fingernails. His shoulders were hunched just a bit, meaning it made him nervous to have me behind him. Which was really tough.

People like this Eastpoole really irritate me. You see them driving Caddies, air-conditioned cars. I love to give them tickets, the bastards, but I know it doesn't do any good. What's twenty-five dollars to people like Eastpoole?

I looked over at the television screens, and Tom and the

secretary were just walking through one of the offices; the one on the top left. I watched them walk, and the secretary had a really nice ass. I like that kind of knit dress she was wearing, it shows a lot about a woman's shape, and this one was built very nice indeed.

I wondered if Eastpoole was getting into that. There wasn't any point asking him; whether he was or he wasn't, he'd deny it. And he'd give me a look, as though he couldn't believe there were such animals as me running around loose. Oh, I know that type. He hired her for her shorthand, that's what he did. Sure. Her shorthand, and his short arm.

It was tough to wait here like this, with nothing to do. I had the urge to needle Eastpoole a little, maybe poke him in the shoulder to see if he was as nerved-up as I was. But I knew I shouldn't do it, I shouldn't do anything that might make him forget to be smart and cool and quiet. It wasn't worth twenty years in a federal penitentiary to get a rise out of Eastpoole.

Twenty years. That thought suddenly brought it home to me; we were doing it! The thing we'd been talking about, building up for, kidding around with, we were actually doing it, we'd passed the stage of maybe yes, maybe no. There weren't any more maybes now. It's like the first time you ski down a real hill on your own; all the chances for thinking it over are gone, and from here on the only thing you can think about is keeping your balance.

I almost hadn't done it. I came this close to not bracing Eastpoole at all. Coming in with him from the recption area, I kept thinking about just running the whole thing through as though it was a gag. I mean, actually look at the windows on the northeast corner, maybe give the employees a lecture about throwing offensive objects onto the people below—I had this whole thing worked out in my head where I'd give a whole speech about shit without ever quite using the word—and then just turn around and walk out again. Pretend that's all I'd ever meant to do, that the whole robbery thing had never been anything but a gag anyway.

If it hadn't been for Tom there with me, that's probably exactly what I would have done. But I could feel Tom there beside me, waiting for me to make the move, and I just couldn't chicken out. Same as with skiing again; there comes that point, you've done your boasting, everybody's watching you, and it suddenly doesn't matter if you break your neck or not. You've got to do it, because if you don't you've made a fool of yourself, and nothing is worse than that.

Twenty years?

Well, almost nothing.

Movement on one of the television screens. I looked over there, and I was aware of Eastpoole tensing up right in front of me.

The secretary had walked into the anteroom. She had her back to me, I couldn't see the expression on her face. Any other time, honey, I'd love to see your ass, but right now it's your face I want.

At least I could see the guard's face. He looked up and gave her a big smile. So far as I could tell, she didn't say anything wrong to him, because the smile didn't flicker for a second. She moved forward, bent over to sign the sheet of paper on his desk, and then walked on into the vault. I kept watching the guard, and he didn't do anything wrong at all. He didn't even bother to look at her signature, just opened his newspaper again the second she was out of the anteroom and into the vault.

Now I could see her on the next screen. She walked into the vault, looked around, and glanced up at the camera. Yeah, honey, I'm watching.

I looked at the screen showing the reception area. The two guards were both leaning on the counter, talking together. Neither of them was looking toward the screens.

Back in the vault, the secretary was opening one of the file drawers. She started to finger through it, and pulled out a sheet of heavy paper like a high school diploma. She opened another drawer and rested the sheet of paper on top of the things in the drawer, then went back to the first one to select some more.

I hoped she was getting the right stuff. I hoped Tom had gotten the point across to her and that she'd understood what it was we wanted. I didn't want to get home later on and find out we'd gone through all this for a lot of paper we couldn't use.

It was taking her a goddam long time. She kept looking at paper after paper, and most of them she just shoved back into the drawer. What was taking so long? Come on, damn it, grab the paper, let's go. We don't want to miss the parade, that's part of our scheme.

I looked out the window again. The astronauts would be the wind-up of the parade, and that's where the stream of ticker tape was coming down. It was closer, but still blocks away. But it wouldn't take forever.

I looked back at the screens again. The girl in the vault was still picking through the file drawer. "Come on," I whispered, too low for Eastpoole to hear me. "Come on, come on."

But she kept doing it. The stack on the other drawer was getting pretty thick now, but she still wasn't finished.

We'd wanted too much, that was all. We should have settled for half of that. Five million, that would get us half a million each. Five hundred thousand dollars, who needs more than that? It's nearly forty years of my salary. We'd been greedy, that's what, and it was taking too long.

Come *on*, bitch, come on!

Movement. I looked at the screen on the top right, the reception area. An elevator door had opened there, and three uniformed patrolmen were coming out of it, moving toward the two guards behind the counter.

I slapped a hand down on Eastpoole's shoulder. He'd seen it, too, he was tensing up like fast-drying concrete. My throat was so dry my voice came out like steel wool. I said, "What's going on?"

The three cops stopped at the counter, one of them talked to the guards. A guard turned toward the telephone.

I squeezed Eastpoole's shoulder, clamping down on it. "*What's going on?*"

"I d-don't know." I could feel him trembling under my hand, the concrete was breaking up. He was frightened for his life, and he had a right to be. "I swear I don't know," he said, and sat there trembling.

The guard was dialing. On the vault screen, that stinking bitch was still picking out papers, one at a time. All the other screens were fine.

The phone rang, on Eastpoole's desk. Eastpoole stared at it. His head was twitching.

So was mine. I fought the goddam holster, I got my pistol into my hand. "By God," I said, "you're a dead man." And I meant it. I thought we were both dead men, and if I was, Eastpoole was.

Eastpoole lifted his hands. He stared at the telephone. He didn't know what to say or what to do. He really and truly didn't know whether to shit or go blind.

I kicked the chair out of the way that I'd dragged around behind the desk before. It went over on its side with a crash, and Eastpoole jumped. I crouched down beside him, so I'd be able to listen on the phone and still watch the television screens. I pushed the pistol barrel against Eastpoole's side. "Answer it," I said. "And be goddam careful."

He had to take a couple of seconds to get some control, so he'd be able to move and talk. I let him have the time he needed, and then he reached out and picked up the phone and said, "Yes?"

I could only make out about half the words the guard said to him. But it didn't seem as though there was any tension in the voice, or any sense of excitement out there in the reception area.

On the other hand, if they were here because they knew what was going on, they'd know we could see them on television, wouldn't they?

But how would they know? There hadn't been any breakdowns, there wasn't any reason for anything to go wrong.

Eastpoole said into the phone, "But do they have to—? Well, one moment. One moment." He put his hand over the mouthpiece, and turned to talk to me. "They're here to check security for the astronauts," he said.

I kept watching the screen. I said, "What do they want?"

"Just to station themselves at windows."

We didn't want cops in here. What the hell was the matter with them, why didn't they pick some other floor? Why didn't they go on the roof, for Christ's sake, that's where your snipers come from. "God damn it," I said. I felt like blowing up into a million pieces. "God *damn* it."

"I'm not responsible," Eastpoole yammered, "I didn't know they—"

"Shut up, shut up." I was trying to think, trying to decide what to do. He couldn't refuse, that wouldn't look right. "Listen," I said. "They can do it, but not in this office. Tell them that."

He nodded, fast and nervous. "Yes," he said, and into the phone he said, "Go right ahead, tell them it's all right. One of you escort them in. But I don't want any of them in here. Not in my office."

I could read the guard's lips on that one, see him say, "Yes, sir." Eastpoole hung up, and so did the guard. The guard turned back to the three cops, said something to them, and then walked around the end of the counter to lead them in.

I looked at the vault screen, and the girl was finally finished. Carrying a double armful of papers like a schoolgirl with her books, she pushed the two drawers shut and turned toward the door.

I jabbed Eastpoole with the pistol again. "Call the vault!" I told him. "I want to talk to that girl."

"There's no phone in the—"

"The anteroom! The anteroom! For Christ's sake, call!"

He reached for the phone. The girl was out of sight of the

vault camera now. On the anteroom camera, I saw her come through the doorway. The stack of papers in her arms was maybe three inches thick, as thick as two ordinary books, but of course stacked somewhat looser. There were maybe a hundred and fifty sheets of paper there.

Eastpoole was dialing a three-digit number. The guard in the anteroom turned his head when the girl walked in, saw the stack of paper she was carrying, and jumped to his feet to open the hall door for her.

I kept jabbing Eastpoole in the side with the gun. "Hurry it up!" I said. "Hurry it up!"

The guard and the girl were both moving toward the camera, they'd be out of sight under it in a second. "Come *on*," I said. I wanted to shoot everything in sight; Eastpoole, the television screens, the astronauts out in the street. The goddam drums were pounding away down there as though I didn't have enough pounding from my heart.

"It's ringing," Eastpoole said, still terrified, still trying to show me he was cooperating. And just before the guard disappeared out of sight, I saw him look back over his shoulder toward the phone on his desk.

But he was polite, he was. Ladies first. He went on, he disappeared. The girl disappeared.

"It's ringing," Eastpoole said again, and from the sound of his voice and the look on his face I thought he was about to cry.

The guard appeared again, alone moving toward the desk and the telephone. I reached over and slapped my free hand down on the phone cradle, breaking the connection. On the screen, the guard picked up the receiver. He could be seen saying hello into it, being confused.

Eastpoole was jabbering, he was going to shake himself right out of his chair. Staring at me, he was saying, "I tried! I tried! I did everything you said, I tried!"

"Shut up shut up shut *up*!" The other cops were long since gone from the reception area. Tom and the girl would be walking through all those offices, Tom having no idea about the three cops.

Eastpoole was panting like a dog. The six screens were all normal. I stared at them, and bit my upper lip, and finally I said, "A phone on their route." I looked at Eastpoole. "What's their route back?"

He just stared at me.

"Damn you, what's their route?"

"I'm trying to think!"

"Anything goes wrong," I told him, shaking the pistol in his face, "God *damn* it, anything goes wrong, you're the first one dead."

Shakily he reached for the phone.

Tom

I stood in that corridor a long time. I must have figured out fifty different ways for things to go wrong while I waited there, and no ways at all for things to go right.

For instance. It was true that Joe could keep an eye on Miss Emerson through the television screens in Eastpoole's office, but what good would that do me if she decided to blow the thing to the guard in the anteroom after all? Joe would see her do it, he'd know what was going on, but he didn't have any way to get in touch with me to warn me. For all I knew, it had already happened, and Joe was out of the building by now, leaving me to stand here and wait to be picked up.

Or say she didn't do it on purpose, Miss Emerson, but her nervousness made her do or say something that got the guard suspicious. Same result; me standing out here as though I was waiting for the bus.

The bus to Sing Sing.

Would Joe clear out, if that happened? If the roles were reversed, and I was the one in Eastpoole's office and saw it all going wrong on the television screens, what would I do?

I'd come looking for Joe, to warn him. And that's what he'd do, too, I was sure of it.

Aside from anything else, it wouldn't do Joe any good to get away and leave me here. Even if I never said a word, how long would it take the investigating officers to get from me to my next-door neighbor, who was also my best friend and also on the force? They'd have us both booked by nightfall.

Where was she, what was taking so long?

But Joe would come looking for me, I was sure of that.

Which didn't mean he'd find me. He didn't know the route from Eastpoole's office to the vault any more than I had. I'd followed Miss Emerson, that's all.

That would be beautiful. Everything gone to hell, me standing here not knowing about it, and Joe running back and forth all over the seventh floor looking for me. That would be too ridiculous to believe, and if that's the way it went we'd almost deserve to be caught.

What was she *doing* in there?

I looked at my watch, but it didn't tell me anything, because I didn't know what time she'd gone in. Maybe five minutes ago, maybe ten. It seemed like a week.

The parade. If she didn't get a move on, we'd miss the parade, and that would screw things up all over again.

You spend your life waiting around for women, I swear to God you do. You'll be late for church, late for the movies, late for dinner, late for the parade, late for everything. You sit out in the car and honk the horn, or you stand in the bathroom doorway and say, "Your hair looks all *right*." Or you stand around looking at your watch, in the middle of committing a felony. Nothing ever changes, men just wait for women and that's all there is to it.

A door opened, farther down the hall. A girl came out, carrying a thick manila envelope. She was short and dumpy, in a plaid skirt and a white blouse, and she looked like the kind of girl who would go on working when everybody else in lower Manhattan was watching the parade. I stood there, clenching my teeth, watching her walk toward me. She gave me a neutral smile on the way by, walked on, and went through another doorway and out of sight. I exhaled, and looked at my watch again, and another minute had gone by.

I'd looked at my watch twice more before the anteroom door opened. I was standing back against the wall to one side, so I couldn't be seen from inside the room, and it's a good thing I was, because apparently the guard had come over to open the door for her. "See you again," I heard him say, with that smile in his voice that men have when talking to a good-looking woman.

"Thank you," she said. Her voice seemed to me too obviously frightened, but he didn't make any connections from it; at least, not that I could tell.

He probably thought it was her period. Any time a woman acts upset or nervous or weepy or anything at all out of the ordinary, everybody always takes it for granted it's her period, and pretends not to notice.

She came out to the corridor and gave me a haggard look, and the guard closed the door behind her. I heard his phone ring as the door was closing. Let it be nothing, I thought.

She had a stack of documents in her arms, held against her chest. I nodded at them and said, "All set?"

"Yes." Her voice was very small, as though she were talking from a different room.

"Let's go, then."

We headed back for Eastpoole's office, retracing the same route as before. Parade noises still thumped in through the open windows, employees were still jammed at all the windows with their backs to us, everything moved along exactly as before.

At the end of one corridor there was a closed door. I'd opened it for her the last time, coming through, and now that her hands were full there was even more reason to do so. I did, and we stepped through into the next office, and I'd gone another pace or two when I suddenly thought about fingerprints.

Now, that would be smart. The most basic thing in police procedure is fingerprints, every six-year-old boy in the country knows about fingerprints, and I was about to go off and leave prints all over two doorknobs; the one going, and the one coming.

"Hold it a second," I said.

She stopped, giving me an uncomprehending look. I went back to the door and smeared my palm all around the knob, then pulled it open and leaned out to do the same thing on the other side. I rubbed it good, and was about to shut the door again when movement attracted my attention. I looked down at the far end of the corridor, and one of the guards from the reception area was coming in, followed by three uniformed cops.

I ducked back into the room and shut the door. I was sure they hadn't seen me. I rubbed the inner knob again, then turned back to Miss Emerson, took her by the arm, and started walking fast. She was startled, mouth open, but before she could speak I said, low and fast, "Don't do anything, don't say anything. Just walk."

The windows were on the right, lined with employees. Band music was loud, making our own movements silent. Nobody saw or heard us.

There was an alcove on the left, full of duplicating equipment; a row of filing cabinets partly shielded it from the main area of the room. I turned that way, steered Miss Emerson in there. "We're going to wait here a second," I said. "Crouch down. I don't want you seen over the tops of the cabinets."

She crouched a bit, but apparently found that too uncomfortable because a second later she shifted position and knelt instead. She knelt in a prim way, back straight, like an early Christian martyr about to get it. She watched me, wide-eyed, but didn't say anything.

I hunkered down, and peeked around the edge of the last filing cabinet. I'd let them go past me, and then follow. That way, if they were headed for Eastpoole's office I'd at least be behind them, where I might be able to do some good.

Did Joe know about the cops being here? He'd have to, he would have seen them come in.

What was he doing now? Had my worst fears come true, was Joe wondering around these offices somewhere looking for me?

God damn it, what a mess.

I could smell the secretary. Fear was making her perspire, and the perspiration was mixing with whatever perfume or cologne or something she had on, and the result was a half-musky, half-sweet scent that brought back the whole sexual thing all over again.

I didn't have time to think about that. I was doing some sweating myself right now.

The guard and three policemen appeared. Past them, a phone rang on one of the desks. The cops all stopped, right in front of me, to talk things over.

On the second ring of the telephone, a girl at one of the windows turned around reluctantly, gave an exaggerated sigh, looked long-suffering, and strolled over to answer it.

The cops had decided one of them would stay in this room. While the others walked on, he went over and forced a place for himself at one of the windows, looking out.

Meanwhile, the girl had answered the phone. "Hello?" She paused, then looked more alert and on-the-job. "Mr. Eastpoole? Yes, sir." Another pause. She looked around, and shook her head. "No, sir, Mr. Eastpoole, she hasn't been through yet." Another pause. "Yes, sir, I certainly will." She hung up, and hurried back to the window.

Now what? How the hell was Eastpoole making phone calls? Where was Joe? What was going on?

And I didn't need that cop at the window, I really didn't.

Well, I had him. Straightening up to look over the top of the filing cabinet, I saw him standing there, having taken a window for himself, and he was looking out, his back squarely to me. If he'd only stay like that, there was still a chance.

I hunkered again, and turned to Miss Emerson, "Listen," I said. "I don't want a lot of shooting."

"Neither do I," she said. She was so sincere it was almost comic.

"We're just going to get up and walk," I told her. "No trouble, no fuss, no attracting anybody's attention."

"No, sir," she said.

"Okay. Let's do it."

I helped her up from her knees, and she gave me a quick nervous smile of thanks. We were developing a human relationship. We came out from behind the filing cabinets and walked down the length of the office, and out, without being seen.

12

The next time they saw one another, they both started talking at the same time. Tom opened the door and ushered the secretary into Eastpoole's office, and Joe snapped around from where he was glaring at the television screens, trying to find out where everybody was.

Tom said, "There's cops out—"

Joe said, "Where the hell—"

They both stopped. There was so much tension in the air they could both have thrown themselves on the floor and started screaming and kicking and thrashing around.

Joe gestured at the phone on Eastpoole's desk. "I tried to call you," he said, "I saw them come in."

Tom had shut the door behind him. Now he walked across toward Joe and the desk and Eastpoole, saying, "I almost walked right into them. What are they doing?"

"Security for the astronauts."

Tom made a face. "Christ," he said. Then, suddenly remembering, he said, "The astronauts! We don't want to miss the end of the parade!"

Joe turned and hurried to the window and looked out. The paper snow was about two blocks away, approaching slowly. He turned back to the room, saying, "We're all right."

"Good," Tom said. He took a blue plastic laundry bag out of his left rear trouser pocket. It was all folded up small, into something about the size and shape of a pack of cigarettes. He shook it open, and it opened out into a good-size laundry bag; big enough to put a couple of sheets in, plus a regular wash.

Meantime Joe had walked over to the other area of the room, behind the white latticework. There was a door there, next to the bar. He pushed it open, reached in to switch on the light, and found a small but complete bathroom in there. Just as it had shown on the blueprints filed downtown. Sink, toilet, shower stall. It all looked very expensive, including the fact that the hot-and-cold-water faucets were in the shape of golden geese; the water would come out of their open mouths, and you'd turn their flared-back wings.

Tom turned to the secretary, holding open the laundry bag. "Dump them in here," he said.

As she dumped the bonds into the bag, Joe came back from his inspection of the bathroom and said to Eastpoole, "Okay, you. Get up from there."

Eastpoole knew enough now to be obedient right away, but he was still terrified. Rising, he said, "Where are you—?"

"Don't worry," Joe told him. "You were a good boy, you'll be okay. We just got to lock you up while we get out of here."

Tom threw the bag over his shoulder. He looked like a thin blue Santa Claus with a blue bag over his shoulder.

Joe wiggled his finger at the secretary. "You, too, honey," he said. "Come along."

Joe led them to the bathroom, then had them precede him into the room. He took handcuffs out of his left hip pocket and said to Eastpoole, "Give me your right hand."

Tom waited in the main part of the office. He didn't think they could see him now, but he didn't want to take any chances.

Joe put the cuff on Eastpoole's right wrist, then told him, "Kneel down. Right here by the sink." When Eastpoole did it, looking both frightened and confused, Joe turned to the secretary and said, "You too. Kneel right next to him."

After the girl had knelt, Joe crouched down with them and pushed Eastpoole's right arm so he could pass the handcuffs around behind the run-off pipe under the sink. Then he took the secretary's left forearm and held it back to where he could hook the other cuff onto her. The position he had to get to, in order to do it, all their heads were close together, like a football huddle. Their breaths mingled, and Joe found himself squinting as he put the cuffs on, as though there were bright lights on both sides of his face. Eastpoole and the secretary both kept their eyes down, looking toward the floor; kneeling there with eyes lowered, they looked like penitents.

Joe straightened, and nodded in satisfaction. They wouldn't be leaving this room, not without help. "You'll be getting out in a few minutes," he told them. "I'll leave the light on."

They watched him now, neither of them saying anything. Eastpoole didn't even say they wouldn't be getting away with it.

Joe went out the door, and paused with his hand on the knob. "Don't bother yelling," he said. "The only one's that'll hear you is us, and we won't come help."

Tom, across the room, standing near Eastpoole's desk, watched Joe in the bathroom doorway, and waited for him to come out and shut the door. When he finally did, Tom turned the laundry bag upside down, grabbed it by the bottom, and shook the bonds out onto the desk.

Joe came hurrying across the room. "They're closed in," he said.

"I know." Tom was looking at the television screens, and there was nothing unusual showing on any of them.

"There's no keyhole," Joe said, "so they won't be able to see what we're doing."

"They better not," Tom said. "How's the parade?"

"I'll take a look."

This was the part they'd argued about, while planning things. It had been Tom's idea to do it this way, and Joe hadn't liked it for a long while. In fact, it still troubled him now, but he did finally agree with Tom that it was the best way to handle things.

Joe headed for the window to look at the parade, and Tom picked up a thin stack of bonds; about ten of them. The top one was plainly marked "Pay To Bearer," and the amount of it was seventy-five thousand dollars. Tom gave the number a happy smile of welcome, shifted the grip of his two hands on the papers, and ripped them down the middle.

Joe was at the window. He looked out and to the right. He saw the parade, but he also saw a cop at another window on this floor. The cop was glancing in this direction, and when he saw Joe he waved. Joe nodded and waved back, and brought his head back in.

Tom was ripping the bonds into smaller and smaller pieces, working quickly but efficiently. Joe came over to the desk, gave the stack of paper a regretful look, and said, "Less than a block away."

"Help me with this."

"Sure."

Joe picked up a dozen bonds and gazed at them. "This one's for a hundred grand," he said.

"Come on, Joe."

"Right." Smiling sadly, shaking his head, he started to rip up the bonds.

Outside, the parade noises were getting louder; mostly the crowd noises, nearly blotting out the sounds of the bands. Turning his head for a fast look at the windows, Tom saw bits of paper already starting to flutter down. And less than a quarter of the bonds had been ripped up so far.

The two of them stood there, ripping paper. Shouting and yelling from down below. Then, in a different broken rhythm, a foot started thudding against the bathroom door.

They looked at one another. Tom said, "Will it pop open?"

"Christ."

Joe dropped the paper in his hands and ran down to the other end of the office. Eastpoole was kicking steadily and strongly at the door; apparently with the flat bottom of his shoe, sole and heel together. The door itself seemed solid enough to hold against that, but the catch could pop at any time and the door swing open.

What Joe would have liked mostly would have been to open the door and start doing some kicking himself; but there was a chance Eastpoole and the girl would be able to see through the latticework what Tom was doing. And the point of all this was that everybody think the crooks had gotten away with the bonds.

Joe looked around, grabbed one of the chairs away from the dining room table, and propped the back of it under the doorknob. He kicked the rear legs to jam them more firmly into the carpet, then stood back and watched. Inside, Eastpoole was still kicking at the door, but there wasn't even a tremor showing around the knob or the chair.

Tom was still ripping paper, back by Eastpoole's desk. Joe trotted over and said, "Fixed. It won't open now."

"Good."

There was a mound of ripped paper on the desk, all little irregular pieces no more than an inch square. Joe grabbed a double handful, carried it over to the window, and leaned his head out slightly first to see if the other cop was still visible down to the right. He was, but he was turned the other way, watching the roofline across the street.

Down below, through thousands of descending specks of paper, Joe could see the three convertibles in a row, each one with an astronaut sitting up on the back, waving and smiling. The lead car wasn't quite opposite this building yet, and they were all moving very slowly, no more than three miles an hour. The air was full of cheers and paper.

Joe grinned, and tossed his handful of ripped-up bonds out the window. The mass went out like a snowball, and disintegrated at once, all the pieces mixing with the rest of the torrent of paper coming down.

Tom's thumbs and wrists were getting sore. The bonds had been printed on heavy paper, and he'd been tearing them up as quickly as he could, the stacks as thick as he could manage. Now he took a break, grabbing up a handful of shreds and turning toward the window.

Joe was coming back. "Be careful leaning out," he said. "There's a cop down the row to the right. Waved at me."

"I'll be careful."

Tom tossed the paper out without showing himself, or trying to see the cop at the other window. When he turned back, Joe was picking up more paper. Tom hurried over, saying, "No, not that. Smaller pieces, smaller. They aren't ready yet."

Joe nodded at the window. "They're going by, Tom. The cars are going by right now."

"Small, Joe," Tom said. "So nothing shows." He pushed a little stack of paper together. "Take this."

Joe gave an irritable impatient shrug, gathered up the stack Tom had made, and carried it over to the window. Tom went back to ripping, and when Joe came to the desk again he also started shredding the bonds that were still left.

For the next minute or so the two of them stood side by side at the desk, tearing the last of the bonds into tiny remnants. Then they threw them all out, double handfuls fluttering down through the paper-filled air, disappearing. The three convertibles had all gone by, were all in the next block by now, but there was still enough paper coming down from all the buildings in this block so that Tom and Joe's contribution didn't show.

Tom gathered up the last few pieces left on the desk, hurried to the window, and tossed them out. Joe walked slowly around the desk, searching the floor, and found half a dozen pieces that had fallen in their hurry to be done. Tom spent time looking at the floor around the window, and found three more pieces that he picked up.

When Joe came over to the window with the few scraps he'd just gathered up from the floor, Tom said, "We can't leave any."

"We won't," Joe said. He tossed the last scraps out. "Let's go," he said. "It's time to get out of here."

But Tom kept prowling around, frowning down at the floor. "If we leave even one little piece for them to find," he said, "it blows the whole thing. They'll know what we've done, and that kills it."

"We've got them all," Joe insisted. "Come on, let's go."

"Hah!" Tom pounced on one last bit of paper midway between desk and window. He hurried to the window, where the snowfall of paper was starting to thin, and tossed the final piece out. "Now," he said.

Joe was already opening desk drawers. He found a stack of typewriter paper in one and pulled out a handful. Tom joined him at the desk, opened the blue laundry bag, and Joe dumped the paper into it. Then they both took a quick last look around.

"Okay," Tom said.

Joe was looking at the television screens. All quiet. "Fine," he said. "Let's go."

They walked out of Eastpoole's office together, through the secretary's office, and down the corridor toward the reception area and the elevators. Tom carried the laundry bag over his shoulder. It was very obvious there, but that was the point; they had to be seen carrying the loot out with them.

Walking along, Tom said, "I wish we knew a way out that wouldn't take us past any of those damn cameras."

Joe nodded. "I know. It'd be better if the guards didn't know we were coming."

"We could try," Tom said. They'd come to an office entrance now, but Tom stopped and said, "There's a camera in there. Why don't we go down this other way instead? Maybe we can go around, come at it from the other side."

"Get lost in here? Wander around until we get picked up?"

"It isn't that big," Tom said. "And if we get lost, we just stop somebody and ask."

Joe grinned at him. "You get funny ideas," he said. "Okay, let's try it, what the hell."

So they went off into new territory. They both had a pretty good sense of direction, and they had a general idea of the way things were set up around here. If they kept to the right for a while, then made a left farther on, they should come at the reception area from the opposite side.

It worked, all right, insofar as getting them to the reception area along a different route was concerned. But it didn't do any good when it came to avoiding television cameras. There had been two along the old route, which left a third, and they found that halfway to the reception area.

They didn't notice it until they were already in the room with it, with the damn thing pointing at them. Then Joe said under his breath, "You see what I see?"

"I see it," Tom said.

They walked through that office, casual and unconcerned, then began to move faster once they were away from the camera. They already knew there was a rule around here that visitors didn't travel unescorted, even if the visitors were policemen in uniform. They were traveling unescorted, from Eastpoole's office; the guards on duty in the reception area might not leap to the conclusion they were thieves, but they'd suspect something was wrong, and they'd start right away to look into it.

First they'd try phoning the boss. They wouldn't get any answer, either from Eastpoole or his secretary, and that would upset them even more. But making the phone call would take time, maybe all the time needed for Tom and Joe to cover the rest of the ground and get them under control.

If not, if they didn't get there in time, what would the guards do next? Would they put in an alarm right away? Since the visitors were supposed to be cops, they might be a little more careful, a little more cautious. They might get in touch with the guard in the vault anteroom. They might send somebody to alert the other three cops up here, the ones assigned to the security detail for the astronauts. They might get in touch with somebody Tom and Joe didn't know about, down at the street level. There were a thousand different things they might do, and Tom and Joe could be pretty sure they wouldn't like any of them.

They hurried, but it still took a while to travel the rest of the way to the reception area, and when they got there only one guard was behind the counter. It was the same one who'd been here when they'd first come up. He looked at them now, and he was very nervous and trying not to show it. They angled across toward the elevators, and he called over, "Where's Mr. Eastpoole?"

Tom gave him a smile and wave of the hand. "In his office," he said. "Everything's okay."

Joe pressed the down button for the elevator.

The guard couldn't keep the nervousness from affecting his voice. He pointed at the laundry bag Tom was carrying and said, "I'll have to inspect that bag."

Tom smiled at him and said, "Sure. Why not?"

Joe stayed behind, by the elevator doors, while Tom walked over to the counter and set the laundry bag atop it. The guard, losing some of his nervousness because they were acting as though nothing was wrong, came down the counter to look into the bag. As he was reaching for it, Tom nodded toward the screens down on the far wall. He said, "The guy in the vault anteroom. Does he have a set of screens like that?"

The guard looked over at the screens. "Sure," he said.

"He can see us?"

The guard gave Tom a warning look. "Yes, he can," he said.

Joe, back by the elevators, was watching the screens very carefully; all of them. The guard in the anteroom was still reading his *Daily News*. On one of the office screens, the other guard from out here suddenly appeared, moving fast.

He wasn't quite running, and he was apparently headed for Eastpoole's office.

Tom, still talking in a conversational tone of voice, said, "Well, if he can see us, I guess you don't want me to show a gun."

The guard stared. "What?"

"If I show a gun," Tom told him, "he'll know something's wrong. Then I'll have to kill you so we can take off out of here."

From his position by the elevators, Joe called to the guard, "Take it easy, pal. Don't get anybody upset."

The guard was scared, but he was a professional. He didn't make any large moves that the anteroom guard might see on his screen. Holding himself in tight control, he said, "You'll never get out of the building. You'll never make it."

Joe said, casually, "It isn't your money, pal, but it is your life."

"Come around the counter," Tom said. "You're going out with us."

The guard didn't move. He licked his lips and blinked, but he had guts. He said, "Give it up. Just leave that bag on the counter and take off. Nobody'll chase you if you don't have the goods on you."

An elevator arrived. Its door sliding open prompted Joe's next remark. "Come on, pal," he said. "Don't waste time. We'd rather do it the easy way, but we don't have to."

Reluctantly, the guard moved, going down to the flap at the end of the counter, lifting it, stepping through. On the anteroom screen, the guard could be seen still reading his paper. He hadn't noticed yet that the reception area was about to be left undefended. When he did, he'd know something was wrong, but it would still take him a minute or two to figure out the right procedure to deal with the situation. He'd try to call Eastpoole, he'd try to call the reception area. He wouldn't want to leave the vault, just in case the whole thing was a stunt to lure him out. His indecision would give them time.

The elevator was empty. Joe was holding the door open and watching the television screens. Tom was carrying the laundry bag again, and watching the guard.

"If you take a hostage," the guard said, coming out from behind the counter, "you run the risk you'll have to shoot somebody."

He meant himself, and all things considered he delivered the sentence very calmly. Joe said to him, "Just get in the elevator."

The three of them stepped into the elevator, and Joe pushed the button for the first floor. The door closed, they started down, and the guard said, "You can still get out of this. Go down to one, leave the bag with me, take off; by the time I get back upstairs you'll be gone. And you won't have taken anything, so who'll be looking for you?"

They already knew the answer to that, far more than he could guess, but neither of them said anything. Tom was watching the guard, and Joe was watching the numbers showing which floor they were passing.

You couldn't hear the parade in the elevator at all. It had Muzak in it, playing some melody they both recognized but neither of them knew the name of.

The guard said, "Listen. With a hostage, you're risking a shoot-out. Plus kidnapping, it's technically kidnapping."

The elevator was passing the fourth floor. Joe reached out and pressed the button marked 2. The guard looked at that and frowned. He didn't know what they were doing, and his bewilderment shut him up. He didn't have anything else to say at all.

The elevator stopped on the second floor. Joe reached over, plucked the guard's pistol out of his holster, and said, "Move."

"You aren't going to—"

"No, we're not," Joe said. He was snappish and in a hurry. "Just move."

The guard stepped out. They made as if to follow him, but

when the door started to slide shut they stepped back again. The guard was turning, open-mouthed, as the door finished closing and the elevator descended to the first floor.

"Christ," Joe said. He took off his hat, showing big beads of perspiration high on his forehead. He used the hat to smear his prints from the guard's pistol, then put the pistol on the floor in the rear corner of the elevator. As he straightened, the elevator stopped, the door opened, and the lobby floor was in front of them.

Clear. They were ahead of pursuit, and if they just kept moving briskly along they'd stay ahead of it.

They walked out across the lobby, Tom carrying the laundry bag. They pushed through the doors and went out to the street, and the parade crowd was beginning to break up. Some paper was still floating down from windows in the upper stories, but not much.

It was tougher to get through the crowd this time; the convenient empty lane between crowd and building fronts had gone, swallowed up by the generalized movement of the crowd away from here.

The pursuit would be slowed just as much, they had to keep reminding themselves of that.

They reached the arcade, and it too was full of people now, though not quite as bad as the street; they moved through at a good pace.

The squad car was right where they'd left it, just as it was supposed to be. A lot of people were milling around, but none of them were interested in two cops. Tom paused by a wire trash can at the curb. He held the laundry bag by a bottom corner, and quietly upended it into the trash can. The typewriter paper fell out, and the weight of it all together in a pack drove it down through the crumpled newspapers and cigarette packages and paper cups, halfway out of sight.

They moved on toward the squad car. Tom squashed the laundry bag into a ball and stuffed it into his pocket.

They got into the car, Joe behind the wheel, and drove away.

Two blocks later, they had to stop at an intersection to let two other patrol cars rush by, sirens screaming and lights flashing. Then they drove on.

13

Once again they changed the license plates and the identifying numbers on the squad car, this time switching everything back to the original way. Their actions were shielded by the highway stanchion and the parked trailer. Joe made the transfer on the rear plate and Tom the front, and then they met at the back of Tom's Chevvy. Tom opened the trunk lid, and they tossed the plates and numbers and the two screwdrivers in with the canvas bag containing Tom's civilian clothing.

Neither of them said anything. They were both feeling very down, very deflated. It was the letdown after all the excitement, and they knew it, but knowing what the trouble was didn't change it.

Tom was making some attempt to shake the feeling off. Pulling the blue plastic laundry bag out of his pocket, he shook it out to its full length and then held it up in front of himself like a doctor holding up a newborn baby. His hand was trembling as he held the bag, and he gave it a shaky, uncertain grin. ''Well, there it is,'' he said.

Joe gave the bag a sour look. He wasn't fighting against his depression at all. "Yeah, there it is, all right," he said.

"Two million dollars," Tom said.

Joe shook his head. "Air," he corrected.

Tom gave him a grin that was supposed to be brave and sure of itself. "We'll see," he said.

Joe shrugged. The gesture meant that he was skeptical, and that he was too weary to give a damn. "Yeah, we will," he said.

Suddenly feeling defensive, Tom told him, "We talked it over, Joe. We agreed this was the way to do it."

Joe shrugged again, and gave an exhausted nod. "I know, I know." Then, seeing Tom's expression, he tried to act more friendly, and to explain himself. "I just wish we had something to show for it," he said.

Tom said, "But that's just what we didn't want. Nothing we had to carry away from the scene, nothing we had to hide, nothing to get caught with, nothing to be used as evidence against us."

"Nothing," Joe said. Then he spread his hands and said, "What the hell, you're right. We did talk it over, we did agree. Come on, let's go. I need a drink."

Tom was going to argue some more, but Joe had turned away, walking back toward the squad car. And Tom thought, what's the point in arguing? We've already done it, and we did it this way, and it was the right way. He dropped the plastic bag into the trunk, and shut the lid.

They got into the two cars, and Joe led the way back uptown to the police garage. The parking space he'd taken the car from was gone now, but there was another one near it. Joe left the car there without doing anything under the hood; tomorrow morning, a mechanic would find the car had mysteriously fixed itself. If he was a normal mechanic, he'd first take it for granted there'd never been anything wrong with the car other than a stupid driver, and second take credit for having fixed it.

Tom was waiting around the corner in the Chevvy. Joe

walked around and got in, and they drove back over to the Port Authority. While Joe stayed outside in the car, Tom went in and changed back to civvies. When he came out, Joe said, "I wasn't kidding about that drink. My nerves could use one."

Tom was agreeable; the idea of a drink was a good one to him, too. "Where do you want to go?"

"Nowhere we're known."

"I'll find a place over in Queens."

"Good."

Tom drove across town and up to the 59th Street Bridge and over to Queens. They found a bar on Queensboro Boulevard with nobody in it except the bartender and an old fellow dressed in striped railroad coveralls. The railroad man was sitting at the bar, watching an afternoon game show on the television set mounted at the end of room. They ordered a couple of beers, and sat in a booth to drink them.

They were both in the mood for a drink, but they had different reasons. Tom was hoping liquor would make him feel happier, more like celebrating their success, and Joe was in the kind of a bad mood that requires a bad-mood drunk. So they sat in a booth and socked it away for a while and did very little talking.

It was about two-thirty when they first went in there. About an hour later, which was five or six rounds later, Tom roused himself and looked around and said, "Hey."

Joe turned his head and stared at him. He was already feeling pretty bleary. He said, "What?"

"We're making a mistake," Tom told him. "We're making one of the basic mistakes of the whole world."

Joe frowned, not following the meaning. He closed one eye and said, "Which mistake is that?"

"That's the mistake," Tom said carefully, "where a fella pulls a job and then goes right out and gets drunk, and while he's drunk he talks about it. Happens all the time."

"Not to us," Joe said. He was a little indignant.

"Happens all the time," Tom insisted. "You know that

yourself. You've picked them up your own self, I know you have. And so have I. My own self, I've picked them up."

"We're smarter than that," Joe said. He drained his glass.

"Well, look at us," Tom said. "What are we doing, if we're smarter than that?"

Joe looked around. There were only the four of them in the bar; railroad man, bartender, Tom, Joe. "Who am I gonna talk to?"

"The night's young," Tom told him. Looking out at the daylight past the front windows, he said, "In fact, the day's still young."

"I'm not gonna talk," Joe said. He sounded a bit belligerent.

"You said that pretty loud," Tom told him. "Also, you're in uniform."

Joe looked down at himself. He wasn't wearing the hat or the badge or the gunbelt, all of which were locked up in the trunk of Tom's Chevvy, but his shirt and pants were identifiably those of a police officer. "Son of a bitch," he said.

"I've got a better idea," Tom said.

Joe looked at him, interested. "I could use one," he said.

"We'll go home."

"Shit, no!"

"No, wait, listen to me. We'll go home, and we'll go down into my bar. I got my own bar, remember?"

Joe frowned, thinking about it. "You mean the basement?"

"It's *in* the basement," Tom said, with dignity, "but it's the bar. It isn't the basement."

Joe studied that one. "It's in the basement," he said thoughtfully.

"That may be true," Tom said. "But it's the bar."

"If you say so."

"It isn't the basement."

Joe nodded, judiciously. "I get the idea," he said.

"So that's where we'll go," Tom said.

"To the bar," Joe said. "*In* the basement."

"In the basement."
"And drink there."
"And drink there," Tom agreed.
"That's not a terrible idea," Joe said.
So that's what they did.

14

Their hangovers were beyond belief, and they both had morning duty the next day. They rode in together in Joe's car, both of them stunned by last night's drinking, and by too little sleep, and by this morning's heat; it was going to be a hell of a day, they could see that already.

They had the radio on in the car, and it was full of yesterday's robbery. The first they heard of it was when the news announcer said, "Two men, disguised as police officers and apparently driving a New York City Police Department car, made off yesterday with nearly twelve million dollars in negotiable securities in what police term one of the largest robberies in Wall Street history."

Tom said, "Twelve million? That's good."

"It's bullshit," Joe said. "They're padding it for the insurance company, just like anybody else."

"You think so?"

"I guarantee it."

Grinning, Tom said, "I'll tell you what we'll do. Ten

million or twelve million, we'll still let Vigano have it for the two million we said to begin with."

Joe laughed, then winced and took one hand off the steering wheel to clutch his forehead. Still holding it, but still laughing, he said, "We're a couple of sports, we are."

"Quiet a second," Tom said, and patted the air.

On the radio, they were still talking about the robbery. The announcer had been replaced by somebody interviewing a Deputy Police Commissioner. The interviewer was saying, "Is there any chance at all that these actually were police officers?"

The Commissioner had a deep voice, and a slow dignified manner of speech, like a fat man walking. He said, "We don't at this time believe so. We do not believe that this was a crime such as police officers would have committed. The police force is not perfect, but armed robbery is not in the pattern of police crime."

The interviewer asked, "Is it possible they really did use a Police Department squad car to make their getaway?"

The Commissioner said, "You mean stolen?"

"Well—" said the interviewer. "Stolen, or borrowed."

The Commissioner said, "That possibility is being investigated. The investigation is not yet complete, but so far we have no evidence of any stolen police vehicle."

"Or borrowed," said the interviewer.

The Commissioner, sounding a little irritated, said, "Or borrowed, yes."

"But that possibility is being investigated?"

Heavily, sounding like a man having trouble holding onto his temper, the Commissioner said, "All possibilities are being investigated."

Joe said, "That wise-ass reporter could lay off on the borrowed for a while."

"We're safe on that," Tom said. "You know we are. We worked it out, and there's no way anybody can figure out what car was used."

Joe said, "We're safe on *that*? What do you mean, we're safe on that? Where aren't we safe?"

"We're safe all over," Tom said. "You were talking about the car, that's all. I'm saying they can't get to us through the car, there's no way."

"I already knew that," Joe said. Squinting out at the traffic, he said, "I should have worn sunglasses."

They both had sunglasses on. Tom looked over at Joe and said, "You are wearing sunglasses."

"What?" Joe touched his face and felt the glasses. "Jesus Christ, it must be bright out there." He lowered the glasses slightly, looked at the glare, and shoved them back into place. "I should have worn two pair," he said.

"Wait," Tom said. "They're still talking about it."

A different interviewer was on now, asking questions of the Inspector from the downtown precinct who was in charge of the investigation. The interviewer was asking him, "Do you have any leads or suspects so far?"

That's the question they always ask, and it's the one question that can never be answered while an investigation is still going on. But they always ask it, and the spokesman has to deal with it somehow. What the Inspector said was, "So far, the best we can say is, it looks like an inside job. They knew exactly what to take, negotiable instruments as good as money."

The interviewer said, "All bearer bonds, is that it?"

"That's right," the Inspector said. "They were very explicit with the girl they sent into the vault to get the stuff for them. They wanted all bearer bonds, no bond worth less than twenty thousand or more than a hundred thousand."

"And that's what they got," said the interviewer.

"Exactly," said the Inspector. "To the tune of almost twelve million dollars."

"And the fact that the robbers wore police uniforms?"

"Definitely a disguise," the Inspector said.

The interviewer said, "Then you're confident the robbers have no connection with the Police Department."

"Absolutely," said the Inspector.

"And that's more bullshit," Joe said. "We'll be lucky they don't run the whole force through the line-up, give Eastpoole a look at us all."

"I'd rather not," Tom said.

"If they do," Joe said, "I hope it's this morning. I don't even recognize myself right now."

"We drank too much last night," Tom said. "We shouldn't do that."

"Not when we got to work."

"Not anyway," Tom said. "That's the way you get fat."

Joe gave him a look, then faced the highway again. "Talk about yourself, pal," he said.

Tom didn't have the strength to be insulted. "Anyway," he said, "a year from now, we won't have to go to work at all anymore. Not ever."

"I want to talk to you about that," Joe said.

"About what?"

"About how long we stick around."

Tom roused himself toward anger. "Are you going to start that again?"

Joe, being low and intense even though it made his head hurt more, said, "A year is too long, that's all, too much shit happens. You do what you want, I'm giving it six months."

"We agreed—"

"Sue me," Joe said, and glowered at the traffic.

Tom stared at him, and for a few seconds he was boiling mad. But then the rage suddenly drained out of him, like water out of a sink, and all he felt was tired again. Looking away, he shrugged and said, "Do what you want, I don't care."

They were both silent for a couple minutes. Then Joe said, "Besides, we've still got Vigano to think about."

Tom kept looking out the side window. He wasn't mad about the six months anymore; in fact he agreed with it, though he'd never admit that. But the Vigano thing was something else. "Yeah, that's right," he said.

"We'll want to give him a call," Joe said. "You call him, right? You know him."

"Yeah, sure," Tom said. "I'm the one he's got the arrangement with, how I'm supposed to call and everything."

"When will you do it? This afternoon?"

"No, not today," Tom said. "It's not a good idea to do it today."

"Why not?"

"Well, in the first place, I've got too much of a headache to think straight. In the second place, we ought to let a couple days go by, maybe a week. Let things quiet down a little after the robbery before we do anything else."

Joe shrugged. "I don't get the point," he said.

"Listen," Tom said, "what's the hurry?" He was getting annoyed again, and that was making the headache worse, and that was making him more annoyed. "We're going to be here six months no matter when I call Vigano."

"Okay," Joe said. "Do it any way you want."

"So there's no reason to rush. He'll keep."

"Fine with me," Joe said.

"Just let me do it at my own pace."

"That's what I'll do," Joe said. "Forget I brought it up."

"All right," Tom said. He was breathing hard. "All right," he said.

Vigano

Vigano slowly turned the pages of the book. He was sitting at a wooden table in the library of his own home, turning the pages, looking at the faces on each page. Marty was also at the table, looking through a second book. The other books were being studied over at a second table by everyone who'd had a look at the guy who'd come here a month ago to ask what he should steal that Vigano would pay two million dollars for.

The messenger who'd brought the books down from New York was waiting in a car in the driveway. It had cost a lot of money to get the loan of these books for the night, and the messenger had to get them back no later than six tomorrow morning. The books contained the official photo of every policeman currently on active duty with the New York Police Department.

During the day, these same books were being looked at by the employees and guards of the stock brokerage that had been robbed. So far, according to Vigano's information, they hadn't come up with anything.

Neither had Vigano. The faces all began to blend together after a while, all those eyebrows, hairlines, noses. Vigano was tired and irritable, his eyes were burning, and what he really wanted to do was kick these goddam books across the room.

If only Marty hadn't lost the son of a bitch the night he was here. Afterwards, it was easy to see the thing had been a set-up, the cop at the head of the stairs in Penn Station had to have been the first guy's partner, but at the time there hadn't been any way for Marty to guess that. He hadn't been present for the conversation, he hadn't known there was a possibility the guy he was following was a cop, nor that he'd spoken about having a partner. Later on, when they'd compared notes back here at the house, it had been easy to see what had been done.

It had been simple and clever, like the robbery. Whether the two of them were really cops or not, they were fast and shrewd, and they shouldn't be underestimated.

Whether they were cops or not. That was the worst of looking through these lousy books, there was still a good chance the guy wasn't really a cop at all. At what point was he disguised as a cop and at what point was he a real cop? He and his partner had been disguised in police uniforms when they'd pulled off the robbery; had his claiming to be a police officer while he was here in this house been simply the same disguise?

All the faces in the books looked alike. Vigano knew he wasn't going to get anywhere, but he believed in being thorough. He would look through all the books, every one. And so would Marty, and so would the others. It wouldn't do any good, but they'd do it.

One way and another, Vigano was determined to find those two. Cops or no cops.

Tom

Sometimes on the night shift Ed and I go out and do a turn around the precinct in our Ford, rather than sit in the Detective Division squadroom and wait for the calls to come in. The night shift is when you get most of your street crime, and it sometimes helps to be out there and in movement; often, when a squeal comes in, we're already in the neighborhood, and can get to it faster with instructions from the dispatcher than if we'd actually taken the phone call from the complainant ourselves.

So that's what Ed and I were doing that night, around one in the morning. This was nearly a week after the robbery. Joe and I hadn't talked about the robbery at all since the morning after in the car, and I hadn't yet made my phone call to Vigano. I hadn't worked out in my own head any reasons for not calling Vigano, I just hadn't seemed to get around to it.

The robbery itself had stayed hot news for three or four days. It was linked up with some department-store holdups in Detroit from a couple of years ago that had also involved guys wearing police uniforms, but that seemed to be about the only lead the authorities had. An interdepartmental memo had come through, asking everybody to think back to the day of the robbery and try to remember anything unusual they might have noticed in connection with any patrol car on that day, or with any other member of the force. That was about the extent of the investigation within the Police Department, but even that was too much for the PBA. The Patrolmen's Benevolent Association, which I must admit is very rarely benevolent about much of anything, raised such a stink about that memo, and the implication it contained that police officers might actually have been involved in the crime, that the Commissioner himself called a press conference to apologize and say the memo had been "ill-judged." And that had been about the last newsworthy item in connection with the robbery; for the last day or two, there'd been nothing about it on television at all.

It was beginning to look as though we hadn't made any mistakes in planning the job or pulling it off. Now all we had to do was not make any of the normal post-crime mistakes, such as getting drunk in public and talking about what a sharp operator you are, or hiding the loot some place where it could be found by the wrong person, or spending the money right away in a big spree, or quitting our jobs and taking off to live a completely different life. We knew all the mistakes, we'd seen them all from the other side. So far, we seemed to have done all right for ourselves.

Before the robbery, I'd thought it would be very tough to come back to work after it, that I'd have a hard time going through the regular grind knowing I had a million dollars salted away. But the fact was, I seemed to enjoy the job more than I had in years. The robbery had been like a vacation. It was true I didn't actually have Vigano's million dollars yet, but I took it for granted I was going to get it, and I didn't care. Except for that morning with the hangover, I'd been actually happy to go to work every day I'd had duty since the robbery.

Partly I suppose it was the vacation idea; committing the

robbery had been such a total break in the routine that it gave the routine a kind of fresh lease on life. But also, for the first time in my life I could look forward to an end of the routine. I mean, an end other than death or retirement, neither of which prospect had ever cheered me very much. But now the routine was going to end at a time when I'd still be young enough to enjoy it. And rich enough to enjoy it, too; a hell of a lot richer than I'd ever thought I was going to be.

Who wouldn't be happy working six months for a salary of one million dollars?

Then there was another thing. Weather affects crime, believe it or not. If it's too hot or too cold, too rainy or too snowy, a lot of crimes just don't get committed; the people who would have committed them stay at home and watch television. This last week had been very hot, and my tours had been quiet and peaceable. I'd caught up with a lot of my back paperwork, I'd relaxed, I'd taken it easy. Even if I weren't being paid a million dollars for it, I wouldn't have minded very much working this last week.

Which changed, all of a sudden. And it was a very small thing that made it change, small and stupid. I never really entirely understood why it made such a big difference inside my head.

It was the night Ed and I were on the night shift, and out driving around in the Ford. Things had been quiet for about an hour until a little after one o'clock a call came in that somebody had been attacked over in Central Park. We were pretty close to the park at the time, so Ed, who was driving, said, "Shall we head on over there?"

The squeal hadn't been directed to us, though we'd heard it on the radio. "Sure," I said. "Let's see what's going on."

"Fine," he said.

There was no urgency, since we weren't the primary team responding to the squeal, so we drove over without siren or red light, and stopped near the park entrance at West 87th Street. We got out of the car, unlimbered the pistols in our hip holsters, left the guns holstered, and walked into the park.

We could see the group ahead of us, down the black-top path and under one of the old-fashioned street lights they have in there. One guy was sitting on the black-top, and three others were standing around him. One of the standing men was in uniform, all the others were in civvies.

When we got a little closer, I could make out the faces. I didn't know the patrolman, but the other two standing men were detectives from my precinct; one was named Bert and the other Walter. They were talking to the guy sitting on the ground.

I recognized him, too. Not individually; I mean I recognized his type. He was a homosexual, young and slender and delicate, wearing tight pale-blue chinos and white sandals and a white fishnet shirt. He was pretty obviously what's called a cruiser, a faggot who hangs around one of the gay areas of the city looking to get picked up. They very frequently get beat up, too, and sometimes they get killed. They also have a higher incidence of VD than any other group in the city. I won't say it's a kind of life I understand.

At the moment, this one was scared out of his mind, terrified, trembling all over. He was so fragile-looking, he looked as though he might break his own bones with all that shivering he was doing.

When we got close enough to hear voices, it was the boy on the ground who was talking. He could hardly speak; his voice was trembling and his throat apparently kept closing up on him. All the time he struggled to talk, his hands kept fluttering around. I hate to say they fluttered like butterflies, but that's what they reminded me of.

He was saying, "I don't know why he'd do it. There wasn't any reason, there was just— There wasn't any reason. Everything was fine, and then—" He stopped talking, and let the fluttering of his hands finish the story.

Walter, one of the plainclothesmen, preferred words to hands. Not sounding at all sympathetic, he said, "Yeah? Then what?"

The hands fluttered to his throat. "He started to choke

me." The street-light glare was in his face as he looked up at us, bleaching out whatever color was left in it, reducing his face to little more than a twisting mouth and staring eyes. With that face, and the gracefully twitching hands, he suddenly also reminded me of pantomimists I've seen on television. You've seen them; they cover their faces with white make-up, and wear dark clothing and white gloves, and they pretend to be in love, or to be an airplane, or to be mixing a martini. This one seemed to be doing a pantomime impression of terror.

Except that he was talking. Hands still at his throat, he said again, "He choked me. He was screaming awful things, terrible, and just choking me." His hands trembled at his throat.

Walter, still not sympathetic, said, "What was he saying?"

The expressive hands came down, flattening out. "Oh, please," he said. "Oh, just terrible things. I don't even want to remember them."

Walter's partner Bert was grinning a little as he watched and listened, and now he said, "What did you say you were doing just before the attack?"

Evasiveness cut through the young man's agitation. Suddenly nervous as much for his present situation as for what had happened to him in the past, he gestured vaguely with both hands, looked away from us all, blinked, and said, "Well—" He stopped, ducked his head, twisted his shoulders around. "We were just talking, just—" He looked up at us again, looking like the heroine of a silent movie melodrama, and said, "Everything was fine, there wasn't any reason at all."

"Talking," Bert said. He jerked his head to the right and said, "Over there in the bushes at two in the morning."

He clasped his hands together. "But there wasn't any reason to *choke* me," he said.

I wondered why he kept reminding me of silent things—pantomimists and silent movies—when he was steadily talking. Of course, as much as anybody was really listening to him, he might as well have been silent. He'd thought he'd found a friend, and he'd been betrayed, and that was most of the pain he was showing us. But we'd all seen it before, and we had other ways to describe it. All Walter and Bert were hearing—and all I'd be hearing, if I was the one who'd have to fill out the report on this—were the facts. Like that old police show on television used to say, all we want are the facts, ma'am.

Walter was saying now, "Can you give us any identification on him?"

"Well . . ." He thought about it, sitting there in the middle of us, and said, "He, uh, he had a tattoo." He said it as though he were proud of having remembered, and expected a gold star.

Ed said, "A tattoo?" The incredulity in his voice was almost comic.

I looked at Ed beside me, and saw he was grinning. Looking down at that poor jerk and grinning. I thought, Ed's a nice guy, he's really a very nice guy, decent and straight. What the hell was he doing grinning down at some poor bastard who's been betrayed and choked and humiliated by some other son of a bitch?

And me, too. I was in the ring around the guy, one of the five cops standing around him, brought out to do our duty to protect him from bodily harm.

I took a step backward, as though to get out of the circle. I really didn't understand it myself, it was just a feeling I had, that I didn't want to be a part of this anymore.

The guy on the ground was explaining about the tattoo. "On his forearm," he said. "His, uh, his left forearm." He pointed to his own left forearm. "It was in the shape of a torpedo," he said.

Walter laughed, and the guy pouted at him. He was getting over his fear now, and his normal mincing mannerisms were returning to him.

That wasn't the way God had made him. And none of us were the way God had made us, either.

I remembered again that hippie talking about what the city does to people, and that none of us had started this way.

Bert was saying, "What about a name? He give you any kind of name before you went off in the bushes with him?"

He raised his eyes again, and clasped his hands in his lap. Christ, he looked like Lillian Gish. Wistfully, remembering having liked the bastard, he told us, "He said his name was Jim."

I took another step backward and looked up at the sky. It was one of those rare nights in New York when you can see a few stars.

Joe

I'd been in a bad mood ever since we pulled it off. Tom didn't feel that way, he was going around happy and chipper and easy in his mind, but as for me, most of the time I felt like punching somebody in the head.

It would have been a different thing if we had the money in our hands. Even if we had the bonds, something we could sell, something we could touch and hold and know that this was the result of our labors. But what did we have? A blue plastic laundry bag full of air.

I'm not arguing. I know the case for doing it that way, and we did it that way, and I agree with it. As Tom said, the Mafia is not going to give away two million dollars if it doesn't absolutely have to, so we can take it for granted when the time comes to make the switch they'll try to double-cross us. And, since they already know this is a one-shot operation, we're never going to be useful to them again, they'd be smart not only to cheat us but also to kill us.

Why not? We're the only connection between the bond robbery and the mob, the only ones that know the whole story. Kill us, and they not only save two million dollars, they protect themselves from getting implicated just in case we should ever get picked up by the law later on.

So they'll try to double-cross us, and they'll try to kill us. We knew that before we went ahead and did the job. Because the next step is, we're the ones who decide the method of transfer. And to bring us to the transfer point, they have to produce the cash, the two million for us to look at and touch. We can make it a part of the arrangement, that we see the cash before we give them the bonds.

They'd expect that. They'd expect us to be careful with them, because they'd expect us to be afraid of them.

What they *wouldn't* expect is a double cross right back.

As Tom said, money isn't just green pieces of paper in your wallet, it's credit cards and charge accounts and all kinds of things. It's bonds. It's anything you *think* is money.

You know what we stole from Parker, Tobin, Eastpoole & Company? The *idea* of ten million dollars. And that's what we figured to sell Vigano. His newspaper and television set would tell him we did the job. He'd have no reason to think we didn't have the bonds anymore. So when the time for the switch came around, they'd have to have real cash, and all we'd have to have was a good plan and a lot of luck.

But the point is, we'd be needing that anyway. Double-crossing them on the bonds wouldn't make any difference, they were going to try to cheat us and kill us whether we showed up with ten million dollars' worth of bonds or two dollars' worth of ripped-up newspapers. It made no difference whether we conned them or not. And in pulling the robbery, it had been easier not to carry the bonds away with us, to destroy them. So that's what we did.

You see, I understand the argument and I agree with it. But that still didn't change the fact I would have liked something in my hand afterward to show me I'd accomplished something. And not having anything meant I was spending my time in a really lousy mood.

For instance. When I was on duty now, I was becoming a

real hard-ass with the tickets. I was giving them out left and right, citing store owners for dirty sidewalks, hitting delivery trucks for driving down streets where commercial traffic was prohibited, even going after jaywalkers. I'm telling you, I was mean.

Paul was out of the hospital now, so that was good, but he wasn't back on duty yet. He'd have a couple months at home for rest and recuperation, the lucky bastard. In the meantime, I still had Lou to contend with.

He wasn't bad, but his attitude needed work. He was over-eager, that was his problem. For instance, Paul would have known how to calm me down when I was out there ticketing the entire population of the Upper West Side, but so far as Lou was concerned I was tough but good. It got so he was becoming pretty nearly as mean as I was, though nobody is ever going to top the time I ticketed the pregnant woman for obstructing the sidewalk with her baby carriage. That's one of those records where you retire the trophy.

As an example, though, of where Lou's attitude went overboard, there was the night about a week and a half after the robbery when we really did lose our car for repairs. Which I already considered ironic.

What happened, late at night we caught sight of these two guys coming out of a jewelry store on Broadway. We yelled at them to stop, and they jumped into a four-door Buick parked in front of the shop and took off southbound. I was driving, and I could keep on their tail but I couldn't catch up with them, not with the piece of crap I was driving. I'd been putting in requests for a new car for eight months, and never even got a response.

Meanwhile, Lou was on the radio. But shit, that time of night, everybody's either already got problems of their own or they're off someplace cooping. You know, having a doze.

The Buick headed straight down Broadway, with me a full block back. I had the siren and flasher going, mostly to make other traffic stop up ahead and keep the clown in the Buick from killing somebody while running a red light. Of course, at that time of night, nearly four in the morning, there's practically never any traffic anyway.

He was a good driver, I'll say that much for him. His brake lights didn't go on until less than half a block before he made his right turn onto a cross-street in the Fifties. His inside wheels left the ground as he shot around the corner, but he made it without losing control, and by the time I came screeching around the intersection after him he'd leveled himself out and was tear-assing away, the other side of Eighth Avenue already, heading due west along a narrow side street with cars parked along both curbs and just barely room for two cars next to one another in the middle.

"Jesus!" Lou yelled. "We're losing him!"

Boy, are you hot to trot, I thought, but I was too busy driving to say anything out loud.

The light was with us both on Ninth Avenue, though it wouldn't have made any difference. We both shot through, him not getting away but me not gaining any ground. What we needed was another car in front of us, to head him off before somebody got hurt.

The block between Ninth and Tenth is mostly red-brick tenement buildings, half of them with shops in the ground floor, but the block between Tenth and Eleventh is warehouses, and there's trucks parked along both sides instead of passenger vehicles. The same thing is true between Eleventh and Twelfth, and after that you can't go any farther west without a boat. That's the Hudson River out there, and you have to turn either north or south.

He wasn't quite as sure as I was on this narrow street, with the parked cars crowding in on both sides, and that was doubly true after we crossed Tenth and he was traveling down between two walls of trucks. The trucks take up more room than cars do, leaving less space down the middle for driving, and I could tell the guy in the Buick didn't care for that. Given another two or three miles of the same kind of street and I probably could have caught up with him. But what actually happened was, he almost creamed a cab on Eleventh Avenue.

The light was red down there. Big-sided trucks were parked along both curbs right down to the corner, restricting everybody's vision, making a kind of tunnel out of the street. The trucks and the warehouses also probably contained my siren too much, so that it couldn't be heard by somebody out on Eleventh Avenue.

And there was somebody out there; a cab, going north, traveling empty. He was probably on his way to check in at one of the garages farther uptown on the West Side, having been out for eight or ten hours hacking around the city. In other words, tired. And alone in the area, so far as he knew. And with the light in his favor.

Well, he entered the intersection just as the Buick did. And he was damn lucky God had given him fast reflexes because he just about stood on his brake with both feet and threw an anchor out back besides. The Buick swerved to its right, just nicked the front bumper of the cab on the way by, swerved to the left again, and kept going toward Twelfth Avenue.

And here was I, half a block away. The cabby had to figure the first guy through was a nut, but with me he could see the flashing red light even if he had all his windows closed and maybe air-conditioning on and couldn't hear the siren. So he had to know I was a cop. And twice in a row he did exactly the right thing.

Because he hadn't managed to completely stop before the Buick went by. In fact, the nose of the cab was still down like a pig looking for truffles, and the vehicle was still in motion. Which put it right directly in front of me.

"Stop!" yelled Lou. As though I could have stopped by then, any more than the cab could. It takes a long distance to stop, hundreds and hundreds of feet—the only time you can stop on a dime is when you're walking.

Besides, the cabby was doing his second right thing in a row. The instant the Buick was past him, he hauled in that anchor, switched both feet away from the brake and over to the accelerator, tromped down hard, and yanked that yellow mother out of the intersection.

I had to swerve left to miss his ass, just as the Buick had had to swerve right to miss his nose. But I did miss, and I never took my foot off the accelerator, and I entered the next block in fine shape.

In a lot better shape than the Buick. The near miss with the cab had loused him up for good. He shot into that next block angled wrong, coming in from the right because of having gone around the cab, and didn't get straightened out in time. He sideswiped a truck on his left, scraping along the body, and then careened off that and headed down the block at an angle to the right, and damn if he didn't hit another truck over on that side. He was like a drunk running down a hallway, bouncing from one wall to the other.

All the sideswiping, and all the struggling to get his car under control, were slowing him down. He did it a third time, over on the left again, and this time his front bumper or fender or something must have got hooked for a second on a truck cab, because all at once the Buick swerved around and jolted to a stop crossways in the street, the front bumper inches from the side of one truck and rear bumper inches from a truck across the way. The driver's side was toward us, and I could see his white face in there in my headlights.

I stood on the brakes myself the second I saw what the Buick was doing, and the squad car dug its nose in and screamed, me fighting a skid to the left every inch of the way.

The passenger door of the Buick, the one on the far side, had popped open the second the Buick came to a stop, and somebody jumped out and laid what looked like a black stick across the roof of the car, pointing at us. That is, it looked like a black stick until the end of it blew up in red and yellow, and the windshield got peppered with a dozen sudden new holes.

Lou yelled, "What the fuck is *that*?"

"Shotgun!" I was still fighting that leftward skid, the squad car was still in motion, I was still praying for it to quit so I could get my head down out of the way of that shotgun. And finally we did shudder to a stop, no more than twenty feet from the Buick.

I hit the switch that turned off the siren, and shoved my door open. The driver's face was no longer showing in the window of the Buick, and the black stick was no longer pointing at us over the top of the car. I leaned my head out to the side, and heard them running into the darkness in the opposite direction.

As I was getting out of the car, I saw Lou jumping out on his side and making a dash for the Buick. "Hey!" I yelled. "Where the hell are *you* going?"

He looked back and saw me standing behind the open door, which would give me some protection if they opened up with that goddam shotgun again. He stopped running forward and crouched there, pistol pointing straight ahead but head still turned around facing me. Looking baffled, he said, "After them. Don't we—?"

I said, "In that darkness? With a shotgun? They'll blow your ass off."

He straightened out of his crouch, all momentum gone, but he still didn't come back. "But we'll lose them," he said.

"We lost them," I told him. I would never have had to explain that to Paul. "Get back here," I said, "and call in."

The footsteps had faded away. Those two were gone for good, and just as well. I came out from behind the door and walked around to look at the front of the car. Very little of the shotgun blast had reached the windshield, so where had the rest of it gone?

Into the radiator, as I'd thought. Red cooling fluid was oozing out of a thousand holes. The headlights had also been smashed. A little higher, I thought, and my face would look like that.

It was in that instant that I knew Tom had to stop fucking around on this Vigano deal. He had to call him, we had to make the arrangements and get the money, and we had to do it and get it over with. I was still willing to hang around the six months before I'd pack up my family and go off to Saskatchewan, but God damn it, I wanted to *see* what I'd accomplished. I wanted that money in my hand, where I could touch it.

Lou was walking by me, heading for his side of the car. I told him, "They shot the shit out of our radiator. When you call in, tell them we need wheels."

"Okay," he said.

I stood there looking at the radiator, thinking about what I was going to say to Tom.

And another thing. After this, they'd *have* to give us a new car.

15

It was a hot day. It would be really muggy and bad in the city, but fortunately they both had the day off and they could sit around on lawn chairs in Tom's backyard, near the barbecue, and drink beer and work on their tans and watch the ballgame on the Sony portable Mary had given Tom for last Christmas.

Tom hadn't been thinking about anything, except how hot it was and how glad he was he wasn't working and how maybe he'd cut out the beer and start losing weight when the hot weather broke, but Joe had been thinking for the last few days, ever since the shotgun incident, how to approach Tom on this Vigano question, and he was beginning to think the only way to do it was straight out, no beating around the bush, dead ahead.

It was a very dull game. Cincinnati had got six runs in the first inning, and nobody had done a damn thing since. In the bottom of the fourth, with a deliberate walk coming up, Joe said, "Tom, listen."

Tom gave him a half-awake look. "What?"

"When do we call your Mafia man?"

Tom looked back at the deliberate walk. "Pretty soon," he said.

"It's been two weeks," Joe told him. "We've already passed pretty soon, we're catching up on later, and I see never dead ahead."

Tom frowned, staring at the television set, and didn't say anything.

Joe said, "What's the story, Tom?"

Tom made a face, shook his head, frowned, shrugged, gestured with his beer can; did everything but talk, or meet Joe's eye.

Joe said, "Come on. We're in this together, remember? What's the problem, what's the delay?"

Tom turned his head and frowned at the barbecue grill. He looked as though he had a toothache. He said in a low voice Joe could barely hear, "Day before yesterday I went into a phone booth."

"Fantastic," Joe said. "Three days from now you drop the dime?"

Tom grinned, despite himself. He looked at Joe, and he surprised himself by being relieved that he was getting this off his chest. He said, "Yeah, I guess so."

Joe said, "So what's the matter?"

"I don't know, it's like—" Tom clenched his teeth, trying to find the way to put it into words. He said, "It's like we already got away with it, you know? Like we shouldn't push our luck."

"Got away with what? So far all we got is air."

Tom shook his head violently back and forth. He was angry at himself, and he let it show. "The goddam truth is," he said, "I'm afraid of that son of a bitch Vigano."

Joe said, "Tom, I was afraid of the robbery. I was scared shitless when we went in there to do that thing, but we did it. It worked, just like we thought it would."

"Vigano's tougher."

Joe lifted an eyebrow. "Than us?"

"Than a stock brokerage. Joe, we're talking about beating them out of two million dollars. You think it's going to be easy with those people?"

"No, I don't," Joe said. "But the other part wasn't easy either. I say we can do it."

"I don't have a way," Tom said. "It's as simple as that. It's easy to say we'll work out a system where they have to bring the money and show it to us and all that stuff, but when it comes right down to it, where the hell's the system?"

"There is one," Joe said. "There has to be. Look; did we steal ten million dollars? We aren't stupid. If we can figure that we can figure this."

"How?"

Joe frowned, trying to think. He looked at the television set and the inning was over, and some actor made up to look like a cowboy was peddling razor blades. Joe shrugged and said, "Disguised as cops."

"We already did that."

Joe grinned at him. "We can't do it again? Treat it the same way, use the equipment and everything just like last time."

"Like how? Doing what?"

Joe nodded, feeling very pleased with himself. "We'll think of it," he said. "I know we will. If we just keep talking about it, we'll work it out."

And a little later that afternoon, they did.

16

They'd gotten off duty together at four in the afternoon. Joe had his Plymouth today, and they drove across town, through the park at 86th Street, and over into Yorkville where they stopped at a corner with a pay phone. Tom called the number Vigano had given him, and asked for Arthur, and said his name was Mr. Kopp. A gravelly voice said Arthur wasn't in, but was expected, and could he call Mr. Kopp back? Tom read off the number of the pay phone, and the gravelly voice hung up.

Then twenty minutes went by. It had been a hot day, and it was gradually becoming a hot evening. They both wanted to go home and take their clothes off and stand in the shower for a while. Tom leaned against the side of the phone booth and Joe sat on the fender of the Plymouth, and they waited, and twenty minutes went by with the speed of grass growing.

Finally Tom looked at his watch for the fifteenth time and said, "It's been twenty minutes."

Reluctantly Joe said, "Maybe we should—"

"No," Tom said. "He told me if he didn't call back in

fifteen minutes, we should try again later. We've waited twenty minutes, and that's enough.'' Joe was still reluctant, because he didn't want to have to nerve Tom up to this all over again, but he gave in without any more argument, saying, ''Okay, you're right. Let's go.''

Even though they now had a plan, Tom hadn't been all that eager to talk to Vigano again. ''Fine,'' he said, and started toward the passenger side of the Plymouth, and the phone rang.

They looked at each other. They both tensed up right away, which Tom had expected but which surprised Joe. He'd had the idea he was under better control than that. ''Go on,'' he said.

Tom had just been standing there. ''Right,'' he said, and turned back, and went into the phone booth. The phone was just starting to ring for the second time when he lifted the receiver and said, ''Hello?''

''Is that Mr. Kopp?'' Tom recognized Vigano's voice.

''Sure. Is that Mister—''

Overriding him, Vigano said, ''This is Arthur.''

''Right,'' Tom said. ''Arthur, right.''

''I expected to hear from you a couple weeks ago.''

Tom could feel Joe's eyes on him through the glass walls of the booth. With a sheepish grin, he said, ''Well, we had to get things set up.''

Vigano said, ''You want me to tell you where to bring the stuff?''

''Not a chance,'' Tom said. ''We'll tell *you* where.''

''Doesn't matter to me,'' Vigano said. ''Give me your setup.''

Tom took a deep breath. This was another of those moments of no return. He said, ''Macy's has a wicker picnic basket. It costs around eighteen bucks, with the tax. It's the only one they've got at that price.''

''Okay.''

''Next Tuesday afternoon,'' Tom said, ''at three o'clock, no more than four people, two of them female, can carry one of those baskets into Central Park from the west at the Eighty-fifth Street entrance to the park roadway. They should turn right, go down near the traffic light, and sit down on the grass there. No later than four o'clock, either I or my partner will show up to make the exchange. We'll be in uniform."

Vigano said, "With another basket?"

"Right."

"Isn't that kind of public?"

Tom grinned at the phone. "That's what we want," he said.

"It's up to you," Vigano said.

"The stuff in your basket," Tom said, "should not have traceable numbers and should not be homemade."

Vigano laughed. "You think we'd palm off counterfeit on you?"

"No, but you might try."

Serious again, almost sounding as though he'd been insulted, Vigano said, "We'll examine each other's property before we make the switch."

"Fine," Tom said.

"You're a pleasure to do business with," Vigano said.

Tom nodded at the phone. "I hope you are, too," he said, but Vigano had already hung up.

Vigano

Vigano slept for most of the trip. He was lucky that way, he could sleep on planes, and for that reason he tried to do as much of his traveling as possible late at night. Otherwise, too much time was wasted going from place to place.

He was riding in a Lear jet, a private company plane owned and operated by a corporation called K-L Inc. K-L's function was to own and care for and run the fleet of six planes that were available around the country to Vigano and some of his associates. The company also leased hangar space in Miami and Las Vegas and two other places, and in addition owned some real estate in the Caribbean. It had been financed by a private stock offering a few years ago, most of which had been bought by various union pension funds. Its assets were the planes and the island real estate, but its expenses were very high and it had never shown a profit, and so had never paid taxes or dividends.

The interior of the plane was comfortable, but not lush, in a kind of motel-lobby style. There was seating for eight, large soft chairs similar to first-class accommodations on a scheduled airliner, except that the front pairs of seats faced backwards and there was an unusual amount of leg room. Aft of the seats was a partition, followed by a dining area; a long oval table that would also seat eight, around three sides, leaving one of the long sides open for passage. A lavatory and galley came next, and farthest back was a bedroom containing two single beds. That was where Vigano traveled, sleeping on one of the beds while his two bodyguards sat up front, joking with the hostess, a girl who used to be a dancer until she'd had to have an operation on her hip. She was a beautiful girl, and her former bosses had done right by her.

The hostess came back finally and knocked on the bedroom door, calling, "Mr. Vigano?"

He woke up right away. His eyes opened, but he didn't move. He was lying on his right side, and he looked around, shifting only his eyes, until he'd oriented himself. He'd left one small light on, over the door, and it showed him the other bed, the curving plastic wall of the plane, the two oval windows looking out on nothing but blackness.

On the plane. Going to see Bandell about the stock market robbery. Right.

Vigano sat up. "All right," he called.

"We'll be landing in five minutes." She said that through the door, not opening it.

Of course they'd be landing in five minutes, otherwise she wouldn't be waking him. "Thank you," he said, and reached for his trousers on the other bed.

He'd stripped to his underwear for the flight, and now he quickly dressed, then opened his attaché case and out of the small separate compartment in it took his toothbrush and toothpaste. Carrying them in one hand and his tie in the other, he left the bedroom for the lavatory.

The hostess was in the galley, doing this and that. She smiled at him and said, "Coffee, Mr. Vigano?"

"Definitely."

He didn't take long in the lavatory, and then he carried his attaché case up front to the regular seats to have his coffee and watch the landing. His bodyguards were sitting facing one another on the right, so he took the forward-facing window seat on the left. The bodyguards were named Andy and Mike, and Vigano never called them bodyguards. He didn't even think the word; they were just the young guys he traveled with. They both carried their own attaché cases, and they were presentable in a tough kind of way, and he simply traveled with them because that's what he did.

Vigano sipped at his coffee and looked out the window at the lights of the city. You could always tell a resort town, it ran much heavier to neon. A place like Cleveland, now, you could hardly see any neon from the air at all.

Andy, grinning, said, "Mr. Vigano, it's a waste of time to come here in the summer. We ought to come for the winter."

Vigano smiled back. "Maybe I'll work something out," he said. He liked these two boys.

It was a smooth landing. They taxied away from the normal passenger terminals and over to the private area. When they rolled to a stop a black limousine drove out to meet them. Vigano and the two young men he traveled with picked up their attaché cases, thanked the hostess, congratulated the pilot on his landing, and stepped out into incredible heat. "Christ," Andy said. "What's it like in the daytime?"

"Worse," Vigano said. The heat lay on his skin like a wool blanket. It made New Jersey seem cool.

They crossed quickly to the limousine, and slid inside, where the air was a cool, dry seventy degrees. The chauffeur shut the door after them, slid behind the wheel, and drove them smoothly to the hotel. It was nearly four in the morning, and the streets were deserted; even a resort city goes to sleep sooner or later.

They had another blast of heat between the car and side entrance of the hotel. They were also put on film, though it didn't matter, by a team of federal agents concealed in a bakery truck parked on a side road just off the hotel property.

It was infra-red film and the faces were blurred, but they already knew who it was they were filming, so there wasn't any problem about identification. This strip of film would eventually join the strip that had been taken earlier tonight outside Vigano's home in New Jersey, and the two strips would establish the fact that on this date Anthony Vigano had gone to a meeting with Joseph Bandell. The fact would never mean anything to anybody, but it would have been established and placed on film and filed away, at a cost to the government of forty-two thousand dollars.

Vigano and his bodyguards rode up in the elevator to the twelfth floor, and walked down the corridor to Bandell's suite, at the end. They went in and Bandell was there with his advisers. "Hello, Tony," he said.

"Hello, Joe."

They spent a few minutes in civilities, taking drink orders and asking after one another's wives and making the couple of introductions necessary; one of Bandell's assistants was a new man freshly in from Los Angeles, named Stello. There were handshakes and general chitchat.

Bandell was stocky and short and gray-haired, a man in his sixties, wearing a dark suit and a conservative tie. The three men with him were in their thirties or forties, tanned, all dressed casually in the style of a resort town. Everybody deferred to Bandell, who sat alone on a sofa with his back to a picture window. Vigano was the only one present who called him Joe instead of Mr. Bandell, but he too deferred to the older man, in smaller ways.

After three or four minutes, Bandell said, "Well, it's nice to see you again. I'm glad you phoned. I'm glad you could take the time to come visit."

He meant the chitchat was done, and he wanted to know the purpose of the trip. Vigano hadn't attempted to explain anything on the phone, had only suggested he make the trip. (The phone conversation was also in a government file now, at a cost of twenty-three hundred dollars.) Now, in guaranteed privacy, Vigano set aside the drink he'd been given and explained the story of the two possible cops and the twelve-million-dollar stock-market heist.

Bandell interrupted once, saying, "It's usable paper?"

"They took exactly what I said, Joe. Bearer bonds, in amounts between twenty and a hundred grand."

Bandell nodded. "All right."

Vigano went on, explaining the payoff terms he'd agreed to. When he was finished, Bandell pursed his lips and looked across the room and said, "I don't know. Two million dollars is heavy cash."

Vigano said, "It'll be back in the bank within two hours." Because that was the point of this meeting; he couldn't draw two million cash on his own say-so, he needed Bandell's approval.

Bandell said, "Why take it out at all? Use a bag full of newspapers."

"They aren't that dumb," Vigano told him. "The caper they pulled shows how cute they are."

"Then use a dressed roll," Bandell said. "Take out a hundred thousand or so."

Vigano shook his head. "It won't work, Joe. They're very cute and very cautious. They'll have to see the two million before they relax. They'll reach in and see what's in the bottom of the basket."

Bandell said, "How about wallpaper?"

"They already talked about that," Vigano said. "They're ready for it."

Stello, the new man, said, "If they're that good, how do you know they won't figure out a way to keep the money?"

"We've got the manpower," Vigano said. "We can smother them."

Another of Bandell's assistants said, "Why not leave them alive? If they did this first job so good they can do more."

"We don't have anything on them," Vigano pointed out. "We don't know who they are, we don't have any handle on them, and they don't want to do any more. They were only interested in the one job. They're amateurs, they said so from the beginning and they acted like it."

"Smart amateurs," suggested Stello.

"Granted," Vigano said. "But still amateurs. Which means they could still make a mistake and get picked up by the law, and that leads right directly from them to me."

Bandell said, "Are they cops or aren't they?"

"I don't know," Vigano said. "We tried to find them in the force, we asked around with our tame cops, nobody knows anything. I myself personally looked at mug shots on twenty-six thousand New York City cops, and I didn't come up with them, but that doesn't mean anything because the guy came to me in a wig and moustache and eyeglasses, and who knows what he looks like with his normal face?"

Bandell's other assistant said, "Why didn't you take the disguise off him when you had him?"

"That was before he pulled the job," Vigano pointed out. "If I broke his security ahead of time, he never would have gone through with it."

Bandell said, "What do you think, Tony? You yourself, personally. Are they cops or not cops?"

"I just don't know," Vigano told him. "The guy who came to me said he was on the force. They pulled the job in uniform and used a police car for their getaway. But I'll tell you, I don't know for sure what the hell they are."

Stello said, "If they're cops, maybe it's not such a good idea to have them hit."

"If they're cops especially I want them hit," Vigano said. "One of them visited me in my own home, remember."

Bandell said, "If you do it, you do it quietly."

"Quietly," Vigano agreed. "But to relax them so I can do it, I need to be able to show them cash."

Bandell considered, pursing his lips again and staring at a spot in midair. Then he said, "What's your setup for the changeover?"

Vigano clicked his fingers at Andy, who immediately got to his feet, opened his attaché case, and brought out a map of Manhattan. He opened the map and stood there being a human easel, holding the map so everybody could see it, while Vigano pointed at it to explain the situation.

"I told you they're cute," Vigano said, and went over to stand next to the map. "Their idea is," he said, "that we'll switch picnic baskets in Central Park next Tuesday at three o'clock in the afternoon. Do you know where the snapper is in that?"

Bandell didn't want to guess; he was strictly business. "Tell us," he said.

Vigano said, "Every Tuesday afternoon, Central Park in New York is closed to automobiles." Gesturing at the map, he said, "There's nothing allowed in there but bicycles."

Bandell nodded. "How do you counter?"

"We can't use cars, but neither can they." Vigano started touching the map with his finger, explaining it all. "We'll put a car at every exit from the park. All the way around, here and here and here. Inside, we'll have our own men on bicycles, all over the place. They'll be in touch with one another by walkie-talkie, back and forth." He turned away from the map, held his hand out in front of himself, palm up, and slowly closed his fingers into a fist. "We'll have the whole park bottled up," he said.

Stello said, "You'll have a thousand witnesses."

"We can smother them," Vigano said. "When we have them at the spot where we make the switch, we can just surround them with our own people. There won't be anybody to see a thing, and we carry them the hell out of there afterwards, and nobody going by on bicycles is going to know a thing about it."

Bandell was frowning at the map. "You have this clear in your mind, Tony? You're sure of yourself?"

"You know me, Joe," Vigano said. "I'm a careful man. I wouldn't get involved in this if I wasn't sure of myself."

"And it's twelve million. In bearer bonds."

"Just under." Vigano looked around at them all and said, "It's a good big pie to slice up."

Bandell nodded slowly. He said, "You want to take the cash out of our accounts in New York, put it together to make two million, show it to them, and then put the cash right back again."

"Right."

"What's the chance of losing the two million to somebody else?"

Vigano gestured at his young men. "Andy and Mike will be with it all the way. And the other soldiers in the operation don't have to know what's in the basket at all."

Bandell shifted position on the sofa, half-turning so he could look out the picture window behind him. The seconds went by, and he continued to show the room only the back of his head. Vigano gestured to Mike, who quietly folded the map again and put it away. Still Bandell looked out at the city.

Finally he turned back. He gave Vigano a level look and said, "It's your responsibility."

Vigano smiled. "Done," he said.

Tom

Joe let me off at Columbus Avenue and 85th Street, and I walked the one block over to Central Park West. I crossed with the light, and the park was now directly in front of me, the grass separated from the sidewalk by a knee-high stone wall.

There are benches along this part of Central Park West with their backs against that low wall, so that if you sit in one of them you're looking at the apartment buildings across the way. I've never understood why anybody would want to sit on a park bench facing away from the park, but there are always plenty of people sitting on them in the warm weather, so there must be an attraction to it that I don't understand. Maybe they like to count the cabs.

Today, I joined them. I sat on an unoccupied bench and counted cabs, and found nothing exciting in it.

I spent nearly an hour sitting there, with a newspaper in my lap and a moustache on my face, waiting for the mob to show up. It was a humid day and the moustache tickled like crazy, but I was afraid to scratch it for fear it would fall off.

Every once in a while when it got to be more than I could stand I'd twitch my upper lip around like a beaver, but I tried to limit that relief to moments of true emergency, since for all I knew that too would make the damn thing break loose, and I didn't want a moustache in my lap when Vigano's people arrived.

The reason I was thinking about the moustache and park benches so much is that I was afraid to think about Vigano and his mobsters, and what we were here to do.

This one was worse than the robbery, a hundred times worse. That other time, we'd been operating against decent civilized human beings, who at the very worst would arrest us and try us and put us in jail. This time, we were operating against thugs who were going to try to kill us no matter what we did. Last time, we were pitting our one-shot plan against a normal company's normal routine. This time, we were pitting our lives against the experience and manpower and malevolence of the mob.

When I did think about it, I simply thought we were crazy. If I'd worked it all out back in the beginning, say when I'd been on the train going to talk to Vigano, if I'd figured it out then that sooner or later we would be making ourselves murder targets for the Mafia, I never would have gone through with it. And Joe the same, I'm sure of it. But all we could concentrate on in the beginning was stealing the bonds, and not what would happen afterwards. And when it did occur to me what Vigano's natural reaction would have to be, I was still so caught up in the other thing that all I thought about was how much easier that would make things for us, since we didn't really have to steal the bonds, just make it look as though we had.

It was the morning after the robbery, while suffering that hangover in Joe's car on the way to work, that I'd first looked the thing full in the face. We had done part one, and we'd done it pretty well. But part two was the crunch. Part two was where death waited for us if we weren't very smart and very careful and very lucky.

But if we didn't do part two, there was no point in our having done part one.

I was in a real funk for a while after that. I couldn't even think about the problem, couldn't concentrate on it. It just seemed more than I could deal with, reaching into the trap and pulling out the two-million-dollar piece of cheese without getting the spring across the back of my neck.

I'd been coming out of it anyway, spurred on by the scene with the homosexual in the park—very near here, in fact—but it was Joe who finally goosed me back into action again. I think Joe probably has less imagination than I do, but that's a good part of his strength. If you can't imagine the things that might go wrong, you won't be afraid of them.

I don't mean that Joe wasn't scared of the mob. Any sane man would be, particularly if he meant to sell them a lot of old newspapers for two million dollars. It's just that Joe was never paralyzed by his fear the way I'd been paralyzed by mine. Joe dealt more with specific things that he could touch and taste. What made me the most nervous was the mob, but what made him the most nervous was that we'd done part one and didn't have anything to show for it. It really pained him when we ripped up those bonds, I know it did.

Well, we'd committed ourselves again. We could still turn around, of course, we could still cop out, but I didn't think we would. We were at the stage now equivalent to when, in the robbery, we'd met Eastpoole but Joe hadn't grabbed his arm yet. We'd set things up with Vigano, we were both in position, but we hadn't yet made contact, we could still change our minds at the last second.

Joe made his first pass twenty minutes after I'd sat down, but I didn't give him the signal because Vigano's people hadn't showed up yet. I watched him drive by, and then I counted cabs some more, and fifteen minutes later he went by again, and still they hadn't showed up.

Weren't they going to? If after all this, after nerving ourselves up to it and working out the best scheme we could think of, the mob didn't show up this time for the transfer, I didn't know what I'd do. I wouldn't be able to stand it, that's all. To have to start all over again, phone Vigano again, set up another meeting, I'd have an ulcer before it was over. Or a nervous breakdown.

But what if they weren't coming at all? What if they'd decided the hell with it, they didn't want to buy the bonds?

Christ, that would be something. Then Joe would really be sore, and at me. Because if we actually had the bonds, and the mob reneged on us, we could maybe go fence them to somebody else. But Vigano was the only person on earth to whom we could sell the *idea* of the bonds. It was him, or nobody.

The arrangement Joe and I had was that he would come by every fifteen minutes until I gave him the signal. Then our second timing sequence would begin, with me making the first move. We hadn't made a contingency plan for what we'd do if the mob never showed up, but I figured if Joe was still circling the neighborhood an hour from now we might as well throw in the towel and go away and see what we could do next.

Get drunk, most likely.

Five minutes before he was due to come by for the third time, the mob arrived. A black limousine came up Central Park West and pulled to a stop in the entrance to the roadway. Gray police sawhorses blocked the road to automobiles this afternoon, and the limousine stopped broadside to the sawhorses, out of the way of northbound Central Park West traffic. Nothing happened for a few seconds, and then the rear door opened and four people got out; two men and two women. None of them looked like the kind of people who normally travel around in limousines. Also, the general practice with limousines is that the chauffeur gets out and opens the door for the passengers, but this time the chauffeur stayed behind the wheel.

A man came out first. He was stocky and tough-looking, and despite the heat of the day he was wearing a light zippered jacket closed about halfway up. He looked around warily and cautiously, and then motioned for the other people to come out.

The two women appeared. They were both in their twenties, both a little too full in hip and breast, both wearing plaid slacks and ordinary blouses, both in full night-style make-up, and both with big bouffant hairdos. One of them was chewing gum. They stood around like collies waiting their turn to appear at a dog show, and the other man came out of the car after them.

He was the one. He looked like the first guy, and he too wore a half-zippered jacket, but the important part was that he was carrying the picnic basket. From the way he held it, the thing was heavier than hell.

Let it be full of the real thing, I thought. Let them not try that kind of fast one, I don't want to have to go through this twice.

The four of them made very unlikely picnickers. There didn't seem to be any coherent connection among them; the men didn't hold the women's hands or elbows, and there wasn't any conversation back and forth. Nor could you figure out which woman was supposed to be with which man. The four of them seemed as arbitrarily joined together as four strangers in an elevator.

They walked off in a group into the park, the second man struggling with the heavy picnic basket. They disappeared from sight, but the limousine stayed where it was. Thin exhaust showed from the tailpipe.

I took the newspaper off my lap and tossed it down to the other end of the bench. In less than a minute a thin old fellow came along and picked it up and walked off with it, reading the stock reports.

Joe came by right on schedule. I didn't look directly at him, but I knew he would see that I didn't have the paper in my lap anymore. That was the signal. He would dope out for himself what the limousine meant, parked sideways in the entrance.

After Joe passed, I got to my feet and walked on into the

park. Strolling down the asphalt path, I saw the four picnickers sitting in a bunch down near the traffic light on the interior road, where I'd said they should be. They had the picnic basket on the ground and they were sitting in a tight circle around it. They weren't talking among themselves, they were all facing and concentrating outward, not even pretending to have a picnic together. They looked like Conestoga wagons waiting for Indians.

Vigano would have other people in the area, to guard the basket and try to keep us from going away with it. Walking around, I spotted four of them, guys sitting or standing at strategic locations where they could watch the picnickers. There'd be more of them, I was sure of that, but four was all I'd seen so far.

I'd probably see more later, whether I wanted to or not.

I kept an eye on my watch. It would take Joe a while to get into position. At the right time, I walked forward across the grass and down a gentle slope toward the picnickers.

They watched me coming. The one who'd first gotten out of the car put his hand inside his half-open jacket.

I walked up to them. I had a smile tacked to my face, as phony as the moustache. I hunkered down in front of the first man and said, quietly, "I'm Mr. Kopp."

He had the eyes of a dead fish. He studied me with them and said, "Where's your stuff?"

"Coming," I said. "But first I'm going to reach into the basket and take some bills out."

His expression didn't change. He said, "Who says?" Both women and the other man kept looking away from us, outward; watching for Indians.

I said, "I have to check them out. Just a few."

He was thinking it over. I glanced away to my left and saw one of the guys I'd spotted earlier, and he was closer now. He wasn't moving at the moment, but he was closer.

"Why?"

I looked back at him. The question had been asked in a flat tone, as though he were a computer instead of a man, and his face was still expressionless. I said, "You know I'm not going to make the deal until I know for sure what you've got in that basket."

"We have what you want."

"I'll have to check it out for myself."

The other man turned his head and looked at me. Then he faced outward again and said, "Let him."

The first man nodded. His fish eyes kept watching me. He said, "Go ahead. A few."

"Fine," I said. As I leaned forward to reach into the basket, I looked down the road. Joe was due about now.

Joe

I let Tom off at Columbus Avenue and 85th Street, went on up to 90th, made a right turn, and headed over to Central Park West. Then I turned south, and drove slowly down alongside the park to consider the situation.

Everything looked normal, as far as I could see. I didn't believe it, but that was the way it looked. There's a long oval road called the Drive that goes all the way around inside the park, and every entrance to it that I saw was blocked with gray Police Department sawhorses; the usual thing for a Tuesday afternoon. People with bicycles were going in past the sawhorses, and wherever I could catch a glimpse of the Drive inside the park it was full of bicycles sailing by. Nobody I saw had a sign on his back that read *Mafia*.

It took twenty minutes to go down to 61st Street and then come back up again, and when I went past 85th Street it was fine by me that Tom was still sitting there with the newspaper in his lap. I wasn't ready to leap into action just yet. To tell the truth, I was getting a late case of cold feet.

Maybe it was because everything looked so peaceful. When

we'd gone up against the brokerage, there had been people around with uniforms and guns, there'd been closed-circuit television and locked doors to go through and all kinds of things to pit ourselves against. But here there was nothing, just a peaceful afternoon in the park, summer sunshine everywhere, people riding bicycles or pushing baby carriages or just lying on the grass with a paperback book. And yet this was a much tougher situation; the people we were up against were meaner, and we were pretty sure they were out to kill us, and they knew we were coming.

So where were they?

Around; that much I could be sure of. Since I'm on the uniformed force I haven't had much to do with stakeouts, but I know from Tom that it's possible to flood an area with plainsclothesmen and not have anything look out of the ordinary at all. And if the Police Department could do it, the mob could do it.

I was supposed to check with Tom every fifteen minutes, so after I saw him I headed over to Broadway and farted around there for a little while. Ran my beat, in fact. I was on duty at the moment, which was the simple straight-forward way I'd gotten hold of a car this time. It had turned out Lou had a girl friend that went to Columbia and lived up near the campus and didn't have any classes on Tuesday afternoons. So for the last three weeks I'd been giving him a couple hours to shack up with her; drop him off at her place, pick him up later. It was an established pattern now, nothing out of the ordinary, and it gave me a couple of hours alone with the car; with the numbers changed again.

Fifteen minutes. I went back over to the park, passed by Tom again, and he still had the newspaper in his lap.

This time, I didn't like it. I was still nervous, I still had cold feet, but my reaction when I'm scared of something is that I want to get it done and over with. No stalling around, building it up, making myself even more nervous than I was already.

Come on, Vigano. Make your play, let's do something.

Because of my nerves, my driving was getting bad. A couple times, if I'd been in a civilian car I would have racked it up for sure; but people pay more attention to police cars, so they saw me in time to get out of the way. But that's all I needed, was to be involved in some fender-bumping argument over on Columbus Avenue while Tom was making contact in the park; so after the second trip past him I didn't do much driving at all, just pulled in next to a hydrant on 86th to wait the fifteen minutes out.

I had the radio on, listening to the dispatcher, though I don't know why. I sure wasn't going to respond to any squeals, not now. Maybe I was listening for something to tell me the whole thing was off, we'd blown it and could go home and forget the whole thing.

In the back seat, directly behind me, was the picnic basket. It was half full of old copies of the *Daily News*. On top we'd scattered some fake diplomas and gag stock certificates we'd picked up in a novelty shop on Times Square. They ought to look good enough for a fast peek, which is all we meant to give the other side before we made our play. If things worked out right.

Fifteen minutes. I pulled away from the hydrant, made a loop around, and passed Tom again, and he didn't have the newspaper on his lap anymore.

All of a sudden I had a balled-up wet wool overcoat in my stomach. I was blinking like a hophead, I could barely make out the numbers and the hands on my watch when I raised my arm in front of my face to check the time. Three thirty-five. All right. All right.

I drove up to 96th Street, the next entrance to the Drive. I stopped with the nose of the car against one of the sawhorses blocking the road, and stumbled and almost fell on my face getting out from behind the wheel. I walked around to the front of the car, lifted one end of the sawhorse, and swung it out of the way. Then I drove through, put the sawhorse back, and angled the car slowly down the entrance road to the Drive.

I was in the only kind of vehicle that could come into the park on a Tuesday afternoon. That was the edge we had; we could drive, and the mob had to walk.

I stopped by the Drive and checked my watch again, and I had three minutes before I should start to move. Tom needed time to make contact.

Bicycles streamed by me, heading south, the same direction I would go. There's no law about it, but most people who ride bicycles in the park treat the Drive as a counterclockwise one-way street, the way it is the rest of the week for cars. Every once in a while somebody would come up in the other direction like a salmon going upstream—usually it was a teen-ager—but most of the traffic was south-bound. Even the women pushing baby carriages were all heading south.

I didn't want any shooting in here today. Aside from what would happen to Tom and me, they could really rack up a score on women and children.

Time. I shifted into drive and joined the stream of bicycles and matched their pace on down toward Tom.

17

They had rehearsed this, they'd gone through it over and over again, they both knew their parts; and still, when Tom looked up from the picnic basket and saw the police car threading its way toward him through the bicycles, he was amazed at the relief he felt. Now that Joe was actually here, Tom could admit to himself the fear he'd been carrying in the back of his mind that for one reason or another Joe would fail to show up.

Joe hadn't had that worry about Tom. The only unacknowledged fear he'd been ignoring was that Tom would already be dead before the patrol car got there. Seeing Tom alive relieved Joe's mind a little, but not much; they were still just at the beginning of this ride.

Joe eased the car to a stop near the picnickers. Tom had half a dozen bills from the basket clenched in his right fist, taken from the top and the middle and the bottom—they didn't want the fakery with old newspapers done right back at them—and now he said to the picnickers, "Take it easy. I'll be right back."

They didn't like it. They were looking at the patrol car and at each other and up the hill toward their friends. They obviously hadn't figured on the patrol car, and it was making them upset. The first man, with his hand still inside his jacket, said, "You better move very slow."

"Oh, I will," Tom said. "And when your hand comes out from under there, it better move slow, too. My friend sometimes gets nervous."

"He's got reason," the picnicker said.

Tom got to his feet and walked slowly over to the patrol car, coming up to it on the right side. The passenger window was open. He bent to put his elbows on the sill, hands and forearms inside the car. A nervous grin flickering on his face, he said, "Welcome to the party."

Joe was looking past him at the picnickers, watching their tense faces. He looked tense himself, the muscles bunched like a lumpy mattress along the sides of his jaw. He said, "How we doing?"

Tom dropped the handful of bills onto the seat. "I spotted five guys so far," he said. "There's probably more."

Reaching for the microphone, Joe said, "They really don't want us to get paid."

"If there's enough of them," Tom said, "we're fucked."

Into the microphone Joe said, "Six six." To Tom he said, "That's the chance we took. We worked it out."

"I know," Tom said. He rubbed perspiration from his forehead onto the back of his hand, and from there to his trouser leg. Half-turning, staying bent, keeping one elbow on the windowsill, he looked around at the sunny day and said, "Christ, I wish it was over."

"Me, too." Joe was blinking again, having trouble seeing things. Into the microphone, he said, "Six six."

The radio suddenly said, "Yeah, six six, go ahead."

Picking up the money from the seat, Joe said, "I got some bills for you to check out."

"Okay, go ahead."

Joe held one of the bills close to his face, and squinted so he could read the serial number. "This one's a twenty," he said. "B-five-five-eight-seven-five-three-five-A"

The radio read the number back again.

"Check," Joe said. "Another twenty." He read off the number, listened to it repeated, and then did the same thing with a third bill, a fifty.

"Give me a minute," the radio said.

Tom muttered, "If we have a minute."

Joe put the microphone away under the dashboard and held one of the bills up by the open window to study it with the light behind it. Squinting at it, focusing with difficulty, he said, "Looks okay to me. What do you think?"

The grin twitched on Tom's face again. "I was too nervous to look," he said, and reached into the car to pick up one of the bills from the seat. He studied it, felt the paper between thumb and first finger, tried to remember the signs of a phony bill. Over on his side of the car, Joe was checking another of the bills, seeing this one a little more easily; he was beginning to settle down, now that something was happening.

"I guess it's all right," Tom said. Irritably he tossed the bill back on the seat. "What's taking him so long?"

Joe dropped the bill and rubbed his eyes, then said, "Go talk to the people."

Tom frowned at him. "Are you really as cool as all that, or is it bullshit?"

"It's bullshit," Joe said. "But it'll do."

Tom's grin turned a little sickly. "I'll be back," he said, and left the car, and walked over again to the picnickers, who were watching him with great suspicion. He hunkered down where he'd been before, and talked directly to the first man, who seemed to be the leader of the group. He said, "I'll be going back over by the car. When I give a signal, one of you carry the basket over there."

The first man said, "Where's the trade?"

"The other basket's in the car," Tom said. "We'll do the switch there. But only one of you come over, the rest stay right here."

The first man said, "We've got to look it over."

"Sure," Tom said. "You bring the basket, you get in the car, you check the other one, you get out again."

The second man spoke up, saying, "In the car?" He frowned at his friend, not liking that.

Tom said, "Let's not make it any more public than we have to." Which was an argument they should appreciate.

They did. The first man said to the second, "It's all right. It's better inside."

"Sure," Tom said. "You stick tight, I'll let you know when." He got to his feet, trying to look nonchalant and sure of himself, and walked back over to the car. Leaning in again, he said, "Anything yet?"

Joe was twitching like a wind-up doll. Waiting was the worst thing in the world for him. "No," he said. "How's it going?"

"I don't know," Tom said. "Their friends haven't come down from the hills yet, so I guess we're still ahead."

"Maybe," Joe said, as the radio suddenly said, "Six six."

They both started; as though they hadn't been expecting that sound. Joe grabbed the microphone and said, "Yeah, six six."

"On those bills," the radio said. "They're clean."

Joe's face suddenly opened into a big wide smile. It was going to be all right, he all at once knew that as a positive certainty. "Okay," he said into the microphone. "Thanks." Putting the microphone away, he turned and gave Tom the big smile and said, "We go."

Tom hadn't been affected the same way. The fact that the money was real just confirmed for him the knowledge that the mob was out to kill them. Counterfeit money or stolen money with traceable numbers might have meant the mob would be content merely to cheat them, but real money meant their lives were definitely at stake. Having trouble breathing, Tom responded to Joe's big smile with a small nervous grimace, and then turned away to make a little waving gesture toward the picnickers.

The women over there were looking a little green, as though the situation had become trickier than they'd been led to believe. They were sitting staring outward, waiting for disaster to strike or relief to come at last. The two men looked at one another, and the first man nodded. The second one got reluctantly to his feet, picked up the basket, and carried it toward the car.

It took him forever to make the trip. Joe kept staring across the car and out the open side window at him, willing him to move faster. Tom watched the slope up toward Central Park West; three of the guys he'd spotted before were clustered together up there now, talking things over. They seemed excited. Was that a small walkie-talkie one of them had in his hand?

"They've got an army," Tom said. All at once, he saw how hopeless it was; the two of them against an army, with army equipment and an army disregard for life.

Joe ducked his head, trying to see Tom's face. "What?"

The guy with the picnic basket was too close. Tom said, "Nothing. Here he comes."

"I see him."

Nervousness could have made both of them irritable right then. If it hadn't been for the pressure of what else they were doing, they could have turned on each other instead, bickering and snarling like a couple of dogs in a vacant lot.

The guy with the basket reached the car. Tom opened the rear door, and saw the guy's face register that he'd seen the other basket in there. But he didn't make a move to enter.

"Get in," Tom said. Up the slope, one of the trio was using the walkie-talkie.

"Tell your friend to open the basket. Lift the lid."

"For Christ's sake," Tom said, and called in to Joe, "Did you hear him?"

Joe was already twisting around in the seat, reaching over the back of it for the basket. "I heard him," he said, and lifted the lid. The gag certificates with their fancy designs showed indistinctly in the shadows.

The men up the hill were moving this way; casually, not hurrying yet. Some other men were also strolling this way from other directions. Tom, trying to keep his voice calm and assured, said, "You satisfied now?"

For answer, the guy shoved his basket ahead of himself onto the back seat, and immediately slid in after it, reaching across it toward the other basket to get a closer look at the papers in there.

Tom slapped the door shut, pulled the front door open, and slid in. "They're coming," he said.

Joe already knew that; there were more of them coming up from the other side of the road, he could see them through the bicycle riders. He had the car in gear already, and at once they rolled forward.

The guy in the back seat yelled, "Hey!"

Tom's hand patted the seat between himself and Joe, found the .32 there where it was supposed to be, and came up with it. Turning in his seat, seeing the guy back there reaching into his jacket, Tom laid the pistol atop the seatback, aiming at the guy's head. "Take it easy," he said.

Vigano

Vigano sat in an office on Madison Avenue with an absolutely clean phone; guaranteed. He had an open line to a pay phone on the corner of 86th Street and Central Park West, across the street from the park. He had a man in the booth, pumping change in, keeping the line open. A second man, outside the booth with a small walkie-talkie no bigger than a pack of cigarettes, was the relay between Vigano and the one hundred and eleven men he had scattered in and around the park. From the phone to the walkie-talkie, he could get an order to any man in the park in less than half a minute.

Aside from the transverse roads, the ones that simply cross the park and don't connect with the interior road, there are twenty-six entrances to and exits from the Drive. Every one of them was covered, with either one or two cars, and a minimum of three men; including the one-way entrances that no vehicle was supposed to use in leaving the park, such as the one at Sixth Avenue and 59th Street and the one at Seventh Avenue and West 110th. His people with the two million dollars in the picnic basket were completely surrounded by

Vigano's men, and six others roamed the general vicinity on bicycles. If the two amateurs with the bearer bonds tried to get away by bicycle they'd be stopped at a park exit. If they tried to cut across the park on foot they wouldn't get twenty yards.

Vigano had the interior people all in position before the basket was delivered, but he held off blocking the park exits until after contact was made with the amateurs; no point scaring them off. He had a conference call hook-up on the phone, so that it broadcast into the room and he could reply without holding the speaker to his mouth, and he sat back in the desk chair, his hands up behind his head, and smiled at the thought that he was the spider, and his web was out, and the flies were on their way.

"One man," the speaker-phone said.

Vigano frowned and sat forward in the chair, bringing his hands down to rest on the empty desk. Over on the sofa, Andy and Mike looked alert. Vigano said, "What's that?"

"One man, civilian clothing, has approached our people."

Just one? Move the cars into position now, or wait for the other one? "What's happening?"

Silence for nearly a minute. Vigano frowned at the phone, feeling tense even though he knew everything had to be all right. But he didn't want anything unexpected now; if he lost that two million, it would be his head.

He wouldn't lose it.

"Mr. Vigano?"

Vigano gave the phone an angry look. Who else would it be? He said, "What's going on?"

"It's one of them all right. He's taken some of the money out of the—Hold on a second."

"Took some money? What the hell are you talking about?"

Nothing. Andy and Mike were both looking as though they wanted to find something cheerful to say, but they'd damn well better keep their mouths shut.

"Mr. Vigano?"

"Just talk, I'm not going anywhere."

"Yes, sir. The other one showed up, in a police car."

"A what? In the park?"

"Yes, sir. In uniform, in a police car."

"Son of a bitch," Vigano said. Now that he knew what was going on, he felt better. Giving Andy and Mike a tight grin, he said, "I told you they were cute." He turned back to the phone: "Move the cars in. Don't change anything, do it all like we figured."

"Yes, sir."

Andy got to his feet in a sudden motion, betraying the nervousness he'd been covering up. He said, "They must really be cops."

"Probably." Vigano felt grim, but confident.

"How do we stop cops?" Andy spread his hands, looking bewildered. "What if they just drive out of the park, order our people to move over?"

Mike said, "We can follow them, take care of them some place quieter."

"No," Vigano said. "There's too many ways to lose them outside. We finish it in the park."

Mike said, "Against cops?"

"They're just men," Vigano said. "They wipe themselves like anybody else. And they can't call their brother cops to come help them, not with two million bucks in the car."

"So what do we do?" Mike said, and at the same instant the phone said, "Everybody's set, Mr. Vigano."

"Listen," Vigano told Mike. He said to the phone, "Spread the word. They stay in the park. If they try to get out, we can force them to stop at our cars. When they do, kill them, take our goods, clear out."

"Yes, sir."

"Hold on, there's more. If they don't try to leave the park, we just keep them bottled up until the park is opened to cars. Then we drive in, surround them, finish it the same way."

"Yes, sir."

"The main point is, they don't leave the park."

"Yes, sir."

Vigano leaned back again, smiled at Andy and Mike, and said, "See? They're cute, but we've got everything covered."

Andy and Mike both grinned, and Andy said, "They've got a surprise coming."

"That's just what they have," Vigano said.

Nobody said anything after that for a minute or two, until the phone suddenly said, in an excited voice, "Mr. Vigano!"

"What?"

"They're crossing us! They took off with our goods and didn't leave anything! And they've got Bristol with them in the car."

"He's gone over to them?" That didn't sound right; the people to carry the money had been very carefully selected.

"No, sir. They must have pulled a gun on him."

"They're headed south?"

"Yes, sir."

Vigano squinted, visualizing the park. If they'd come in to try a double cross, they had to have some method for getting away again. Where would it be? Vigano said, "Cover the transverse roads. They might decide to cut across the grass and out that way."

"Yes, sir."

"Pass that one on."

While the man was gone from the phone, Vigano kept thinking. How fast would a car move, surrounded by bicycles? It was no good settling for holding them in the park now; they had to be stopped, as quick as possible.

"Mr. Vigano?"

"All spare men," Vigano said, "get over to the section of the Drive on the east side, just south of the bridge over the first transverse road. Block the road there. Don't let them through, finish them off."

"Yes, sir."

"Move!"

Andy and Mike were both leaning on the desk, giving him worried looks. Andy said, "What's going on?"

"They're starting from 85th Street," Vigano said, "going south. The Drive takes them down to 59th, and then across the bottom of the park. They can't move fast, not with all those bikes. Our people get over to the east side of the park first, block the road there. If they try to get out before then, they're stopped. If they last that long, they're stopped."

"Good," Andy said. "That's good."

"They've been cute for the last time," Vigano said.

18

They were in motion. Joe faced front, steering the patrol car southward along the Drive, while Tom faced the rear, holding the .32 aimed at the guy in the back seat.

Joe tapped over and over on the horn, and ahead of him the bicyclists reluctantly got out of the way, their front wheels waggling back and forth as they glared at the automobile immorally in here during their special time.

From left and right, as they started away, they could see men running after them. There weren't any guns in plain sight yet, but there might be any second. The other male picnicker was running along in their wake, leaving the two women sitting on the grass behind him, looking stunned.

They'd only been moving ten seconds or so. To both of them, every instant now seemed a distinct and separate thing, as though they were working in slow motion.

Tom said to the guy in the back seat, "You've got a gun under there. Take it out slowly, by the butt, with your thumb and first finger, and hold it up in the air in front of you."

The guy said, "What's the point in all this? We're making the payoff."

"That's right," Tom said. "And all your friends were here because they like fresh air. Take the gun out the way I said and hold it up in the air."

The guy shrugged. "You're making a big thing over nothing," he said. But he pulled a Firearms International .38 automatic from under his jacket and held it up in front of himself like a dead fish.

Tom switched his own pistol to his left hand, and took the automatic away with his right. He dropped that on the seat, switched the pistol back to his right hand again and, still watching his prisoner, said to Joe, "How we doing?"

"Beautiful," Joe said grimly. By keeping up almost a steady honking, he was managing to get bicycles and baby carriages out of his path without running over anybody, and was up to maybe twenty miles an hour; twice as fast as the general flow of bicycle traffic, and four times as fast as the men chasing them on foot.

The 77th Street exit was a little ways ahead. They couldn't afford to stop and unload their passenger until they got out and away from the park, but that shouldn't be long now.

Joe started the turn, seeing the sawhorses down at the other end of the feeder road, and just in the nick of time he saw the green Chevvy and the pale blue Pontiac across the road, just beyond the sawhorses. Three men were standing in front of the Chevvy, looking this way.

Joe hit the brakes. Tom, startled but not looking away from the guy in the back seat, said, "What's the matter?"

"They got us blocked."

Tom snapped his head forward and back, taking a quick look out the windshield. The patrol car was stopped, cyclists were streaming by on both sides of it. They couldn't stay here. "Try another one," Tom said. "We can't get through there."

"I know, I know." Joe was twisting the wheel, tapping

the accelerator, leaning on the horn. They slid away from that exit and headed south again, hurrying through the cyclists.

Both of them—Tom by looking out the back window and Joe by looking at the rear-view mirror—saw the three men who'd been standing by the Chevvy suddenly run around the end of the sawhorses and come trotting after the patrol car. They couldn't catch up, obviously, but that didn't mean much; they acted as though they knew what they were doing. Tom remembered the walkie-talkie one of them had carried back by the picnickers, and the army imagery seemed stronger than ever all of a sudden; they must have a central-command post somewhere, with men reporting in from all around the park.

If there'd been a way to call the whole thing off, Tom would have done it right then and there. Just give it up, forget it, make believe none of it had ever happened. As far as he was concerned, they'd had it, they were defeated already, and only going on because there wasn't anything else to do.

But not Joe. His sense of combat had been aroused, he was feeling nothing but the warring instinct. As a little kid, his comic-book hero had been Captain America; shield and fist against entire swarming armies of the enemy, and he won out every time. Joe hunched over the steering wheel, weaving the car through all the people with small taps on the accelerator, tiny shifts of the wheel, steady pushing at the horn, feeling himself the master of his machine in a slow-motion Indy 500.

It was almost no time at all to the next exit at 72nd Street, even at these slow speeds. Joe felt no surprise, only a sense of grim determination, when he saw the two cars parked broadside beyond the sawhorses. "That one, too," he said, and swung away, still heading south.

Tom turned his head to the left and saw the blocked exit. Grimacing, staring at the guy in the back seat again, he said to Joe, "Then they're all blocked."

"I know," Joe said.

The guy in the back seat grinned a little, nodding. "That's right," he said. "Give it up. What's the point?"

Tom's mind was scrambling. He was sure they were going down in defeat, but he'd keep bobbing and weaving all the way to the bottom. "We can't just drive around," he said. "We've got to get out of here."

Frustration was making Joe angry; things were supposed to work differently from this. Thumping a fist against the steering wheel, he said, "What the hell do we do now?"

The guy in the back seat finally reached into the other basket, and pulled out a handful of phony stock certificates and pieces of newspaper. He looked surprised for just a second, then held the papers up, gave Tom a pitying grin, and said, "You two are really stupid. I just can't believe how stupid you are."

"You shut your face," Tom said.

Joe abruptly slammed on the brakes. "Get him out," he said. "Get him out or shoot him."

Tom gestured with the gun. "Out."

The guy pushed open the door, making a passing cyclist wobble onto the grass to avoid an accident. "You're all through," the guy told them, and slid out of the car, and Joe hit the accelerator while he was still departing. The door, snapping shut, nicked him on the left elbow, and Tom saw him wince and grab the elbow and trot away toward Central Park West.

Tom faced front. Fifty-ninth Street was just ahead of them, with the spur road angling off toward Columbus Circle. Cars there, too.

"There's got to be a way out," Joe said. He was clutching the steering wheel hard enough to bend it. He was enraged and bewildered because he was the hero of his life, and the hero always has a way out.

"Keep rolling," Tom said. He expected nothing anymore, but as long as they were moving it hadn't ended yet.

They swept around the curve at the southern tip of the park, the car moving through the cyclists like a whale through trout. They passed the Seventh Avenue turn-off and there were cars out there, too, but they expected that by now.

The Sixth Avenue entrance was ahead of them, on the right. Sixth Avenue is one-way, leading uptown toward the park, so there's no automobile exit there, just an entrance. It was blocked anyway, with two cars parked across it.

The Drive was curving again, leftward, starting up the other side of the park. The Sixth Avenue entrance angled in ahead of them on the right. Farther along, up by the bridge, they both suddenly saw maybe fifteen or twenty men, standing around in the roadway.

Just standing around. Some with bicycles, some not. Talking together, in little groups. Leaving enough room between them for bicycles to get through, but not enough for a car.

"God damn it," Joe said.

"They blocked—" Tom stopped, and just stared.

It wasn't any good. Run those people down and it wouldn't be the mob they had to worry about anymore, it would be their own kind that would get them. The park would fill up with law in nothing flat.

But they couldn't stop.

Joe hunched lower over the wheel. "Hold tight," he said.

Tom stared at him. He wasn't going to plow through those guys anyway, was he? "What are you going to do?"

"Just hold tight."

The Sixth Avenue entrance was right there, the long approach road curving back southward to the edge of the park. Suddenly Joe yanked the wheel hard right; they climbed a curb, cut across grass, bounced down over another curb, and were headed toward Sixth Avenue, due south, with Joe's foot flat on the accelerator.

Tom yelled, "Jesus Christ!"

"Siren," Joe shouted. "Siren and light."

Pop-eyed, staring out the windshield, Tom felt on the dashboard for the familiar switches, hit them, and heard the growl of the siren start to build.

The patrol car lunged at the sawhorses, and at the two cars parked sideways beyond them. They blocked the road from curb to curb.

But they didn't block the sidewalk. Siren howling, red light flashing, the car raced at the roadblock, and at the last second Joe spun the wheel leftward and they vaulted over the curb, slicing through between the blockage and the stone park wall.

"Move!" Joe yelled at the people running every which way on the sidewalk. Even Tom couldn't hear him, with the siren screaming, but the people moved, diving left and right, yanking themselves out of the way by their own shirt collars. Traffic going east and west on 59th Street abruptly jammed up as though they'd hit a wall, opening a line across like the path through the Red Sea. The hoods at the roadblock were clambering into their cars to give chase, and the patrol car wasn't even past them yet.

Lamp post. They shot across the sidewalk, Joe nudged the wheel a bit to the right, and they flicked by between the post and one of the parked cars. They both felt the jolt when the right rear of their car kissed off the bumper of the other; and then they were through.

And Joe headed straight south. Tom threw his hands up in the air and screamed at the top of his voice, *"Holy jumping Jesus!"*

Sixth Avenue is one-way north, and five lanes wide. The patrol car was heading south, and three blocks ahead was a phalanx of traffic spread completely across the avenue, coming this way, moving along at about twenty-five miles an hour, following the sequence of the staggered green lights. They covered the road from left to right, they were coming in a tight mass like a cattle drive, and Tom and Joe were tearing toward them at about sixty, and accelerating every second.

Joe was driving one-handed, waving the other hand at the oncoming traffic, yelling at them under the siren, while Tom pressed against the seatback and braced the heels of his hands against the dashboard, and just stared.

Cabs and cars and trucks down there veered left and right as though an atomic bomb had just gone off in Central Park. Cars climbed the sidewalks, they practically climbed each other's shoulders, they went tearing away down side-streets, and hid behind parked buses, and jay-walkers ran for their lives. A lane opened up down the middle of the street, and the patrol car went down it like a bullet through a rifle barrel. Open-mouthed drivers flashed by in cars on both sides. Joe wriggled and squiggled the wheel and tight-roped past taxi bumpers and the jutting tails of trucks.

Elation suddenly grabbed Tom and lifted him up into the sky. Still bracing himself with one hand, he pounded his other fist on top of the dashboard and yelled, "Yeah! Yeah! Yeah!"

Joe was grinning so hard he looked as though he was imitating all those automobile grilles out front. He was practically lying on top of the steering wheel, hunched around it so tight he was driving as much with his shoulders as with his hands. He was concentrating like a pinball player on a streak, goosing the ball past all the dangers toward the big winner.

Three blocks, four blocks, and they were out of that swarm, with the next bunch half a dozen blocks ahead, coming up with the next traffic-light sequence. "Siren and light off!" Joe yelled. He couldn't be heard, so he pounded Tom's leg, and jammed a finger toward the switches, simultaneously making a screaming two-wheel left turn onto West 54th Street.

Tom hit the switches as they shot around the turn, and then braced himself again, because Joe was standing on the brake with both feet. He brought them down to about twenty, and they rolled the rest of the way to the traffic waiting for the light at Fifth Avenue, and came to a gentle stop behind a garment delivery truck.

They grinned at one another. They were both shaking like a leaf. Tom said, with both admiration and terror, "You're a madman. You're a complete madman."

"And that," Joe said, "is how you don't get followed."

19

They both had day shift, so they were with the rush-hour traffic again on the Long Island Expressway, heading toward the city. Joe was driving, and Tom was beside him, reading the *News*.

This was about a week after the business in the park. When they'd gotten the picnic basket home that night, they'd found it had the full two million dollars in it, to the penny. They'd split it down the middle, and each of them had taken his share for safekeeping. Tom put his in a canvas bag he'd once kept gym equipment in, and locked it away in a cabinet behind the bar in his basement. Joe put his in the blue plastic laundry bag they'd used during the bond robbery, moved his pool filter (which was on the fritz once more), dug a hole under it, put the bag in the hole, filled it up again, and put the filter back on top.

The main result of the activity in the park was a notice on the bulletin boards in all the Manhattan precinct houses, a couple days later, urging caution if anybody ever had to travel the wrong way on a one-way street. The Department surely would have liked to find out who had done that stuntman number on Sixth Avenue, but there was no way they were going to do it, and they probably didn't even try.

They'd been sitting there in Joe's Plymouth in silence for a pretty long while, inching along in stop-and-go traffic, when Tom suddenly sat up and said, "Hey, look at this."

Joe glanced at him. "What?"

Tom was staring at the newspaper. "Vigano's dead," he said.

Joe glanced at him. "What?"

Tom was staring at the newspaper. "Vigano's dead," he said.

"No shit." Joe faced front again, and moved the Plymouth forward a little bit. "Read it to me."

"Uhh. Crime kingpin Anthony Vigano, long reputed to be an important member of the Joseph Scaracci Mafia family in New Jersey, was shot to death at ten forty-five yesterday evening as he emerged from Jimmy's Home Italian Restaurant in Bayonne. The killing, which Bayonne police say bears all the earmarks of a gang-type slaying was done by an unidentified man who stepped from an automobile parked in front of the restaurant, shot Vigano twice in the head, and left in the automobile. Police are also seeking the two men who had been with Vigano in the restaurant and who left with him but who had disappeared before police reached the scene. Vigano, who was still alive when the first police officers responded to a call from the restaurant owner, Salvatore "Jimmy" Iacocca, died in the ambulance en route to Bayonne Memorial Hospital. Vigano, fifty-seven, first attracted the attention of the police in nineteen—uhh, the rest is all biography."

"Is there a picture?"

"Just of the restaurant. A white X where he got it."

Joe nodded. A small smile of satisfaction was on his face. "You know what that means, don't you?"

"He lost the mob's two million dollars," Tom said, "and they didn't like it."

"Besides that."

"What else?"

"They can't find us," Joe said. "They've tried, and they can't do it, and they gave up."

"The mob doesn't give up," Tom said.

"Bullshit. Everybody gives up, if there's nothing left to do. If they thought they could still find us and get the money back, they wouldn't kill Vigano. They'd let him keep looking." Joe gave Tom a big smile and said, "We're free and clear, buddy, that's what that thing in the paper means."

Tom frowned at the newspaper report, thinking it over, and gradually he too began to smile. "I guess so," he said. "I guess we are."

"Fucking A well told," said Joe.

They rode along in silence again for a while, both of them thinking about the future. A little later, Joe glanced toward Tom, and beyond him he saw the next car over, stopped like they were, and it was a gray Jaguar sedan, one of the big ones. The windows were rolled up, and the middle-aged guy inside there was neat and cool in his suit and tie. As Joe looked at him, the guy in the Jaguar turned his own head, met Joe's eye, and gave him that quick meaningless smile that people invariably flash when they cross glances with somebody in another car. Then he faced front again.

Joe smiled back at him, but with something savage in it. "That's right, you bastard, smile," he said to the Jaguar driver's profile. "Six months from now you're going to be six months closer to your coronary, and I'm going to be in Saskatchewan."

Tom looked at Joe while he was talking, puzzled; then turned and saw the Jaguar driver and understood. The surf on a beach in Trinidad crashed lazily in his mind, and he smiled.

It was going to be a hot day. They sat there in the car, their elbows out the open windows, reaching for a little breeze. Endless stalled traffic stretched away into the hazy distance, and far away they could just make out the scum-covered smoky island of Manhattan, squatting there like that portion of Hell zoned industrial.

The car in front of them moved a little.

RAVES FOR *The Fugitive Pigeon* and Donald E. Westlake

"The suspense novel that is genuinely funny without sacrificing its status as a mystery thriller is one of the most difficult kinds to bring off successfully.... Westlake manages the feat triumphantly in *The Fugitive Pigeon*."
—New York Post

★

"A gem."
—Pittsburgh Press

★

"He has glimpsed the comic potential of tossing the sand of petty frustrations and human fallibility into the well-oiled machine of the thriller. The results have brought new life to a neglected sub-genre: the caper novel."
—Time

★

"Intricate whimsy."
—Saturday Review

★

"It's all there. A mystery to remember."
—Richmond Times Dispatch

★

more...

"*The Fugitive Pigeon* is so good that the time-old question arises, what can Donald Westlake possibly do for an encore?"

—Book Week

★

"Through sheer craftsmanship, Westlake makes us say 'of course' to the most preposterous of happenstances . . . a writer of uncommon talent, imagination, flair and unpredictability."

—Los Angeles Times

★

"Westlake's comic eye is hilariously perceptive and ruthlessly unsparing . . . he works with an elegance that might be the envy of many an ambitious writer."

—Washington Post Book World

★

"Westlake is always original."

—Elmore Leonard

★

"If there is any funnier mystery novelist around, I can't imagine who it might be."

—USA Today

★

"Westlake doesn't miss a comic beat or a funny line."

—Playboy

★

"Westlake has no peer in the realm of comic mystery novelists."

—San Francisco Chronicle

★

"Westlake can wring humor out of a situation until an appreciative chortle becomes a hopeless snort of oxygen deprivation."

—Newsday

★

"The master of the rolling scam."

—James Grady

★

"Westlake is among the smoothest, most engaging writers on the planet."

—San Diego Tribune

★

"Westlake sets off plot twists and surprise endings like so many firecrackers."

—Booklist

★

"Donald E. Westlake [is] the Noel Coward of crime.... He displays an excellent ear for bitter-salty urban humor, composed of equal parts of raunch and cynicism."

—Chicago Sun-Times

★

"Westlake probably is the best practitioner we have of the craft of writing about subjects that should be grim and tense but turn out only to be ridiculous."

—Kansas City Star

★

"Donald Westlake keeps showing me people I'd like to meet."

—Rex Stout

★

By Donald E. Westlake

NOVELS

Humans • Sacred Monster • A Likely Story
Kahawa • Brothers Keepers • I Gave at the Office
Adios, Scheherazade • Up Your Banners

COMIC CRIME NOVELS

Trust Me on This • High Adventure
Castle in the Air • Enough • Dancing Aztecs
Two Much • *Help* I Am Being Held Prisoner
Cops and Robbers • Somebody Owes Me Money
Who Stole Sassi Manoon? • God Save the Mark
The Spy in the Ointment • The Busy Body
The Fugitive Pigeon

THE DORTMUNDER SERIES

Don't Ask • Drowned Hopes • Good Behavior
Why Me • Nobody's Perfect
Jimmy the Kid • Bank Shot • The Hot Rock

CRIME NOVELS

Pity Him Afterwards • Killy • 361
Killing Time • The Mercenaries

JUVENILE

Philip

WESTERN

Gangway (with Brian Garfield)

REPORTAGE

Under an English Heaven

SHORT STORIES

Tomorrow's Crimes • Levine
The Curious Facts Preceeding My Execution and Other Fictions

ANTHOLOGY

Once Against the Law (edited by William Tenn)

DONALD E. WESTLAKE

THE FUGITIVE PIGEON

THE MYSTERIOUS PRESS
New York • Tokyo • Sweden
Published by Warner Books
A Time Warner Company

MYSTERIOUS PRESS EDITION

Cover design by Jackie Merri Meyer
Cover illustration by Wilson McLean

This Mysterious Press Edition is published by arrangement with the author.

Mysterious Press Books are published by
Warner Books, Inc.
1271 Avenue of the Americas
New York, NY 10020

A Time Warner Company

Printed in the United States of America

First Mysterious Press Printing: April, 1993
10 9 8 7 6 5 4 3 2 1

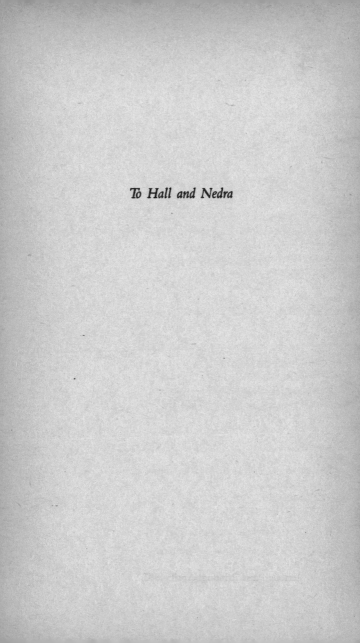

To Hall and Nedra

But oh, beamish nephew, beware of the day,
If your Snark be a Boojum! For then
You will softly and suddenly vanish away,
And never be met with again!

Hunting of the Snark, Lewis Carroll

★

He shall not live; look, with a spot I damn him.

Julius Caesar, William Shakespeare

★ It was a slow night, like any Tuesday. The late late show was *High Sierra* and there's always a couple of Bogart fans around, in fact I'm a Bogart fan myself, so I figured to stay open till the movie was over and then lock up and go upstairs and get some sleep. After one-thirty I only had two customers, both regulars, both sitting at the bar, both watching the TV, both beer drinkers. I stood down to the far end of the bar, with my arms folded and my white apron on, and I watched the TV myself. Commercials, one or both customers had refills. I don't drink on duty, so it was none for me.

My name is Charles Robert Poole, everybody calls me Charlie. Charlie Poole. Just so you know.

High Sierra ended with the cop shooting Bogart in the back and Ida Lupino glad society couldn't treat Bogart bad any more, and I said, "Okay, gents, time to drink up. I need my beauty sleep." It's a neighborhood bar, regular customers, I like to keep an informal atmosphere.

These two were both good about it, not like some which come in mostly on weekends and want the night to go on forever. But not these two, they drank up and said, "Night, Charlie," and out they went, waving to me.

I waved back and told them good night and rinsed their glasses and set them on the drainboard, and the door opened again and two guys came in with suits and topcoats, the topcoats all unbuttoned so you could see they were wearing white shirts and ties. Not what you mostly get in a bar in Canarsie two-thirty on a Tuesday night.

I said, "Sorry, gents, just closing up."

"Yeah, that's okay, nephew," said one of them, and they came over and sat down on stools at the bar.

I looked at them then, and they were both grinning at me. Tough-guy types. I recognized them both, associates of my Uncle Al, they'd both been in before to drop off a package or a message or to pick one up. I said, "Oh. I didn't recognize you at first."

The one that talked said, "You know us, though, don't you, nephew? I mean you know us to see, am I right?"

Calling me *nephew* like that was a kind of a playful insult. I got it from Uncle Al's associates all the time. What it meant was, I wasn't really a part of the organization, I only had this job here because of Uncle Al, if it wasn't for my Uncle Al I'd probably starve to death. I knew that's what this one meant when he called me *nephew*, but I didn't get sore or anything. In the first place, these two and all the others in the organization were very tough mean nasty types. In the second place, facts are facts, it was the truth; I was born a bum and I've been a bum twenty-four years, and if it wasn't for my Uncle Al and this job running this bar I would starve to death in a minute. So what was the point of starting an argument, just because a guy calls me *nephew?*

So all I said was, "Sure, I know you. I recognize you now. You been in here before."

The other one said, "He recognizes us."

The first one said, "Well, sure. We been in here before."

Life imitates art. And yet I'd bet neither one of them had ever read Hemingway.

I said, "Is there anything I can do for you?" I was hoping it was just a drop, just a package they wanted to leave and then they'd go away. I was tired; if it hadn't been for *High Sierra* I'd have closed the place at one o'clock.

The first one said, "Yeah, nephew, there is. You can tell me if this looks okay." He reached into his topcoat pocket and came out with a small white card, like a calling card, and put it down on the bar between us, kind of slapped it down under his palm and then took his hand away. "How's it look?" he said.

It had my name on it, and a thing like an ink blot. It looked like:

I said, "What's that supposed to be?"

They looked at each other. The second one said, "Is he kidding?"

The first one said, "I don't know." He looked at me with a lot of mistrust. "You don't know what that is?"

I just shrugged, and shook my head. I kept looking back and forth, from the card to their faces to the card to their faces. I was kind of almost-grinning, because I figured it was some kind of a gag or something. Every once in a while one of Uncle Al's associates thinks it's funny to pull a gag on me, on the useless bum of a nephew. It's what I have to put up with for the soft berth.

The first one shook his head after a minute and said, "He don't know, he honest to Christ don't know."

"What a nephew," said the second one. "Nephew, you are the biggest nephew that ever lived. You're all the nephews in the world rolled into one, you know that?"

"What's the joke?" I said. "I give up, what's the joke?"

"Joke," said the second one. He said it flat, like it was too incredible to believe.

The first one tapped the card. He had thick fingers and dirty fingernails. He said, "That's the spot, nephew, get me? That's the spot, the black spot, and you're on it."

The second one said, "He still don't get it. Would you believe it, he still don't get it."

"He will," said the first one. His right hand reached in fast inside his coat and came out with a gun, a huge black thick right-angled glittering gun with a hole full of poison in the end of it and the hole pointed straight at me.

I said, "Hey!" I threw my hands up in front of my chest, or something like that. And I still had in the back of my mind that this was a gag, they were trying to scare the nephew. "Hey!" I said, therefore. "You want to hurt somebody?"

"Open the cash register," said the first one, still

pointing the gun at me. "The bit is, this has to look like robbery, you know? Do you know what I mean, nephew?"

"He don't," said the second one. "He don't know a thing."

"That's right," I said, giving them a chance to tell me what it was all about. "I don't know a thing."

"The spot means you're done," said the first one. "You're all through. Go on over there and open that cash register."

"Hurry, hurry," said the second one. "Nephews should do like they're told."

I still didn't get it. But on the other hand maybe the best thing was play along with them, and sooner or later they'd get tired of kidding around and they'd tell me what this was all about. So I went over and hit the No Sale key and the register drawer popped open and I said, "There. It's open."

"Pull the bills out," the first one said. He was still holding that gun. "Put them on the bar there."

There weren't very many bills. The Rockaway Grill barely makes enough a week to pay my salary, never mind upkeep and stock and six per cent profit and all that. But it's all right, nobody wants the Rockaway Grill to make any money, don't ask me why. I asked my Uncle Al three, four times, and the first couple times he tried to explain it, something about taxes, on the books the Rockaway Grill makes a profit that is actually money the organization made somewhere else, something like that, but every time my Uncle Al explains something to me it winds up he's hitting himself on the forehead with the heel of his right hand so I don't ask him any more.

Anyway, there was just this little stack of bills, most of them ones, and I put them on the bar, and the second one came over and took them and stuffed them away in his topcoat pocket.

I said, "Hey, wait a second. That isn't funny."

"That's right," said the first one. He looked mean, and he was still aiming the gun at me.

For the first time I began to take it serious. I said, "You aren't going to *kill* me."

"You got it," said the other one.

"And here it comes," said the first one, and Patrolman Ziccatta, the cop on the beat, came in saying, "Hey, Charlie. You're open late."

So what should I of done? Should I of said, "Patrolman Ziccatta, these two men just come here to rob and murder me, and that one there has my night's proceeds in his topcoat pocket and that other one there just stuck a big mean-looking gun quick back in his topcoat pocket when you came in," is that what I should of said? You think so? These associates of my Uncle Al, I should finger them to the police, never mind what for? You think so?

That just shows you don't know the situation.

My Uncle Al would *kill* me, I blew the whistle on two of his associates like that. I mean with no fooling around, *bam!*

I mean, it's all well and good with Patrolman Ziccatta right there and everything for the moment, but what about tomorrow? What about next week? How do I live? Where do I live? What do I do with myself?

More important, what does Uncle Al do with me?

These two guys, now, they weren't kidding, they'd come here to kill me, I finally got that through my head, but let's sit down and think about this thing a minute. There's no reason why the organization should want me killed, so it's got to be somebody made a mistake somewhere, right? Now, with somebody makes a mistake what you do is you don't throw the baby out with the bath water, what you do is you see can you rectify the mistake. Right?

So what I had to do was I had to stay alive some way or another until I could get to a telephone and call my Uncle Al—which he would really love, two-thirty in the morning and everything, but this time I would say I got a legitimate excuse, I mean after all—and then I could tell my Uncle Al what was up and he could maybe rectify the mistake.

So I didn't say anything to Patrolman Ziccatta except, "Just closing up now, just this minute." Then I looked at the two mean types and I said, "Sorry, gents, you got to go now."

They looked from me to the patrolman, and then they looked at each other, and I could see everything they were thinking. They were supposed to kill me, but they couldn't kill me right this minute unless they killed Patrolman Ziccatta too, and killing a uniformed policeman in the performance of his duty is a very dangerous thing to do and maybe going too far just as a sidelight in the rubbing out of a nephew, so maybe for the moment they should call it off. Maybe for the moment they should go outside, and wait for Patrolman Ziccatta to go away, and then they could come back and kill the nephew in the privacy of his own home.

I saw this going through their heads and running back and forth between their eyes, and then the first one said, "Okay, barkeep. See you later."

"Yeah, barkeep," said the second one. "See you later."

They went on out, and Patrolman Ziccatta came over and leaned on the bar and said, "There's quite a wind blowing up out there."

Now, it was only the eleventh of September, and it might have been breezy outside but it wasn't exactly the North Pole, but I knew what Patrolman Ziccatta really meant and what I was supposed to do about it, so I said, "Let me give you something to warm your bones."

"Well, thanks, Charlie," he said. He always acted surprised, and we ran through this same business almost every night.

I got a four-ounce glass from under the bar, and filled it about two-thirds with bar bourbon, and slid it over in front of the patrolman. He kind of slouched against the bar, and turned his back to the big plate-glass window that faced the street, and he held the glass in close against his chest so it couldn't be seen from outside, and he took quick nips from it, one right after the other. Nip. Nip. Nip. Like that.

Past him, I could see those two guys across the street, standing in front of the men's clothing store over there and talking together like they were any two guys you might see anywhere.

I said, "I'll be right back."

"I'll hold the fort, Charlie," he said, and went nip, nip, nip.

I walked on down to the end of the bar, and raised the flap and went through, and past the jukebox and the shuffleboard bowling machine game and the restroom doors, and through the rear door with NO ADMITTANCE printed on it, and into the back room, piled high with beer and whiskey cases. One thing I always had, I always had a good inventory.

I turned on the light back there and checked the back door that the two locks and the bar were all secure, and checked the double locks on the three windows, and everything was okay. I left the light on and went back up front and Patrolman Ziccatta was standing by the front door. "You left your cash register open, Charlie," he said, and pointed his nightstick at it.

"Oh, yeah," I said. "Thanks a lot."

"One of these days, you'll get yourself robbed here," he said. "Well, good night, Charlie."

"Good night," I said.

He went out and I locked the door right after him. Those two guys were still across the street. Patrolman Ziccatta strolled away down the sidewalk, practicing with his nightstick. He was getting so he could twirl it pretty good now, didn't drop it very much at all any more.

I turned off the neon beer signs in the window, and walked down the long narrow room to the back again, and switched off the indirect lighting there, so now only the backbar displays were still lit and those were left on all night. I looked down the long dim length past the plate-glass window and across the street, and saw the two of them step down off the curb and start this way. There wasn't any traffic out there, there wasn't anybody but those two guys.

I went into the back room, where the light was already on, and up the creaking stairs to the second floor. I could actually hear my heart. In my ears, I could hear it.

Up on the second floor I had this really very nice little three-room apartment, with a living room in front and a kitchen in back and a bedroom in the middle. The only way up there was the staircase from the storeroom downstairs to the kitchen upstairs, and then you had to walk through the bedroom to get to the living room, all of which didn't help any romantic mood any time I took a girl up there, but I didn't get to take too many girls up there anyway so it didn't make that much difference. The only thing, it was a pretty nice place, and convenient, but no playboy penthouse.

I went up there now and turned on the kitchen light before I clicked the switch at the head of the stairs that turned off the light down in the storeroom. I shut the door at the head of the stairs and turned the key in the lock and left the key in there to delay them if they figured to pick the lock. Except why should they pick the lock when they could just shoot it off?

Well. I hurried through to the living room, where the phone was. The whole place was its usual mess—the bed unmade, magazines all over the floor, the door standing open and ugly between the bedroom and the bathroom, underwear scattered around—the whole usual mess I was always telling myself I would clean up the next chance I got and never did. But this time, of course, I never even noticed the mess or thought about it or anything. I just hurried into the living room, turning on every light I came to, and quick called my Uncle Al at his apartment on East 65th Street in Manhattan.

Seven rings it took; I counted them. I knew my Uncle Al would be boiling, this hour of night, but even he would have to admit this call had a reason.

Finally he answered. I recognized his voice, sleepy and irritable. ''Lo? What? Who the hell?''

''Uncle Al,'' I said. ''It's me, Charlie.''

All at once he was wide awake, and very formal. ''Albert Gatling is not in,'' he said.

I said, ''Uncle Al? Didn't you hear me? It's me, your nephew, Charlie Poole.''

''Albert Gatling is not in,'' he said. ''He's out of town.''

What was going on? I said, ''What are you talking about? I recognize your voice, you're Uncle Al.''

"Albert Gatling," he said, "is in Florida. He'll be there at least a week. This is the butler talking."

"Let me talk to Aunt Florence," I said. I didn't know what Uncle Al was up to, but Aunt Florence would snap him out of it. Aunt Florence is my Uncle Al's wife, and my mother's sister. Uncle Al is actually only my uncle by marriage.

"Albert *and* Florence Gatling," he said, "are both in Florida."

"Uncle Al," I said, and he hung up.

That is, I thought he'd hung up. But then when I tried to call him back, there wasn't any dial tone or anything, no sound at all in the telephone. I knew what that meant, it meant those guys had cut the wires outside so I couldn't phone for help.

What was I going to do? I had these wild visions of getting the frying pan from the kitchen, and hiding behind the door at the head of the stairs, and when they came in I'd let them have it, *bonk! bonk!* But that was no good. Even if I wasn't afraid to do something like that, and believe me I was far too afraid to hide behind the door at the head of the stairs even if I had a machine gun, but even if I wasn't afraid, that was no good. Because all this was a simple mistake, and once it was all straightened out everything would be okay again, same as before. Except if I were to do something to one of those guys, like kill him or hurt him bad so he went to the hospital or something like that. I mean, even though it would be self-defense and the result of a mix-up that wasn't my fault at all, I would still be in trouble with the organization.

The way it worked out, they could shoot at me or whatever, but I didn't dare do a thing to them. Not a thing. Not if I wanted to go on living the same old life like always.

On the other hand, I didn't dare just sit here, not if I wanted to go on living period.

So what to do?

This question was given a sudden sense of urgency because of the crash from downstairs that meant they'd just come in the back door. Two, three minutes, moving along cautiously like they naturally would, and they'd be up here, right up here in front of me. And if Patrolman Ziccatta should all of a sudden walk into my living room after two-thirty in the morning, it would be the very first time.

What I had to do, it was clear as could be, what I had to do was get out of here. What I had to do was get to Manhattan, and to my Uncle Al's apartment, and find out what was going on, and make him help me correct this no doubt honest mistake before I turned out mistakenly killed.

But there was only one way down from here, and that was the staircase, and the odds were very heavy that those two guys were already occupying the staircase, coming *up*.

I looked around the messy living room, feeling frantic, wishing there was a dumbwaiter so I could go down to the basement, or a chimney so I could go up to the roof, or anything at all so I could get the dickens out of here.

Well, of course there was something.

The window.

I looked at it. Was it possible? Was there any chance at all I could go out that window and survive?

Well, on the other hand, there was no chance at all I could stay inside and survive, so that pretty well decided the issue.

I jumped to my feet and ran over to the bedroom doorway and shut the door. There was no key in the keyhole, but the sofa was right next to the door, and I pushed it over in the way in hopes it would anyway slow them down a minute. Then I turned the lights out and went to the front window.

Outside, there was nothing but the dark and windswept street. A page of the *Daily News* blew by. I opened the window and felt the cold breeze and realized I was just in my white shirt and apron, and my jackets were all hanging in the bedroom closet.

Well, it was too late to go back for them. I took my apron off and sat on the window sill, and as I lifted my legs over I heard the door at the head of the stairs crash open.

There was a kind of a ledge under the window a couple of feet, with metal letters along it that said ROCKAWAY GRILL. I stepped over the W and on the other side there were only a couple of inches to spare. I bent down and grabbed the letters and brought my other foot over, and AWAY gave away, and down I went.

It was only about a ten-foot drop. I landed on hands and knees, and AWAY went clattering away, and just a second or two later so did I.

★ I suppose it would be fair to say that all my life I've been a bum. First, when I was a kid growing up, I was a bum on my mother. Now, these last few years I've been a bum on my Uncle Al.

It was just my mother and me while I was growing up. My mother worked for the telephone company, it used to be sometimes it was her voice on some of those recorded announcements all about how you just dialed a particularly stupid number, and she made pretty good money, the telephone company isn't all that bad to work for. Later on she wanted me to go to work for the company too, but somehow or other I just never felt right about it. I had this feeling, I guess, I'd wind up being thrown out on my ear, and it would be a bad reflection on my mother and all, still working there.

Anyway, the jobs I did get, after I got out of high school and the Army wouldn't take me because of this something or other in my inner ear which I didn't know anything about before then and which to this day has never once bothered me, the jobs I did get I never lasted with, not one of them. I'd work a month or two, and then I'd loaf around the house a month or two. And my mother, she was in the habit of supporting me anyway, she'd done it all my life, so she never complained about me being home and not working or making any money. She'd been my sole support because my father disappeared the day after my mother found out she was pregnant with me, and my father has not been heard of from that day to this, and it is my mother's theory that he's in jail or worse.

In any case, it got so I was twenty years of age, twenty-one, twenty-two, and I was still a bum, loafing around the house all the time, reading science-fiction magazines, not settling down or accepting my responsibilities or doing any of those things my Uncle Al likes to talk about as being the attributes of maturity, and I'd had eleven different jobs in three years, and the longest I'd stayed at any of those jobs was nine weeks. My mother got me a couple of jobs, and Uncle Al got me a few more, and the rest I got through the *New York Times*.

And then one day Uncle Al came around and he said he'd finally found the job that was perfect for me, it was the job I'd been born for, and it turned out to be running the Rockaway Grill out in Canarsie, which is a section way out at the end of Brooklyn that vaudeville comedians used to make fun of all the time. New Jersey and Canarsie, those were the two places vaudeville comedians used to make jokes about. Anyway, this job was I was to run the bar all by myself. I could open at any time before four o'clock in the afternoon, and close at any time after midnight, the actual hours were up to me. I would work a seven-day week, but I'd get paid a hundred and twenty dollars a week and I'd get this three-room apartment to myself upstairs.

At first I didn't think it was a good idea, because I thought my mother wouldn't want me to move out of our apartment, she'd get lonely or something. But she took to the idea right away, seemed almost too pleased by it, and that's how I wound up running this bar in Canarsie.

It wasn't much work to run. No one ever checked up on me to see did I open before four o'clock or did I dip into the cash register from time to time. Then, there were already a few longer-established bars in the immediate neighborhood that took most of the local clientele, so I never did have a crowd in there, not even on weekends. I had a few regulars, and now and then a transient or two, and that was it. The bar lost money and nobody cared. I ran it loose and sloppy and nobody cared. My Uncle Al was right; it was the job I was born for.

Of course, there was the other little part of it. Every once in a while some friend of Uncle Al's from the organization would come around and give me a package or an envelope or some such thing, and I was supposed to put it in the safe under the bar until someone would come in and say such and such a code phrase, like in spy movies, and then I'd hand over the package or whatever it was. I got something like this to do once or twice a month, and always checked with Uncle Al on it to be sure there wasn't any problem, and all in all it wasn't exactly what you'd call hard work.

Then, too, sometimes I closed the bar on a Monday or a Tuesday night, and went to a movie or something like that. I still knew a couple girls I could ask out from time to time, girls I'd known since high school. Generally speaking it was a pretty comfortable life. All I had to do was just drift along.

Until those two guys came in and showed me the black spot. And all at once my drifting days were done.

★ The way in and out of Canarsie, if you don't have a car, is by subway, which is called the Canarsie Line, and which you get at the end of the line on Rockaway Parkway by Glenwood Road, about eight blocks from the Rockaway Grill. I ran that eight blocks till I got a stitch in my side, and then I kept running even with the stitch because I'd rather have a stitch in my side than a bullet in my head any day. I didn't know how close those two guys were, or even if they were running after me; I was too busy to look.

I got to the station and it took forever to find change in my pockets and buy a token and run out on the platform. A lit sign said NEXT TRAIN and pointed an arrow at the only train there, on the right side of the platform. All the doors were open. I ran aboard, and then ran from car to car till I found one with four people already in it, and there I collapsed into a seat and panted and held my side where the stitch was now nine.

In one way I was lucky. Less than a minute after I ran aboard, the doors slid shut and the train started for Manhattan.

Making a getaway by subway is not good for the nerves. The train just barely gets rolling pretty good when it slows down again, and stops, and the doors slide open in a very ominous way with nobody near them. Two killers do not get aboard, and the doors close, and the train starts forward, only to go through the whole thing again two or three minutes later.

There are twenty-one stops between Rockaway Parkway and Union Square on the Canarsie Line, in case you want to know.

I couldn't really believe, when I left the train at Union Square, that I'd escaped from them. Even though I hadn't seen them yet, I was sure they were still on my tail. Scurrying, looking over my shoulder, I ran along the deserted passageways that led me to the Lexington Avenue Line, and stood on the platform there behind a soft-drink machine, waiting.

It was ten minutes before a local came in, and in the meantime every sound of footsteps on the concrete platform took another year or so off my life. But the local finally did show up, and I leaped from cover behind the soft-drink machine, ran low and zigzag across the platform the way they do in war movies, and barreled aboard the train like a one-man rush hour.

The Lexington Avenue local makes seven stops between Union Square and East 68th Street. I was seeing a lot of subway platforms.

I never know which way is which when I come up out of the subway in Manhattan. I was at 68th and Lex, and I wanted to be at 65th and Fifth, which meant south and west, but I had no idea which way was south. I finally took a chance on a direction that looked right, walked up to 69th Street, read the street sign there, and walked back again.

I told myself this was actually just as well; if anyone was tailing me, doubling back this way would confuse them and help me spot them. But of course I didn't spot anyone tailing me, and didn't really think I would.

The walk to Uncle Al's apartment building was long and dark and scantily populated. A few solitary hunched walkers passed me, our separate fears mingling for just a second as we went by, but nothing happened, and I got to Uncle Al's building at last, a tall and white and narrow building with a brightly lit little entranceway. I went in there, and pushed the button beside the name A. *Gatling*.

There was no answer. For a long while there was no answer, and then I pushed the button again, and then there was no answer some more.

I stood there shifting from foot to foot. Where was he, why didn't he answer? Could it be he really *was* in Miami?

No. He suspected it was me at the door, that's all. He didn't want to answer because he figured it was probably me.

I pushed the button again, and just left my finger on it, and stood there that way. I leaned on the button, and glanced out at the street, and a long black car was pulling to a stop out front. They got out of it, those two guys. They looked up at me, and then they looked at each other, and they came walking toward me.

I stopped pushing Uncle Al's button, and pushed all the other buttons instead. I stood there like the cashier at a supermarket cash register, pushing buttons. The two guys came across the sidewalk and up the steps. They were looking at me with no expression on their faces, and they were taking their time. I guess they figured they had me cornered. That's the way I figured, too.

But I kept pushing buttons all the same. The round grille beside the row of buttons began shouting in a variety of sleepy angry voices, but I didn't answer. I just kept pushing buttons.

One of the two guys looked at me through the glass, and reached for the knob of the outer door, and at last the buzzing sounded I'd been waiting for. I pushed open the inner door, slammed it behind me again, and for just a second I was safe.

But what I could do they could do. I ran across the little lobby and pulled open the elevator door and pushed yet another button; this one numbered 3, for the floor my Uncle Al's apartment was on.

A very expensive building, this, seven stories high, with only two apartments on each floor. The elevator moved much faster than they do in buildings on the West Side. When it stopped, I pushed the 7 button and got out. The elevator went on up to the seventh floor, which would delay those two guys and might even fake them out.

Two white doors in the cream wall faced me across the white rug. The one on the right, with the brass B on it, belonged to my Uncle Al. I went over and knocked on it.

Because I didn't expect an answer right away, I just kept on knocking. I even kicked the door once or twice, making black marks on the white, which couldn't be helped.

Behind me, with a whirring sound, the elevator went by on its way back to the first floor.

Why didn't they take the stairs, why wait for the elevator? I tried to figure it out, while I kept knocking and kicking at Uncle Al's door, and then I realized what had happened. The city fire laws, see, make apartment houses have staircases even when they have elevators, but most expensive East Side apartment houses are as embarrassed about staircases as if they had to have outhouses in addition to the indoor plumbing, so they put the staircases in and then put walls around them and blank doors leading to them and they hope nobody will ever notice them. Which nobody ever does.

In a minute they'd be coming up, via elevator. Would they stop at the third floor, or would they go on to seven? Did they know my Uncle Al lived here? They had to, there was no other reason for them to come here. They hadn't followed me, I was sure of that. While I'd taken my route here by subway, they'd taken their route by car.

So they'd stop here, just to be sure, on the third floor.

Whirr, they were coming up.

I've been coming to Uncle Al's apartment since I was a kid, and kids always know geography better than adults. Kids know apartments better, buildings better, neighborhoods better. So I knew the door to the right of the elevator led to the staircase. I gave off kicking and knocking, and went through that door, and fixed a matchbook so the door didn't close all the way. Through the narrow vertical slit, I could see Uncle Al's door.

I'd been right; they got off the elevator at the third

floor. Peeking one-eyed through the crack, I could see their backs, broad and black-coated. They didn't just stand, they hulked.

They walked across the white carpet without any noise, and knocked on Uncle Al's door. It was a special code-type knock, and anyone could tell that; one, and then three, and then one.

The door opened right away, and Uncle Al stuck his head out and said, "You got him?"

Uncle Al is a big hefty guy, about two-thirds bone and muscle, about one-third spaghetti. He has black hair so thick and shiny most people think he's wearing a toupee, and his face is a normal collection of mouth, eyes, eyebrows, cheeks, chin and ears positioned around a nose the size and shape of the bald eagle's beak on the tail of a twenty-five-cent cigar. In the summer, when he pitches softball in his undershirt at clambakes, you can see he has black hair growing all over his chunky arms and chunky shoulders and chunky chest. I don't know about his chunky stomach, but I suppose he has black hair growing all over that, too. When he sits in an overstuffed armchair and crosses his legs, another hairy region pops into view between the top of his black sock and the cuff of his black trousers.

Normally, Uncle Al has a voice to go with all this chunkiness and hair, a bass voice that makes him a natural for the barbershop quartets at the aforesaid clambakes, but right now, as he said, "You got him?" that voice had gone up maybe two octaves. It was the first time I'd ever seen or heard my Uncle Al scared.

One of the two guys said, "Not yet. Is he in there?"

Uncle Al said, "Are you kidding?"

The second one said, "You wouldn't cover up for him, would you? Agricola wouldn't like that."

"I'm keepin' out of it," my Uncle Al said. "I want no part of it, no part of it." All that showed of him in the hallway was his head, looking scared.

Standing there in the yellow stairwell, my feet on concrete and my forehead against the edge of the door and my eye blinking at the narrow vertical strip of corridor, I began at last to understand a couple of things. Way back in Canarsie, when those guys out there had first come after me, my immediate reaction had been to call Uncle Al, the only one I personally knew in the organization. I'd been too scared and excited myself to understand the meaning of his response on the phone; at the time, it had only meant to me that Uncle Al was being difficult to talk to. And the same again, when I'd been kicking futilely at the door. My relationship with Uncle Al has always involved a degree of difficulty in communication for both of us, so there was no reason this time should be any exception.

But now, seeing his face hanging disembodied in the hallway, hearing his voice, I understood I'd made this trip for nothing. Uncle Al wouldn't help me because he couldn't help me. He was too scared.

Out there in the corridor, while I was making my discouraging discoveries, they were still talking. The first one was saying, "He come up here." Like it was an indictment of Uncle Al, an open-and-shut case.

"Would I cross Agricola?" my Uncle Al asked them. He pronounced it A-gric'-o-la. "Am I a dumbhead?" he asked them.

That was one of his favorite expressions. When he was young he used to drive a cab, and when he talks about it these days he says, "Drive a cab all my life? Am I a dumbhead?" The answer is supposed to be no.

The first one, meanwhile, was repeating, "He come up here. And he didn't go back down."

Uncle Al said, "What about the roof?"

They both shook their heads. "It don't figure," the first one said. "He come here looking for you."

"Invite us in," said the second one.

Uncle Al said, "Listen, I got trouble enough. The wife don't know nothing about this, you follow me? The brat's her sister's kid, you know what I mean? How do I explain you two, this time of night?"

"We want the kid," said the second one.

The first one, still working the same idea, said, "He come up here."

Uncle Al said, "Maybe he went back down."

"How?" said the second one. "We took the elevator ourselves. There it is." He half-turned, and pointed at it.

Uncle Al said, "The stairs, maybe he took the stairs."

"What stairs?" They both said it, while I was thinking to myself that I understood about how he couldn't help *me* but it struck me he was going too far when he started helping *them*.

Uncle Al brought an arm out into the corridor to go with his head. He pointed the arm right at me, and said, "Those stairs there."

They turned and looked in my direction, and looked at each other, and came forward.

That was all. Down the stairs I went, two and three at a time. I had to sacrifice either speed or silence, and I opted for speed. So I guess they could hear me going just as plain as I could hear them coming.

Doors, nothing but doors. I burst out the groundfloor door into the foyer, out the foyer door into the entranceway, out the entranceway door into the street. Their long black car was still double-parked out front, with nobody in it. I turned left, toward Central Park, and ran.

★ When I was sure they'd given up and gone away, I crawled out from under the bush again and headed across the park toward the West Side.

Now that the heat of the chase was gone, at least for a while, I was beginning to freeze. It was now about quarter to four, Wednesday morning, the twelfth of September. I don't know exactly what the temperature was, but it was too low to be out walking around Central Park in just shirt sleeves. Walking briskly westward, I flapped my arms around like a drunk arguing with himself, while I pondered a future that now appeared to be as short as it was uncertain.

Where could I go now, what could I do? I'd escaped the killers for the moment, but I knew enough about the organization from newspapers and television to know I wasn't free of them for good. They wouldn't give up, no matter how far or how fast I ran. I was a marked man; the tentacles of the organization would reach out to deal me swift vengeance wherever I might try to hide.

My only goal had been Uncle Al. From him I had expected sanctuary, in him an ally, through him an explanation of why I'd been put on the spot. It still had to be a mistake, some sort of error; all I had to do was find the error and rectify it.

But now what? I was safe for the moment, but that was all. I had no coat, not much money, and now that the excitement was temporarily over I could realize I was exhausted. I should have been asleep hours ago.

Walking across the park, flapping my arms and jumping up and down and running in little circles to keep warm, I tried to figure out what to do next. More than anything, I needed some place to sleep, some place to get warm in, some place where I'd be safe.

What about my mother's apartment? There were even a couple of my old high school jackets there. I could sleep, get warm, eat something, and decide tomorrow what had to be done.

But that wasn't any good. Hadn't those two killers come direct to Uncle Al's? Didn't that mean they knew about me, knew who I'd go to, where I'd run next? They were probably on watch at my mother's place this very minute, waiting for me to show up.

Somewhere else, then, somewhere else. Like where?

I hadn't thought of anywhere yet by the time I reached Central Park West. I came out of the park between 62nd and 63rd streets, stood on the sidewalk there a minute, and then crossed CPW and walked down 62nd Street. Not that I had any destination in mind, it was just too cold to stand still.

Somewhere, somewhere. Somebody, in fact. There had to be somebody I knew, somebody who would take me in for what was left of the night.

Then I remembered Artie Dexter. I hadn't seen Artie for seven or eight months, since the last time he'd dropped around the Rock Grill. Artie and I went to high school together, which is when he started playing conga drum in rhythm groups weekends. Later on he spread out to guitar and folk songs, and also sold marijuana and different kinds of pills sometimes, or at least that's the impression he'd give. I don't know how much was true and how much was just showing off. I know sometimes he'd seem to have a lot of money, and other times he'd be completely broke. Like the last time he came out to see me in Canarsie he borrowed ten bucks from me. That's thirty-five he owes me. I know he's good for it.

My relationship with Artie is kind of an odd one. He was a colorful character back in high school, and colorful characters always have these hangers-on that cluster around them. I was one of the hangers-on, except for some reason Artie always liked me, so we were closer than your normal run of hero and hanger-on. After high school we still kept it touch, very occasionally, mostly with Artie showing up all of a sudden, inviting me to a party or stopping out at the bar or something like that. I suppose we could have been real good friends if I could have gotten over feeling like a hanger-on, but I never could.

Of all the people I knew, which wasn't very many when you got right down to it, the one I figured I could most likely barge in on at four o'clock on a Wednesday morning was Artie Dexter. Nodding, flapping my arms, clicking my heels together, I moved westward across 62nd Street with a sudden new surge of purpose.

Artie lives in the Village, of course. I walked over to Broadway now, and turned left, and walked down to Columbus Circle, having taken the long way around to get there, and went down into the subway to take the first IND train that came along. The Sixth Avenue and Eighth Avenue trains separate just south of Columbus Circle, but they come back together again down at West Fourth Street and that was the stop I wanted.

It was an A train came in first, the one Billy Strayhorn wants everybody to take to Harlem. I took it the other way. The car already had about ten people in it, sour-faced guys in work clothes and two youngish bums sleeping with their mouths open.

I didn't mind the stops (six of them) so much this time. I felt reasonably safe, for the time being.

Authors who come to New York from Majorca once every ten years to buy a new bathing suit always put down in their books that the big city never sleeps, but that's what they know. New York sleeps, all right, from about four-thirty in the morning till about quarter after five. That's maybe only forty-five minutes, not very long to be asleep, but it can seem like forever if you're one of the few people awake during it. And it's most noticeable in places like Times Square, that are so fully awake the rest of the day. Sixth Avenue is like that, right around 8th Street, at Village Square. The movies and bars are closed, the luncheonettes are closed, everything is closed. There's no traffic, no pedestrians, and the streets westward radiating away like a fan are all narrow and dark and empty.

I hurried through this empty space, over the wide bumpy blacktop of Sixth Avenue and down a street to take me to Sheridan Square. Everything seemed so small, so narrow, it was like walking on an old movie set.

Artie Dexter lives on Perry Street, which I reached via Sheridan Square and Grove Street and a couple other streets. I don't know half the street names in the Village and I don't believe anybody else does either. I do know the two really great intersections in the Village, because Artie told me about them. One of them is where West Tenth Street crosses West Fourth Street, which is enough right away to make a tourist turn around and go back uptown where he belongs, and the other, which I passed on my way to Sheridan Square, is the intersection of Waverly Place and Waverly Place. You don't have to believe me if you don't want, but it's true.

Anyway, hurrying through these empty artificial streets, with cold breezes ruffling my shirt sleeves, I wondered what Artie would think of me waking him up in the middle of the night like this.

I needn't have wondered. Half a block from his place I began to hear the noise, the singing and shouting and music. It was either a party or a presidential convention. I moved closer, jazz and hilarity wafting out onto the night air as though New York hadn't gone to sleep after all but had called in all its forces into this one tiny corner of itself to keep the old pulse going till daylight. I looked up, and saw the brightly lighted windows, and it looked as though that was Artie's apartment.

It was. When I rang the bell downstairs, the buzzer sounded almost immediately. I pushed the door open and went upstairs to the second floor.

Party noises filled the hallway, so loud it seemed as though the partygoers must be here, in the narrow hall, all around me, invisible. I walked to the end of it and knocked on the door, but that was ridiculous. No one could hear knocking, not in there. I pushed the door open and went in.

Artie has two and a half rooms. The half is a wide closet in the living room, full of kitchen appliances. The bathroom, which doesn't count in the "two and a half" description, is bigger than the kitchen, very, very long, with a bathtub on a raised tile platform, and with doors leading both into the bedroom and the living room.

The living room is furnished mostly in shelving, rickety shelving sagging under the weight of LP records.

There's a fireplace, with shelving over it and on both sides of it. There are two windows overlooking Perry Street, with shelving between them and under them and beyond them, and with great big speaker cabinets on top of them. Shelving flanks the hall door, the bedroom door, the bathroom door, the kitchen-closet doors. Not all of this shelving bears LPs; there are a few books, and some knickknacks and whatnots, and hi-fi components, all mixed in here and there.

With shelving on all the wall space, the furniture—a spavined sofa and a few miserable mismatched chairs and tables—is all clustered in the middle of the room, on and around an old green and yellow fiber porch carpet. The speaker systems scattered around the room all bisect amid this furniture.

At the moment, fifteen or twenty people filled the doughnut-shaped area between the furniture and the shelves, all holding drinks and all holding forth. I didn't see anybody listening. I didn't see anybody sitting either.

Artie himself suddenly popped up in front of me. He's half a foot shorter than me, about five four, and since he had his teeth capped he smiles all the time, brilliantly. He never looks at any one spot for more than a tenth of a second, glances always darting here and there, so that sometimes he looks as though he's doing a trick or maybe exercising the eye muscles. He bounces a lot, being musical, and keeps jabbing around with his hands.

"Baby!" he said, looking quick at my right shoulder, my left ear, my widow's peak, my right elbow, my left nostril, and the stain on my collar. He jabbed his hands around. "Glad you could make it!"

"I need a place to sleep," I shouted.

"Anything, baby!" he shouted back. He looked at nine

parts of me, said, "Make yourself at home!" and disappeared.

Fine. It was almost four-thirty in the morning by now, I was too tired to stand up straight. I moved through the people, most of whom gave me half a sentence or so on the way by, and opened the bedroom door. It was dark in there, which seemed like a good idea. I closed the door, but didn't turn the light on, and groped my way to the bed.

But there were people in it, I'm not sure how many. A voice growled, "Watch it, you."

"Sorry," I said. There was a rug on the floor. I lay down on it and closed my eyes. The party noises went away.

★ The funny thing is, I knew I was dreaming, but I didn't know *what* I was dreaming. That was the damnedest dream ever; to be dreaming, and know you're dreaming, and know it's a bad dream, a terrifying dream, and not to know what the hell the dream's all about.

I guess that was the most frightening part of it. Terror of the unknown and all. I wanted so hard to know what I was dreaming about that I popped myself out of sleep like a cork out of a champagne bottle.

I was lying on a floor, in a swatch of sunlight.

This was wrong. My bedroom windows face north; I get an acute angle of sunlight, a narrow beam, only at the very peak of summer. Besides, in my bedroom I sleep in bed, not on the floor. This was very wrong.

The body wakes up first, and then the mind. I opened my eyes, and moved my arms, and remembered everything.

I sat bolt upright. My back twinged as though someone had just yanked my spine out. I said, ''Ngahh,'' and lay down again. Sleeping on the floor isn't a good idea at the best of times.

I got up more slowly on the second try, and this time made it all the way to my feet. I stood there, bent forward a little bit, and surveyed the room.

There was still someone in the bed, but now it was Artie and he was alone. On every flat surface in the room—dresser, night tables, straight chairs—there were half-empty glasses. The closet door was open, and clothing was lying in a heap on the floor in front of it.

There was the smell of coffee in the air. I followed it from the bedroom, and at the kitchen-closet I found a sloe-eyed raven-tressed beauty in dungarees and black turtleneck sweater, scrambling eggs. She was barefoot, and very short, and she had that Chinese-French-Negro look that Jewish girls get when they go to the High School of Music and Art.

She was the first to speak. ''You were asleep on the floor,'' she said. Matter-of-fact, the way you'd comment on the weather.

''I guess I was,'' I said. My back hurt, my hands were greasy-feeling, my mouth was furry, and I remembered perfectly why I wasn't in my own safe apartment above the Rock Grill. I said, ''Could I have some coffee?''

She pointed at the pot with a fork that dripped scrambled egg. ''Help yourself. You're hung over, huh?''

"No," I said. "I didn't drink last night. What time is it?"

"Little after two."

"In the afternoon?"

She looked at me. "Sure in the afternoon," she said. She went back to stirring the eggs. "Must have been some party," she said.

"You weren't here?" I was opening cupboard doors, looking for a cup.

"They're all in the sink," she said. "No, I'm the morning after girl."

"Oh," I said.

It was close quarters there, her at the stove and me at the sink. I picked a cup out of the pile of dishes in the sink, washed it as best I could, and poured coffee in it.

She said, "I never saw you around before."

"Oh," I said. "Well, I don't get up here very much."

"Up here from where?"

"Canarsie," I said.

She made a face like I'd just told a very corny joke. "Come on," she said.

"No, it's true."

She already had a plate for herself. She scraped the eggs into it and put the pan back on the stove. "You want eggs, you got to make them yourself," she said. Not being nasty about it, just letting me know.

"No, that's all right," I said. "Coffee's enough for me."

She carried her eggs and coffee over to the cluster of furniture in the middle of the room and sat down. Artie had no kitchen table. I followed her and sat down facing her and sipped at my coffee, which was still too hot to drink. She didn't pay any attention to me, but just shoveled scrambled egg in the way you might shovel coal into a furnace, just scoop, scoop, scoop. Like Patrolman Ziccatta and his nip, nip, nip. Steady, machine-like.

I said, "When do you figure Artie'll get up?"

"When I'm done breakfast," she said. "You don't have to stick around."

"Oh, but I do," I said. "I have to talk to Artie."

Now she did look at me. "What about?"

"A problem," I told her. "A jam I'm in."

"What's Artie supposed to do about it?"

"I don't know," I said, which was the truth. There just wasn't anyone else I could think of to talk to.

"If it's money," she said, "he's broke. Believe me."

"It isn't money," I told her. "I need his advice is all."

She looked at me over the vanishing eggs and went scoop, scoop, scoop. Then she paused a second and said, "What is it, you need an abortionist?"

"Oh, no," I said. "Nothing like that."

She said, "If it isn't money and it isn't sex, then I don't know. You aren't a junky, are you?"

"Me? No, not me." The idea was as surprising as the idea that two professional killers might have been sent out to practice their profession on me. Me a junky? Me a threat to the organization?

"I didn't think so," she said. "You look too healthy." It was a comment that could almost have been an insult, delivered matter-of-fact between mouthfuls of scrambled egg.

"It's just some trouble I've got," I said. I drank some of the coffee, and walked around the room a little. I'd slept in all my clothes, and I had that swollen puffy moist feeling you get when you've slept in all your clothes. I felt as though I'd just slept my way through a cross-country bus ride. "I'm sorry if I'm being mysterious," I said. "But I don't think I ought to talk about it too much."

She shrugged, finished the eggs, and got to her feet. "I don't care," she said.

As she went over to dump the plate in the sink, I remembered something I *could* tell her. "My name's Charlie," I told her. "Charlie Poole."

"Hi," she said, standing at the sink, her back to me. She didn't offer me her name. "You want to wake Artie now?" she asked me.

"Is it okay?"

"If you don't," she said, "I do."

"Oh. Okay."

"Don't take too long," she said.

"Okay."

I went back into the bedroom, carrying the coffee cup, still half full. Artie was lying on his stomach, arms and legs spread out in a pale twisted swastika. He looked like he was sleeping five miles down.

I said, "Artie? Hey, Artie."

Surprise. He opened his eyes right away, flipped over on his back, sat up, looked at me, and said, "Chloe?"

"No," I said. "Charlie. Charlie Poole."

He blinked, and then flashed a great big smile and said, "Charlie baby! Nice to see you, long time no see, baby!"

"I came in last night," I reminded him. I wasn't entirely convinced he was awake.

He kept smiling the big smile, looking at me with bright eyes. "Great party!" he said. "What a great party!" Then he blinked again, and the smile slipped, and he looked at the floor. "You slept on the floor," he said, the way he might have said, "You walked on the water." Incredulity, but muted by awe. He said it twice, the same way both times. "You slept on the floor. You slept on the floor."

"Artie," I said, because I figured now he really was awake, "I'm in a kind of a jam. I need help, Artie."

He looked up from the floor, and his smile this time was puzzled, his eyes sort of glassy. "Charlie Poole," he mused. "Little Charlie Poole. Slept on the floor. Got himself in a jam. Little Charlie Poole."

"I need help," I repeated.

He spread his hands. "Tell me, baby," he said, more quietly and sincerely than I'd ever heard him say anything. "Tell me all. Begin."

Begin. Begin where? Two people were trying to kill me, that was part of it. The whole explanation about Uncle Al and the organization and the bar in Canarsie, that was part of it. Being out with little money and no coat, that was part of it. But where was the beginning of it?

Then I remembered the name I'd heard in the conversation between Uncle Al and the killers last night: Agricola. Agricola was the beginning of it, I supposed, the man who'd ordered the killers to kill me. So I said, "Artie, do you know of anybody named Agricola? In some kind of criminal organization or something."

"Agricola? The Farmer? Hell, yes."

"You do know him."

"Farmer Agricola," he said. "Everybody knows him. Knows of him, anyway. I never met him myself, of course, he's too big. Besides, he stays out on his farm on Staten Island most of the time."

"Staten Island," I said.

"Sure. I knew about him back when I used to sell the pills, you know? He's way up in the higher echelons there, maybe he runs the whole thing for all I know. Did you know I quit selling them things? I saw this documentary on television, the evils of narcotic addiction, and let me tell you, baby, it was like a revelation. You're looking at a new Artie Dexter, a new man, believe it or don't. I am now so loaded with social conscience you—"

"Agricola," I said.

"If you're thinking," he said, "of making an extra kopek, peddle the pills like at that bar you run out there, take my advice and don't do it. Some morning you'll look at yourself in the mirror, you'll say—"

"No," I said, "that isn't it. This guy Agricola sent—"

But then the door opened and the sloe-eyed raven-tressed beauty came in and said, "Time, gentlemen, please."

Artie shouted, "Chloe!" He threw back the covers and spread out his arms. "Come to Papa!"

"I hope to Christ not," she said.

Artie didn't have any pajamas on at all. Feeling that old adolescent blush staining my cheeks like the Sherwin-Williams paint can had just been dumped on my head instead of the globe, I said, "Well, uh, Artie, uh, I'll, uh, talk to you, uh, later on, uh . . ." Meanwhile backing up. I left the room by the other door, the one leading to the bathroom, because that way I didn't have to get closer to Chloe, who was taking off her dungarees and ignoring the dickens out of me.

I felt much better when I had the closed bathroom door between us. I heard Artie shout, "Ah hah!" and then there was silence from in there.

As long as I was in the bathroom anyway, and nothing to do, I washed. I didn't take any clothing off, because I would have had to put the same dirty clothing on again and I didn't want to have to do that. I knew, for instance, that my shirt collar must be black by now, but it didn't bother me as much as it would if I were actually to see it. So I simply washed my face and hands, brushed my teeth with toothpaste and my finger, gargled a little bit on general principles, and left the bathroom by the other door feeling somewhat better.

As I was going out to the living room, I heard the telephone ring. I looked around, but the phone was in the bedroom, and I heard Artie bellow, "Every time! Every goddam time!" The phone didn't ring any more, so I guess he answered it.

I searched the living-room shelves, found in amid the record albums an old paperback of Charles Addams' cartoons, and sat down with it to distract myself from thoughts of violence and mayhem.

Somehow, I think I picked the wrong book.

After a while Artie and Chloe came out, both dressed now, both looking bouncy and healthy. Artie rubbed his hands together briskly and said, "Now! Charlie boy, you wanted to talk."

Chloe said, "Coffee?"

"Right," said Artie. "A round of coffee. Coffee for me and my troops. Charlie?"

"Fine," I said.

"Great," said Artie. He clapped his hands together and came over and sat down in a chair facing me. "We begin," he said.

"And," said Chloe from the kitchen-closet, "you can tell your Uncle Al he's got a rotten sense of timing."

I said, "My Uncle Al?"

Artie frowned and said to Chloe, "That was supposed to be a surprise, schmo. He didn't want us to tell him."

"I forgot," said Chloe. "Sorry."

I said, "What is this?"

Artie said, "Let's talk. You had a problem, you wanted to talk. Something about Farmer Agricola, right?"

"No, wait," I said. "This is important. What about my Uncle Al?"

Chloe said, "Forget it, will you? I'm sorry I spoke up, I didn't mean to ruin anything."

"The bit's blown," Artie told her. "It don't matter any more, idiot, you already opened your big mouth." But the manner wasn't as harsh as the words. It was as though he couldn't really be mad at her right now.

She said, "So sue me," and went back to making the coffee.

I said, "So tell me."

"That was your Uncle Al on the phone," Artie told me. "He wanted to know were you here, and I said yes did he want to talk to you, and he said no he'd come on down and pick you up but don't tell you because he wanted it to be a surprise. So when he comes in, will you act surprised?"

★ You read about it in the papers all the time. A city bus driver, bored and bedeviled by years of driving back and forth over the same restricted route, all at once makes a left turn and drives to Columbus, Ohio, instead. Not that he wants to go to Columbus, Ohio, or even knows anyone there. It is only that Columbus, Ohio, is off that damn bus route. You remember reading about things like that, right?

Well, some day it's going to happen on a Staten Island ferry. Some day the guy at the wheel of the Staten Island ferry is going to get sick of going back and forth between Staten Island and the Battery, and he's going to turn left and steam to Nantucket instead. It hasn't happened yet, but you mark my words; some day.

Riding the ferry to Staten Island now, and thinking about it, I was wishing today would be the some day, and this ferry the ferry that would do it. Nantucket, Bermuda, even the Azores. Or, Fidelistas hijack airplanes and take them to Cuba, why not ferryboats?

I don't know why not, but they don't. Or didn't, not the one I rode. The one I rode went to Staten Island, of all places, and I got off and went looking for Farmer Agricola.

I had left Artie's place, of course, in a hurry. But first there'd been a few more things to say; I'd borrowed a jacket from him, and swore him to secrecy about where I was going and that I knew the name Agricola. "Don't tell my Uncle Al," I said. "Don't tell anybody."

"Baby, tell me what's going on," he said.

"No time, no time. I'll come back when I can, I promise."

"Right," he said. "My lips are sealed. Hers, too." He looked at her. "Right, big mouth?"

"Sure," she said. She shook her head at me. "Don't worry, Charlie," she said. I'm not sure, but I thought she seemed more interested in me now than before.

Anyway, "I'm off," I said, and got into the black basketball jacket Artie was loaning me. The arms were too short, so the sleeves of my white shirt stuck out halfway from wrist to elbow, and I couldn't close it across to zip it up, but it was better than nothing.

I ran back down to the street, and two blocks away I saw them, the killers, rolling slowly along in their black automobile with my Uncle Al between them on the front seat. They didn't notice me; they were too busy looking at street signs, trying not to get lost in the Village.

I picked up the Seventh Avenue subway at Sheridan Square, took it to South Ferry, the end of the line, and got aboard a Staten Island ferry, which set sail for Europe but only got as far as Staten Island.

It was a beautiful day for a sea voyage; a cloudless sky, a bright warm sun, a brisk but not cold breeze. I stood out on the upper deck, at the front, where if for one reason or another I should go over the rail I would land on a car roof and not in the Atlantic Ocean, and I tried to build up some spirit of adventure from the voyage and the weather and the mission, but all I was was scared.

And hungry. When the ferry docked at St. George I walked up to the main street, built diagonally across one of the steep hills that Staten Island has so many of, and found a luncheonette, and had myself a hamburger and a cup of coffee. When I paid, I had seventeen dollars and thirty-eight cents left.

The luncheonette boasted a phone booth. I went over to it and looked in the narrow Staten Island directory, not expecting to find anything, but Agricola, A.F. was practically the first entry. It didn't give a street address, just a town, Annadale.

This wasn't necessarily the right Agricola, but on the other hand, how many people named Agricola would be operating farms on Staten Island? If it turned out to be the wrong one, maybe he'd know where I could find the right one.

I asked the man behind the luncheonette counter how I would get to Annadale, and he told me what bus to take and where I'd find it.

Staten Island is a very odd place. It's one of the five boroughs of New York City, just as much a part of the city as Manhattan or Brooklyn or the Bronx, but on the other hand, it's this crazy island tucked in next to New Jersey, and until the Verrazano-Narrows Bridge you couldn't even drive to Staten Island from any of the other boroughs. It's still the only borough with no subway, and it has no skyscrapers, and there are great expanses of it that are just scrubby weedy fields. It has slums, because every place has slums, but the slums don't look like New York City slums, they look like Poughkeepsie slums or the back part of Belleville, Illinois. And even though the whole island is only one-fifth of a city, it itself is a collection of little towns, separated by countryside and woods. There's St. George, where the ferry lands, and Port Richmond and Howland Hook, and New Dorp and Eltingville, and Pleasant Plains and Richmond Valley, and Bulls Head and New Springville, and Annadale, where a man named Agricola lived.

Annadale is a pleasant underpopulated town between Arthur Kill Road and Drumgoole Boulevard, in case you'd like to hear two street names that didn't make me feel any better.

The old-time comedians that made so much fun of Canarsie and New Jersey mostly just left Staten Island alone. Maybe it was out of sympathy for the Islanders, or maybe it was because Staten Island is so improbable, in concept and appearance, that even a comedian couldn't think of anything to say about it.

My bus let me off where Arthur Kill Road and Drumgoole Boulevard meet at Richmond Avenue. There was a Gulf station there, and I stopped in and asked the man if he knew where I'd find the Agricola farm. He didn't, but he suggested I walk down Drumgoole Boulevard a ways and inquire again.

Drumgoole Boulevard was built during the Second World War by the United States Army in order to move troops quickly from New Jersey, via Outerbridge Crossing, across Staten Island to the embarkation points along the northeastern coast. From the looks of it, it hasn't been repaired since, not once. It gets very little traffic, and for the most part there are just woods and fields on both sides of the road. Now and again I'd pass a cluster of houses built all in a row, four or five of them, usually of brick, very nice-looking but lonely. Now and again a car would pass me, headed west toward Outerbridge Crossing, or coming the other way. The cars all drove in the left lane, because the right lane was in such bad shape, the concrete all crumbling and pitted. There were no sidewalks, so I walked down the grass islands in the center of the road, weaving in and out of the tree trunks and streetlight poles.

I'd walked quite a ways, not having seen a gas station or store of any kind, and beginning to wonder who I was going to ask about Farmer Agricola next, when a black car raced by me, headed west.

It was *the* car, I knew it the second I saw it. Yes, and the two of them in it, both in the front seat. I stood where I was, on the island, and watched the car shoot up to the top of a long gradual hill ahead of me, and there turn right.

Had they questioned Artie, threatened him, perhaps threatened his girl? Had one or the other, Artie or Chloe, told them what I knew, that I knew the name Agricola and that I was coming to Staten Island in search of him?

Or had they merely come back for further instructions? They wouldn't dare use the telephone for a matter like this, not with all the wiretapping going on these days. They maybe went to Artie's place, found me gone, and knew they'd lost my trail again. So back they came to Staten Island to confer with Agricola, to decide what to do next.

They must know by now they couldn't use Uncle Al any more to betray me, that I would be defending myself against Uncle Al's phone calls from now on.

This was twice they'd gone by me today without noticing me. Having gone past me this second time seemed to prove that neither Artie nor Chloe had talked; if the killers had known I was on the Island they would surely have checked everyone they saw who could possibly be me.

So they must be returning to Agricola. Which meant Agricola's farm must be off to the right, at that intersection up ahead.

I didn't know how long they would be with Agricola, or how soon they would come rushing back, so I left the center island and went over to the right edge of the road and walked along the grass and weeds there by the curb, where the sidewalk would have been if the Army engineers had expected us to win the Second World War.

The intersection was at a street called Huguenot Avenue. Naturally. I turned right and kept walking.

For some reason all of Staten Island, even the most expensive parts like Princess Bay, has a faintly grubby look, as though everyone had given up years ago in the attempt to keep the place looking bright and cheerful. The most fiery red, exposed a brief while to the aura of Staten Island, fades into a pedestrian tone, modest and a little grimy. The Island, from end to end, has the same feeling as the ferries that service it.

Huguenot Avenue had this aura, in buckets. I walked along past just slightly seedy homes, and past just slightly scuffy fields and copses, and now and then a stretch of farmland, sometimes with dead cornstalks in faded cream rows. A couple of times I passed dirt roads, with rural delivery mailboxes on poles at the edge of the road.

Rural delivery mailboxes, in New York City!

The names were on the mailboxes: Guyon, Hyland, Barrett, Agricola . . .

The dirt road went off to the right, fenced in barbed wire on both sides. On its left was a cornfield, on its right a grazing pasture. Ahead, the road ran into a copse of trees.

I didn't want to go in that road, on which I would be open and exposed and trapped, while there was any chance I'd meet those two killers coming the other way. So I went past the entrance, and down the road a ways farther, and where a tree had fallen over to make a natural bench beside the road I sat down to wait.

It was getting to be late afternoon now, the sun losing some of its warmth, the breeze adding to its chill. I lit a cigarette, and scuffed my feet around a little in the dirt beside the road, and sat on the fallen tree, and wondered what I was doing here.

Trying to save my life, I supposed.

Though it did take some of the heart out of the expedition to have Uncle Al turn traitor that way. And having those two guys in their black car show up everywhere I went was beginning to give me the willies.

What if I couldn't convince Agricola? What if he wouldn't listen to me? What if he took one look at me, realized who I was, and started shooting?

If only I had a gun of my own, I could hold it on him and force him to listen to me while I talked. If I had a gun. And if I wouldn't be too scared to use it, which I would be.

Sitting there on the tree, thinking about things, I began to get myself more and more frightened and more and more depressed. Surely the best thing for me to do was go away to Mexico or Tierra del Fuego. Regardless I had only seventeen dollars and twenty-three cents. I could stow away on a ship, on a plane. I could hitchhike to Mexico. In Brasilia perhaps I could find a job, learn the language—could Portuguese be learned?—and build a new life for myself.

But I knew it was a false dream. Wherever I might try to hide, from Aabenraa, Denmark to Zywiec, Poland, they would find me. From Zululand to Afghanistan, from Etah to Little America, the wrath of the organization would seek me out. There was no use trying to run away from the organization. All I could hope to do was convince the right people that I wasn't someone they wanted to kill after all.

Down the road, the black car nosed out into view. I tensed; they were returning to action, armed with fresh orders from their boss, off again in their search for me.

The car turned right. Toward where I was sitting.

My first instinct was to throw myself on the ground behind the fallen tree, put my face in the grass and my arms up over my head, and await my end in as cowardly a manner as possible. But I resisted; all was not lost, not all, not entirely. They couldn't be expecting to see me here, and that was to my advantage.

So all I did was fold my arms in front of myself, to hide the shortness of the jacket sleeves, and lean forward with my head slumped as though I were asleep. I was well aware what an inviting target I made for a hit-and-run accident, my bent head sticking out there just at headlight height, but I locked every nerve and every muscle and every joint, and I waited.

The black car rolled by me, with a purr of engine and a hiss of tires. I sagged a bit, in relief, but otherwise held my pose until I was sure they were out of sight. Then I sat up, and looked to left and right, and I was alone on the road.

Now there was no longer any excuse to stall. The black car was gone, I was all alone and unobserved. I had come here to see Agricola; now was the time.

I got to my feet, heavy-footed with reluctance, and started walking.

★ It was a long way in. The first part, between the pasture and the cornfield, I felt as obvious and exposed as the last house standing in the Dust Bowl, and when I got to the cover of trees without incident I had to stop a minute to calm my nerves and wipe my brow and wind my courage up again.

Also to get off the dirt road. This copse of trees was thick with underbrush, but I preferred to fight my way through a thicket or two than be caught on that road by Agricola or any of his henchmen. So I labored along, not as quiet as a Cooper Indian nor as fast, but progressing.

What I was blundering through was a slender arm of

forest reaching down between two cleared sections. The farmhouse, when I finally saw it through the trees, stood in lonely grandeur in the middle of a huge clearing all its own. I looked at it, and depression got a fresh new grip on me.

The building itself didn't register with me at all, to begin with; only that blank open grassy expanse stretching between me and it. Agricola, I knew, must have had this in mind when he moved into yon house; the business he was in, it must be reassuring to know no one can sneak up on you.

So what to do? Wait till darkness? But it was now barely three-thirty in the afternoon, and besides, if this was Agricola's defense against a brutal world in the daytime, what would his defense be like at night? Floodlights at the very least, and maybe armed guards. Visions of slavering dogs leaped in my head.

Better in than at. I struck out across the open ground toward the house.

Every nerve-ending in my body developed radar, and they all detected the same thing: machine guns in every window of the house, all aimed at me, all waiting for me to get just a step closer, two steps closer, just a little, little closer...

I kept walking. Nothing happened, and I kept on walking, following again now the dirt road, and ahead of me the house loomed larger and larger.

It was a farmhouse, that's all, of the afterthought variety. Someone had built an ordinary rectangular farmhouse, two stories high, with a bit of a porch in front, and with an A-shaped roof sloping front to back, the roof bulging with two dormers, and then rooms and rooms and rooms had been added as afterthoughts. A chunk had been stuck on at the left side, as full of windows as the bridge of a Staten Island ferry; possibly a solarium or a hothouse or who knew what. Another chunk on the right, windowless. A chunk on the top of the solarium, with modern crank windows instead of the old-fashioned kind on the rest of the house. More chunks, here and here and here, most of them in approximately the same clapboard as the original house, but with a final concrete-block addition on the left and something that looked like aluminum siding used on one second-story chunk on the right. The result, sort of Grant Wood flaccid, had been painted maroon and left for dead.

The dirt road, in its last stages toward this stack of building parts, stopped being a dirt road and started being a blacktop road. The pasture, too, having been pruned and watered, had graduated to a lawn. The blacktop road cut across this lawn, turned right at the house in order to go past the front door, and turned left again to go around the side of the house to the back. A gray Lincoln Continental was parked in the sunlight at the side of the house, facing me with Chinese eyes and a grille that laughed in evil anticipation.

I attained the blacktop. No gunshots, no guards, no slavering dogs. Nothing but silence and sunshine and the maroon house and me walking forward and the Oriental Continental. I kept walking, breathing from time to time through an extremely narrow opening in my throat.

I got all the way to the front door, and still nothing had happened. I stopped there at last, close enough to the door to touch it, and wondered what I should do next.

Just knock, and wait? But a servant, I assumed, would answer, or maybe a bodyguard. Anyway, not Farmer Agricola himself, that was for sure. And whoever it was, I could visualize the conversation:

"Mr. Agricola, please." "Who's calling?" "Charles Poole." *"Bam! Bam!"*

Some other way then. The thing to do was sneak into the house somehow and see if I could find Agricola alone. Then, if only I could talk fast enough and convincingly enough, maybe he'd listen.

I moved away from the front door, off to the right, where the drive went around to the back of the house. I went past the gleaming gray Lincoln and around boxy maroon house additions, and going around the final corner at last I came to the rear of the house, where the blacktop spread out into a solid black pool, a parking lot. A bulky sagging dirty red barn and a low shiny white aluminum four-car garage stood next to one another, both uncomfortable at the association. Beyond the blacktop, varicolored slabs of slate formed a large patio full of tubular lawn furniture in green and yellow. There was no one in sight.

A door just at the corner of the house attracted my attention. I went over to it and opened it and it led into a narrow sort of entranceway with coats and hats and jackets and sweaters hanging from nails stuck into the walls along both sides. Overshoes and rubbers were lined along the floor, and a snow shovel leaned in the corner.

I stood thinking of science fiction. Until I started running the bar, I used to spend a lot of my unemployed days flat on my back, reading science fiction. There's a particular science-fiction story that was written over and over again and that I always enjoyed, about a young man in some future society who goes through a lot of dangerous adventuring, with mysterious people after him and various threats on his life and some sort of secret organization in the background, and at the end of the story you find out nobody ever really meant to hurt the young man at all, the whole thing was a kind of test to see if he was good enough to join the secret organization, and of course he always is.

As I had opened the door of the house, I remembered those stories, and in a sudden rush of fantasy I had told myself that on the other side of this door would be Uncle Al and Mr. Agricola and Patrolman Ziccatta and Artie Dexter and Chloe and the two men from the black car, and they'd congratulate me, I'd passed the test with flying colors and I was now a member of the organization. But what did I actually find, within that door? Overshoes and sweaters.

Secret organizations may menace people for the fun of it in future societies, but in the society we live in now they only do it if they mean it.

Well. There was another door, directly in front of me. I opened it, and it led me to a huge old farm kitchen full of huge new city-kitchen appliances. Like everything else around here, the kitchen was empty. I crossed it, to a swing door that stood open, and moved on tiptoe down a hall.

Now at last I did see someone. In a room to the right of the hall, three people sat around a table talking. The colored woman the size of a barrage balloon would be the cook, the white-haired red-nosed man in the gray uniform would be the chauffeur, and the husky broken-nosed man in the white shirt and a gun in a shoulder holster would be someone I didn't want to meet right now. Or ever.

They were talking about graduated income tax, and they all seemed to be opposed to it, though what they thought it was doing to them I didn't stick around to find out. None of them was looking in my direction, so I flitted past the doorway like the lover in a French bedroom farce, and continued on down the hall.

Ahead of me, someone was playing an awful lot of lush piano very badly. I moved closer, down the hallway. Rooms to left and right were all empty.

The piano-playing was coming from within a room shut off by double sliding doors. But the doors didn't quite meet; leaning close and peeking between them, I could see a girl in billowing pink sitting at a piano in a band of sunlight, playing with fingers that twinkled and spun. Her hair was yellow bright, and long, and in thick delicate waves like yellow mist reflecting the sunlight. Her face was pretty as a greeting card, and it seemed to me, though I couldn't see all that clearly, that her eyes were blue. She was slender, with slender arms and a narrow waist, and long slender legs tapering to tiny thoroughbred ankles down where her toes in pink pumps touched the piano pedals. She was, I suppose, eighteen or nineteen, and as lovely a vision as could be imagined.

She was playing the sort of thing Liberace plays, only far worse. And from the dreamy expression on her face as she played, I could only assume she dreamed of the Scarlet Pimpernel.

I turned away. Although I'd only been able to see a narrow pie-slice of that room, the expression on her face had been enough to tell me she was alone there.

Stairs on my left led upward. There were still rooms I hadn't seen on the first floor, I was sure of that, but I didn't know exactly how to get to them. Simply because it was easiest, I chose to continue my search upstairs.

And hit the jackpot on the first try. At the head of the stairs—carpeted happily—was a hall, and on the right a door slightly ajar. I looked in there, and it was a den or office, with bookcases on the walls and a desk and leather sofa and bar and filing cabinet. The man sitting at the desk, glowering in irked thought at the door, must be Farmer Agricola. Husky, fiftyish, jowly, with the arrogant look of the wealthy and powerful, this could be no one but the head of the house.

I ducked back before he saw me, and took the time to gather what few wits and what tiny shreds of courage I could find, erecting them into a shaky substitute for a backbone. I stood there three or four minutes in the hall, at the head of the stairs, taking deep silent breaths and letting them out just as silently, with the faint sound of that lovely girl's rotten piano-playing in my ears, and finally I forced myself to move, striding forward and pushing the door open the rest of the way and marching directly into the path of that glower.

"Mr. Agricola," I said, talking fast, "I'm Charlie Poole, and I've got to talk to you because you're making a terrible mistake."

He didn't move. No surprise showed in his features at all. He glowered at me as thought I'd been standing in front of him like this for hours and he was beginning to get bored with me.

Had he known all along? Was there someone behind me, waiting only for the nod from that heavy head?

"Mr. Agricola," I said, and turned my own head quickly, but there was no one behind me at all. I looked back. "I've got to talk to you, Mr. Agricola," I said.

Nothing.

Suspicion struck me, horrible suspicion. I said, "Mr. Agricola?"

I moved forward, across the room. His eyes did not follow me. He kept glowering at the doorway.

Ripples were running up my back, shivering that had

nothing to do with cold. My teeth even began to chatter a little bit. "Mister," I said. "Mister."

The room wasn't very brightly lit, not very brightly lit at all. Heavy draperies across the windows cut down the sunlight to a mere bronze memory of itself, and the massive dark furniture with which this study was furnished seemed to absorb what light was left. In the semi-dark, only his eyes were oases of light, glowering in fury at the doorway.

I moved around the desk, beside him, and I could see that the hilt of the knife in his back had caught in the back of his chair, holding him upright. As though he'd been standing behind the desk when he'd been stabbed, and had dropped into the chair, hooking the hilt and hanging himself there in final impotent rage.

This was the first corpse I'd ever seen without a camera between me and it, so I don't know how long I stood there, fascinated by the knife and the balance of the body the way a bird is fascinated by the snake, but I hadn't moved when the voice from the doorway said, "Hey!"

I was startled out of reverie. I turned my head, and saw the broken-nosed man just unlimbering the gun from its shoulder holster. I put my hands up in the air and said, "Don't shoot."

He pointed the gun at me, but he didn't shoot. "I got him, Mr. Agricola," he said.

"Uhhh," I said, wondering how to break the news gently.

But I didn't have too. This broken-nosed man surely had more experience than me with corpses; at any rate, it took him less time to understand he was in the same room with one. He said, "Oh ho?" And then, "All right, you."

"I didn't do it," I said. Talk about whistling in the dark.

★ "Don't move," said the broken-nosed man. His gun said the same thing.

I didn't move. I stood there with my arms up over my head and wondered what was going to happen now. My arms almost immediately had gotten tired, and the broken-nosed man hadn't told me to put them up in so many words in the first place, but I didn't want to take a chance on lowering them. I stood there and sweated and smiled like a Dale Carnegie dropout.

The broken-nosed man took two steps backward, through the doorway and into the hall. Still watching me, he shouted, "Tim! Hoy, Tim!"

From far away downstairs came an answering shout, with a question in it.

"Come up here a minute!" shouted the broken-nosed man.

I heard sliding doors slide, somewhere downstairs, and a clear and beautiful voice called, "Clarence? What's the matter up there?"

The broken-nosed man—whose parents had apparently been such poor prophets they'd named him Clarence—called back, "It's all right, Miss Althea, there's nothing the matter."

Heavy footsteps thudded up the carpeted stairs. I

hoped they belonged to Tim rather than Miss Althea; lovely young girls shouldn't clump like that.

Tim it was, the white-haired red-nosed chauffeur. He was red-cheeked now, too, from the climb, but the red drained from his cheeks and faded on his nose when he saw his employer. He said, "For God's sake, what's happened?"

"This bird killed Mr. Agricola," Clarence told him.

I shook my head, between my upraised arms. "He was dead when I came in here," I said.

"For God's sake," said Tim.

Clarence said to me, "That won't do, you. Nobody did Mr. Agricola in but you."

"No. Really."

Clarence shook his head and looked as though he pitied my feeble brain. "There's nobody in the house," he said, "but me and Tim and Ruby the cook and Miss Althea, and we all been downstairs."

"Those two guys in the black car," I said. "That just drove away, maybe they did it."

Clarence shook his head some more. "Let me just show you it's no good," he said. "You made your try and it didn't work. Mr. Agricola came downstairs with those two boys, and then went back up again after they left. We all saw him."

Tim, who was still recovering from his first shock, started abruptly and nodded, saying, "That's right. He came to the doorway where we were all sitting, the three of us."

"So it's you," said Clarence.

I knew it wasn't me, but Clarence was sure convincing. I said, "How do you know there's nobody else in the house? I got in, why couldn't other people?"

"Sure," said Clarence.

Miss Althea was suddenly in the doorway, saying, "What's wrong? What's the matter? Clarence? Daddy?" I was right, her eyes were blue. They were also very wide right now.

Of all the people in the world, Miss Althea was the one I most wanted to know I was innocent. I said to her, with as much sincerity as I could put into my voice, "I didn't do it."

Clarence and Tim, meanwhile, were both trying to get her to go back out of the room, but she wouldn't go. She said, "Daddy? Daddy?" Her eyes just kept getting wider and wider.

Clarence bellowed, "Ruby! Come up here and get Miss Althea!"

Miss Althea, at that point, screamed and fainted.

I still knew I hadn't done it, but I couldn't help feeling as though I was somehow the cause of all this trouble and commotion, and I was feeling embarrassed and foolish about the whole thing. I stood there with strained arms and pained expression and wished desperately I was somewhere else. Even in the back seat of the black car, even that much, if it meant I wasn't here.

There were two or three minutes of confusion. Tim carried Miss Althea away, and Ruby arrived and immediately trundled off to see to Miss Althea, and Tim came back, and throughout it all the black eye of the gun in Clarence's hand kept watching me.

When Tim came back, Clarence said, "Frisk him."

I said, "I swear I didn't do it."

"Sure," said Clarence. "We went through that already, remember?"

Tim came around behind me and went through my pockets, taking everything out and piling it up on the desk beside us. There wasn't much: my wallet, my keys, a pack of Pall Malls and a folder of matches, twenty-three cents in change, and a pocket pack of tissues.

Clarence said, "What's the wallet say?"

I said, "Can I put my arms down, please?"

"Go ahead."

I did, and said, "Thank you."

Tim had opened my wallet in the meantime. "His name's Charles Robert Poole," he said. "He lives in Brooklyn."

"Poole?" Clarence looked at me with new interest. "You're the nephew runs the bar?"

"Yes. I came—"

"Who would have thought," he said. "You showed guts, kid. Not much brains, but lots of guts."

"Listen," I said desperately, "I really didn't—"

Tim interrupted me, saying to Clarence, "Should I call the law?"

"No," said Clarence. "If this is the nephew, he knows too much. We can't have him talking to the law."

Tim waved his hands, saying, "I don't want to know nothing about that. I'm a chauffeur, that's all I am. I don't want to know nothing about nothing."

"Sure," said Clarence. To me he said, "Put your stuff back in your pockets."

I put my stuff back in my pockets. I wanted to ask him what he was planning, what he was going to do, but I was afraid if I asked him he'd tell me, so I kept my mouth shut.

Clarence backed out of the room again and motioned with the gun. "Let's go," he said.

Tim said, "What do I do about Mr. Agricola?"

"Leave him be. Call Mr. Gross, tell him the farmer bought the farm. You got that? The farmer bought the farm."

"The farmer bought the farm," said Tim.

Clarence said, "His number's in the pad there, on the desk."

"Right," said Tim.

Meanwhile I had come out to the hall. Clarence turned his attention to me again and said, "Downstairs, you."

We went downstairs, me in the lead. I said, "If you'd just let me explain," and paused because I expected to be interrupted. But Clarence didn't say a word, so I went on, saying, "I didn't kill Mr. Agricola. I really didn't. I'm the wrong type to do something like that, you can see that just looking at me. All I wanted to do was talk to—"

"Turn right."

We were at the foot of the stairs. I turned right, and walked toward the kitchen.

"—Mr. Agricola about what was going on, why anybody would want to kill me, because I didn't do anything. Somebody was making a mistake somewhere, and all I wanted to do was talk to Mr. Agricola."

"Through that door there," he said.

I opened the door and stepped out into the sunlight. That blacktop, that sunlight, the silence and emptiness made me think of firing squads.

"Over to the barn."

I walked toward the barn.

"I wouldn't kill him," I said. "Honest to God, I wouldn't kill him. I wouldn't kill anybody. Why would I do something to Mr. Agricola? I wanted him to tell those two guys not to kill me, what good would it do me—"

"He couldn't do that," Clarence said. "He had his orders, like anybody else. Open the door and go on in."

I pulled open the barn door, which creaked and groaned, and went on in to darkness and a musty smell.

"Orders from who?" I said.

"Never mind," said Clarence. "Walk straight ahead."

The barn wasn't being used for anything. Empty stalls, empty bins, empty nails stuck in the walls, empty loft up above. Sunlight gleamed in cracks in the outer walls, filling the interior with soft vague indirect lighting as though we were underwater in a lagoon.

The left rear corner had been closed off into a tiny windowless room lined with rough-plank shelves. This was empty now, but not for long; Clarence pushed me in and shut the door behind me. I heard a hasp lock click shut. I was alone.

Now what? I supposed Clarence had decided he couldn't do anything about me on his own account, and so he'd just locked me away here for safekeeping until he found out what was what from Mr. Gross. I also supposed Mr. Gross was the man higher up, the one Mr. Agricola had taken his orders from.

So it was Mr. Gross I should be trying to see, not Mr. Agricola.

Well, it didn't look as though I'd get to see him. If anybody wanted to set up a Charlie Poole pool, I would put my money on the two guys in the black car for the next people I'd be seeing. And the last.

A rotting old barn like that, there wasn't any reason I couldn't escape from it. I kicked at one of the exterior walls, experimentally, and managed only to hurt my big toe. I hit my shoulder against the door, and hurt my shoulder. I hit my palm against one of the interior walls, and hurt my palm.

While there were still a few parts of me that didn't hurt, I decided to quit.

How long would it take? Clarence and Mr. Gross would have to talk together, guardedly, on the telephone.

Then Mr. Gross would have to get in touch with the two men in the black car, and they'd have to drive on out to Staten Island again. An hour at least, maybe two hours.

I sat down on the dirt floor, and gave myself up to depression.

It was only fifteen minutes before I heard someone unlocking the door out there. I scrambled to my feet, and my mouth got dry while my palms got wet. I kept clearing my throat and clearing my throat; when that door opened, I was going to have to talk faster than I had ever talked before in my life. And I wasn't even sure what I was going to say.

The door swung open at last, and it was Miss Althea standing there, as beautiful and improbable as a Disney heroine, but distorting her beauty was a terrible frown of grief and rage that stroked her face with heavy angry lines. In the right hand she raised toward me was, incredibly, a gun, a great big automatic. Her hand was barely large enough to hold it, and she had to bring her left hand up to help keep it steady.

''Hey,'' I said. ''What are you doing?''

''You killed my father,'' she said. Her voice was hoarse with strain.

''No, no,'' I said. ''No, I didn't, no.''

''I'm going to kill you,'' she said, and pulled the trigger.

★ The noise alone, in that confined space, was practically enough to kill me. The gunshot went POWwwrrranginggg, reverberating around inside the tiny room and my tiny head like J. Arthur Rank falling over his gong.

I thought for sure I was shot, killed, done with. What confused me was that I wasn't falling down. I stood there, stunned, baffled, and all my mind was capable of doing was wondering why I wasn't falling down.

Could it be I *wasn't* shot?

POWwwrranginggg! She did it again, frowning now as much in concentration as in either rage or grief. Her tongue stuck out a corner of her mouth, her slender shoulders were hunched up with effort, and she just kept squeezing that trigger.

Twice. Was it even remotely possible I was still alive? With no more than six feet separating us, with that huge piece of machinery spitting authoritative pieces of metal at me, was there any reason at all to suppose I was still alive?

Of course, the gun barrel was weaving back and forth like the head of a cobra. And it was certainly true that I still wasn't falling. So maybe, just maybe now, she was missing.

But could she keep missing forever? I was in front of her, six feet away. No matter how bad a shot she was, sooner or later one of those bullets she was sending out into the world was going to find a home in a portion of me.

I jumped her.

She was slender, but strong, and she had an amazing number of sharp edges. Her elbows, for instance, were very sharp, very sharp. So were her teeth, which were imbedded briefly in my wrist. So was her knee, which kept trying to prove she wasn't a lady.

I was hampered not only by the sharp parts of her, but also by the soft parts, which I tried to avoid touching. But if you think you can take a gun away from a sharp-toothed sharp-elbowed girl without touching any soft parts, you're crazy. I wouldn't behave with an old girl friend in a movie balcony the way I behaved with Miss Althea. And believe me, I got no pleasure out of it. I found the whole incident embarrassing and painful and not a little dangerous.

Anyway, I finally got the gun. My left wrist was bleeding, where she'd bit me, and I was limping because she'd kicked me on the right shin, and my left eye was watering because she'd stuck her finger in it, and my kidneys would require a long quiet time to forget her elbows, but at least I had the gun.

She stood there in front of me, gasping for breath, glaring at me defiantly. High spots of color shone in her cheeks, and she was cupping her right hand with a left as though *I'd* hurt *her*.

"You'll pay for this," she said. Do I have to mention she said it through gritted teeth? I thought not.

"Now, listen," I said. "I did not kill your father, I swear it. I never killed anybody in my life. Your father was trying to have *me* killed, if you want to come right down to it."

"That's ridiculous," she said.

"What about those two guys in the black car? They're the ones that tried to do it."

"Those are my father's business associates," she said.

"You're darn right they are. And they—"

But that was as far as I got. The gunfire had apparently been heard in the house, because at that point the barn door burst open and Clarence came barreling in.

There's a time for chivalry, and there's a time for practicality. This was a time for practicality. I immediately ran around behind Miss Althea, grabbed her around the throat, stuck the gun in the delicately magnificent small of her back, and shouted, "One step closer and I plug her!" If my voice hadn't gone falsetto about midway through that sentence, the whole performance would have been very impressive.

Nevertheless, it was impressive enough to stop Clarence in his tracks. "Let her go," he said, but he knew I had the whip hand.

"Back on out of the barn," I told him. "Go on, move."

He backed on out of the barn, looking like Lon Chaney, Jr., making up his mind to turn into the Wolf Man. I followed, pushing Miss Althea ahead of me. I switched my grip from her neck to her arm, and out to the sunlight we went. I could feel her trembling, but whether from rage or fear I couldn't tell.

Outside, there was another surprise. A tableau: Tim, still in his chauffeur's uniform and now with the addition of his cap, holding a small pistol aimed at Artie Dexter, who stood sheepish and worried in the middle of the expanse of blacktop.

Artie Dexter!

First things first. I shouted, "Drop that gun! Drop it!"

Tim just gaped at me. So did Artie.

Clarence said, "Do like he says. He's got a gun on Miss Althea."

Artie said, "Charlie! What's come over you, baby?"

Tim dropped the pistol.

"Pick it up, Artie," I said.

"Right."

To Clarence I said, "Is Mr. Gross coming out here?"

He said, "What? Are you kidding?"

"They were going to kill you, Charlie," Artie told me. "They got their orders on the phone, I heard them talking. They were going to kill you and bury you out back. And when they got me, they figured to kill me too."

"That's a lie!" cried Miss Althea. "Clarence?"

"I can't do nothing, miss."

"We've got to get out of here, Artie," I said.

"Take her along," he suggested. "For a hostage."

"Good idea. You two get into the barn. If I see either one of you coming after me, I'll plug Miss Althea."

Of course I knew I wouldn't shoot Miss Althea, but they didn't. Red-faced with anger and embarrassment, Tim and Clarence went reluctant and pouting on into the barn.

"Come on," said Artie.

We went around the house, me still keeping a tight grip on Miss Althea, who from time to time wasted breath by telling me things I wouldn't get away with. To Artie I said, "Where'd you come from?"

"After you left my place," he said, "two tough-looking guys showed up, asking for you. They acted kind of odd when I told them you were gone. I got to thinking about it, you saying you were in a jam, and asking about Agricola, and then those two guys coming along, so after a while I figured maybe I better come look for you. You said you were coming to Staten Island to talk to Agricola, so here I am. I tried to sneak up on the house, see if you were around, but those two plug-uglies caught up with me."

"I don't know what you two are trying to do," Miss

Althea said, "but you're wasting your breath. You can't fool me."

Artie said, "What's she talking about?"

I told him about Agricola being dead and this being his daughter who thought I had killed him.

"And you did!" she cried.

"Quiet," I told her.

Artie looked back at the house. We'd just about reached the trees by this time. "We better hurry," he said.

"Maybe we should have taken the Continental," I said.

"Car thieves too!" Miss Althea cried.

"I've got wheels," Artie assured me. "Don't worry."

"Killers!" cried Miss Althea. "Murderers!"

Artie leaned close to me, so we walked a moment shoulder to shoulder. In a confidential tone he said, "Did you, Charlie? You know, did you do the old guy?"

"For Pete's sake!"

"He did, he did! You're an accomplice!"

"Oh, shut up," I told her. She was a real pain sometimes. I said to Artie, "You know me better than that, for Pete's sake."

"I thought I did, baby," he said, "but all of a sudden you're like wow, you know what I mean? Like sleeping on the rug all night, like you're in a jam with the rackets bosses, like here we are with a chick for a hostage, this isn't exactly the same old Charlie Poole from New Utrecht, you know?"

"You do what you got to do," I said.

"Killer!" she yelled.

I pinched her arm to make her shut up. I told Artie, "She don't know about her father, I guess. About him being in the rackets."

She shouted, "Are you *insane?* My father was a

farmer! You two are crazy, you're both crazy! Help! Help!''

I had to really twist her arm a good one before she'd quit hollering. I didn't want to do it, but there wasn't any choice. ''Walk faster,'' I told her, ''and keep your mouth shut.'' And I kept her arm twisted up behind her a little, so she'd do both and not give me any more trouble.

We hurried on out to Huguenot Avenue and Artie went off to the right, saying, ''Down this way. Hurry!''

Parked down the road, next to the fallen tree on which I had been sitting not too long ago, was the most nefarious automobile I had ever seen. It made the killers' black car look like a churchgoer. This one, purring a bit with the engine on and a trickle of white smoke at the exhaust, was a black 1938 Packard limousine, with the bulky trunk and the divided rear window and the long coffin-like hood and the headlights sitting up on top of the arrogant broad fenders. It was as gleamingly polished all over as a toy from Japan, with sparkling white sidewalls and glittering chrome hubcaps and door handles that semaphored the sun. And there was Chloe inside, sitting at the wheel, like advance scout for a foray from St. Trinian's.

''Where?'' I said. ''Wha.''

''My aunt's,'' Artie explained. ''She lets me borrow it sometimes.''

Miss Althea said, ''You can get the electric chair for kidnapping, you know.''

''Anything to keep from being shot,'' I said.

We reached the car and Artie pulled open the rear door. ''Put her in there,'' he said.

I did, and followed her in, and Artie shut the door and got into the front seat. ''Get out of here fast,'' he said.

Chloe said, "Hi, Charlie," and asked no questions. We roared off.

"Our best bet is Jersey," Artie said. "Take your next left."

"Right."

"The Mann Act," said Miss Althea.

"What do I care?" I said. "I'm going to the electric chair anyway."

I have been in apartments smaller than the interior of that Packard. There was enough floor space between the front and back seats for a crap game, all softly carpeted and softly clean. Everything in the car was clean, spotless. The upholstery, which had to be the original stuff, was scratchy gray plush, as new-looking as the enraged girl sitting grim-faced beside me. There were leather thongs at the sides, for elderly ladies and gangsters to hold on to, and small green vases containing artificial flowers hung in little wire racks between the doors.

The steering wheel of this monster was itself nearly as big as Chloe, who drove with the nonchalance of one who knows she cannot die. I, lacking that assurance, sat and cowered like the coward I was. If death didn't come from behind me, in the shape of Clarence and Mr. Gross and all the other minions of the organization, it would surely come from ahead of me, in the shape of something hard and immovable for Chloe to drive headlong into.

"You'll never get away with this," Miss Althea told me.

As if I needed reminding.

★ At the tollbooths to the George Washington Bridge, Miss Althea stuck her head out the window and screamed, "Help! They're kidnapping me!"

The toll taker in his uniform looked blankly at her.

"They're kidnapping me!" she insisted.

The toll taker made a disgusted face, to show what he thought of modern kids, out running around with no sense of values, making noisy senseless jokes. He took the half-dollar from Chloe, and we rolled on past there.

"He's in the plot, too," I said.

"Oh, shut up," she said. She flounced back in the seat, folded her arms, and glared furiously at the back of Chloe's head.

We had taken an extremely roundabout way of returning to New York, leaving Staten Island by the Outerbridge Crossing and driving up past the Holland and Lincoln tunnels and all the way up to the George Washington Bridge, just in case the car had been seen by anyone who could describe it to the organization's underlings, who were surely by now all in hot pursuit of us and our hostage.

As to the hostage, we were keeping her because we felt safer with her to hide behind. It seemed unlikely any organization tough would gun down the daughter of Farmer Agricola in order to get at an unimportant nephew like me.

On the trip up the Jersey coast, after filling Artie and Chloe in on the details of what had happened to me since last night—and that it had all occurred in less than sixteen hours, including time out for sleep on Artie's bedroom floor, was itself as astonishing as anything else—I made a long and unsuccessful attempt to explain to Miss Althea Agricola just who and what her father had been and why I had gone out to the farm to see him. But she refused to believe any of it, and nothing I said would shake her firmly seated ignorance.

At first it had seemed incredible that she could have remained unaware of her father's true self, but in the course of her denials, facts about her life came out which helped to explain it. In the first place, her mother had died when Miss Althea was still an infant, so Farmer Agricola was her only parent. In the second place, she had spent practically all of her life in boarding schools, and was only rarely at home on the Staten Island farm. Summers had been spent with other relatives in various parts of the world. She was only at home now because there was a two-week hiatus between the end of her summer visit to an uncle and aunt in Southern California and the beginning of the fall semester at the girls' college in Connecticut at which she would be a junior this year.

So if her father told her he was a farmer, why shouldn't she believe him? And if he told her he had his money invested in stocks and real estate that gave him a good high return, what was wrong with that? And if he told her Clarence wasn't a bodyguard but was hired to run the farm, he was hardly any more improbable a foreman than some she'd seen on television or in the movies. And if men like the two in the black car, who stopped by occasionally to confer in private with her father, were announced as either old friends or business associates, why should she disbelieve?

I know it isn't exactly the same thing, but I myself didn't really know what Uncle Al did for a living till I was twenty-two years old, and then I only found out because he got me a job at the bar, which by all rights I should have been in Canarsie opening instead of riding across the George Washington Bridge with a gun in my hand, a hostage in my hair, and—for all I knew—a price on my head.

Approaching the New York side of the bridge now, Chloe spoke up for nearly the first time, saying, "Where to?"

Where to? I didn't really know. "Mr. Gross," I said. "I guess I have to find Mr. Gross."

"But which way do I go?" Chloe wanted to know.

"I don't know," I said. "I don't know where to find Mr. Gross."

"Let's put it this way," Chloe said. "The end of the bridge is coming up. Do I take the Henry Hudson Parkway or do I take local streets? See the signs?"

I saw the signs, but I didn't really know what to tell her. Artie took the decision out of my hands, saying, "We'll want to go downtown anyway. Take the Parkway."

"Fine," said Chloe. She changed lanes, terrifying an orange Volkswagen, and we left the bridge.

Artie turned in the seat to say to me, "About Mr. Gross I can't help you. From what you say, from what I heard those guys say, he's got to be higher up in the rackets than Agricola was, and Agricola was the highest up I ever even heard of."

Miss Althea said, "Why don't you just give up? It isn't going to do you any good. I don't believe you and I won't believe you, so why don't you stop?"

"Shut up," I asked, "I've got to think."

"How about your Uncle Al?" Artie suggested.

"What about him? I tried to get him to help me before, and he betrayed me instead."

"You didn't have a gun last time," Artie pointed out.

"Hmmm," I said.

"You're all insane," Miss Althea said. "Insane."

"All right," I said. "Back to Uncle Al."

★ There was a fire hydrant just down the block from Uncle Al's building. Chloe carefully parked the Packard next to it and Artie said, "We'll keep hold of the hostage, don't worry."

"I appreciate this, Artie," I said. "I really do."

"Don't be silly, baby," he said. "Since I quit peddling the pills, life has been dullsville."

"If a cop makes us move," Chloe said, "I'll circle the block."

"You're all insane," Miss Althea said. She'd tried to jump out of the car when we were stopped for a light at 72nd Street and West End Avenue, and I'd had to slap her face to calm her down, and since then she'd maintained an insulted and dignified regality, like a member of the French court on the way to the guillotine. Had I been Madame Defarge, I might well have blanched a bit in her presence.

However. "I'll hurry," I said, and got out of the car, and returned to Uncle Al's building.

I didn't want him to know I was coming until I was

right at his door, so I didn't push the button next to his name this time but pushed the button for apartment 7-A instead. When a male voice came out of the grille, wanting to know who it was, I said, "Johnny."

"Johnny who?"

"Johnny Brown," I said.

"You got the wrong apartment," he said.

"Sorry," I said, and rang the bell for apartment 7-B.

There was no answer at all from 7-B, so I tried 6-A. This time it was a female voice that answered, one of those voices that sounds as though its owner has been drinking rum and writhing nude on a bearskin rug just to get warmed up for your arrival. "Who's there?" she asked, making those two nondescript and pedestrian words reek with suggestiveness.

"Johnny," I said.

"Well, come on in," she said, and the buzzer sounded.

Isn't that always the way it is? The really great opportunities to connect with sex bombs always come along when you're already tied up with something else. That, I suppose, is the difference between fiction and reality. In fiction the sexy voice says, "Come on in," and the guy goes on in, whereas in reality the guy has seven minutes to get to work and the boss told him if he's late one more time he's fired and he can't afford to lose this job because he's still paying off his *Playboy* subscription. In fiction, if you want to know something, it's a good thing the sexy voice does speak up, because the guy doesn't have a *thing* to do, and if it wasn't for that unexpected sexy voice he would undoubtedly have dropped dead from boredom in another two, three days.

So much for philosophy. I did not go to apartment 6-A, once I'd gained entrance to the building, but went to apartment 3-B instead. I remembered the way those two guys had knocked last night, the code knock, one and then three and then one, so that's the way I knocked now. Then I put my hand inside the pocket of Artie's jacket, where I had the pistol we'd taken from Tim. It was smaller than the automatic I'd gotten from Miss Althea, so Artie and I had switched guns before I left the car.

I waited so long after knocking that I was beginning to think this time Uncle Al and Aunt Florence really were in Florida when at last the door pulled open and Uncle Al's astonished face appeared before me. He saw who it was, and saw the gun in my hand, and promptly started to close the door again.

But I said, "No, Uncle Al," and pushed forward, across the threshold.

If he had taken a firm stand, if he had told me to get the hell out of here or had demanded to know just what I thought I was doing, I'm not sure what would have happened next. Having grown up without a father, I'd had no one but Uncle Al to look to for a symbol of male strength and confidence. I was used to Uncle Al ordering me around, used to Uncle Al weighing me in the balance and very loudly finding me wanting, used to Uncle Al shouting at me to get out of his sight. I was so used to it that if he'd done the same thing now, I might even have obeyed him. Only for a second, maybe, but anyway long enough for him to shut the door again in my face, and certainly long enough for him to get control of the situation.

But I was learning something about Uncle Al. He respected power above all things, with a respect born of fear and a fear born of utter cowardice. Just as he had been terrified of the two men who had come here last night, too terrified of them and Agricola and the organization to even talk to me much less help me, so now he was terrified of the little pistol in my amateur hand, and as I moved forward across his threshold he moved backward into the apartment, and in that instant the old relationship between my Uncle Al and me was gone forever.

I shut the door behind me. "We've got some talking to do," I said.

Belatedly he tried to get a grip on the authority he'd just forfeited. Shaking a quaking finger at me, he said, "You little punk, you realize the spot you put me in? You know what you've done to me?"

"Don't be a moron, Uncle Al," I told him. "Nobody's trying to kill you, with the possible exception of me. Let's go into the living room and sit down."

He looked startled, and held his hands out as though for quiet while he half-turned his head and seemed to listen. "Your Aunt Florence," he whispered. "She doesn't know."

"Maybe it's time she found out," I said.

"Charlie boy, don't. Maybe you got it in for me, maybe you got every right, but I ask you on bended knee to don't."

He didn't ask me on bended knee, actually, but I knew what he meant. I said, "We'll talk it over."

"Sure, Charlie. We'll talk it over."

"In your den," I told him. "We won't be disturbed there."

"Right, in my den. We won't be disturbed there."

I wasn't sure which threat worried him most, the pistol or Aunt Florence. In any case, the combination of the two was enough to pull Uncle Al's string and make him as quiet and agreeable as a new minister with the church elders.

Uncle Al's apartment is a triumph of money over background. Aunt Florence knew just enough about taste to know her own was too uncertain to carry her safely through the furnishing of an entire apartment, so she handed a great big wad of Uncle Al's money to a pretty young man with an extremely limp wrist, told him she wanted "quiet elegance," and turned him loose. The only thing wrong with the result was that when you saw Uncle Al standing in the middle of it you figured he had to be a burglar; he couldn't possible be somebody who *lived* in this place. The pretty young man, unfortunately, had been given free rein to choose everything about the apartment but its occupants.

The den had been done in mahogany, ebony and burlap, all brought together by a rich green carpet on the floor. A black leather sofa was the most ostentatious item of furniture, but it blended so well with the rest of the room that even a Communist couldn't have any real objection to it. The bookcases, which had been filled according to the strange but not at all uncommon literary criterion of the color of the book spines, gave a comfortably spurious air of age and solidity to the room, making it difficult to believe that this entire place had not stood here, exactly like this, for at least a hundred years. The den, in fact, had been done seven years ago.

Once we were in this room with the door shut, Uncle Al began to talk. I let him go on awhile because I wanted to see if he'd say anything of use to me.

"You got to understand, Charlie," he said to begin with. "You got to understand the position you put me in. I get this phone call from this person, which you can see why I don't want to mention any names, that tells me my nephew's on the spot and what do I got to say about that, and what do I say? Charlie, you know me, I'm your Uncle Al, I done the best I could for you all your life. Your old man run out on you before you was born, to the best of my ability I tried to help take his place, you know that."

I didn't know any such thing, but I was letting him talk, so I said nothing.

"Your Aunt Florence and me," he went on, patting himself on the chest with all his fingertips, "we wasn't blessed with children, in a lot of ways you're like my own kid, my own flesh and blood."

I didn't say anything to that one, either, though my mother had told me one time about a confidence she'd been given by Aunt Florence, to the effect that Aunt Florence had wanted children but Uncle Al hadn't, Uncle Al even going so far as to tell Aunt Florence to be warned by what had happened when her sister—meaning my mother—got herself knocked up, referring of course to my father having deserted. But to this bit of twaddle, too, I remained silent.

"You know I always done my best for you," Uncle Al went on, "even getting you the job out to Canarsie there. I went out on a limb for you that time, Charlie, you know that? You realize the kind of limb I went out on for you that time, you not even in the organization or anything? But there's a limit, you got to see that, there's a point where I got to say, 'No, Charlie, no more. I know I'm your uncle, Charlie, I know you're my nephew, but eventually comes the time I got to think of myself, I got to think of your Aunt Florence, I got to be practical. I help you out whenever I can, Charlie, but if you ever get in a serious jam with the organization there's nothing I can do, not a single thing I can do.' And it's happened, right? You're in trouble. You done something, I don't know what, I don't even want to know what, and you got the organization down on you. So what can I do? I get this phone call, 'Your nephew's on the spot,' what can I say? I got to say, 'I'm sorry to hear it,' that's all. There's nothing else I can do."

The time had come to break in. "You couldn't even ask why? You couldn't even find out what I was supposed to have done?"

"If they want me to know, Charlie," he said, "they'll tell me. If they don't tell me, I don't ask. That's one thing I had to learn about the organization, if they want you to know some—"

"Wait, wait," I said. "Wait, now. Stop for a minute."

"Charlie, I'm only—"

"Shut up, Uncle Al."

He did, too, for just a second. The surprise did it, I guess. But then he pointed a finger at me and said, "I'm still your uncle, boy, and you—"

I pointed the pistol at him and said, "Shut up, Uncle Al."

A pistol is more forceful than a finger any day. He shut up.

I said, "You are my Uncle Al because you're married to my Aunt Florence. Other than that, the relationship between us is kaput."

"That's perfectly all right with me," he said. "If you think I—"

"Shut up, Uncle Al."

He shut up again.

"Now, let me tell you something," I said. "I didn't do anything to the organization. They're making a mistake. I didn't talk out of turn to anybody, I didn't lose a package or steal anything, I didn't do a thing. It's a mistake, and all I want to do is correct it."

"The organization don't make mistakes," he said. "An organization as big as—"

"Shut."

He shut.

I told him, "This time the organization *did* make a

mistake. Now, what I want to do is find out what they think I did wrong, and then maybe I can convince them it wasn't me that did it.''

He was shaking his head back and forth and back and forth. ''Never in a million years,'' he said. ''You'll never—in the first place, you can't even get to the men in charge, I couldn't do it myself.''

''I almost go to talk to Farmer Agricola,'' I said, ''but he was—''

''Who?'' Astonishment made him look for a moment even dumber than he is. ''What did you say?''

''Farmer Agricola.''

''How did you find out about him? Charlie, what have you been up to?''

''Never mind,'' I said. ''The point is, I couldn't talk to him because he was killed. But I did—''

''What what what?''

''Killed,'' I said. ''Listen faster, Uncle Al, I don't have much time. I went to see Farmer Agricola, but somebody killed him before I got to him. Stuck a knife in his back. But I did find out—''

''The Farmer's dead? Is this on the level?''

''Uncle Al, I don't have much time. Yes, the Farmer's dead. His bodyguard and chauffeur think I did it, but I didn't. I've got his daughter for a hostage, and now I've got to—''

''Charlie!'' He just stared at me, about the way Artie stared at me when I came out of the barn back at Agricola's farm. ''What's come over you?''

''I don't know,'' I said. ''Maybe it's self-preservation. Now, be quiet a minute and listen to me. I found out the name of the man above Mr. Agricola is Mr. Gross. Now, Mr. Gross is the man I got to talk to, and you're the one has to tell me where I find him.''

"Me! Charlie, you don't know, you can't—" He sputtered, and gestured, and carried on, and finally got a complete sentence out: "I'd get gunned down in a minute if I told you that."

"If you won't tell me," I said, "you'll tell Aunt Florence. I know she'll help me." I backed toward the door, still aiming the pistol at him.

He said, "Charlie, you wouldn't. Charlie, for the love of God don't tell your Aunt Florence!"

"Either you tell me right now where I find Mr. Gross, or I call for Aunt Florence. And if I call for Aunt Florence, I tell her everything."

Times have changed since my Uncle Al told my Aunt Florence he'd leave her if she got pregnant. That was twenty years ago or more, and my Aunt Florence has learned since then how to control her lunk of a husband. Until last night I'd been under the impression my Uncle Al was afraid of nothing in this world with the exception of Aunt Florence. Of course, now I knew better, and Aunt Florence's accomplishment in housebreaking Uncle Al no longer seemed quite so incredible, but the accomplishment still remained in effect.

I could see Uncle Al thinking madly. He gnawed on his lower lip, stared in torment at the floor, rubbed his hands nervously together. Which was he more afraid of—the organization or Aunt Florence?

To help him decide, I said, "Nobody knows I came here, and nobody has to know. Nobody has to know I got the address from you. I got to Agricola's farm out on Staten Island, and you didn't tell me that."

"If they ever found out," he said, "I'd be done for."

"They won't find out from me."

"Charlie, you don't know what you're asking."

"So I'll ask Aunt Florence," I said, and reached for the doorknob.

"Nonono, wait!"

I hesitated.

"All right," he said. "All right. But don't get me in a jam, whatever you do. You know I'd help you if I could, if you say you didn't do nothing to earn the spot I believe you, I know you wouldn't lie to me, boy, but my hands are tied. You can see that. They know you're my nephew, they figure I'm prejudiced in your favor, so what could I do?"

"The address," I said.

"Yeah, yeah. Wait, I'll write it down."

He hurried over to the desk and I said, "Don't open any drawers, Uncle Al."

He looked at me. His feelings were hurt. "My own nephew?"

"Just don't open any drawers."

Wounded, he said nothing. But he didn't open any drawers. There was a memo pad on the desk, with "From the desk of *Albert P. Gatling*" at the top of each sheet, and an ornate penholder set with a marble base and two fountain pens. Using these, he wrote the address and handed me the paper.

I said, "If this is a false address, Uncle Al, I'll come back here, you can count on it. And I'll go straight to Aunt Florence."

"Charlie, I'm giving you the goods, I swear I am. I can't help you, I told you that, but you're like my own son, my own flesh and blood, and the least I can—"

"Sure," I said. "But don't call Mr. Gross after I'm gone."

"*Call* him? Are you nuts? Call him and tell him I gave his private address to a kid with a grudge and a gun?

Charlie, the minute you leave here your Aunt Florence and I go straight to Florida."

"No, you don't. You stay here in town. If I have to phone you in Florida, it's Aunt Florence I talk to."

"Charlie, let me build up an alibi!"

"No. I may need to know something else before this is done."

He looked very gloomy when I left, and he didn't walk me to the front door.

★ The Packard was still parked next to the fire hydrant, but now Artie was in the back seat with Miss Althea. I slid into the front seat next to Chloe, and Artie explained, "She tried to duck out again."

She was being silent and grim at the moment, sitting hunched into the corner, staring straight ahead and ignoring everybody.

I said, "She's more trouble than she's worth. Maybe we ought to get rid of her."

"She's insurance, Charlie," Artie said. "She's our hostage."

I wasn't all that sure a hostage would stop Mr. Gross and his organization, particularly when the hostage's father was already dead and couldn't complain, but if it made Artie feel safer it was worth it. I'd already come to depend on Artie's presence, not to do anything in particular to help me but just to be there to talk to, and I wouldn't want to see him scared away. So I said, "All right, we keep her."

Chloe said, "Did you get the address?"

"Right." I took the paper from my pocket and read the address aloud: "One twenty-two Colonial Road, Hewlett Bay Park, Long Island."

Chloe said, "Hewlett Bay Park. Where's that?"

"On Long Island, I guess," I said. "Have you got a map?"

"I don't know. Look in the glove compartment."

There was nothing in the glove compartment but a pair of ladies' black gloves and the automatic I'd taken from Miss Althea.

From the back seat, Artie said, "We need gas anyway. Get a road map at the gas station."

"Fine," said Chloe. The motor was already running, purring away as though it were brand-new and born to be in a getaway car. Chloe turned the wheel, ignored the traffic coming down 65th Street from behind us, and pulled away from the curb. She was a very individualistic driver, Chloe, and I wasn't at all surprised when I learned, some time later, that the State of New York refused to give her a driver's license.

We were already on the East Side, so we decided to drive on over to the 59th Street Bridge, go over to Queens, and find a gas station there, which we did. Miss Althea told the attendant we were kidnapping her, but we were used to that sort of thing from her by then, so we all laughed it off and the attendant got a chuckle out of it, too. He wasn't a sourpuss like the toll taker at the George Washington Bridge. Artie bent Miss Althea's thumb back, to make her stop yelling, and then everything was fine. I got a road map of Long Island, paid for the gas, and we drove away from there.

Hewlett Bay Park turned out to be on the south shore of Long Island, in the midst of a little flurry of places named Hewlett. There was Hewlett Harbor and Hewlett Neck, Hewlett Bay and Hewlett Point, and even a town just called Hewlett.

From where we were there didn't seem to be any sensible way at all to get to Hewlett Bay Park, or any other Hewlett. With all of us but Miss Althea studying the map and making suggestions, we finally decided on what looked to be the simplest route of all. By a complex series of local streets, we got from Queens Boulevard, on which we were now situated, to the Long Island Expressway, which we took to Grand Central Parkway, which we took to the Van Wyck Expressway, which we took to the Belt Parkway (at this point for some reason called Southern Parkway), which we took to Sunrise Highway, which we took to Central Avenue in Valley Stream, which we took to the general vicinity of the Hewletts, at which point we would ask directions.

Of course, it didn't work that way. It was now a little after six, and we were caught up in the tail end of the rush hour, and evening was beginning to edge toward us from the east, and Chloe kept getting confused by the signs, and so we managed to be lost more often than not. Still, by fits and starts we approached our target.

We'd been approaching it for an hour and a half, and had attained Sunrise Highway, when, at about seven-thirty, while we were stopped for a traffic light, Miss Althea caught us all by surprise—she'd been quiet as a mouse for nearly an hour—and got the car door open and leaped to the street.

Artie shouted, "Hey!" and leaped out after her.

She was off like a deer across the highway and down the side street. Artie pelted after her, shouting, "Hey!

Hoy! Hey!'' And there were Chloe and I, just the two of us, with the light turned green in front of us and several drivers turned dangerous behind us. With the horns honking away, I said, ''You better pull forward. Get over to the side of the road as quick as you can.''

Of course, we were in the farthest left lane of three, so it took us nearly half a mile to get over to where we could pull off the road—in a discount carpet center's parking area—and try to figure out what to do next.

Chloe gazed worriedly out the rear window. ''He won't know where we are,'' she said.

I said, ''What if he doesn't catch her? In fact, what if he does? He can't drag her screaming and kicking along beside a big highway full of cars.''

Chloe squinted and squinted. ''I don't see him coming,'' she said.

''He'll be along,'' I told her.

But he wasn't. We waited fifteen minutes, and he never showed up. I was feeling pretty impatient anyway, this whole trip taking so blasted long, and sitting there fifteen minutes, in an unmoving automobile and waiting for somebody who continued not to show up, was getting to me.

Finally I said, ''He's not coming back, you know.''

''He'll be here any minute,'' she said, squinting away out the rear window.

I said, ''If he was going to get back here, he'd have done it by now. Either he's chased her so far away he figures there's no point looking for us here any more, or she's managed to get him arrested.''

''Arrested?'' She looked worried. ''Are we out of the city limits?''

''I don't know, I think so. Why?''

"Artie has to avoid the city police," she said, and let it go at that.

I said, "Well, in any case, he wouldn't expect to find us here any more. He knows I'm in a hurry, I'm trying to protect my life, so he'll naturally expect us to go on. He knows the address where we're headed, maybe he'll meet us there."

"How will he get there?" she wanted to know.

"How do I know? Maybe he'll take a cab. I wouldn't be a bit surprised if he got there before we do."

"And what if he isn't there?" she said.

"Then he'll meet us back at his place, after I see Mr. Gross."

"Do you want to try to see Mr. Gross alone?"

"I didn't count on Artie coming in with me anyway," I told her. "I wouldn't want him to risk getting himself killed on my account."

She stopped squinting out the rear window at last, and looked rather searchingly at me. "Do you mean that, Charlie?" she asked me.

"Well, sure," I said. It was true; I hadn't expected Artie would come in with me. I'd assumed he'd wait out in the car, the same as at Uncle Al's.

"You're really something, Charlie, you know that?" she said.

"No, I'm not," I said. "If I had my way, I'd be right back in Canarsie this minute, behind the bar, watching television. This isn't the life for me, believe me."

"I know that," she said. "That isn't what I meant."

"We'd better get going," I said.

She turned her head and looked out the rear window again. "Do you really think so?"

"He'd have been here by now," I said.

She sighed. "I suppose so." She faced front. "I hope

nothing's happened to him. He's an awful sweet guy, you know.''

''I know that,'' I said.

''He looks up to you,'' she said.

I stared at her. ''Artie? Looks up to me?''

''What's wrong with that?''

''I thought it was the other way around,'' I said.

She laughed. ''You don't know yourself at all, Charlie,'' she said. Looking neither to left nor right, she started the Packard rolling forward and angled it out into the traffic.

★ Nine o'clock.

There didn't seem to be any way into Hewlett Bay Park. We'd found the general area an hour ago, and we'd been circling around and around it ever since, always coming back to the same street, a dark street with a barrier halfway across it and a stop sign on it and another sign saying ONE WAY DO NOT ENTER. So far as I could tell, the other side of that barrier was Hewlett Bay Park, but I just couldn't find the way in.

The fourth or fifth time we came back to that same place, a Cadillac ahead of us drove nonchalantly around the barrier and on down the street. I looked at Chloe and Chloe looked at me and it hit us both at the same time. The barrier and signs were phoney; it was just an exclusive town's cute way to keep tourists and other rabble out.

"Anything a Cadillac can do," I said, "a Packard can do. Onward."

"Right," she said, and around the barrier we went.

This was another world. Head-high hedges surrounded the homes, each of which sprawled in moneyed elegance on an insultingly large plot of land. There were few streetlights, but many of the driveways we passed were lit with blue or amber lights. There was no sidewalks, of course, because who in this area walked? The street names were lettered vertically on green posts set discreetly at each corner, and the intersections were free of vulgar traffic lights. In the ten minutes it took us to find Colonial Road we saw no other moving automobile.

One twenty-two was a house to fit the road; Colonial, with a bit of plantation thrown in. White pillars marched across the front of the house, which was of white clapboard with black shutters. Lit carriage lamps flanked the wide front door, and more lamps of the same style, on poles, were spaced along the curving driveway. There was the normal tall hedge all around, and more lawn than any one house could possibly need. The ground-floor windows were lit, the upstairs windows dark.

I said to Chloe, "Drive on by. Park beyond the next corner."

There was a streetlight at the intersection, as dim as a cocktail lounge at midnight. We went past it, and Chloe stopped the Packard up close to the hedge in the next pool of darkness.

"If I'm not back in half an hour," I said, "you better not wait for me. I'll try to get back to Artie's place as best I can."

"Be careful," she said.

"Well, sure. I'm no daredevil."

The hedge being so close, I had to get out on her side.

We stood together a second beside the car, while an odd feeling came over us, or at least over me, and then I said, "I'll be back in a little while."

"Please be careful, Charlie," she said, with a funny kind of emphasis on "please."

It made me uncomfortable. "I'll do my best," I said.

She got back into the car and I walked down to the intersection and through the halo of yellow light there and beyond. It was almost like walking along a country road; the darkness and the high hedges obscured the signs of civilization. There was no sound anywhere but the scruff of my own shoes on the pebbles at the edge of the road. The back of my neck was cold, where the hairs were standing up.

My right hand was in the pocket of Artie's jacket, holding tight to the little pistol I'd gotten from Tim. The pistol should have made me feel better—safer, more secure, more in control—but it did just the reverse, serving as a cold metal tangible reminder that I was kidding no one but myself. In fact, not even myself.

I looked back, and at first I couldn't see the Packard, but then I caught an evil glint of chrome in the darkness back there. That car was the mechanical Sydney Greenstreet.

The driveway entrance to Mr. Gross's house was at the far end of the frontage. I crunched along, seeing his house lights vaguely through the hedge on my left, and after the road's darkness his driveway, when I stood in front of it, seemed as bright as Times Square. It was wide, and four or five cars were parked along it, all new and expensive.

Would he have dogs? It seemed to me a place like this required dogs, huge loping animals who'd galumph over and bite your leg off without the least malice in the world. I stood a minute peering into the property in search of them, but all I could see were driveway and lights.

What I was worrying all the time about dogs for anyway I'll never know, since it was mostly human beings who'd been trying to do me in the last twenty hours.

Finally, reluctantly, I stepped onto Mr. Gross's property. I skirted the driveway and all its lights, and came around at the house from the other side. Light spilled from the windows to guide my way across turf as soft as a Persian rug. These windows were too high for me to look in them and see anything but ceilings, which was just as well; it made it less likely anyone on the inside would glance out and see *me*.

I moved around to the rear of the house, where I tiptoed across a slate patio alive with metal furniture. There were no rooms alight at the rear of the house, so I moved in utter darkness here, and my progression across the patio, ricocheting from metal chair to metal table to metal chair like a complex billiard shot, was a series of tiny magnificently distinct noises. When I came at last to a door, a possible entry, I simply leaned against it for a minute to listen to the blessed silence.

But the job was to get in. After I'd caught my breath and my wits, I tried the knob and the door proved to be unlocked. I could hardly believe my luck.

Well, it wasn't luck. I pushed open the door, stepped through in unbroken silence, shut the door as silently behind me, and forty lights went on.

I was in a smallish dining room, with secretaries and highboys against the walls and a sturdy English-looking table in the center. Leaded windows overlooked the patio and, I suppose, a garden. Quiet elegance bespoke itself softly in this room, just as in my Uncle Al's apartment, and similarly, too, the human element provided the only discordant note.

In this case it was the Three Stooges, one of whom had turned on the lights, principally a crystal chandelier suspended above the table. I say the Three Stooges, but of course I mean only an imitation of the Three Stooges. But for all that, a pretty good imitation.

Moe, in a black chauffeur's suit, held an automatic, pointed more or less at me. Larry, in a butler's tux, had armed himself with a baseball bat. And Curly, in white apron and tall white chef's cap and blackface, hefted a meat cleaver. All three glared at me with the belligerence of fear.

This was the last thing I'd expected to find in the house of Mr. Gross—amateurs like myself. They were, in their own way, more frightening than professionals. Like dogs, there was no reason to suppose they could be talked to.

I raised my hands over my head. "Don't shoot," I said. "Don't hit. Don't cut."

They advanced.

★ From the window I could see the driveway and lawn and hedge, and down to the right, beyond the hedge, I could make out the streetlight at the intersection. Just beyond there, I knew, Chloe sat waiting in the Packard. I stared off that way, but of course I couldn't see the car.

The Three Stooges had grabbed me up like blockers on the kickoff forming around the man with the football. They'd run me up a narrow flight of stairs—back stairs, service stairs, whatever they call them—up here to the second floor, and locked me away in this bedroom facing the front of the house. Larry, the butler with the bat, had frisked me and relieved me of Tim's little pistol—which he handled with complete terror—and then they'd backed out of the room, bumping into one another and watching me with round eyes. I heard them talking through the door, deciding Larry and Curly, the cook, should stand guard at the door while Moe, the chauffeur, went downstairs to tell Mr. Gross what they'd caught.

Well. I was in the Gross house, under the Gross roof. There was even a chance I was going to see Mr. Gross himself in a minute or two. And wasn't that what I wanted?

Of course it was.

Then why did I keep looking around for some place to hide, some way to escape? I didn't *want* to escape, did I?

As a matter of fact, I did. Hopelessly, miserably, but certainly.

The room I was in seemed to be a spare bedroom, reserved for guests. The bed was a high wide ornate old thing with a canopy, dominating the room. Flowers and vines and so on were carved into the wooden headboard, and the same motif was followed through on the dresser, the vanity table, the writing desk, and the night tables. Paintings of fox hunts graced the walls. Heavy drapes framed the windows.

Yes, a guest room. The dresser drawers I opened were all empty. I don't know why I expected to find a Gideon Bible in one of them, but its absence surprised me.

A key turning in the lock made me start and slide shut

a dresser drawer with embarrassed haste. As though that counted! Poking into empty dresser drawers was hardly something to agitate Mr. Gross; aside from having already broken into his house, there was whatever else he thought I'd done that had made him put me on the spot in the first place.

I turned and the Three Stooges popped through the opening doorway all at once and spread out, and after them came Mr. Gross.

Up till then I'd assumed that "Gross" was the man's name, but it was his description. He looked like something that had finally come up out of its cave because it had eaten the last of the phosphorescent little fish in the cold pool at the bottom of the cavern. He looked like something that better keep moving because if it stood still someone would drag it out back and bury it. He looked like a big white sponge with various diseases at work on the inside. He looked like something that couldn't get you if you held a crucifix up in front of you. He looked like the big fat soft white something you might find under a tomato plant leaf on a rainy day with a chill in the air.

He was beautifully dressed, but in his case it was a mistake. Had he worn overalls, a dirty flannel shirt, it would have been better. But the tailored black suit, the crisp white shirt, the narrow dark tie, the gleaming black shoes, the golden cuff links and the broad plain wedding band and the large flat wristwatch with its gold expansion bracelet, all they did was to emphasize the grossness and pallor and sickliness of white parts that bulged out at collar and cuff.

Stuck on that face like raisins on a cake were two expressionless eyes. They looked at me, the fat lips twitched, and out of them came a cracked soprano, a voice so high and foolish I inadvertently looked at the Three Stooges to see which was the ventriloquist. But it was Mr. Gross speaking, in his own voice:

"What did you want in here? Are you a burglar?"

"No, sir, Mr. Gross," I said. I tried to keep looking him straight in the eye, to show him I was honest, but it was just impossible. He was so vile-looking it was embarrassing, I had to keep looking away.

Falsetto, cracking, there-are-sharks-in-these-waters voice: "One thing I cannot stand is incompetence. Incompetence. How could you expect to break in with the house full of people?"

"I wanted to see you, Mr. Gross," I said. Looking everywhere at once, like Artie when he first sees you again, the way he did last night when I showed up at his party. And now doing the same thing myself, because Mr. Gross was as painful to the eye as a wrong piano chord is to the ear. Did I say he was bald? With a head that looked as though if you squeezed it, it would stay squeezed.

He held up Tim's gun in a tubby white hand. "With this?" What an idiotic voice. "You wanted to see me with this?"

"For protection," I explained.

"I have little time," he said. "I am dummy this hand. We have three tables tonight, all close personal friends. You are an embarrassment to me."

"I'm sorry," I said.

"If you want to see me—"

"Her-bert!" A shout, from downstairs.

His face twitched. Indecision, and then the mind made up. "Keep watch," he told the Three Stooges. To me he said, "I will return. When next I am dummy."

He went away, and the Three Stooges settled down to

watch me. I told them, "I'm not going to try and get away. I want to talk to Mr. Gross."

But I don't think they believed me.

While they stood grouped near the shut door, I went back over to the window. Nothing had changed down below. I stood gazing, and all at once a shadow flitted, out at the end of the driveway, by the edge. I blinked, but it was gone.

Behind me, the Three Stooges were talking together, deciding to send one of their number for a deck of cards. Larry, the butler, was the one to go.

I watched and watched. Was that motion along the hedge, in the darkness? I couldn't be sure.

Moe, the chauffeur, said, "You."

He had to mean me. I turned and pointed at myself.

He said, "You play bridge?"

"A little," I said. "I'm not very good."

"That's all right," he said. "We need a fourth."

"All right."

But Larry hadn't yet returned with the cards. I turned and looked out the window again, and now I did see her, following my route exactly—Chloe, pussyfooting across the lawn toward the house.

"You," Moe said. "Come on, we got the cards."

★ It just so happened we were both dummy at the same time. When Mr. Gross came in I was sitting at the table with my arms folded, watching my partner, the cook—whose name was not Curly but Luke—take a perfectly sensible contract of five hearts and grind it beneath his heel. I had always thought I was one of the world's worst bridge players, but now I knew three worse.

Mr. Gross came in then, and I got to my feet. He said, "If you want to see me, why not merely ring the front doorbell?"

It struck me he'd picked up our conversation exactly where it had been interrupted last time. And this time, would it be interrupted the same way, or would the interruption be screams and crashings as Chloe was discovered? It had been ten minutes since I'd seen her out the window, and so far not a sound.

Just as I had been forcing myself to concentrate on the cards, now I forced myself to concentrate on what I had to say to Mr. Gross. "I was afraid you wouldn't talk to me. It's a matter of life or death."

"Life or death?" His mouth twitched; clearly, a fastidious distaste for melodrama. But how on earth could such a face convey fastidiousness about anything? And that wedding band on his left hand—what sort of female horror did it imply downstairs?

He said, in that voice again, "Whose life or death? Mine?"

"No. Mine."

"Yours? But you came here with a gun."

"To defend myself."

"Rather than that," he said with twitching lips, "explain yourself." The lips made a smile, in appreciation of the joke. His teeth looked soft, like bread.

"My name is Poole," I told him. "Charles Robert Poole. Two men came—"

But he already knew the name. He took a step backward, his eyes widened, and if his face hadn't already been as white as the belly of a fish, I think he would have blanched. "You killed the Farmer!"

"No! No, I didn't, Mr. Gross. I want to explain—"

"And you came here to kill me!"

"Mr. Gross—"

"Damn!" said Luke. Our contract had just sunk without a trace, only a bit of oil skim on the water.

Mr. Gross said, "What possible point can there be in these murders? Do you think you can kill the whole organization?"

"Mr. Gross, I didn't kill anybody. I swear I didn't."

"Her-*bert!*" Again from downstairs.

But this time he ignored it. "Of course it was you," he said. "Who else would kill the Farmer? Who else would dare? Who else would want to?"

"*I* didn't want to. Why would I kill him? I didn't even know him."

At the table, Luke was shuffling with unnecessary noise. The three of them sitting there were watching me with ill-concealed impatience. In any game, the worst players are always the ones most in a hurry to get at the next hand.

Mr. Gross was saying, "You found out he was the one who had sent Trask and Slade to kill you. Foolishly, you thought you could save your own life by ending his."

"No, no. I just wanted to talk to him. I know better than that, Mr. Gross. I know it wouldn't do any good to kill Mr. Agricola. Or those two men, either."

"Trask and Slade."

"Yes, sir, Trask and Slade. There would just be somebody else come after me, somebody else to send them, I know that."

Gross frowned, making creases in his cheeks that

looked as though they'd never pop out again. He agreed with what I was saying, but if that was what I already believed, then something had to be wrong somewhere. He said, "And if you were to kill me? Do you think *then* you would be safe?"

"No, sir. Even less safe. The whole organization would be out looking for the man who killed you."

This was heady flattery indeed. He preened before me. "That is very—"

"Herbert!" Shouted this time from the doorway.

We both turned to look, and the woman there was undoubtedly six foot three in her bare feet, but at the moment she was wearing four-inch heels. She looked to be in her late twenties, a statuesque blonde, leggy and magnificent, with a body of a somewhat slimmer Anita Ekberg: a Copacabana chorine if there ever strutted one. Facially she had a cold Scandinavian beauty; ice-blue eyes and hollow cheeks and wide mouth and smooth complexion. Just as Gross's ugliness was embarrassing, making you turn away in spite of yourself, this woman's beauty had the same effect. It was too much beauty, larger than life, overpowering. It would take a man with absolute confidence in himself to climb into bed with her.

Or a fistful of money? Because this was surely the woman heralded by that wedding band.

Gross himself seemed impressed by her. He waved flaccid hands helplessly, saying, "Something's come up, my dear."

"I doubt that," she said, with utter scorn.

Had Gross had blood in his veins, I'm sure he would have blushed. As it was, his face turned just slightly green. Formaldehyde? He said, "You must carry on without me, this cannot wait."

"Bridge," she told him, "is played with four players."

He looked around helplessly, and saw Luke and the other two sitting at the table in silent agreement of the lady's observation. "Joseph," he said. "Go down and take my place for the moment. I will return as soon as possible."

Joseph was the butler, whom I had initially thought of as Larry. And the chauffeur was not Moe but Harvey.

The quick look I now caught between Joseph and the lady of the house led me to believe this was not the first time, nor the first circumstance, in which Joseph had taken Mr. Gross's place for the moment. In fact, it seemed to me I saw a similar exchange of glances between the lady and Harvey. Luke, I noticed, resolutely watched his hands shuffle the cards.

I had almost come to think of myself as invisible, the hidden observer, the one who sees everything but is himself unnoticed. I was, therefore, looking straight at the lady's ice-blue eyes when they turned and looked straight back at me.

It was like being hit in the forehead with a piece of cold pipe. The eyes saw me, catalogued me, weighed me, considered me, and set me aside as being, at least for the moment, not worth the trouble. She turned—did I say her gown was low-cut, floor-length and shimmering gold?—and strode out of the doorway, followed immediately by Joseph.

Mr. Gross now sat down at the table at which we'd been playing cards. "You two," he told Luke and Harvey, "stand over there by the door. If this young man tries anything, stop him."

"Yes, sir."

"I won't try anything," I said.

"Come over here and sit down," he ordered.

I went over and sat down, opposite him.

He raised a finger like a white sausage. "Nothing," he said, "is senseless. That I learned long ago. If a fact is presented which appears to be devoid of sense, it means only that we must look again." He paused, as though wanting comment.

I nodded and said, "Yes, sir."

He pointed the white sausage at me. "You," he said, "are discovered in perfidy. Trask and Slade are sent to dispatch you. You escape. You appear at the Farmer's place, and the Farmer is murdered. You appear here, with a pistol in your pocket. The conclusion seems inescapable—you killed the Farmer and you intended to kill me."

I shook my head vigorously. "No, I didn't," I said. "I didn't—"

"Wait." Five white sausages raised up to halt me, with a gesture like a traffic cop. "I told you, nothing is senseless. And yet, from appearances, your behavior is utterly devoid of sense. You know that killing Farmer Agricola will not save you, that killing me will not save you. The obvious course of events, therefore, is not necessarily the true course of events. Some other, or some further, explanation will be required."

"That's what I'm trying to—"

"No, no." The sausages waggled; I had the uneasy feeling his fingers would fall off, but they didn't. He said, "Let me do this in my own way. Order out of chaos. Now, if you did not kill Farmer Agricola, then someone else must have. And you must have had some purpose for going to see him other than his murder. And you must have had some purpose for coming here other than *my* murder. Now, the question is, what other purpose? And who else would want to kill Farmer Agricola?"

I'd always understood that big wheels in the organization were awash in enemies prepared to do them in, that violent ends were common among them and the practice of keeping bodyguards no mere affectation, but Mr. Gross seemed to think otherwise, and he was after all a big wheel in the organization himself and should know. So I let that question go, and tried the other one: "What I wanted to see—"

But it wasn't my turn yet. "Ah ah ah," he said. "One moment. Allow me please to see if this problem can be worked out with no more information than that which I already possess."

I sat back and allowed him.

He thought it over, pursing his lips, which was a disgusting sight. After a minute he said, "There is, of course, also the daughter, who aided your escape. Her name?"

"Aided my—"

He snapped his fingers. It sounded like hitting two pork chops together. "Her name," he said.

"Miss Althea," I said. "But she—"

"Yes. Althea. Is this the explanation?"

I said, "She didn't aid my escape, Mr. Gross. In fact, she tried to kill me. She thought I killed her father, and she came—"

"Please," he said. "If you must lie, do so intelligently. The Farmer's bodyguard, who himself has questions to answer, locked you away for safekeeping. This Althea person, the daughter, released you and gave you a gun. Further, she went away with you. The only term for this in my lexicon is 'aided your escape.' Yes?"

"No," I said. "That's all wrong. She—"

"Is undoubtedly somewhere nearby," he said, "waiting for you to dispatch me and return to her arms."

"But why?" I said. "Why would I *do* anything like that?"

"That," he told me, "is the question with which I am currently engaging myself. *What* has been done is clear and obvious. *Why* is more complex."

"Mr. Gross, I swear—"

"Don't. Be still."

I was still.

The wait this time was a longer one. Mr. Gross sat there with hooded eyes, like a white frog waiting for some beauty's kiss to turn him into a green prince, and thought and thought, while I sat all atremble with corrections and emendations I wanted to make to his misinformation and incorrect conclusions.

Finally he spoke again: "Perhaps I begin to understand. The Farmer had tried always to keep the truth of his occupation from his daughter's ears, which never ceased to strike me as snobbery. If a man's own family cannot be taken into his confidence and be expected to spur him on in his professional endeavors, then God help us all. Be that as it may, to each his own, the Farmer wished his daughter to believe he was a farmer. An idiosyncrasy."

He looked at me expectantly, but so far he hadn't said much of anything, so there was nothing for me to reply to. I kept my silence, waiting for him to get to the parts that counted.

After a few seconds he nodded as though we'd come to agreement on something, and went on: "Somehow, the daughter learned the truth. Hearing it from outsiders, undoubtedly in a distorted and prejudiced manner, and at a highly impressionable age, the truth affected her badly. Particularly since the Farmer had given credence to the idea of his guilt and ill feelings by hiding this truth from his child so many years. A vigilant feeling came over the child. She must atone for her father's sins by destroying the organization herself, and with her own two hands.''

Again he stopped, and this time I did have something to say. ''That's wrong, Mr. Gross. She still doesn't believe the truth. I tried to tell her, but she wouldn't listen to me.''

He smiled, pityingly, which was horrible to see. ''You are very young,'' he said, ''and inexperienced at lying. However, let us go on. This daughter, this child, this young girl, feeling herself helpless to destroy such a large and powerful organization, sought assistance in her scheme, that's where you came in.''

''Mr. Gross! For—''

''Be still! When I have done, you may speak, you may rebut, you will be given your chance.''

All right then. I shrugged, and folded my arms, and sat back in the chair, all in an attempt to give the impression I was listening to utter nonsense and would be able to prove my case in a twinkling once my turn to speak had come. I wondered if I could.

Mr. Gross said, ''Somewhere you two had met, the beautiful daughter of the gangland leader and the drifter, the ne'er-do-well, the useless nephew in his useless job. You understand, I mean nothing personal.''

I shrugged. It wasn't yet my turn to speak.

''I am only,'' he explained, ''being vivid. In any case, you two met. She, purposeful, strong, beautiful. You, purposeless, weak, willing to be led. The two of you formed an alliance, and began your efforts to undermine the organization, and ultimately to destroy it.''

I shook my head, but didn't say anything.

''At first,'' he said, ignoring my shaking head, ''you were content to be an informer, passing information on to the police, but after a—''

"No! I didn't, Mr. Gross, I did not! What infor—"

"Be *still!* When I am *done* you may speak!"

I subsided. "I'm sorry," I said, more calmly. "That was just . . . I'm sorry."

"Very well." He had himself become a bit ruffled. He smoothed his lapels—how astonishing that his hands didn't leave a trail of white slime on the black cloth! —and took a deep breath. "After a while," he said, "it became evident this was not enough. I cannot guess what your plans were before last night, but once you realized we were on to you, you suddenly intensified your program of attack. You attempted first to murder your own uncle, but were foiled. You then"—he gazed at me sternly till I stopped sputtering—"proceeded to Staten Island, murdered the Farmer, joined forces with your beautiful partner, and came here to kill me. That, as I see it, is the sum and essence of your activities."

I said, "May I speak now?"

He waved two clusters of sausages airily. "The floor is yours."

"All right. Number one, I did not come here to kill you. I came— No. That isn't number one."

"Take your time," he said. "Organize your thoughts."

"May I stand up?"

"Certainly. Pace the floor if you wish. Except near the door, of course."

"Thank you."

Moe and Curly—I mean Harvey and Luke—had been fading away into somnolence over by the door, but now that I was on my feet they suddenly became very alert again, standing shoulder to shoulder in front of the doorway, gripping their guns tightly, glaring at me as though daring me to get funny. It was my own personal feeling that if I said, "Boo," to those two, they'd turn tail and run to Montauk Point, but that didn't matter. My job wasn't to escape, but to plead my case.

How to do it, though, how to do it? I prowled around the room, trying to think. After a minute I stopped and said, "Can I ask a question?"

"Certainly."

"Is that why you sent your two men to—"

"Trask and Slade."

"Yes. Trask and Slade. Is that why you sent them to kill me? Because you believed I was giving information to the police?"

"Naturally," he said. "An adequate enough reason, I believe."

"Sure. Can I ask another?"

"Ask as many as you wish."

"What made you think it was me? That was giving information to the police?"

He shook his head, with that pitying smile on it again. "We checked," he said. "Naturally. The police were obviously in receipt of information concerning shipments of various commodities. There were at least two instances, and perhaps more, when particular shipments went through your hands, and which were perfectly safe before reaching you, had developed a police tail after leaving your hands."

"You mean packages I kept in my safe."

"Certainly."

"What makes you think it was me?"

"As I say, we checked. I spoke to Mahoney myself, asked him to find out, and the word came back it was the bartender. You."

"Who's this Mahoney?" I said. "I don't know any Mahoney."

"Our liaison on the police force."

Mahoney. It was a name I wanted to remember, for future reference. But I would also want it narrowed down to more than that, so I said, "Would that be Michael Mahoney?"

"No," he said. "Patrick." Then he frowned, as though wondering why he'd told me that.

Before he could think long enough to realize he'd been psyched, I said, "How can you be sure you can trust this guy Mahoney?"

"Of course we can trust him. We bought him, years ago."

I said, "Well, this time he's lying, Mr. Gross, before I got that job out at that bar, I was just a drifter, just a bum, living off my mother all the time. My Uncle Al got me that job, and it just suited me right. All I wanted out of life was to go on running that bar. I never looked inside any of the packages or envelopes I was asked to hold for a while, and I never asked anybody any questions about what was inside them or about anything else, because I didn't want to know. I never wanted a lot of money, I never wanted revenge, I never wanted anything but to go on running that bar."

"Until," he said, "Miss Althea Agricola came into your life."

"No, sir. No, sir, that isn't right."

He shrugged and shook his head. "Tell your story," he said.

"Just let me get it straight. I want to tell you everything in chronological order."

"Take your time."

I went over by the window and glanced out, and here came the black car, the same old black car. I stared, and saw it pull to a stop with the other cars parked out front, and they got out of the car, the two of them, and hitched their trousers and shifted their shoulders inside their coats and pushed their hatbrims around a little and looked at each other and up at this window and moved toward the front door.

Trask and Slade.

So I couldn't take my time after all. Before he'd come back up, Mr. Gross had contacted Trask and Slade, told them to come out here.

I turned and said, "Trask and Slade. They just drove up."

But he waved a fat hand to indicate it didn't matter. "They'll wait downstairs until called for," he said. "Go on with your story. In chronological order, I believe you said."

"Yes, sir."

I went back to the table and sat down, and started: "Like I said, I never gave information to the police because I never had any information to give them and never wanted to give them any information anyway. So last night when those two guys—Trask and Slade—when they came in and put that card with the black spot down on the bar, I thought they were kidding. It was just dumb luck I got away. I went to see my Uncle Al to ask him to help me, because the organization wanted to kill me and I didn't know why, because I didn't do anything wrong, but he was too scared to even talk to me. So I went to see Mr. Agricola to find out from him—"

"Excuse me," he said, holding up a wad of bread dough shaped somewhat like a hand. "If you were so devoid of information, how did you know to find the Farmer's farm? From the Farmer's daughter, perhaps?"

"No, sir. Trask and Slade mentioned the name to my Uncle Al, I heard them when I was hiding in the stairwell. Then I went to a friend of mine, he used to sell pills for Mr. Agricola and he knew he lived out on Staten Island, and so I went out to Staten Island and found him in the phone book."

"The phone book?" He seemed startled.

"Yes, sir."

"The Farmer was listed in the Staten Island phone book?"

"Yes, sir."

He shook his head. "One never knows. Very well, go on."

"Yes, sir. When I got there, he was dead. That was the first time I'd ever seen him or his daughter or that farm. A man named Clarence locked—"

"The bodyguard," he said, in a tone that indicated trouble for the bodyguard in the near future.

"Yes, sir. He locked me in the barn, and then Miss Althea came with a gun and unlocked the door and tried to shoot me, because she thought I'd killed her father. She took two shots at me."

"And missed you."

"Yes, sir."

"How very fortunate for you."

"It happened," I said.

He smiled—pityingly, again—and said, "Go on, go on."

"I got the gun away from her, and outside I found my friend that had told me where Mr. Agricola lived, he'd come after me to see if I was okay, and we got away together. We took Miss Althea with us for a hostage, but she wouldn't believe me when I told her the truth about her father, and she got away back on Sunrise Highway and my friend went after her and I haven't seen him since. Either of them."

"How sad. I never, never had the privilege of meeting

the Farmer's child, and I had been looking forward to your introducing us. Is this the end of your story?"

"I came here," I said, "to talk to you, to find out why you wanted me killed, and to try to convince you I didn't do whatever it was you thought I did. I didn't give anybody any information, I'm not in cahoots with Althea Agricola, I didn't kill Mr. Agricola or anybody else, and I didn't come here to kill you. I don't know about this Mr. Mahoney, if he's lying on purpose or he just made a mistake, but whatever it was what he said is wrong."

"I see. Is that all?"

I could tell by his face, by his voice, that he didn't believe me. "And to ask you," I said, "to give me a chance to clear myself."

"Very touching," he said. "In other words, you would like me to let you go."

"Yes, sir. So I can prove I'm telling the truth."

"Surely you can see—"

"All right, everybody!" shouted a female voice from the doorway. "On your feet and get your hands up!"

Mr. Gross and I both scrambled to our feet and stuck our hands in the air. Behind me, over by the door, I could hear two thumps as Luke and Harvey dropped their guns, one of which was Tim's little pistol.

The female voice said, "Not you, dummy, you're on my side, remember? Put your hands down."

I turned around and it was Chloe there in the doorway, as wild and beautiful as a cheetah, holding the automatic in both hands. I smiled at her, put my hands down, and picked up both guns.

"Ah," said Mr. Gross. "The beauteous Miss Althea. How do you do?"

★ Chloe said, "I been listening in the hall, Charlie. You told him your story, and he wouldn't believe you. Now let's go."

I said, "We've got to be careful. Trask and Slade are downstairs."

"Who?"

So she hadn't been listening that long. "The two guys," I explained, "that've been looking for me."

Mr. Gross said, "Young lady, I was aware the younger generation had gone astray, but to be a willing accomplice in the cold-blooded murder of your own father is, it seems to me, carrying bohemianism too far."

Chloe gave him a look of scorn. "Don't be any more of a moron than you have to be," she told him.

I said, "Wait a minute. She didn't mean that, Mr. Gross."

She frowned at me. "I didn't?"

"When this is all over," I told her, "I'm going to want my job back in the bar. I'm not out to fight the organization." I turned to Mr. Gross. "You're making a mistake, Mr. Gross," I said. "And I'm going to prove it to you. All I want is the job I had, and to be left alone."

"If the facts weren't so clear, the conclusions so inescapable," he said, "I could almost believe you. You should have been an actor."

I said, "Mr. Gross, if I came here to kill you, why

don't I do it right now? If that's Miss Althea there, why doesn't *she* kill you right now?''

''Because of Trask and Slade downstairs,'' he said reasonably. ''As you just told the Farmer's daughter, their presence means you'll have to be careful. You can't risk the noise of a shot.''

Chloe was looking gimlet-eyed at Mr. Gross. ''What did he mean by that crack?'' she wanted to know.

We both looked at her. ''What crack?'' I said.

''That crack about the farmer's daughter.'' She stared daggers. ''Just what did you mean by that, Fatso?''

Mr. Gross looked insulted, which on him meant his face got a greenish tinge again. I said, ''It wasn't a crack. He didn't mean anything by it. I'll explain it later.''

''He better watch his lip,'' she said.

I said, ''I'm sorry, Mr. Gross, but I'm going to have to tie you and gag you. So we can get away.''

Mr. Gross said, ''Harvey, call for help, Luke, you too.''

Harvey opened his mouth and said, ''HELP!''

Luke did, too.

Now, that wasn't fair. Chloe and I were the ones with the guns, we were the desperate characters. According to the rules, Mr. Gross and Luke and Harvey should all have been very quiet and very obedient and very meek. Instead, Harvey and Luke were both saying, ''HELP!'' not quite in unison, and under the racket Mr. Gross was looking at us with the patient smile of an inevitably victorious Lucy about to play another game of checkers with Charlie Brown.

We had our choice. We could shoot everybody and run, or we could just run.

We just ran.

''This way!'' I shouted, over the shouting of Harvey and Luke, who leaned closer together in the style of barbershop quartets and who were practically making a theme song out of HELP. I shouted my own shout, and waved my arms, and ran from the room at full tilt. Chloe came along in my wake.

I figured Trask and Slade would be coming up the front way, along with everybody else, so I headed for the back stairs, the ones I'd been brought up earlier. We leaped down the steps three and four at a time, and behind us we could hear Luke and Harvey yelling at the top of their lungs, now having worked into a kind of tempo, a sort of Sonja Henie skating-music beat. Mr. Gross was yelling, too, by now, shouting directions to somebody to do something. I could guess what.

Still, there was a chance; we did have a lead on them. At the foot of the stairs, I made a false start toward the rear door I'd come in, but then I changed my mind and my direction and headed for the front of the house instead, Chloe willy-nilly in my wake. They would all, I was hoping, figure us to go out the back way, so they'd go out the front and circle the house on both sides to get us. If we followed them out the front way, we might have the slight advantage of surprise.

I slowed down a bit, going through the ground-floor rooms, and Chloe at last caught up with me, panting and tugging at my arm. She whispered, "What are we going this way for?"

But there wasn't time for explanations. I shook my head, and motioned for her to stick with me and ask no questions.

Ahead of us there was a closed door. I opened it, cautiously, and entered an unpopulated room full of card tables, with playing cards scattered all over their surfaces. Folding chairs stood back from the tables, as though they'd been vacated by people abruptly getting to their feet and hurrying away. Across the way, past a wide doorway, there was a hall leading to left and right, and a hubbub of conversation but no one to be seen.

I led the way, tiptoeing now, across this empty room to the doorway. I stuck my head around the corner, and down to the right I saw a cluster of people grouped around the foot of the stairs, some looking up the staircase and others looking toward the front door, which was just beyond the cluster and which was standing open. There was no more shouting now, from anywhere. Mr. Gross's bigger-than-life wife was prominent in the middle of the cluster, a head taller than anyone else. She looked somewhat offended.

I brought my head back into the card room and whispered to Chloe, "We're going through those people out there. Through them and out the front door and straight down the driveway and back to the car. It's still in the same place?"

"Yes."

"Holler and wave your gun around while we're leaving the house," I told her. "It'll help clear us a path."

She nodded. She looked intent, and excited, and very High School of Music and Art. I could have been giving her directions to find a Communist cell meeting, or a Blass Mass, or a pot party, or the Egyptology room in the Fifth Avenue library.

"Get set," I whispered. I felt, myself, very Robert Mitchum. I had to stifle an urge to synchronize watches.

We stood poised at the threshold, like ski jumpers at the top of the slide. I hefted the guns in my two hands—my old pistol in my right, and Harvey's automatics in my left—and then I hollered, "Let's go!" and went racing around the corner, yelling, "Yah! Yah! Yah!" I also waved my firearm-full hands around quite a bit. Behind me I could hear Chloe shrieking like a banshee.

The card-party guests exhibited for our bemusement a catalogue of startled white faces, and then whisked those faces away to left and right like the skeletons in a black-light ride at Disneyland. A path opened between us and the door, and we tore through it.

Trask and Slade appeared in the doorway, side by side, filling it. Black suits, black topcoats. Black guns in their hands, black scowls on their faces, Menace, menace.

I couldn't have stopped if I'd wanted to. Whooping, I lowered my head and kept on going.

My shoulders caught them amidships, my left shoulder thudding into the breadbasket of Trask or Slade and my right shoulder chunking into the midsection of Slade or Trask. I heard, "Oooff!" in stereo, and then I was through the doorway and there was nothing pressed against my shoulders any more, and I was flailing forward in a wild attempt to get my feet back under my torso where they belonged.

I ran for the next little space of eternity completely off balance. My feet pumped and pumped, trying to catch up with the rest of me, and it seemed certain I was about to dig my nose into the gravel driveway and maybe ream out a furrow twenty feet long. At the same time I was trying to catch up with myself, I was also trying to run around all the cars parked in front of Mr. Gross's house, having no desire to run *into* any of them, not at my current speed, which I later estimated to have been about Mach point nine. I don't think it was much higher than that because I didn't hear any sonic boom.

What I did hear was a lot of shouting and hirruping, all from behind me. Ahead, once the last parked car had been cleared there was only the lit driveway and the lovely blank hole in the hedge that led to the street. Flailing, flying, I hurtled toward it, and on through.

Unfortunately, I couldn't make the necessary right turn. I kept on going, turning in a slight arc that would have had me complete a right turn somewhere out around Montauk Point, and if it hadn't been for the hedge on the other side of the road I don't know where I might have gone.

Where I *did* go was into the hedge. *Thunk!* I got my arms up in front of my face just in time, and the hedge stopped me the way all that cotton batting stops bullets in ballistics test boxes in the movies.

I hung there, exhaling, for a second or two, until somebody pulled me by the back of Artie's jacket, and Chloe's voice said, with shrill insistence, "Come *on!* Come *on!*"

I came on, out of the hedge and off again. There had been no shots at all, and so far no one had come out as far as the road after us, but I thought I heard a car being started in there and that had to mean Trask and Slade were after us again. Now, I guessed, more than ever.

We pelted down the road, through the dim light at the intersection and into the lovely darkness beyond. I'd gotten into the lead again by then, having long legs and no sense of chivalry, and so I was first into the car, through the door on the driver's side and across past the steering wheel, which caught me a good one in the ribs.

Chloe leaped in after me, slammed the door, and jammed the key into the ignition. Looking back I could see four headlights coming out of Mr. Gross's driveway. You might know those guys would drive with their highs on.

"Hurry!" I said.

But as I said it the car leaped forward, and I cracked

my head on the back of the seat, biting my tongue severely.

"They'll never get us now!" Chloe cried, and crouched over the wheel with the smile of competition on her lips and the glint of motor madness in her eyes.

I closed my own eyes, and awaited the worst.

★ Chloe said, not without pride, "I've lost them."

It was the first word either of us had said in ten minutes or more. Not that the intervening time had been soundless, oh no; the shriek of tires and squeal of brakes had filled in nicely for the lack of dialogue.

I had spent the time—I never have claimed to be anything but a coward, I hope you've noticed that—with my eyes shut. Even so, I could visualize our screaming progress through the tiny towns of Long Island, the long bulky black 1938 Packard roaring down the night-dark streets, the natives peering fearful and open-mouthed from their cottage windows, the whole thing straight out of Carol Reed. I was so caught up in my imagery that now, when I did at last open my eyes again, I was surprised to see the world not in black and white.

Chloe said, "Where to?"

"Back to the city," I said. That much thinking I'd been able to do down there behind my shut eyelids, while the world had squealed and teetered around me. "I've got to find a policeman named Patrick Mahoney."

"That should be easy," she said. "I doubt there's more than fifty Patrick Mahoney's on the force."

"Well, I've got to find mine," I said.

"Why?"

There was no quick answer to that. I had to fill her in on everything I had said to Mr. Gross, and everything he had said to me, and when I was finished with all that I said, "The way it looks to me, I've got to prove I didn't inform to the police, and I've got to prove I didn't kill Mr. Agricola. If I can prove I didn't inform, that ought to help prove I didn't do the killing."

"Maybe," she said. She sounded doubtful.

I said, "What's wrong?"

"It all sounds too complicated," she said. "You don't know any of these people or what the real situation is or anything else. If you didn't give information to the police, then somebody else did. And if you didn't kill Mr. Agricola, then somebody else did that, too. Maybe the same somebody, maybe a different one. The point is, you don't know who these people are or what they're doing or what they're after. You're probably just a sidelight to them, one little corner of some great big thing that's going on."

"I'm learning," I told her. "What else can I do? I keep moving, from name to name, from fact to fact, and I hope after a while I find out what's going on and I get everything straightened out, and then I can go back to the bar and forget all this mess."

"Do you think so?" She glanced at me, and then back out at the road again.

I didn't get what she meant. "Do I think what?"

"After this is over," she said. "Even if you get everything straightened out the way you want, do you think you'll be content to go back to your old life again?''

''Ho ho,'' I said. ''You bet your sweet—you're darn right I will. Content is hardly the word. Those cows on that evaporated milk can are nervous wrecks in comparison.''

She shrugged. ''If you think so,'' she said.

''I know so.'' I looked around, out the windshield and the side window. ''Where are we?''

''I'm not sure. On Long Island somewhere.''

''That much I knew already.''

''I think we're going north,'' she said. ''If we are, we'll cross one of the expressways sooner or later, and we can take it back into the city.''

''Fine.''

She said, ''Charlie, something else.''

''Something else?''

''I don't know if you've thought about this or not,'' she said, and stopped.

''Neither do I,'' I told her. ''Maybe I will after you say it.''

She said, ''If Gross thinks I'm Althea, and he thinks you and I are in cahoots, and he thinks we're out to wreck the organization, where do you suppose he thinks we're going now?''

''I don't know.''

She shook her head. ''He told you, Charlie, about a crooked cop, what he called the liaison between the organization and the police force. Charlie, he's sure to think we're on our way to kill Mahoney.''

''Oh,'' I said.

''If we do find him,'' she told him, ''we'll probably find Trask and Slade right along with him.''

"They can't be everywhere at once," I said, though by now I wasn't so sure.

"All they have to be," she pointed out, "is where you are."

I shook my head. "Well, I've got nothing else to do. Mahoney's the man I've got to see next, that's all."

"All right, fine. You're in charge. Yeah, there's Grand Central."

Grand Central is a parkway. Chloe tooled the mighty Packard around the long curve down from the street we'd been on, and joined the rest of the night traffic streaming toward the city.

One question Chloe hadn't brought up, but I'd been thinking about anyway, was how we were going to find Patrick Mahoney. All I knew about him was that he was a policeman. He could be a uniformed cop, or a detective in plainclothes. He could be stationed in a precinct in any one of the boroughs, or he could work out of the main Headquarters on Centre Street in Manhattan.

Although, come to think of it, the odds were pretty good he was well up there in the police hierarchy. A uniformed cop on a beat somewhere was hardly in a position to be what Gross had called the "liaison" between the organization and the police force. It seemed to me likeliest that Mahoney was some sort of wheel and would most likely be found at Centre Street.

But how to find out for sure, that was the problem.

A patrol car passed us, exceeding the posted speed limit, and I gazed after it wistfully, wishing we could catch up with it and flag it down and just ask the cop driving it if he could tell us who Patrick Mahoney was and how to—

Ah hah!

I said it aloud: "Ah *hah!*"

Chloe jerked, and the Packard lunged into another lane. "Don't *do* that!" she said.

"Canarsie," I told her. "Never mind Manhattan, drive to Canarsie."

"Canarsie? Are you kidding?"

"No, I'm not kidding. Drive to Canarsie."

"I couldn't find Canarsie," she told me, "with a troop of Boy Scouts to help."

"I could. Stop the car and let me drive."

"You sure you know how to drive this kind of car?"

Coming from her, that was an insult. But I let it pass. "Yes," I said simply. "Pull over to the side."

She did, and we switched places, she sliding over and me running around the front of the car. It was a very large car, with a very long front and a very high hood. I got behind the wheel and immediately felt like a member of Patton's Third Army. Tanks, you know.

What a dream that car was to drive! It was like driving a big old mohair sofa, equipped with a lot of tiny highly oiled ball bearings. It was the first time in my life I ever wished I smoked cigars. I can see why gangsters and little old ladies are assumed to drive cars like this; such a car gives a gangster a feeling of power and importance he can't possibly get in, say, a Cadillac you can barely tell apart from some minor hood's Chevrolet, and a lot of time at the wheel of this sort of car would surely keep the bloom of youth in the cheeks of any reasonably hip little old lady.

"No wonder we got away from those guys," I said, as we rolled merrily along. "This car has too much self-respect to be caught by some four-eyed piece of tin with plastic seat covers."

"Thanks a lot," said Chloe.

"The driver helped, too," I assured her, but I only said it to be polite.

★ I found Patrolman Ziccatta walking along East 101st Street, practicing with his nightstick. He wasn't doing too well tonight, so I heard him before I saw him: Clatter, and "Damn!"

We'd been driving around the neighborhood for fifteen minutes, moving very slowly with all the windows open. It was heading toward midnight and all Canarsie was, as usual, comatose. My competition, the other two neighborhood bars, were both open, of course, their windows full of red neon, but if they were not comatose they were at least somnolent. My own bar, the ROCK GRILL, was comatose; it was strange to drive by and see it closed and empty. How I wished I could get out of the car and go in there and open the place up, light it up, turn on the TV, put my apron on, maybe have a little small-talk with a customer or two, assuming a customer or two might come by.

The late show tonight, I remembered all at once, was *Kiss of Death,* where Victor Mature wants to go straight and Richard Widmark won't let him and pushes the old lady down the stairs in the wheelchair. And the late late show was going to be *It's a Gift,* the old W. C. Fields comedy, where Fields buys the orange grove in California.

That was an awful lot of good television to be missing,

all on account of somebody making a stupid mistake some place.

So anyway, we drove around the neighborhood about fifteen minutes before the clatter and damn told me I'd found Patrolman Ziccatta. I stuck my head out the window and, keeping my voice down as much as possible, said, "Hoy!"

"Eh?" I could see him on the sidewalk, in the darkness midway between two streetlights, bending over to pick up his nightstick. Staying bent over, he swayed this way and that, like somebody involved in a religious ritual of some kind, looking around to see who'd called him.

"Over here," I said. "It's me, Charlie Poole."

I'd meanwhile brought the Packard up to the lefthand curb, near him. Patrolman Ziccatta looked over at me, finally found me and recognized me, said, "Oh! It's you, Charlie," picked up his nightstick, straightened, and came over to the car. "You buy this?" he asked.

"What? Oh, the car. No, I just borrowed it."

"I noticed the placed closed before," he said. "I was wondering were you maybe sick or something."

"I had things I had to do," I said. 'I can't talk about it right now, if you don't mind. No offense."

"Not at all," he said. "Why should I stick my nose in your private business?" And he bent forward again to smile past me at Chloe and raise his uniform hat. 'Good evening," he said.

She smiled back, and nodded her head, and said, "Good evening."

"Patrolman Ziccatta," I said, going through the amenities although my heart wasn't in it, "this is Chloe—uh—"

"Shapiro," she said.

"Shapiro," I said. "Chloe Shapiro. Chloe, this is Patrolman Ziccatta."

They both said, "How do you do?"

I was beginning to feel impatient. Any minute we'd be serving tea and chocolate-chip cookies. I said, "Patrolman Ziccatta, there's a question I wanted to ask you."

"Sure, Charlie. Name it."

"In confidence," I said. "And I can't tell why I have to ask this question."

He put his left hand on his badge, though I guess he meant the gesture to be hand on heart, and said, "I don't snoop, Charlie, I don't pry. Why should I be a nosy parker?"

I said, "Fine. What I want to know is, there's a man somewhere on the police force named Patrick Mahoney, and what I—"

"I'd be surprised if there wasn't," said Patrolman Ziccatta, and laughed. He bend forward again, and looked twinkle-eyed at Chloe, and said, "Wouldn't you, miss? Be surprised if there wasn't?"

The smile she gave him this time was perfunctory, I'm happy to report. I said, "This is serious, Patrolman Ziccatta, it really is."

He sobered immediately, and straightened till he was practically standing at attention. "Sorry, Charlie," he said, "It just struck me funny, that's all. You can see that."

"Sure," I said. "The question is, I want to find this guy Mahoney. I think he's probably stationed at Centre Street, but I'm not sure."

"What is he, a wheel?"

"I think so. But maybe not."

"So what do you want from me?"

"Could you find out some way if there is a Patrick Mahoney stationed at Centre Street, or a Patrick Mahoney who's a wheel stationed somewhere else? And find out on the quiet, so Mahoney doesn't get wise?''

He frowned at me. ''Charlie, are you up to something you shouldn't? I don't want to talk like a cop now, you know that, I want to talk like a friend. If you're involved in something you shouldn't, your best bet is get out of it, right now, before it's too late.''

''I'm not involved in anything I shouldn't,'' I told him, which wasn't exactly true but on the other hand was true for what he'd meant. I said, ''I'd appreciate it if you wouldn't ask me about this.''

He spread his hands, and shrugged his shoulders, and said, ''All right, Charlie, I don't snoop, I don't interfere. Your business is your business.''

''Thanks.''

''And I'll do what I can,'' he said. ''You'll stay here?''

''Yes.''

''I'll walk by the station house,'' he said, ''see what I can find out.''

''Quietly,'' I said.

''Naturally.''

''I could drive you over to the station house,'' I said. ''That might be quicker.''

''I got to walk,'' he reminded me. ''But I'll meet you there. It's over on Glenwood Road, you know?''

''I know. I'll park down the block from it.''

''Fine.''

''Thanks a lot,'' I said.

''I haven't found out anything yet,'' he told me.

We waved at each other and he walked on his way, practicing some more. I put the Packard back in gear and headed for the 69th Precinct station house on Glenwood Road.

Chloe said, ''He's sort of sweet, isn't he? For a cop.''

"He's a nice guy," I said.

She said, "I bet you've got a better class of friends than somebody like Artie."

"What do you mean? *Artie's* my friend."

"Sure. But you're one of the best people he knows, and he's one of the worst people you know."

"Artie? What's wrong with Artie?"

"Never mind," she said. She patted my hand the way a teacher might pat the hand of a kid who'd just stayed back in kindergarten. "You just be yourself."

If there's one thing I can't stand, it's to be patronized. But I couldn't think of a really good comeback line, so I just hunched over the steering wheel and fumed.

Neither of us said anything more until I'd parked the car down the block from the station house, a converted frame one-family house that didn't look any more like a police station than like a moon rocket. Then Chloe said, "I wonder where Artie is now."

"Home, I suppose," I said. "But what about Miss Althea, that's what I wonder."

"We're better off without her," Chloe said. "She was all trouble, and no use to anybody."

"Listen," I said. "About that crack you made about Artie before."

"Charlie, you know Artie as well as I do. Why talk about it?"

"Well, you're his girl friend, for Pete's sake. Why do you say things like that about him?"

She smiled crookedly. "That isn't the question," she said. "The question is, I say those things and they're true, so why am I Artie's girl friend? And I'm not really even his girl friend, Charlie. At the best I'm one of his girl friends, and at the best he's one of my boy friends. I'm his morning-after girl, I told you that."

I said, "Why?"

She cocked her head to one side and seemed to consider the question. After a minute she said, "I'm twenty-three years old, Charlie. Puberty struck me when I was twelve. That's eleven years. When I was seventeen I got married, to a boy eighteen, believe me he was a mistake. Two years later I got a divorce for reasons of desertion. Not here, over in Jersey where we lived in Elizabeth. Maury worked in the Esso refinery until he ran out. Is this beginning to sound like a true-confessions story just a little bit?"

I said, "If you don't want to tell me about it, I don't—I mean, it's your personal business, I've got no right . . ."

"No, let me. I'm started now, so let me go. You've been taking a very simplistic attitude about me, Charlie, it's time you got a more complicated picture. Like for instance I've got a five-year-old daughter, Linda, my parents have her up in the Bronx."

I said, "Oh."

"Oh," she said. "You're darn right oh. One thing I'm happy about, I didn't let Maury talk me into quitting high school the middle of my senior year. I finished, I got my diploma. The last four years I've been working here and there, going to night school at NYU, sometimes I keep Linda and sometimes my parents keep her, and so it goes. You got a picture in your head now?"

"Sort of," I said.

"Good," she said. "Now, here's another point. After Maury, after getting married too early, one thing I haven't been in any hurry for is adult responsibility, you follow. That's why I unload Linda on my parents every chance I get, that's why I hang around with people like Artie and his crowd where there's no responsibility at all, you know what I mean?''

"I never got married when I was seventeen,'' I said, "but I guess my job at the bar is the same thing. Avoiding responsibility.''

"All right, so you understand that part. Now, one last point, and I hope I don't make you blush. Remember puberty at twelve. Married at seventeen. A mother at eighteen. I'm long since no virgin, Charlie, and I've got drives and needs just like anybody else. So I've got these drives and needs, and I don't want responsibility, so I wind up Artie Dexter's morning-after girl. You got the picture?''

"You didn't have to, uh,'' I said.

"Shut up, Charlie,'' she said. "I just want you to know what Artie is to me and what I am to Artie. And that I know what Artie is and it's just the weaknesses in Artie that made me connect with him.''

I said, "Well, uh, what about this social-conscience thing, this TV special and not selling the pills any more and all?''

"I know,'' she said. "There've been a couple of other signs like that. Like him looking up to you like he does these days. Maybe he's growing up, maybe pretty soon I'll have to be somebody else's morning-after girl.''

I said, "Couldn't you—''

"Don't say anything dumb, Charlie,'' she said. "Look, there goes your cop friend.''

I looked and there went my cop friend all right, into the station house.

Chloe said, "To get back to business, can I make a suggestion?''

"Sure.''

"After this, we call it quits for tonight. It's getting

late, Mr. Gross probably has men looking all over for us, we'd probably be smartest to hole up somewhere until morning. Besides, I'm getting tired and you should be, too."

"I guess I am," I said. "But—"

"You're not going to find this Mahoney in the middle of the night," she said.

"Where do I hole up?"

"Same place as last night. Artie's. I've got a key. We should be safe there till morning."

"We?"

She made a disgusted face. "Don't start a foolish argument, Charlie," she said. "I'm sticking with you. I'll drive the getaway car, I'll do whatever you need. I already came in handy once, remember?"

"I remember," I said. And I thought to myself, there was no point arguing with her. She was right about my waiting till morning before going on, and right about my holing up at Artie's place in the meantime. If Artie was there, or showed up by morning, we could all talk over who'd do what from there on. If Artie didn't show, the morning would be time enough to tell Chloe I'd feel better going off on my own.

Not that I would feel better. It just seemed as though that's what I ought to say.

A few minutes later Patrolman Ziccatta came back out of the station house and began walking back and forth, looking for us. We were across the street and down a ways to his left, in plain sight, with a streetlight just down at the corner behind us. I rolled my side window down and waved my arms at him, but he just kept walking back and forth and he couldn't find us.

All in all, Patrolman Ziccatta was not an ideal cop. He couldn't twirl his nightstick worth a damn, he didn't like poking his nose into other people's business, and he couldn't find a 1938 Packard parked directly across the street under a streetlight.

I finally had to holler, "Hey!"

He looked up, looked around, and saw us. In fact, he pointed at us, as though showing us to himself. He smiled, pleased to find us at last, and came across the street.

I said, *sotto voce*, "Did you find out anything?"

"Did I?" he said. "You bet I did." He leaned a forearm on the Packard, above my side window, and leaned down so his face was framed in the window. He smiled past me at Chloe and said, "Hello, there."

She smiled back, a little more sweetly than necessary I thought, and said, "Hello again."

"Hello, hello," I said, somewhat snappish. "What did you find out?"

"This might not be the right Patrick Mahoney," he said. "There's probably more Patrick Mahoney's on the force than you could shake a stick at."

"I don't want to shake a stick at anybody," I said. "Tell me about the Patrick Mahoney you've got."

"Well, he's a wheel," he said. "He's a deputy chief inspector, and that's right under an assistant chief inspector."

"Wow," I said snidely. "What does he deputy chief inspect?"

"He's in the Mob & Rackets Squad," he said. "He'd be second in command under Assistant Chief Inspector Fink."

"What's the Mob & Rackets Squad?"

"It's something they started after all that stuff came out on television about the Cosa Nostra. It's a special squad to be on the lookout for organized crime in New York City."

"I wonder if they find any," I said.

"I don't know if he's the Mahoney you want," Patrolman Ziccatta said.

I told him, "I'll be mightily surprised if he isn't. Where's he stationed, at Centre Street?"

"No. At Headquarters out in Queens."

"Queens," I said.

"It's probably in the phone book," he said. "Somewhere out in Queens."

"Queens."

He nodded. "Yeah. Queens."

"The Mob & Rackets Squad is out in Queens."

"Well, you know. It's a bureaucracy, Charlie, you know that."

"Sure. Thanks a lot, anyway. I really appreciate it."

"Any time, Charlie. And if there's anything I can do, whatever the problem is here, I don't want to pry but you know I'll do all I can to help."

"I know that," I said, and I did. Patrolman Ziccatta really was a first-rate guy. How he ever got on the force I do not know.

"Thanks again," I said.

He lowered his head so he could smile past me at Chloe again. "Well," he said to her, "good-bye again."

"So long," she said, and smiled upon him once more.

Ostentatiously I started the engine. "I don't want to keep you from your appointed rounds," I said.

"That's mailmen," he said, but he backed away from the car and the conversation was over.

As we drove away, Chloe said, "He's sweet."

I said nothing. I was feeling mixed emotions.

★ All the streets in Greenwich Village are one way the other way. I pushed the Packard around most of the Village, like a landlocked Flying Dutchman, and finally came on Perry Street from the rear. "Almost there," I said.

"It's about time."

"If you knew a quicker way," I said, "all you had to do was speak up."

"You're driving," she told me. For some reason, we'd been snapping at each other since Canarsie.

I was about to answer—about to say, in fact, "Thanks for the information"—when I saw the black car, the famous black car, parked by a fire hydrant directly across the street from Artie's apartment. I almost missed it, almost passed it by, because there was only one of them in it, either Trask or Slade, and I had come to think of them as inseparable, like the Doublemint girls. But there was no reason they wouldn't split up from time to time, for one to rest or go get fresh orders or some such thing. In this case my guess would be the other one was with Deputy Chief Inspector Mahoney.

Chloe, still blissfully unaware, said, "There's a parking space. Isn't that incredible?"

It was, but I went on by. The next intersection was West Fourth Street—this was two blocks north of where West Fourth crosses West Tenth and one block south of where West Fourth crosses West Eleventh, if you're keeping a crime map—and West Fourth Street is one way west, or south, so I took it.

Chloe said, "Hey! That was a *parking* space!"

"Trask or Slade," I said.

"What?"

"The killers. One of them is parked across the street from Artie's place."

She turned around in the seat and looked out the back window, although we'd now turned the corner and gone an additional block, so it was unlikely she could see in front of Artie's place too clearly. She squinted and said, "Are you sure?"

"I'm sure. I know those guys pretty good by now."

"In front of *Artie's* place? How come they're in front of Artie's place?"

"They're ubiquitous," I said.

"They're what?"

"That means you told Uncle Al I was there once before."

"Oh." Then one beat late, she took offense: "What are you talking about? How was I supposed to know—"

"All right, never mind. The point is, what now?"

"I'm tired, Charlie," she said. "I can't tell you how tired I am."

"Were there any lights in Artie's windows, did you notice?"

"No. I was looking for parking spaces."

I had come to Seventh Avenue and a red light. I was just as pleased to stop, since I had no idea where I was going. I said, "Is there any back way into his building, around from the next street?"

"I don't know. How would I know?"

"I don't know how you'd know. I'm tired too."

She said, "Isn't there any place else?"

I shook my head. "Artie was the only guy I could think of last night. What about your place?"

"Sorry. I've got two roommates, and they're both schizo enough as it is. I'm not about to bring a man in, in the middle of the night."

"Then I don't know."

The light turned green. Seventh Avenue is one way south. I turned that way, went about five feet, and was stopped by another red light.

Chloe said, "What about across the roofs?"

"What?"

"We'll go in the building on the corner, and up on the roof, and along the roofs to Artie's building, and down inside to the apartment."

I said, "How do we get into the building on the corner?"

"Oh," she said.

This light also turned green, and once again I turned right, this time onto Grove Street, which I took to Hudson Street, where the light was red.

She said, "We could drive around like this all night, you know."

"Please, I'm trying to think."

"Then we're lost," she said.

"Ha ha," I said. "Very funny."

The light, as they all do, turned green, and yet again I turned right. Hudson Street is one way north. I drove one block, to Christopher Street, and got stopped by a red light.

"This is ridiculous," Chloe pointed out. "There's got to be some way to get in there."

I said, "Such as."

We were both silent. We sat and watched the red light, and after a while it did guess what. I drove north up Hudson Street, past West Tenth Street—hello, West Tenth Street!—and past Charles Street, and past Perry Street—

hello, Artie's apartment, a block and a half to our right—and between Perry and West Eleventh I found a parking space. It was a little small, and I stuck the Packard in it like someone putting a marshmallow in a ring box. When it was at last within walking distance of the curb, I turned everything off and said, "All right. The apartment is two blocks from here. Let's think of a way in."

So neither of us said anything for a while. I sat with arms folded and stared gloomily out at the hood, glinting evilly in the night. I couldn't think of a thing. In fact, I had trouble thinking about thinking about the problem. I kept going off into reveries in which none of this had happened, in which I was at this very moment standing behind the bar in the ROCK GRILL, watching Baby LeRoy, on television, throw the can of clams at W. C. Fields.

Chloe said abruptly, "Maybe . . ."

Wrenched back from Baby LeRoy—now spilling the molasses on the floor—I turned my head and said, "Maybe what?"

With maddening slowness she said, "It might work." She was gazing out at the street and frowning in concentration.

A trifle impatient, I said, "What might work?"

"Neither one of them," she said thoughtfully, "got a good look at me. You're the one they know by sight."

"So?"

"In fact," she said, "Mr. Gross thinks I'm Althea, and Trask and Slade know what Althea looks like, so I'm perfectly safe. Perfectly safe."

"I'm happy for you," I said. She seemed less irritated now, no longer waspish, but I was having trouble making the adjustment.

"No, listen," she said, letting sarcasm pass for the first time in over an hour. "I'll go first. I'll walk along like I'm drunk, and when I get to his car I'll make a racket. I'll sing or something, or fall all over his car. I'll make a great big fuss and distract him, and you duck inside. Then I'll come in."

"What if he gets suspicious?"

"Why should he get suspicious? A drunk girl in Greenwich Village at one o'clock in the morning? What could be more natural?"

"I don't like it," I said.

"You think you should disapprove," she told me, "because I'm female and because Errol Flynn would disapprove."

"Then go right ahead and do it," I told her, cut to the point where I hoped she *would* get into a jam with Trask or Slade. "Have a big time," I told her.

"Don't be snippy. I know we're both tired, but control yourself."

"Fine," I said. "I'm controlling myself."

"Good. Now, here's the key. It unlocks both the downstairs door and the apartment door."

"Last night," I said, "the downstairs door wasn't locked."

"Oh?" She didn't seem very interested. She opened the door on her side. "Leave your jacket in the car," she said. "I'll wear it when I come back around, so he won't know I'm the same girl."

I said, "You really want to do this?"

"Yes. I'm tired, and it's perfectly safe, and we haven't been able to think of anything else."

I shrugged and got out of the car. I took my jacket off and left it on the front seat, then locked the door on my side and walked around to the sidewalk, where Chloe was standing and waiting for me. I said, "Maybe we ought to get a hotel room some place instead."

She looked at me. "There are so many things wrong with that idea," she said, "I hardly know where to begin."

"Like what?"

"Like number one, for instance, we couldn't get *a* hotel room, we'd have to get *two* hotel rooms."

"You could sleep at your own place."

"If I leave you alone, God knows what you'll do. Number two, neither of us have the money to waste on hotel rooms. Number three, we still want to get back in touch with Artie, and how do we do that if we don't go to his apartment?"

I said, "All right. You convinced me." I locked the door on this side of the car and gave her the keys. "Good luck," I said.

"Watch me," she said, and winked.

We walked down to the corner of Perry and Bleecker streets together, and I stationed myself against the corner building, where I could peek around at Perry Street and see what was doing. Chloe said, "Wait till I've got him good and distracted."

"Right."

"See you," she said, and walked around the corner. She began at once to sing, very loud and not on key: "*'Hail to the bastard king of England . . .'*" And so on.

I'd never heard that song all the way through before. That was really a very dirty song.

Singing, waving her arms in grandiose gestures to amplify the song, Chloe tottered down the block and angled across the street toward the black car. In her dungarees and black turtleneck sweater and long straight black hair she was every Greenwich Village free-love cliché ever spawned, and I didn't see how Trask or Slade could be anything in this world but distracted out of his mind.

Chloe, however, was taking no chances. Still singing, she brought up against the front left fender of the black car, and stood swaying there a few seconds, studying the obstruction. I couldn't see Trask or Slade from where I was, but it seemed a safe bet he was looking at Chloe and not across at Artie's building. I took a deep breath and prepared to make my dash.

Then Chloe took her sweater off.

The clown; she distracted *me*. I just stood there and gaped.

"'Now I lay me down to sleep,'" Chloe bellowed, top of her voice, and climbed up on the black car's hood. She arranged her sweater as a pillow and curled up on the hood like a cat on the hearth.

She wore a black bra.

Lying there, she finished the prayer, allowed a second or two to go by for reverence' sake, and then began to sing that song again.

Trask or Slade abruptly came boiling out of his car, shouting and hollering and waving his hands, like an orchard owner shooing kids out of his apple trees. "Get offa there! Come on, come on, get offa there!"

Chloe told him something I will not record, and rolled over on her other side.

At last I moved. I ran, like unto the wind. Chloe and Trask or Slade continued to shout at each other—I'm not sure but what I heard Chloe mention rape, as a matter of fact—and I did a Roger Bannister halfway down the block, turned left, up the steps, and into the building.

The downstairs door was unlocked tonight, too. I

thundered up the stairs and unlocked my way into Artie's apartment.

There was no light on in here, and I had to leave it that way. If Trask or Slade looked up and saw light from these windows, he'd surely come and investigate. Still, there was faint illumination from outside, and I made my way around the perimeter of the furniture lumped in the middle of the room, and when I got to one of the windows I looked down and saw a very rumpled-looking Chloe standing on the sidewalk next to the black car, pulling her black sweater on. Trask or Slade stood on the street side of the car, still making shooing motions with his hands. The two of them were still hollering at one another.

No one came out of any buildings to see what was going on. No police showed up. Everything was nice and private.

I watched, and Chloe finally went shuffling away, still singing and doing her drunk act. Trask or Slade stood in the street and glared after her till she'd rounded the far corner, and then he turned and looked up at me—that is, at the window behind which I was cowering—and then he got back into his car. I watched, and a few seconds later a match flared in the car as he lit a cigarette to calm his nerves.

Six hundred seconds went by, one at a time. I stood at the window and watched the street.

A young guy in work clothes—dungarees and a black jacket and a cap on his head—came walking down the street from the direction in which I had come. A cigarette dangled from his mouth, and his hands were in his jacket pockets. A rolled-up newspaper jutted out of a hip pocket of his dungarees.

He came down the street and stopped in front of this

building and flipped his cigarette in the street and I saw it was Chloe. I also saw the pale face of Trask or Slade across the way, looking at her and satisfying himself she wasn't me. Then she trotted up the steps and out of my line of vision.

I waited at the hall door for her. She came to the second floor, grinning, taking the newspaper from her pocket and the cap off her head. All of her hair had been stuffed into the cap one way or the other, and it now fell all asnarl around her face. She brushed it away, came into the dark living room, and said, "Well? How'd I do?'

"Great," I told her, "But the Hayes office made us cut the scene."

"Come on in the bedroom," she said. "We can turn the light on in there."

"Right."

I had grown somewhat used to the darkness by now, so I led the way, talking Chloe by the hand. We went through the doorway into the bedroom, I shut the door, and she switched on the light.

Artie didn't believe in cleaning up. The bed was unmade, the whole room was still the disreputable mess it had been when last I'd seen it. But it was a relatively safe place, and it contained a bed, and its only window faced on an airshaft, so I didn't object too much.

Chloe, taking off the jacket, said, "Well. He'll remember *me* awhile."

"Where'd you get the hat?" I asked her.

"Off a drunk sleeping on Charles Street," she said. She looked at it in disgust and threw it in a corner. "I hope I don't get bugs from it." She ruffled her already-ruffled hair. "Well," she said, "you slept on the floor last night, so you can have the bed tonight. I'll sleep out on the sofa."

"I thought you said I was Errol Flynn," I reminded her. "This is more the Cary Grant bit, isn't it? He was always the one spending the night in the same room with a woman and they're not going to do it."

"That's right," she said offhandedly, "we're not going to do it." She'd been looking around the room. "No note in here," she said. "Maybe there's one in the living room, we'll look when it gets light."

I didn't say anything. Sex had just hit me in the stomach and I was having trouble inhaling.

I couldn't tell you the last time that had happened to me, and after all this time with Chloe that it was happening now was as surprising as it was inconvenient.

It was the damnedest thing. This morning I'd seen her take her dungarees off, and nothing. Tonight I'd seen her take her sweater off, and nothing. In between, I'd ridden all over the Greater New York area in the Packard with her, and nothing. Just a minute ago I'd taken her hand to lead her through the dark living room, and still nothing.

I think it was ruffling the hair that did it. She stood there in that messy bedroom, a rumpled sexy elf looking warm and distracted and tired, and she raised her right arm and ruffled her hair, and there it was. What they call in books a heightened awareness came over me.

A heightened awareness. Yeah, I'll say. I was suddenly so aware of Chloe as a female body, a collection of feminine parts, that I was paralyzed. I couldn't think, I couldn't move, I could hardly breathe.

Flashback: The summer that I was fourteen, I worked as a messenger boy for a deli in midtown Manhattan, carrying coffees and sandwiches into the office buildings along Fifth and Madison avenues. One afternoon, having left an order in an office in the Longines-Wittnauer Building, I boarded a crowded down elevator, and the next floor down three very sexy busty hippy blondes got on board. I guess there was a talent agency on that floor or something. Anyway, we were all crammed together in that elevator, and I had one of those girls pressed against my front, and another one pressed against each side. By the time we reached street level I was so shaken I went over to a White Rose on Sixth Avenue and lied about my age and had my very first shot of bar whiskey. I hated it.

Until tonight, with Chloe, I had never had the old heightened awareness that much ever again. And now the intervening ten years, all the dates with girls, the rare—I'm ashamed to say how rare—scores, all were washed away as completely as though a dam had burst. I was fourteen again, crowded into the elevator again, afraid again to tremble.

Chloe raised her arms over her head and stretched. "Well," she said, while I died. "Anything you want to talk about, or shall we just go to bed?"

"Bed," I said.

"Good. I'm too tired to think, anyway. I'll have to turn this light out before I open the door."

I nodded.

One hand on the doorknob, the other on the light switch, she looked over at me and smiled and said, "You're a real nut, Charlie."

I roused myself, flashed her a nervous smile of my own, and managed to say, "You're something of a goober yourself."

"Huh." She switched off the light, opened the door, and went out to the living room. "Good night," she said, in the dark, and shut the door again.

"Good night," I mumbled, though she couldn't hear me.

I didn't get as much sleep as I needed.

★ I smelled eggs. Frying, scrambling, omeleting, perhaps even poaching. At any rate, eggs.

Naturally, I opened my eyes. Naturally, that woke me up.

I was lying on my back on Artie's bed, dressed only in shorts. I'd gone to sleep covered by a sheet, but sometime in the night I must have kicked it off; I could remember having had several strenuous dreams, the details of all of which had happily been lost.

Ersatz daylight grayed the airshaft window, revealing but not enriching the bedroom. I sat up and looked around the gray lumpy mess everything was in, just like my own bedroom over the bar in Canarsie—so far and far away!—and I found myself feeling as maudlinly homesick as a Third Avenue Irishman. I was beginning my third day as a fugitive.

A clatter of crockery from the other room reminded me of the egg aroma that had awakened me, and all at once my stomach started growling in a determined and irritable manner, and what with one thing and another the day had begun.

I left Artie's bed reluctantly, and shuffled over to the bathroom, where I abluted, after which I borrowed some too-small underwear from Artie's dresser, put on my shoes and trousers, and went out in my undershirt to the living room.

History repeats. The same sloe-eyed raven-tressed dungaree-clad barefoot beauty stood at the same stove scrambling eggs. A cigarette dangled from her lips, to complete the impression of jaded wanton evil. In a silent movie, the first shot of Chloe would inevitably have been followed by a slide reading:

THE OTHER WOMAN

The Other Woman said, "How do you like your scrambled eggs, wet or dry?"

Until that moment I'd thought I was hungry, even starving. My stomach, in fact, was continuing unabated to growl. But being faced first thing in the morning with a decision between wet scrambled eggs (ugh) and dry scrambled eggs (gah) was too much for me. Therefore, "Coffee," I said.

She looked at me in surprise. "You don't want any eggs?"

The more I woke up, the worse I felt, like coming out of novocaine. "Maybe later," I said, in re eggs, more to soothe Chloe and get her to stop talking about eggs than out of any conviction that I might at some future date begin to eat food again. "Just coffee now," I explained further, to nail it all down, and went over to the complex of furniture in the middle of the room, where I sat down in the general direction of an armchair.

The Other Woman suggested, "How about toast?"

Toast. I squinted, to show I was trying to think. The mention of the word toast didn't immediately repel me, so I said, "All right. That sounds all right."

But she wasn't done with me. She said, "How many slices?"

I frowned. I rubbed my nose. I blinked several times. I

scratched my left ankle bone with the edge of my right shoe. I said, "I don't know."

"Two? Can you eat two?"

She insisted on an answer, that's all there was to it. Little did she care that my mind wasn't functioning. I said, "I guess so. No, maybe not. Or, wait a second . . ."

"I'll make one," she said.

I nodded. "That's good."

"If you want another one after, you can have it."

"That's fine."

"With your eggs, if you want eggs after."

"That's wonderful."

She went back, at last, to her chefery. But not for long; a minute later she wanted to know did I want jelly on my toast. When I said no to that, she wanted to know if I wanted honey on my toast. When she got another no, she announced she though it might be a good idea if I had orange marmalade on my toast, what did I think of that?

"Shut up, Chloe," I decided.

She turned around and looked at me. "What?"

"Stop talking," I amplified. "Stop questioning. I don't want anything on the goddam toast, not anything."

"Not even butter?"

I got on my feet and threw sofa cushions at the walls.

Chloe stood watching me. When I was finished, she said, "I know what's the matter with you. And it's your own fault."

"What?"

But now—*now*—now she was done talking. She turned an eloquent back on me and finished scrambling her eggs.

While waiting for my toast and coffee, I walked around the room picking up sofa cushions again and putting them back where I'd found them. I also found twenty-seven cents in the sofas, so it wasn't a total loss.

The food and I were done at the same time. Chloe carried everything over to the furniture, put the plates and cups downs on end tables, and sat in haughty silence directly in my line of vision while she went scoop, scoop, scoop with her eggs. I nibbled at my coffee and sipped my toast.

When I could stand the silence no longer, and even though I knew I was putting myself at a perhaps fatal disadvantage, I finally said, "What did you mean by that?"

"Mean by what?" she lied.

Oh. I could see the conversation stretching out ahead of us like one of those landscapes with the neat straight perspective lines meeting at infinity, the kind of thing done by schoolchildren in composition books and Salvador Dali in the Museum of Modern Art. I would say youknowwhatI'mtalkingabout, and then she would say noIdon'tknowwhatyou'retalkingabout, and then I would say youknowexactlywhatI'mtalkingabout, and then she would. . .

But why go on? I avoided it, the whole thing, tons and tons of words in bales, by saying instead, "You said you knew what was the matter with me, and you said it was my fault. What did you mean by that?"

"You know what I meant," she said.

So. She was determined to have that conversation no matter what.

Well, I was determined too. I nibbled some more coffee and said, "Well, I don't. If you feel like telling me, fine. If you don't, never mind."

She frowned around her egg scooper and let the silence mount up in uneven blocks between us. I sipped at my toast—on which she had put butter, after all—and felt myself beginning, just beginning, to come back to life.

Chloe said, "Your grumpiness, that's what I mean."

I looked attentive, but didn't say anything.

"It's because," she said, "you didn't get enough sleep last night."

And then, for the first time since waking up, I remembered how last night had ended, the awareness that had washed over me and which had kept my little mind churning away until practically dawn, running pornographic movies on the white inner surface of my skull.

I could feel the blush starting. I held the toast and coffee cup up in front of my face for camouflage, and mumbled, "I don't know what you're talking about." All at once I *wanted* that round-and-round conversation.

We could never want the same thing at the same time. She brushed my attempt at verbosity aside and said, "It's because you've got a letch for me, that's why."

"Nonsense," I swallowed. And then, in one last-ditch attempt: "I don't know what you mean."

"And," she went inexorably on, "you kept thinking about me in that bed in there with Artie Dexter, in that same bed you were sleeping in all alone, and me just one room away out here."

"Don't be silly," I said bravely, into my coffee cup. "I was asleep before my head hit the pillow."

"I heard you tossing around in there. Until practically dawn."

"I thrash around in my sleep."

"Funny you didn't thrash the last few hours."

I would have answered that in short order, but I seemed to have a mouthful of toast.

She said, "You're a snob, that's what you are."

I pushed the toast out of the way long enough to say, "*What?*" I was legitimately astonished.

"A snob," she repeated. Bright circles of color were burning angrily on her cheekbones. I saw with some surprise that she'd been, all this time, holding back a real fury. She said, "You wanted to start something with me last night when you took my hand. And you wanted to come out here afterwards, after we'd both gone to bed. And you didn't do it."

"Uh," I said.

"I thought at first," she said, "it was because you were shy, bashful. I thought that was kind of cute. But that wasn't the reason at all. The reason was, you're a snob. Because I've been to bed with Artie Dexter, you think I'm not good enough for you, that's the reason."

"Oh, no," I said. "No no, that isn't—"

"Shut up, you." She got to her feet. "Let me tell you something," she said. "You may think because I'm not a virgin I'm not good enough for you, but if you *are* a virgin you damn well wouldn't be good enough for me. So you can just go to hell, that's what you can do."

What was there to say to *that*? Nothing; exactly what I said.

When she was done glaring at me and listening to my silence, she picked up her plate and cup and stalked over to the sink and busied herself there.

As for me, I stuck the rest of the toast in my mouth and ruminated.

Chloe's charge, it seemed to me, broke down into sections, which would have to be dealt with separately. Part one: that I had slept poorly out of an awakened lust for her body. Part two: that I had done nothing to ease this lust because of moral snobbery.

Very well. As to part one, I could admit that much to

myself as being true, though whether or not I would be able to make the same admission to Chloe was another matter. But as to part two, that was as wrong as it could be. I had done nothing about my lust, that was true, but it was simply and entirely because it hadn't occurred to me there was anything I *could* do.

Well, was there? Had there been? Could I have approached Chloe last night? I still wasn't entirely sure that was what she meant. She could just as easily, women being what they are, have meant she'd expected an approach from me that she would have repulsed. Not that she had wanted it but that she had expected it, and was insulted when it hadn't been forthcoming.

Now she was at the sink, banging Artie's dishes around dangerously. And what was there for me to say to her? I tried, "I'm sorry."

That got no response.

I stood up and moved closer, though not too close. "Chloe," I said to her back. "I really am sorry."

Still no response. She seemed to be washing all the dishes in the sink, not just the ones she'd used for breakfast.

"What I did," I said, "or that is, what I didn't do, or what I didn't try to do, it wasn't because I'm a snob, it really wasn't. It was because I'm dumb. It was out of ignorance that I did it, or didn't do it, or didn't try to do it."

She turned, soapy halfway to the elbow, and gave me an eye as cold as a caveman's toenail. 'Now," she said, "you're laughing at me."

"Laughing at you? For Pete's sake, Chloe, I'm trying—"

"You certainly are," she said. She waggled a sudsy finger at me. "Let me tell you something Charlie Poole.

You're in no position to take any high moral attitudes, an underworld underling like you."

"Hey now! Whadaya mean, underworld underling? I'm no—"

"Yes you are. You ran that bar for the underworld, and you held packages for the underworld, and you helped the underworld get out of paying its taxes."

"I don't even *know* the underworld! My Uncle Al—"

"Don't talk to me about your Uncle Al." She'd waggled practically all the suds off her finger by now. "It's *you* I'm talking about. You, Charlie Poole. You can't just say you don't *know*, and your Uncle *Al*. You can't say, 'Not me, Chloe, I just work here, I don't have to take a moral stand, Chloe,' because that's Adolf Eichmann talk, that's what that is, and I don't think I have to tell you what I think of Adolf Eichmann."

I was getting mad. Adolf Eichmann! Talk about blowing things out of proportion! "Listen," I said. "Talk about—"

"I'm done talking," she said, and turned her back on me again. *Splosh* went her hands into the water. "Shouldn't you get going?" she asked, busy with the dishes. "You've got to find your friend Mahoney, remember."

I squinted at her back. "You're not coming along?"

"I've got my own life to live," she told the sink. "I'm supposed to go up and see my Linda today. Besides, I want to get back to my own place and see if there's any mail."

"So," I said, "You're not coming along."

"No. I'm not coming along."

"Well, then," I said. "In that case, you're not coming along."

She said nothing. Taking her silence to mean she wasn't coming along, I left the living room and went into the bedroom to get my shirt, which looked as though it had been washed in Brand X.

No. It was too dirty, that's all. I rooted around and found a clean white shirt of Artie's. It was too small, of course, but by leaving the collar open and rolling the sleeves up to my elbow I made it fairly presentable. I also found, in the bedroom closet, a black raincoat which must have been too big for Artie because it practically fit me to a T. I saw that it had been made with a removable inner lining, which had been subsequently removed, so maybe that was the explanation; with the lining in, it would fit its owner. Particularly if the owner—Artie—were wearing a suit coat or jacket under it. Sans coat and lining it was Charlie-size.

I stuffed the little pistol in the raincoat pocket, left the larger automatic behind, and went back out to the living room. Chloe was standing at the window now, working away at another cigarette and glowering down at the street. I said, "Well, I'm going."

"Good-bye."

So? What did she want from me? I'd already apologized once, that was enough. Besides, that Eichmann line still rankled. "Good-bye," I said.

I was almost to the door when she said, "Dummy."

I stopped. "What?"

"You don't even know if they're still watching the apartment. You didn't even look out the window first."

She was right, I'd forgotten about Trask or Slade, parked by the fire hydrant across the street. But I said, "If they're still there, I'll go the back way."

She shook her head. "They're not there," she said, with affected weariness, as though to say she'd had all she could bear of me.

Well, the feeling was mutual. "Thanks a million," I said. "Good-bye." I went out and closed the door.

It was true Trask or Slade was gone. Standing at the front door, I could see the fire hydrant across the way, shining in the noon sun. I went down the steps and turned left, toward West Fourth Street. I didn't look up to see if Chloe was still standing at the living-room window.

I was on my own.

★ You'd think the restaurant at Grand Central Terminal would have to be good; look at all the trains parked out front. Well, they're wrong.

Or maybe it was my fault and not the fault of the restaurant that everything I put in my mouth tasted like sand. I know I was emotionally awash, and there's nothing like an upset mind to cause an upset stomach.

The upset in my mind involved two very different people: Chloe Shapiro and Patrick Mahoney. I was still mad at Chloe, and yet at the same time last night's hankering hadn't left me, and besides that I was uneasy at continuing my odyssey without her, and over all, there was a layer of perplexity because I didn't really understand what the girl was all about. As to Mahoney, I wanted to find him and I wanted to avoid him, in more or less equal parts. If you remember Volto, the old-time Grape Nuts Martian, whose left arm repelled and whose right arm attracted, you'll have some idea what Deputy Chief Inspector Patrick Mahoney meant to me.

Well, like a visit to the dentist, the best thing to do about Patrick Mahoney was get him over with. So I paid for my sand, left the restaurant, and went out to the main part of the terminal, where, under a Kodak electronic poster as complicated as a Sally Rand striptease, I found a beehive of telephone booths. At the rear of the beehive were the directories I'd come to Grand Central to consult. Eating sand had been secondary, the result of my having redeveloped hunger on the subway trip uptown.

I'd come to Grand Central because it was the first place I thought of that would have telephone books for all the New York City boroughs, and I wanted those telephone books because I had a plan for tracking down my man Mahoney.

Watch:

First I went through the phone books for Mahoney, Patricks, and Mahoney, P's, and found four in Queens, seven in Brooklyn, three in Manhattan, five in the Bronx. Then, armed with a handful of dimes from the restaurant cashier, I went into one of the booths and began dialing. Each time a man answered I said, "Chief Inspector Mahoney?" and each time a woman answered I said, "Is Inspector Mahoney at Headquarters now?" I got a variety of answers, all of them negative for my purposes and a couple of them pretty comical in their own way, until at last one woman said, "Yes, he is. He'll be there all day."

Ah hah. But was this actually my Patrick Mahoney's household, or merely the household of a relative who would be aware of my Mahoney's whereabouts? So said, "Will he be home before six?"

"I doubt it," she said. "Why not call him at Headquarters?"

"All right," I said. "I will."

"Who shall I say—" she said, and I hung up.

See? Simple. Now I knew where to find him, the particular Patrick Mahoney out of the general class of Patrick Mahoneys. His home address, according to the telephone company, was 169-88 83rd Avenue, in Queens.

The success of this stratagem filled me with confidence, partially restoring a faith that had been slipping badly. I hurried onward, while the momentum lasted.

A bookstore tucked away in an echoing corner of the terminal sold me a street map of Queens, on which I found that the corner of 169th Street and 83rd Avenue was in the section called Jamaica, and only a few blocks from a station on the Independent subway line. So it was back into the subway for me, quite a letdown after riding around in that soft if felonious Packard all yesterday.

The IRT Flushing line clattered me into Queens and a junction with the IND, which took me the rest of the way to Hillside Avenue and 169th Street in Jamaica. I came out to pleasant sunlight, walked up the hill along 169th Street, and turned right on 83rd Avenue.

The neighborhood was pleasantly residential, middle-class, quiet. Most of the houses had been built before the Second World War, most were one-family, most were on fairly good-sized lots. Number 169-88 was similar to its neighbors, a two-story broad gray clapboard house with attached garage. Slightly unkempt shrubbery lined the front of the house, the lawn was somewhat dried out but had been recently mowed, and a sign with reflector letters on the lawn read: MAHONEY.

Was this the right man? Accepting bribes from the syndicate and living in a place like this?

Well, where would he live? I suppose up till then I hadn't really thought about it much, where a crooked bribe-taking policeman would live. I guess I'd supposed he'd live in a night club somewhere, with Merry Anders on one knee and Barbara Nichols on the other. Balloons in the background. Everybody laughing coarsely as the champagne is poured.

But he lived here, in a moderately neat one-family clapboard house on a quiet residential side street in the Jamaica section of Queens. That was a little scary.

I slowed as I passed his house, but I didn't stop. It was barely three o'clock now, and Inspector Mahoney wasn't expected home until sometime after six. So I walked on to the next corner, and turned right, and went back down to Hillside Avenue and went for a stroll.

Hillside Avenue went from bad to worse. The first couple of blocks was banks and delicatessens, but then there came several blocks of store-front real-estate offices, one right after the other, small and gaudy and chiseler-looking. Some of them, to give you the idea, had signs up reading, "We specialize in repossessed houses." I mention this in case you ever wondered what those old-time Scottish body snatchers Burke and Hare have been doing since Dr. Knox laid them off.

After the real-estate offices came the used-car lots. I stopped and turned around, because I didn't want to know what came next.

Back by the subway entrance I went into a luncheonette and sat at the counter and had coffee and cheese danish. Munching danish, I tried to work up a plan.

I might as well admit right now I didn't yet have one. I'd had the plan for finding out where Mahoney lived, but after that everything was still a blank. I knew I wanted to talk to Mahoney, I knew I wanted to find some way to force him to tell me what I wanted to know, and I knew I wanted to accomplish all this without falling into the hands of Trask or Slade, either or both of whom were probably keeping close to Mahoney night and day.

So. I could wait some place where I could see Mahoney's house, and after he got home go straight to the front door and start talking. I assumed he was married, and there was a good chance his wife didn't know the full story of his perfidy, so maybe I could work the same threat that had helped with Uncle Al.

On the other hand, maybe I ought to go to the Mahoney house right now, tie up anybody I found there, and be already inside when Mahoney got home. That way Trask and Slade wouldn't know I was around. Unless they came in with Mahoney, that is.

Or, maybe I should wait till he was home, then phone him and give him some reason for leaving the house again, and then hide in his car and not brace him till we'd left the neighborhood.

I didn't really like any of those plans, but I still had three hours or more to think, and I kept telling myself I'd be sure to come up with something good pretty soon.

The luncheonette had a phone booth. Just for something to do, I went over and looked in the directory for Queens Police Headquarters. The address was 168-02 91st Avenue.

Hey! That was right nearby. Five blocks away, that's all.

So I decided to go take a look at it, just to kill some time. I left the luncheonette, walked down 169th Street to 91st Avenue and turned right. A big municipal parking lot was on one side of me and a department store on the other.

Police Headquarters was smaller than I'd expected, a

squarish five-story building down at the far corner. The first two floors were done in gray stone and the top three in brick. The ground-level windows were tall and wide, with arched tops; inside, green shades were pulled all the way down.

The double-doored entrance—wooden doors with little windows clustered in the upper part—was flanked by the traditional green lights, and white lettering over the doorway read: *103rd Precinct*.

Police Headquarters in Queens wasn't such a much, in other words.

I strolled on by, looking at the building, up at the windows on the upper floors. Deputy Chief Inspector Patrick Mahoney was behind one of those windows, I supposed, at this very moment.

I went on around the corner, and down to the next street, which was Jamaica Avenue. I turned left and walked all the way around the block and pretty soon I was coming to Police Headquarters again. Or the precinct house, which is what it really was.

This time, though, I didn't keep on by. With no plan at all in my head, with nothing there in fact but impatience and nervousness and a hearty desire to have it all over with, I made a sharp left turn and pushed open the double doors to Precinct One Hundred and Three and stepped inside.

A uniformed patrolman was standing just inside the door, in a little airlock sort of arrangement between outer and inner sets of doors. He looked at me with a startled face and said, "What do you want?" He really acted astonished that anyone would come in here.

Hand-lettered notices on the inner doors told police officers they must without fail show identification to the patrolman at the door, and civilians—that's what the sign said: civilians—civilians had to tell this man their business before going any farther.

I was taking too long to read the signs and think of something to say. The patrolman glared with increasing suspicion and said, "Well? What do you want here?"

I had to say something. The space between outer and inner doors was small, keeping us close together. I opened my mouth and stammered a little and finally blurted, "Mahoney."

He lowered suspicious eyebrows. "What?"

Well, this was wrong, all wrong. It was at his home that I intended to meet Mahoney, in silence and privacy, not here in the crowded danger of this police station.

But it was done, and no going back now, so, "Mahoney," I fatalistically repeated. "Deputy Chief Inspector Patrick J. Mahoney." The middle initial I'd picked up from the telephone book.

Comprehension was seeping into the gatekeeper. He said, "You want to see him?"

No, I didn't, not at all, but what I said was, "Yes. I want to see him."

"What name?"

What name. Ah, yes, there's something to think about. What name indeed.

Well, if I was going to rush in where I feared to tread, I might just as well go the whole way. With practically no hesitation at all, I announced, "Charles Poole."

"Charles Poole." He nodded, implying that the name had spoken volumes to him. "Wait here," he said and went abruptly away, pushing through the inner doors and leaving me alone in the airlock—that's all my old science-fiction reading coming out again, excuse it please—with my thoughts and the notices.

It promptly occurred to me to run away. I could do it,

no trouble at all; just out this door and down to my right and into the department store. It's in department stores that people running away always manage to elude their pursuers in the movies on the late show, and I'd seen enough late shows in the last few years to have the method just about letter-perfect.

Still, I didn't go anywhere. I reminded myself I'd felt this way just before going in to see Mr. Agricola, and also prior to invading Mr. Gross's house, and in both cases I'd overcome my feelings and somehow survived, so why not this time.

'Three times and out,'' I muttered to myself, voicing an old superstition that should never have been invented. Three on a match. Three strikes and you're out. Bad things happen in threes.

The inner doors swung open again, happily breaking my trihedral reverie, and the policeman returned, saying, ''Someone will be right down.''

''Thank you.''

For the next few minutes he proceeded to ignore me, glowering fixedly out at the street instead. It's a very odd feeling to be ignored by someone standing with you in a space four feet wide and three feet long, and I wasn't at all sorry when another uniformed policeman stuck his head into our airlock and said, ''Mr. Poole? Would you come with me, please?''

Very pleasant man, this one, very reassuring. Thinning hair, shiny forehead, pale spectacles, mild manner. I went with him unhesitatingly, through rooms and upstairs to the third floor.

What could happen to me in a police station?

★ "Boo, chum," said Trask or Slade.

"Nephew, you sure give us a merry chase," said Slade or Trask.

The uniformed policeman had shut the door behind me. Trask and Slade were in front of me, standing on the gray carpet, smiling at me. Behind them was a desk, and behind the desk a man who had to be Mahoney. The office, medium-sized and somewhat dark, was what you'd expect to contain a deputy chief inspector of something or other.

I said, "I want to talk to Mahoney."

"You never give up, nephew, do you," said Trask or Slade.

"That's one of the qualities about him I like best," said Slade or Trask.

The man at the desk said, "You keep him quiet, you two. This is dangerous." He sounded nervous; as though *he* had anything to be nervous about!

Trask or Slade said, "Don't worry, there. We know our business."

"Take him out the back way," said the man at the desk. "I'll let you know when it's clear."

I said, "Inspector Mahoney, I want to talk to you."

Slade or Trask said, "Last time we heard from you, nephew, you were heeled. You heeled now?"

"No." I said, while the pistol began to gain weight in my raincoat pocket.

"Let's just see. Put your hands up on top of your head."

Neither of them had a gun in sight. All I had to do was reach into my pocket, pull the pistol out, and start blasting away. So what I did was put my hands up on top of my head.

Slade or Trask came over and patted me here and there and took the pistol away. He looked at me and grinned and shook his head, hefting the little pistol on his palm. "You could hurt yourself with this, nephew," he said.

The man at the desk said, "Why don't he call?"

Trask or Slade told him, "Relax. Everything'll be hunky-dory."

I took a deep breath. "No, it won't," I said.

They all looked at me. Trask or Slade said, "You ain't thinking of doing nothing stupid, are you, nephew?"

"Inspector Mahoney," I said, "you better listen to me. You're in worse trouble than you know."

Well, he wasn't. I was the one in trouble, and I was well aware how much. But Mahoney was acting nervous, and I leaped on it, ready to try anything that might help me get what I wanted.

Trask or Slade said to me, "Shut your face, nephew."

But it was too late. Mahoney had reacted big to what I'd said; he was sitting at the desk looking like a man thirty seconds this side of a heart attack. He was a man of about fifty, with sandy graying hair and soft pale Irish flesh well distributed with freckles. Freckles on his cheeks, freckles on the backs of his hands. It was a foregone conclusion he'd have freckles on his meaty shoulders. His face was somewhat jowly from overweight and bore the expression of anxious friendly mendacity of a wardheeler at a clambake, the expression Ed Begley does so well.

He stood up now, behind his desk, and said, "What do you mean by that? What sort of trouble?"

Trask or Slade told him, "It's bushwah. He's got a whole song and dance if you'll let him."

Slade or Trask tossed my little pistol into the air and caught it again. "This is the whole story," he said. "This toy cannon here. He come to kill you, like he killed the Farmer and tried to kill Mr. Gross."

Mahoney was weakening. He didn't know what to think. I said, "What if they're wrong, Inspector? I know where you live, One sixty-nine dash eight-eight Eighty-third Avenue. If I wanted to kill you I wouldn't come here to the police station to do it, I'd go wait near your house."

Trask or Slade came over close to me and poked a stiff finger into my chest. "I thought I told you shut your face."

Mahoney said, "Wait. Hold it, Trask. Let him talk."

Trask. The relief of finally knowing which one was Trask and which one Slade was almost too much for me. I practically forgot what I was here for and what I was trying to do.

But Trask reminded me. He rapped me on the shoulder, a good one, and said, "Okay, nephew, you got your wish. The floor's yours."

Slade—definitely Slade—added, "Give us your song and dance, nephew. You want we should hum along?"

Mahoney said, "Be quiet. Let him talk."

"Thank you," I said.

Mahoney pointed a freckled finger at me. "It better be good."

I said, "Somebody's been passing information to the authorities, and these people think it's me. Somebody killed Mr. Agricola, and they think that was me, too. But what if it wasn't? If it wasn't me, getting rid of me won't do any good. Whoever's squealing will go right on squealing, and sooner or later he'll squeal on you, Inspector Mahoney."

Mahoney scrunched his face up. He was watching me like a hawk, and thinking hard.

I said, "If I didn't kill Mr. Agricola, then whoever did kill him is still wandering around loose, nobody looking for him or even thinking about him, and maybe he does want to kill you, too."

Slade tossed the pistol in the air. "How about this, nephew? What's the rod for, ballast?"

"Self-defense. All you people keep trying to kill me."

Mahoney said, 'Only one thing so far makes sense. Why come here to bump me off if you know where I live?"

So I'd made an opening. I nodded enthusiastically, saying, "Sure. You can see the whole idea falls apart right there."

"Does it? In that case, what I—"

He was interrupted by the ringing of the telephone. He glanced at Trask and Slade, and then picked up the phone and spoke into it. "Hello? . . . Hold on." He cupped his hand over the mouthpiece and said to Trask and Slade, "It's all clear now."

Trask said, "Fine. So we take the nephew."

"I'm not done listening to him," Mahoney said. But he looked doubtful.

I said, to keep him convinced. "You've got more at stake than these two. You can give me five minutes."

He nodded. "Five minutes." He said the same thing into the telephone: "Give us five minutes, then let us know the next time it's clear." He hung up and looked at me, long and thoughtful. Then he sat down behind his desk and said, "Okay. You got one point on your side.

Now I got a question. If you didn't come here to bump me off, how come you're here?''

''For information,'' I said.

''You *want* information? You're supposed to be the one *gives* information.''

''But that's just it, I've never given anybody any information about anything. The reason I went to Mr. Agricola and Mr. Gross was to find out why the syndicate was down on me, because I hadn't done anything. Mr. Gross told me it was because you said I was being an informer. But I wasn't, so I came here to ask you who told you I was?''

''That's easy,'' he said. ''Tough Tony Touhy.''

''Who?''

''Lieutenant Anthony Touhy, Mob & Rackets Squad, know as Tough Tony. He's the one been getting the information on that bar you run, and when I asked him where the dope was coming from he said straight from the bartender, from the guy that runs the place for the syndicate.''

''He said—'' But I couldn't go on. I was dumfounded. I had never in my life heard of Tough Tony Touhy. Why should he say such a thing?

Mahoney said, ''Tough Tony is an honest cop, a non-bought cop. I'm his superior officer. When I ask him where he gets his information from, he tells me. He's got no reason to lie.''

I said, ''But he did lie.''

Mahoney held up two soft palms, making believe they were scales. ''On the one side,'' he said, ''we got the fact it don't make any sense you should come to the station to try to kill me. On the other side we got the fact it don't make any sense Tough Tony should lie to me.''

Trask said, "The nephew killed Farmer Agricola. We know that for sure."

Slade said, "And I was there not half an hour before that. It makes me feel bad to think of it."

Mahoney still mused over his upturned palms. "Over here," he said, "we got to add the fact Tough Tony has never lied to me before, and we got to add the fact everybody agrees it was you bumped off Farmer Agricola, and we got to add the fact you come here toting a gun, and we got to add the fact you was in the best position of anybody to give us the information that was passed over." The hand he was considering was sinking lower and lower under the weight of all the things he felt he had to add to it. Now, after a quick glance at me, he turned his attention to his other hand, which was way up in the air all by itself. "On this side," he said, "we got nothing to add, nothing at all. So maybe you did come here to kill me instead of waiting outside my house, and maybe you tried it this way because you're a dumbbell or you figured on the element of surprise or something."

Trask and Slade both nodded. Slade said, "That's it, nephew. That's the way it adds up, all right."

"Somebody," I said, rather shakily, "somebody is using me for a fall guy. I never said a word to Tough Tony Touhy in my life. I never even heard of him until just now. Either he lied to you or you're lying to Mr. Gross, and I wish I knew which."

Mahoney actually looked insulted. "Me lying? What the hell for?"

"Maybe it was your fault that information got into the wrong hands," I told him. "And you've been trying to cover up by putting the blame on me."

"That's about all I want to hear," Mahoney said.

I appealed at once to Trask. "It's possible," I said.

"You must have talked with Mr. Gross by now, you must have compared descriptions and you know that wasn't Miss Althea with me last night."

Trask frowned. "So what?"

"So Mr. Gross figured I was in cahoots with Miss Althea and that's why I was squealing to the police and killing people. But if I'm not in cahoots with Miss Althea, what's my motive?"

Slade said, "Maybe it's just plain orneriness."

Trask said, "It ain't our business to worry about your motive."

I told him, "It's your business to worry about whether the syndicate is running right or not. What if it *is* Mahoney behind this whole thing, covering up like mad for something he did wrong? So you take me out and kill me and it doesn't change a thing, everything's still all loused up. And Mahoney picks somebody else to be his fall guy next time, maybe even one of you two, and it just goes on and on and on."

Mahoney got to his feet, rather hurriedly, crying, "Now, wait just a damn minute there!"

Trask, without looking away from me, waved a hand at Mahoney to shut up and sit down. Trask was looking both amused and interested, and he said, "All right, nephew, keep it up. What else you got to say?"

"I'm being used for a fall guy," I told him, "that's all I know for sure. Maybe it's Mahoney, maybe it isn't."

Trask said, "What if it isn't?" Like he was just killing time, just humoring me until the phone should ring again.

All right, I had the time, no matter what his reason for giving it to me, so it was up to me to use. it. I said, "Did it ever occur to you, maybe the police force has caught on to Mahoney. Maybe they're not sure, but they suspect he's sold out to the syndicate, so just to be on the safe side they don't give him any information that could make trouble. Like not telling him who the real informer is in a case like this, when the informer might still have more things to tell."

Mahoney was gaping at me open-mouthed. Trask, still looked amused, now turned his head and said, "Well, Mahoney? What do you think of that?"

"I think," said Mahoney, somewhat strangled, "I think that's a lot of crap, that's what I think."

Slade said, "There's one quick way to check."

"Good," I said, turning to him. "Fine. Let's do it."

Mahoney looked at him somewhat warily. "What's that?"

Slade said, "Is Touhy around?"

"I think so," said Mahoney. "He should be in his office, yes."

"Trask and I'll get out of sight. You call Touhy in here. The kid says he's never seen Touhy, never heard of him before this. Let's see if Touhy recognizes him, see what Touhy says to him."

"All right," I said quickly. "That's good." And it was, it seemed to me, very good. Step by step I was coming around the circle to find the charges against me and the name of my accuser. From Uncle Al to Agricola to Gross to Mahoney, and now to Touhy. If only this could be at last the end of the line.

Mahoney seemed less pleased by the idea. "What if he spills the beans? What if he starts talking to Touhy?"

Trask smiled and shook his head. "He won't. He'd only be killing Touhy, because we'd have to shut him up. You wouldn't want to do that to poor Touhy, would you, nephew?"

I shook my head. "No. I won't say anything."

Mahoney said, "Shoot Tough Tony? Right here in my office?"

Slade told him, "I got a silencer. And we can carry the body out when we get the all-clear on the nephew."

"Besides," Trask added, "there won't be any need for any shooting. Will there, nephew?"

"No," I promised.

Mahoney, doubtful, said, "Well . . ."

"Come on," Trask told him. "We don't have much time."

Mahoney shook his head; he still didn't like it. But he said, "Let me see if Touhy's in his office."

We waited and watched as Mahoney used his phone. From his talk, Touhy was in. Mahoney wanted to know could he stop by the office for a minute. Then he hung up and said, "He'll be right in."

Trask and Slade receded toward a door on the far side of the office. "Remember, nephew," Slade said, and Trask grinned at me, and they both slid out of sight.

Mahoney and I stood facing one another, both of us nervous, both of us silent. Time hung in midair, like a pendulum stuck at one end of its swing.

There was a single sharp rap at the door, and then it opened, and a tall black-haired tough-looking lantern-jawed big-knuckled guy came in, the sort that's called the Black Irish. A cross between John Wayne and Robert Ryan.

Mahoney started talking before this big fellow was halfway in the door. "Something's come up, Tony, I'll have to talk to you later, an unexpected visitor, I'll get back to you in about half an hour, sorry to call you away like this for no reason at all."

"Oh, that's all right." He waved a big hand, then looked at me for the first time. "Well, Charlie!" he said, and grinned wide in surprise and pleasure. "Fancy seeing you here! You giving the dope straight to the boss these days, us hired hands ain't good enough for you any more?"

I opened my mouth, but nothing came out but air.

This big bastard poked me playfully on the upper arm. "That's okay, Charlie," he said. "I understand. You don't have to say nothing. I'll see you around, okay?"

And he was gone.

I stood there and stared at the door through which he had entered and exited. Behind me I heard Trask and Slade coming back into the room, but I didn't turn to look at them. I stared at the door and tried to understand what had just happened to me.

In the silent room, the phone rang. Mahoney's voice said, "Hello?" And then silence again, and then, "Okay, good." And the sound of the receiver clicking into its cradle, and Mahoney saying to Trask and Slade, "Okay, it's clear now."

Their hands were on my upper arms. One of them murmured, "Don't make no fuss now, nephew."

Fuss? I couldn't make a fuss. I was just trying to figure out what had happened.

We were moving, the three of us, along a corridor and down some stairs and out to a blacktop driveway. The black car was there, the famous black car. They had me lie down on the floor in back and they threw a knitted afghan over me that smelled for some strange reason of horse. In multicolored darkness under the afghan, bewitched, bothered and bewildered, I rolled away on the last ride.

★ If ever you have a problem, I mean a real knotty problem, a first-class puzzler, like the square root of two, for instance, or who really killed Farmer Agricola and why, allow me to recommend a long ride in the country, lying on the floor behind the front seat of an automobile, covered by a varicolored knitted afghan smelling pleasantly of horse.

The trip took well over an hour, most of it happily on good roads. At first, I admit, I gave myself up to a stunned absence of mental processes, a blank mindlessness of shock, but slowly I began to thaw down from that frozen plateau and I began to get in there and do some no-holds-barred thinking.

There was so much to think about. Who had killed Farmer Agricola, and why, and how? Who had been informing to the police, and why? Why had Tough Tony Touhy identified me as the informant?

I poked at it the way I occasionally poke at the crossword puzzle in the Sunday *Times*. You struggle and struggle, trying to get just a couple good long words to give you a kind of grip on the problem, and from there on with any luck at all you can get half or two-thirds of the puzzle lickety-split. Lying there under the afghan I poked and pried at everything I knew, everything that had happened, everything I understood and everything I failed to understand. There was a lot of that last-mentioned stuff.

I also did a lot of thinking about the people involved, all the people I'd come up against the last three days. My Uncle Al, and Farmer Agricola and his daughter Miss Althea, and Mr. Gross, and Inspector Mahoney, and Tough Tony Touhy, and Trask and Slade. And the ones who'd helped me, willingly or not: Artie Dexter and Chloe and Patrolman Ziccatta. I wondered, for instance, where Artie and Miss Althea were by now. And I wondered where Patrolman Ziccatta would get his quick nips on windy nights from now on, and would it ever occur to him to start an official inquiry into my disappearance, and I shook my head because I supposed it never would, not with his habit of keeping his nose out of other people's business. And I wondered why Tough Tony Touhy had lied, and why and how and by whom Farmer Agricola had been killed, and who had really passed the information on to the police.

I kept coming back, time and time again, to the killing of Farmer Agricola. It seemed to me that had to be connected with my own plight some way, that his having been killed in the short interval between his talking to Trask and Slade about me and my own arrival at the farm was too pat for coincidence. But where was the connection, where did it connect, that was the problem.

Lying there in multihued darkness, like being inside a cathedral in late afternoon under the stained-glass windows, lying there under the afghan, breathing the smells of afghan and horse, I kept chewing it, chewing it, chewing it. Was it possible Farmer Agricola had been killed by the same person who was really giving information to Tough Tony Touhy? Could the connection between the killing and my plight be quite that specific?

What if . . . What if Agricola hadn't been entirely satisfied that I was the squealer? Yes, and what if he'd done some additional investigating, and he'd discovered that I was not, in fact, the squealer? And what if he'd been about to call off the hunt for me and redirect his killers, Trask and Slade, at the real squealer. Wouldn't the squealer, if he knew about it, kill Agricola in self-defense? Of course he would.

Except, how could he possibly have known? Or, knowing, how could he possibly have gotten there and committed the crime? At the time Trask and Slade left him he apparently still believed I was the squealer, and it was less than half an hour later that I found him murdered. In the interim, I didn't see how anyone could have come to the farm without having been seen by me. And the three servants in the house, Clarence and Tim and Ruby, alibied one another.

Unless . . . Now, what if, what it . . . What if the killer was the killers? What if Trask and Slade were the ones themselves? Agricola had begun to suspect I wasn't the squealer, so he told them to lay off me while he did some more investigating. So they killed him and then went on hunting me just the same in order to cover themselves. The bodyguard at the Agricola farm, Clarence, had told me Agricola was still alive after Trask and Slade left, but one or both of them could have snuck back into the house, followed Agricola upstairs, and stuck the knife into him, using the knife instead of their more-accustomed guns because a gun might have been heard by the others in the house.

Scrunched down on the floor, feeling the road vibration all over me like one of those agitator beds in the new hotels, I thought about that possibility, and the more I thought about it the less I liked it. It would explain the knotty problem of how Agricola had been killed, of course, but for the rest of it, it didn't make sense. Trask and Slade were hardly squealers in the first place, and besides that they wouldn't kill Agricola just for not suspecting me so much any more. They'd play a waiting game, see how things were going.

No, it wasn't Trask and Slade. Somebody else, somebody else.

I ran through more theories, possibilities, suggestions, but none of them were any good. I tried coming at the problem through Tough Tony Touhy, and I tried coming at it through the reason for killing Farmer Agricola, and I kept on getting nowhere. I also returned time after time to the *how* of the killing of Farmer Agricola, how someone had managed to get there and kill him between Trask and Slade's departure and my arrival, which in many ways was the most baffling part of all.

I could understand it if Trask and Slade had done the killing. They leave the house, Agricola stops to say something to Clarence and then goes upstairs, Trask or Slade sneak back in, follow him up, kill him, go back down, leave the house again, and they drive away. But they hadn't done it, they just hadn't done it, of that I was positive.

Then I saw it.

It hit me so hard I sat up, shedding afghan on all sides. Bright sunlight angling low through the back window blinded me—we were going east, which didn't help me much, except to tell me we were somewhere on Long Island—and I squinted against it and pointed at Trask. Both of them were in the front seat, Slade driving. To Trask I said, "You didn't go along!"

He turned his head and scowled at me, "Down, nephew," he said.

"Tell me," I insisted. "When Slade went to see Mr. Agricola, you didn't go along. You stayed watching Artie Dexter's place, or my mother's place."

Trask said, "So what? Lie down and cover up."

To Slade I said, "Who went with you? Who did you take to see Farmer Agricola?"

It was the answer of course, the ultimate answer. But I wasn't to receive it, not that easily. Slade didn't say a word, and Trask reached over a big-boned hand with a big hard gun gripped in it and clonked me gently on the head with the barrel. "I said down, nephew."

So I went back down, pulling the afghan up over myself.

There was the answer, locked away in Slade's head. Trask and Slade hadn't gone to see Farmer Agricola, Slade had gone with someone else. That someone else had seen or heard or said something that was dangerous to him, so when they left he said to Slade, "Forgot my cigarettes," or, "Remembered something I wanted to ask the Farmer," or, "Hold it, I got to go back and use the head." Something, anything. Slade waited, the other guy went back in, killed Agricola, came out, rode away with Slade.

And they might have suspected him, Slade at any rate might have remembered and suspected him, if I hadn't come blundering onto the scene a few minutes later, taking all the blame and suspicion onto myself.

I should have realized it long ago, but I was too used to thinking of Trask and Slade as a team, inseparable. But hadn't they been separate last night, one of them watching Artie's place while the other was probably with Inspector Mahoney? If only I'd stopped to think then of the implications, that Trask and Slade *could* work in different places, *could* survive for short periods of time away from one another, I might now be a lot closer to the solution than I was.

Still, it was something. I knew how Agricola had been

killed, and I could guess why. All that remained now was the knotty question of who.

And just before the car stopped I realized who it had to be. Had to be, absolutely had to be. There wasn't anyone else in the world who could have known the proper things, who could have been in the right places at the right times, who could have handled this whole mess with such a teetering combination of panic and cunning, desperation and wiliness.

The car had left the road, was moving slowly now across something that crunched beneath the wheels. Sand, it sounded like. More and more slowly, rising and falling over uneven ground, the big black car finally settled to a stop.

Doors opened and then shut again. Feet crunched through sand. Another door opened, the one by my feet. Trask's voice said, "Okay, nephew."

I pushed the afghan away and sat up. "It's all right," I said. "I know now."

"Let's go for a walk, nephew," Trask suggested.

He wasn't listening to me. "But I've figured it out," I said. "Everything's all right now, I've got it doped out."

Trask showed me that big hard gun again. "Come out of the car, nephew," he said.

I looked at him. I looked past him, and saw nothing but Slade.

I had it all figured out, and these two knobheads couldn't care less. I knew the whole thing, and I'd run the course anyway.

"Nephew," said Trask. "Come along. We're goin' for a walk."

★ Pardon me if you will, but I intend to drop into third person narration for just a little while now. This next scene is far too nerve-racking for me to relive in first person. I want to view it all from as great a distance as possible—the middle of Long Island Sound, for instance.

Therefore . . .

The setting is a bit of sandy beach not far from Orient Point, one of the two eastern tips of Long Island. The other, Montauk Point, farther to the south, is better known, duller to look at, and more heavily commercialized. A ferry leaves Orient Point three times a day in summer, bound for New London, in Connecticut. In summer, also, pleasure boats cruise these waters, swimmers and sunbathers dot these beaches, but after Labor Day pockets of emptiness appear and grow, and by the first snowfall Orient Point is virtually deserted.

This particular stretch of beach is one of these pockets of emptiness, or was until a few minutes ago, when an automobile came driving slowly across the rolling sand from the direction of the invisible road. A big black car, new and gleaming, reflecting the mid-September sun. It stopped about a city block from the water's edge, and two tall men in dark clothing got out. They wore dark topcoats and the sea wind whipped the coat tails around their legs.

A minute or two later a third man got out of the car, somewhat shorter and thinner than the first two, this one wearing a black raincoat which also whipped around his trouser legs.

The three began to walk away from the car, in single file, the one in the raincoat coming second. The other two walked hunched and stolid, their hands in their topcoat pockets, but the one in the middle appeared to be talking; his arms were in constant motion, like an erratic windmill, and his head bobbed with the speed and intensity of his words. The other two appeared not to be listening to him.

In their dark clothing, in the wind, in the sunlight, silhouetted against the light tan of the sand, the three walkers were impressive, curious, somehow frightening. They moved across the sand in a deliberate way, the two bigger ones picking their feet up high and leaning forward and moving their shoulders a great deal, the way men will walk through sand when their hands are in their topcoat pockets and they have a specific place to go. The one in the middle slid around in the sand more, seeming to be constantly on the verge of throwing himself off balance with his waving arms.

They walked at an angle in relation to the water, not directly toward it but rather off to the right away from the car, toward a small break in the beach where the ocean had eroded away a tiny cul-de-sac of water, a minuscule pool or cove or lagoon, walled in by sand. Gray driftwood choked this cul-de-sac, and more gnarled twisted pieces of driftwood up on the sand ringed it in.

As the procession moved closer to this cluster of driftwood the walker in the middle seemed to grow more and more agitated, as though the driftwood held for him a significance he found both unpleasant and impelling.

His rapid, disjointed half-sentences rang out across the water, whipped away by the wind.

The trio reached the driftwood. The two taller men situated the talker where they wanted him, standing at the edge of the little drop to the water, standing amid the driftwood, his back to the water. They moved away from him, still facing him, and both took small machines from their pockets.

The one standing shin-deep in driftwood talked louder and faster than ever, and an occasional whole sentence blew out across the water: "What if I'm right? What if you're wrong and I'm right? How did I know who went with you to the farm?" And other comments, loud and rapid and urgent in tone.

The other two raised the machines in their hands and pointed them at the talker. But then one of them lowered his machine and said something to his partner. The two of them spoke briefly together. They seemed undecided.

The talker kept talking, waving his arms. The wind blew his raincoat around him and the sun gleamed on his perspiring forehead.

The other two finally came to a decision. They motioned to the talker, who came back out of the driftwood and walked with them across the sand again to the car they'd arrived in. While the talker and one of the other two stood beside the car, the third man opened the door, slid behind the wheel, and operated an automobile telephone mounted under the dash.

A name was spoken, blew out over the waves: "Mr. Gross."

There was a brief telephone conversation on the part of the man in the car, and then he handed the telephone receiver to the talker, the one who had just recently been standing amid the driftwood. The talker began to talk again, this time into the telephone, but just as urgently and rapidly as before. He stopped talking to listen and then he talked again. The telephone was handed to one of the others to speak a word of corroboration to the man at the other end, and then handed back to the talker to talk into some more.

The wind blew. The sun shone. The water lapped at the beach. The black auto gleamed. The talker talked. The other two stood stolid and patient, dispassionate, not caring whether the talker convinced the man on the other end of the phone line or not. One of them lit a cigarette, hunching his back and cupping his hands to protect the match flame from the wind. The white smoke blew away, out to sea, along with the words of the talker, along with anything else that might be left here.

The talker was finished. He handed the telephone to one of the others, who spoke into it briefly, listened, nodded and spoke again, and then put the receiver back on its hook under the dashboard.

The trio got into the car, all in the front seat, the talker—now silent—in the middle. The car made a wide U-turn and drove away from the beach, toward the invisible road.

★ Phew!

Let me tell you, that was close. Down among the driftwood there, I thought it was all up, all over but the shooting. I talked like Broderick Crawford in a hurry, I said everything five or six times fast, and I kept jumping up and down and waving my arms to try to attract their attention, and for a while it looked as though I might as well have been talking French. But I just kept at it, telling them who had killed Agricola, and why he'd done it, and how come he had to be the one who'd really been giving the syndicate information to Tough Tony Touhy, and pointing out how I'd guessed he was the guy Slade had taken with him to see Agricola, and then going over the whole thing all over again, and after a while it finally did begin to seep into their skulls, like rain through concrete.

It was Trask who finally said, "What can it hurt? Let him talk to Gross. If Gross says he's on, he's on."

Slade said, "I didn't want to take a lot of time."

"This won't take long," Trask told him.

So that was how it was. We walked on back to the car, and I figured at first it meant we'd be taking another long ride together, back across the Island and south to Hewlett Bay Park, but it turned out the car had a telephone in it. I'd heard about that before, telephones in automobiles, but this was the first time I'd ever seen one.

You'd think, with my reading in science fiction and all, I would have thought about the wonders of science and like that when I saw the telephone in the black car, but that wasn't what came into my mind at all. The black car on the sand dunes, the deserted area, the tough type calling his boss on a telephone in the car—it was exactly like a scene from one of those movie serials I used to watch on Saturday afternoons when I was a kid. I looked up into the sky for Superman or Spy Smasher, but nobody showed.

Except Mr. Gross, of course, on the other end of the telephone. Trask had made the call, while Slade stood next to me with his hand suggestively in his pocket.

After a minute or two of fiddling with the phone company, Trask finally reached Mr. Gross and told him the situation. He and Gross talked back and forth a minute, and then he handed me the phone and said, "He wants to hear it. Tell him the story."

So I went through the whole thing again, in as orderly a manner as I could manage under the circumstances. Mr. Gross asked a few questions, and I answered them as best I could, and then he said, "It sounds possible. Not necessarily true, you understand, but possible. An alternative explanation. We will have to learn which explanation is accurate. Put Trask back on."

"Yes, sir."

I handed the phone to Trask, there was another brief conversation, and then the call was over. Trask said to Slade, "We're supposed to bring him to see Mr. Gross."

I exhaled. It was, I believe, the first time I'd exhaled in about three minutes.

Slade shrugged. "So we'll never get done with this job," he said. But he didn't seem irritated, just fatalistic about it all.

Trask motioned a thumb at me. "Come on, nephew," he said. "Back in the car."

"Under the afghan again?"

They looked at each other. Slade shrugged and Trask said, "No. Climb in front."

I was happy to. Not only did I anticipate a much more enjoyable ride sitting on the seat in the open air than lying on the floor under an afghan, but letting me sit up there was kind of letting me know they pretty much believed me.

Slade drove again, and Trask sat on my right. Slade steered the car around in a wide U in the sand and headed back for the highway. As we reached it and turned west, toward the late afternoon sun, Slade put the visor down and said, "I hope you're telling the goods, nephew. I never did like that bastard anyway."

"Neither did I," said Trask.

I agreed with them both.

★ There was quite a group waiting for us when we got to Mr. Gross's house. Aside from Mr. Gross himself, there was my Uncle Al, there was Farmer Agricola's bodyguard Clarence, there was Inspector Mahoney, and there were two tough-looking types I'd never see before. Uncle Al and Clarence and Inspector Mahoney all looked worried, and the two tough-looking types looked like all other tough-looking types: tough-looking, uninterested, and not very bright.

We came in, Trask and Slade and me, and Mr. Gross said, "Ah. Here you are. We've been waiting for you."

This was the room where three bridge games had been in progress the last time I'd been in this house. The card tables were gone now and rather frail-looking chairs and end tables were spotted here and there around the room. On the floor was a very clean oriental rug.

Mr. Gross had gotten to his feet as we came in, and now he motioned me to a chair where I'd be the inevitable center of attention. "Sit down, Mr. Poole. Make yourself comfortable."

I sat down, but I wasn't very comfortable. Would I be able to convince them?

I felt all the eyes on me and I was feeling a fright that was only partially stage fright.

Mr. Gross said, "I called these people here to listen to your ideas. I want you to tell it all again, just like you told it to me over the phone. They can tell us if the story holds together right."

Mahoney said, "This is dangerous, Gross. I shouldn't be here, this is endangering my usefulness to you and myself and the whole organization."

Gross waved a sausagy hand at him. "Relax, Mahoney. Just sit and listen."

Uncle Al said to me, "Charlie, what are you up to now? How much trouble you want to get yourself in?"

"That's enough," Gross said. He sat down, like a white toad settling himself under a mushroom, and crossed pudgy hands over his white-shirted black-suited torso. "Begin," he said.

I said, "Two things happened, and you thought I did both of them. Somebody gave away secrets to Tough Tony Touhy, and somebody killed Farmer Agricola. You were wrong about me doing them, but you were right it was the same person did both. The reason you thought it was me was because you had Inspector Mahoney find out where the leak was coming from, and he asked Touhy, and Touhy said it was from me." I turned to Mahoney. "But at first," I said, "he didn't say precisely that I was the one talking to him. You said to him something like, 'Where's this information coming from?' And he said something like, 'It's coming from the bartender at the Rockaway Grill.' Isn't that right?"

Mahoney shrugged and spread his hands and looked at Gross. "How do I know?" he said, talking directly to

Gross. "How do I know what exact words was used? What difference does it make?"

"The difference," I told him, "is you asked one question and Touhy answered a different one. Most policemen keep the identities of their regular informants secret as much as they can, at least that's what I've always read, so I guess Touhy didn't even think you wanted to know the name of the informant. You asked him where the information was coming from, and he thought you meant what was the ultimate source in the organization, and that was me. But he didn't mean I was telling him anything directly. What he meant was, the guy who passed the information on to him first got it from me."

Mahoney said, "So you worked through an intermediary. What's that supposed to mean?"

"Not an intermediary," I said. "There was only one person I ever talked to about organization business, and I only talked to him because it was supposed to be safe to talk to him, he was a member of the—"

Uncle Al jumped to his feet and shouted, "Wait a goddam minute!"

Mr. Gross pointed a sausage finger at him. "Sit down, Gatling."

But Uncle Al stayed on his feet. "What is this, a goddam railroad? You think you can pull—"

Mr. Gross made a small gesture with the sausage. The two tough-looking types had already moved over close behind Uncle Al's chair. Now they reached out and put their hands on his shoulders and pushed him very slowly and quietly back down into his chair. He went down, mouth open, and just sat there. He watched me, and his mouth was open, but he didn't interrupt any more. And the two tough-looking types left their hands on his shoulders.

I said, "Touhy got something on Uncle Al, I don't know what. But instead of pulling him, he used Uncle Al to give him information about syndicate business. Including dope about shipments of things going through my bar. Every time I was with my Uncle Al we'd talk about how I was doing at the bar, how much work there was, what the story was with shipments and packages and all that. He knew as much about what was going on there as me, and he was the only one I ever talked to."

Mahoney was watching me at last, instead of Mr. Gross. He said, "That's just your word against his. He's been a trusted member of the organization for years, so why should we believe you?"

"Because he killed Mr. Agricola," I said.

Clarence spoke up, saying, "Not so's you'd notice it. You're the one killed Mr. Agricola, and nobody else."

"No, I didn't. When I got away from Trask and Slade the second time, at Artie Dexter's place in Greenwich Village, they had Uncle Al with them. They phoned Mr. Agricola, and he said Trask should keep watch some place or other, and Slade should come out for further instructions, and bring my Uncle Al along to fill him in on his nephew Charlie Poole." I turned to Slade. "Isn't that right?"

Slade nodded. "Right."

"I should have figured that out long ago," I told them, "but I kept thinking of Trask and Slade always together, like Siamese twins. Anyway, while they were there Uncle Al let something slip, something that Slade wouldn't know about but that Agricola would, something that Agricola didn't catch right away. I don't know what it was, but Uncle Al realized he'd made the mistake, and knew Agricola would catch on sooner or later, so after he and Slade went out to the car he made some excuse to go back inside—''

Slade said, ''He forgot his cigarettes.''

Uncle Al shook his head, abruptly, once, but he didn't say anything.

I said, ''He went back upstairs and killed Mr. Agricola with that knife. I don't know where he got it.''

''It was in the room,'' Clarence said. ''A letter opener is what it was. But I still say you were the one used it.''

I asked him, ''Did you know Al Gatling had come back into the house?''

He frowned a little and shook his head. ''No. So what?''

''Wouldn't you have heard him if he'd made a normal amount of noise? I mean, after all, you were supposed to be guarding the place.''

''I'll hear anybody that comes in the front door,'' he said, getting truculent now. He didn't like being reminded he'd failed in his duty. He was like a watchdog after a successful burglary; so irritated and embarrassed he's liable to bite any leg that comes close.

I told him, ''You didn't hear Albert Gatling come in, though.''

He shrugged, sullen. ''So what?''

''That means he must have been moving extra special quiet, doesn't it?''

''If he came back in.''

Slade said, ''He went back in, I saw him go. I waited for him.''

Mahoney said, ''But why kill Agricola? What's the point?''

''Maybe Uncle Al will tell us,'' I said, and looked at him, but he just glared and wouldn't say a word.

Slade said, "Listen, there's a name you said before."

I turned to him. "Me?"

"Yeah. A cop or something."

"Touhy?"

Slade nodded. "Right. Gatling mentioned that name."

"To Agricola?"

"Yeah. I remember. Something about he had no idea why his nephew would pass news like that on to this guy Touhy."

I turned back to Gross. "Would that do it? Should there have been any way for my Uncle Al to know which policeman was getting the information?"

Mr. Gross shook his head. "Not unless Mahoney told him."

Mahoney said, "Why should I tell him? No point in it. I never dealt with him at all."

"So that's why," I said. "Uncle Al realized he'd made the mistake, and he was afraid Agricola would catch on a little later, and he panicked. He's been running scared the last few days, terrified out of his head. Trask and Slade can tell you. From the time he found out the organization was after me for the squealing he'd been doing he didn't know what to do. He couldn't take the rap for me, and he was even too scared and panicky to try to help me. He made a mistake with Agricola, and killed him because he was so panicky. And since then he's just been sitting around waiting for the whole thing to be over."

Mahoney said, "From the look on Gatling's face, and from everything everybody's said, it looks like you're telling the truth, kid. Except for one thing."

"What thing?"

"Tough Tony." Mahoney pointed a finger at me. "He identified you in my office this afternoon. Not your Uncle Al, you."

"The only thing I can figure," I told him, "is that he suspects you. He's on to you now."

"That's right," said a voice from the doorway. We all turned out heads, and there was Tough Tony Touhy smiling in the doorway, a revolver in each hand and a hall full of cops behind him.

"Stick 'em up, gents," said Tough Tony. "It's the end of the road."

★ Riding toward New York in the back seat of the police car, sitting next to Tough Tony Touhy, I got the rest of the story.

"We've been on to that Rockaway Grill for months," he told me. "For instance Patrolman Ziccatta isn't really a patrolman at all. He's a detective third grade, working out of the Mob & Rackets Squad, on special detached duty to the 69th Precinct in Canarsie so he can keep an eye on the Rockaway Grill. There's nothing like disguising a cop as a cop to allay suspicion." He laughed, a big healthy hearty sort of a laugh, and slapped his own knee.

I said, "You mean, all this time he's been watching me?"

"Not you so much," Tough Tony said. "The bar, the customers, that's what he's been watching. The other night, when he saw Trask and Slade in there, he figured they were just coming by to make another drop or pick up another package. But a little later, when he saw part of the sign knocked down, and saw the back door broken in, and saw you nowhere around the place, he began to think there was something up, and he called me right away."

I said, "So you've been hanging around me the whole time."

"Well, not exactly," he said. "To tell you the truth, we didn't know where you were or what the hell was going on till last night, when you showed up in Canarsie again, asking about a policeman named Patrick Mahoney. Ziccatta called me and then tried to stall you until we could get a tail on you. Up till then none of us could figure out what was going on, but when you asked about Mahoney dawn began to break. I remembered telling him you were the source of the dope we'd been getting, and I could see how he'd get the idea I meant you were the one talking to us, and slowly the pieces began to fit into place."

"So," I said. "You've had people watching me ever since last night."

"No, not precisely," he said. "Ziccatta didn't manage to stall you long enough, so you were gone before our man could get there from Queens. But we knew you were going to try to reach Mahoney, so we surrounded him with men and waited for you to show up. That was easy, surrounding him with men, since there he was right in Police Headquarters anyway." He laughed again and slapped his knee some more.

"Well," I said. "So you had me in view from the time I got to Police Headquarters."

"I wouldn't entirely say that," he said. "To tell you the truth, we didn't expect such a direct approach from you, and none of our special-detail men even knew you were in the building. If Mahoney hadn't called me to come into his office, where I could get a look at you, I don't know what would have happened. Still, all's well that ends well. And when I saw you there, I knew exactly what was going on, and I knew Mahoney wanted to see if I'd recognize you or not, so naturally I said what I did, in order to keep Mahoney from getting suspicious. I figured then we'd watch you, see where you were taken and what happened next.''

'Ah,'' I said, breathing a sigh of relief. ''So you were on hand the whole time out at Orient Point and I really wasn't in danger at all.''

''Well, no,'' he said. ''The fact of the matter is, they moved you on out of Headquarters faster than we expected. We lost you again practically as soon as we'd found you.''

I said, ''Then how did you show up at Mr. Gross's house?''

''We followed Mahoney.''

''Oh.'' I looked out the window and we were in Queens. ''You can let me off at the subway,'' I said. ''Any subway.'' I looked at him. ''You *can* find the subway, can't you?''

He gave me a tough look. ''Is that supposed to be funny?'' he said. ''We saved your life.''

''Oh, yeah,'' I said. ''I forgot.''

★ It was rush hour. When the train reached West Fourth Street I had to claw my way through a mass of sullen humanity to get through the door and out onto the platform. That was possibly the most dangerous moment I'd lived during the past week.

But I did make it to the platform, and all the doors snicked shut behind me, and the subway raced its squirming mass of innards southward through the black tunnels. I went up stairs, and up stairs, and up stairs, and eventually got to the street. I walked west through the beginning of evening, through the Village.

I didn't know her home address, and I didn't know her parents' address in the Bronx. This was the only place I knew her, so this was where I came.

I walked down Perry Street and I saw light gleaming in those windows, but did that mean Chloe or did it mean Artie back at last from his unexplained disappearance? Although I wanted to know what the hell Artie had been doing the last couple of days, at the same time I wished desperately for it to be Chloe up there.

Murder wasn't the only thing I'd been figuring out this afternoon. I'd also been figuring Chloe. I'd come to some realizations about Chloe, and I was eager to get started acting on those realizations.

Like for instance her telling me her life story last night, all about her marriage and her little girl and everything. She wouldn't have told me all that if she thought we were just a couple of ships passing in the night. No, it meant she was interested in me, and willing to see where the interest might lead.

And also, like for instance, her telling me she knew I had a letch for her because she heard me tossing and turning until practically dawn. What I didn't stop to realize at the time, what I only figured out hours later when my brain was all tuned up and figuring out everything that came its way, was if she had heard me tossing and turning until practically dawn that had to mean *she was awake until practically dawn herself*. And what did that mean?

You betcha.

So I hurried across Perry Street toward those lighted windows, second-floor front, hoping it was Chloe and not Artie, and I dashed up the steps outside the building, found the door unlocked yet again, and bounded on up the stairs to the second floor. I knocked on the door, and waited, and knocked again, and at last it opened.

Chloe.

She had changed clothes. She was wearing a black skirt that flared out over her hips, with a lot of fluffy petticoat sort of things underneath to make the skirt stand out even more, and she had a scoop-neck white blouse on that did nothing bad at all for her breasts, and she was wearing stockings and high heels, and she had a good moderate amount of make-up on, and she looked absolutely fabulous.

I suddenly felt raunchy. Still in the same slacks I'd been wearing since this thing started. Same shoes too. Borrowed underwear. Borrowed white shirt that was too small for me. Borrowed raincoat.

I wished I'd thought to stop off at my place in Canarsie first to get cleaned up.

She looked at me standing there in the hallway, and she smiled in a tentative kind of way and said, "You looking for a place to hide out, mister?"

I shook my head. "It's all over," I said. "We won."

"What? Really?"

So the first thing I had to do was come in and sit down and have a cup of coffee and tell her what had happened, tell her the whole day in the tiniest detail. Which I did, and she made suitable comments here and there, and when I was done she said, ''So you came back to get your own clothes and leave Artie's stuff here, is that it?''

I shook my head again. ''No. I came back here to get you.''

''Me?'' Said as though she had no idea what I was talking about.

So I reached out and pulled her close and kissed her. We melted awhile, and then we split and looked at each other and both started giggling. ''And here I'd given up on you,'' she said, giggling.

''The hell you did,'' I said.

''What do you know about it?''

''Plenty.'' I kissed her again, and then I said, ''Shall we spend the night here or at my place down in Canarsie?''

''We? What do you mean, we?''

''You know what I mean.''

She disengaged herself from my arms, backed up a couple of steps, and looked me over. ''You're going to run that bar again?''

''I guess not,'' I said. ''The organization won't be operating it any more, and my contract with the organization ended with Uncle Al. I guess I'll just have to settle down and find myself a sensible job somewhere with good pay and nice fringe benefits and a top-flight retirement plan.''

''You're overstating it,'' she said. ''But you do really mean to settle down and start behaving like an adult.''

''Definitely,'' I said.

''In that case,'' she said, ''I imagine you'll ask me that question again a little later this evening, in a more acceptable manner.''

''I imagine I will,'' I said. ''And how would you like to eat dinner in a real restaurant?''

"Fine. Just—"

The doorbell rang.

We looked at each other. Chloe said, "Do you suppose that's Artie?" Her voice was hushed.

I said, "I don't know."

"What if it is?"

"You mean, because of us?"

She nodded.

"I'll talk to him," I said. "Don't worry, I know Artie pretty well. He never had any long-term plans with you anyway, you or anybody else."

"I know," she said.

So I went over and opened the door and it wasn't Artie, it was a Western Union boy. He handed me the envelope and went away, and I shut the door and opened the envelope and Chloe came over and put an arm around my waist and rested her cheek against my upper arm, and we read the telegram together.

It was from Huntsville, Alabama. It was addressed to both Chloe and me at this address, and it said:

ALTHEA AND ME MARRIED HERE THIS AFTERNOON STOP FLYING SWITZERLAND MORNING STOP WHY DON'T YOU TWO GET TOGETHER QUESTION MARK

ARTIE

"Oh!" said Chloe. "If that isn't the end!"

She was right.

ABOUT THE AUTHOR

DONALD E. WESTLAKE, winner of multiple Edgar Allan Poe Awards and Oscar nominee for his screenplay to the hit film *The Grifters*, is celebrated as one of America's top comic novelists. Among his most recent novels are *Humans, Drowned Hopes, Sacred Monster,* and *Trust Me on This*. Mr. Westlake lives in New York.